Bridgerton
Romancing Mister Bridgerton

BY JULIA QUINN

THE BRIDGERTON PREQUELS SERIES

Because of Miss Bridgerton

The Girl with the Make-Believe Husband

The Other Miss Bridgerton

First Comes Scandal

THE BRIDGERTON SERIES

The Duke and I

The Viscount Who Loved Me

An Offer From a Gentleman

Romancing Mister Bridgerton

To Sir Phillip, With Love

When He Was Wicked

It's in His Kiss

On the Way to the Wedding

The Bridgertons: Happily Ever After

THE SMYTHE-SMITH QUARTET

Just Like Heaven

A Night Like This

The Sum of All Kisses

The Secrets of Sir Richard Kenworthy

THE BEVELSTOKE SERIES

The Secret Diaries of Miss Miranda Cheever

What Happens in London

Ten Things I Love About You

THE TWO DUKES OF WYNDHAM

The Lost Duke of Wyndham

Mr. Cavendish, I Presume

AGENTS OF THE CROWN

To Catch an Heiress

How to Marry a Marquis

THE LYNDON SISTERS

Everything and the Moon

Brighter Than the Sun

THE SPLENDID TRILOGY

Splendid

Dancing at Midnight

Minx

Bridgerton

Romancing Mister Bridgerton

Julia Quinn

HARPER LARGE PRINT

An Imprint of HarperCollinsPublishers

"Romancing Mister Bridgerton: The 2nd Epilogue" was originally published as an e-book.

"Romancing Mister Bridgerton: The 2nd Epilogue" copyright © 2007 by Julie Cotler Pottinger.

Meet the Bridgerton Family teaser excerpts copyright © 2000, 2001, 2002, 2003, 2004, 2005 by Julie Cotler Pottinger.

Originally published as *Romancing Mister Bridgerton* in 2002 by Avon Books.

Meet the Bridgerton Family and Bridgerton Family Tree designed by Emily Cotler, Waxcreative Design

FIRST HARPER LARGE PRINT EDITION

ISBN: 978-0-06-314452-1

Library of Congress Cataloging-in-Publication Data is available upon request.

21 22 23 24 25 LSC 10 9 8 7 6 5 4 3 2 1

*For the women on avonloop, colleagues and friends
all—thanks for giving me someone to talk to
all day long. Your support and friendship have
meant more to me than I could ever say.*

*And for Paul, even though the closest thing
you'd ever find to a romance in his field is a
lecture called "The Kiss of Death."*

Acknowledgments

With utmost thanks to Lisa Kleypas and Stephanie Laurens for the gracious use of their characters.

Prologue

On the sixth of April, in the year 1812—precisely two days before her sixteenth birthday—Penelope Featherington fell in love.

It was, in a word, thrilling. The world shook. Her heart leaped. The moment was breathtaking. And, she was able to tell herself with some satisfaction, the man in question—one Colin Bridgerton—felt precisely the same way.

Oh, not the love part. He certainly didn't fall in love with her in 1812 (and not in 1813, 1814, 1815, or—oh, blast, not in all the years 1816–1822, either, and certainly not in 1823, when he was out of the country the whole time, anyway). But his earth shook, his heart leaped, and Penelope knew without a shadow of a doubt that his breath was taken away as well. For a good ten seconds.

Falling off a horse tended to do that to a man.

It happened thus:

She'd been out for a walk in Hyde Park with her mother and two older sisters when she felt a thunderous rumbling under her feet (see above: the bit about the earth shaking). Her mother wasn't paying much attention to her (her mother rarely did), so Penelope slipped away for a moment to see what was about. The rest of the Featheringtons were in rapt conversation with Viscountess Bridgerton and her daughter Daphne, who had just begun her second season in London, so they were pretending to ignore the rumbling. The Bridgertons were an important family indeed, and conversations with them were not to be ignored.

As Penelope skirted around the edge of a particularly fat-trunked tree, she saw two riders coming her way, galloping along hell-for-leather or whatever expression people liked to use for fools on horseback who care not for their safety and well-being. Penelope felt her heart quicken (it would have been difficult to maintain a sedate pulse as a witness to such excitement, and besides, this allowed her to say that her heart leaped when she fell in love).

Then, in one of those inexplicable quirks of fate, the wind picked up quite suddenly and lifted her bonnet (which, much to her mother's chagrin, she had not tied properly since the ribbon chafed under her chin) straight into the air and, splat! right onto the face of one of the riders.

Penelope gasped (taking her breath away!), and then the man fell off his horse, landing most inelegantly in a nearby mud puddle.

She rushed forward, quite without thinking, squealing something that was meant to inquire after his welfare, but that she suspected came out as nothing more than a strangled shriek. He would, of course, be furious with her, since she'd effectively knocked him off his horse and covered him with mud—two things guaranteed to put any gentleman in the foulest of moods. But when he finally rose to his feet, brushing off whatever mud could be dislodged from his clothing, he didn't lash out at her. He didn't give her a stinging set-down, he didn't yell, he didn't even glare.

He laughed.

He laughed.

Penelope hadn't much experience with the laughter of men, and what little she *had* known had not been kind. But this man's eyes—a rather intense shade of green—were filled with mirth as he wiped a rather embarrassingly placed spot of mud off his cheek and said, "Well, that wasn't very well done of me, was it?"

And in that moment, Penelope fell in love.

When she found her voice (which, she was pained to note, was a good three seconds after a person of any intelligence would have replied), she said, "Oh, no, it is I who should apologize! My bonnet came right off my head, and . . ."

She stopped talking when she realized he hadn't actually apologized, so there was little point in contradicting him.

"It was no trouble," he said, giving her a somewhat amused smile. "I—Oh, good day, Daphne! Didn't know you were in the park."

Penelope whirled around to find herself facing Daphne Bridgerton, standing next to her mother, who promptly hissed, "What have you done, Penelope Featherington?" and Penelope couldn't even answer with her stock, *Nothing,* because in truth, the accident was completely her fault, and she'd just made a fool of herself in front of what was obviously—judging from the expression on her mother's face—a very eligible bachelor indeed.

Not that her mother would have thought that *she* had a chance with him. But Mrs. Featherington held high matrimonial hopes for her older girls. Besides, Penelope wasn't even "out" in society yet.

But if Mrs. Featherington intended to scold her any further, she was unable to do so, because that would have required that she remove her attention from the all-important Bridgertons, whose ranks, Penelope was quickly figuring out, included the man presently covered in mud.

"I hope your son isn't injured," Mrs. Featherington said to Lady Bridgerton.

"Right as rain," Colin interjected, making an expert sidestep before Lady Bridgerton could maul him with motherly concern.

Introductions were made, but the rest of the conversation was unimportant, mostly because Colin quickly and accurately sized up Mrs. Featherington as a matchmaking mama. Penelope was not at all surprised when he beat a hasty retreat.

But the damage had already been done. Penelope had discovered a reason to dream.

Later that night, as she replayed the encounter for about the thousandth time in her mind, it occurred to her that it would have been nice if she could have said that she'd fallen in love with him as he kissed her hand before a dance, his green eyes twinkling devilishly while his fingers held hers just a little more tightly than was proper. Or maybe it could have happened as he rode boldly across a windswept moor, the (aforementioned) wind no deterrent as he (or rather, his horse) galloped ever closer, his (Colin's, not the horse's) only intention to reach her side.

But no, she had to go and fall in love with Colin Bridgerton when he fell off a horse and landed on his bottom in a mud puddle. It was highly irregular, and *highly* unromantic, but there was a certain poetic justice in that, since nothing was ever going to come of it.

Why waste romance on a love that would never be returned? Better to save the windswept-moor introductions for people who might actually have a future together.

And if there was one thing Penelope knew, even then, at the age of sixteen years minus two days, it was that her future did not feature Colin Bridgerton in the role of husband.

She simply wasn't the sort of girl who attracted a man like him, and she feared that she never would be.

On the tenth of April, in the year 1813—precisely two days after her seventeenth birthday—Penelope Featherington made her debut into London society. She hadn't wanted to do it. She begged her mother to let her wait a year. She was at least two stone heavier than she ought to be, and her face still had an awful tendency to develop spots whenever she was nervous, which meant that she *always* had spots, since nothing in the world could make her as nervous as a London ball.

She tried to remind herself that beauty was only skin deep, but that didn't offer any helpful excuses when she was berating herself for never knowing what to *say* to people. There was nothing more depressing than an ugly girl with no personality. And in that first year on the marriage mart, that was exactly what Penelope was. An ugly girl with no—oh, very well, she had to give herself *some* credit—with very little personality.

Deep inside, she knew who she was, and that person was smart and kind and often even funny, but somehow her personality always got lost somewhere between her heart and her mouth, and she found herself saying the wrong thing or, more often, nothing at all.

To make matters even less attractive, Penelope's mother refused to allow Penelope to choose her own clothing, and when she wasn't in the requisite white that most young ladies wore (and which of course didn't flatter her complexion one bit), she was forced to wear yellow and red and orange, all of which made her look perfectly wretched. The one time Penelope had suggested green, Mrs. Featherington had planted her hands on her more-than-ample hips and declared that green was too melancholy.

Yellow, Mrs. Featherington declared, was a *happy* color and a *happy* girl would snare a husband.

Penelope decided then and there that it was best not to try to understand the workings of her mother's mind.

So Penelope found herself outfitted in yellow and orange and the occasional red, even though such colors made her look decidedly *un*happy, and in fact were positively ghastly with her brown eyes and red-tinged hair. There was nothing she could do about it, though, so she decided to grin and bear it, and if she couldn't manage a grin, at least she wouldn't cry in public.

Which, she took some pride in noting, she never did.

And if that weren't enough, 1813 was the year that the mysterious (and fictitious) Lady Whistledown began publishing her thrice-weekly *Society Papers*. The single-sheet newspaper became an instant sensation. No one knew who Lady Whistledown really was, but everyone seemed to have a theory. For weeks—no, months, really—London could speak of nothing else. The paper had been delivered for free for two weeks—just long enough to addict the *ton*—and then suddenly there was no delivery, just paperboys charging the outrageous price of five pennies a paper.

But by then, no one could live without the almost-daily dose of gossip, and everyone paid their pennies.

Somewhere some woman (or maybe, some people speculated, some man) was growing very rich indeed.

What set *Lady Whistledown's Society Papers* apart from any previous society newssheets was that the author actually listed her subjects' names in full. There was no hiding behind abbreviations such as Lord P——or Lady B——. If Lady Whistledown wanted to write about someone, she used his full name.

And when Lady Whistledown wanted to write about Penelope Featherington, she did. Penelope's first appearance in *Lady Whistledown's Society Papers* went as follows:

Miss Penelope Featherington's unfortunate gown left the unfortunate girl looking like nothing more than an overripe citrus fruit.

A rather stinging blow, to be sure, but nothing less than the truth.

Her second appearance in the column was no better.

Not a word was heard from Miss Penelope Featherington, and no wonder! The poor girl appeared to have drowned amidst the ruffles of her dress.

Not, Penelope was afraid, anything that would enhance her popularity.

But the season wasn't a complete disaster. There were a few people with whom she seemed able to speak. Lady Bridgerton, of all people, took a liking to her, and Penelope found that she could often tell things to the lovely viscountess that she would never dream of saying to her own mother. It was through Lady Bridgerton that she met Eloise Bridgerton, the younger sister of her beloved Colin. Eloise was also just turned seventeen, but her mother had wisely allowed her to delay her debut by a year, even though Eloise possessed the Bridgerton good looks and charm in abundance.

And while Penelope spent her afternoons in the green-and-cream drawing room at Bridgerton House (or, more often, up in Eloise's bedchamber where the two girls laughed and giggled and discussed everything under the sun with great earnestness), she found herself coming into occasional contact with Colin, who at two-and-twenty had not yet moved out of the family home and into bachelor lodgings.

If Penelope had thought she loved him before, that was nothing compared to what she felt after actually getting to know him. Colin Bridgerton was witty, he was dashing, he had a devil-may-care jokester quality to him that made women swoon, but most of all . . .

Colin Bridgerton was nice.

Nice. Such a silly little word. It should have been banal, but somehow it fit him to perfection. He always had something nice to say to Penelope, and when she finally worked up the courage to say something back (other than the very basic greetings and farewells), he actually listened. Which made it all the easier the next time around.

By the end of the season, Penelope judged that Colin Bridgerton was the only man with whom she'd managed an entire conversation.

This was love. Oh, this was love love love love love love. A silly repetition of words, perhaps, but that was precisely what Penelope doodled on a ridiculously expensive sheet of writing paper, along with the words, "Mrs. Colin Bridgerton" and "Penelope Bridgerton" and "Colin Colin Colin." (The paper went into the fire the moment Penelope heard footsteps in the hall.)

How wonderful it was to feel love—even the one-sided sort—for a nice person. It made one feel so positively sensible.

Of course, it didn't hurt that Colin possessed, as did all the Bridgerton men, fabulous good looks. There was that famous Bridgerton chestnut hair, the wide and smiling Bridgerton mouth, the broad shoulders, the six-foot height, and in Colin's case, the most devastating green eyes ever to grace a human face.

They were the sort of eyes that haunted a girl's dreams.

And Penelope dreamed and dreamed and dreamed.

April of 1814 found Penelope back in London for a second season, and even though she attracted the same number of suitors as the year before (zero), the season wasn't, in all honesty, quite so bad. It helped that she'd lost nearly two stone and could now call herself "pleasantly rounded" rather than "a hideous pudge." She was still nowhere near the slender ideal of womanhood that ruled the day, but at least she'd changed enough to warrant the purchase of a completely new wardrobe.

Unfortunately, her mother once again insisted on yellow, orange, and the occasional splash of red. And this time, Lady Whistledown wrote:

Miss Penelope Featherington (the least inane of the Featherington sisters) wore a gown of lemon yellow that left a sour taste in one's mouth.

Which at least seemed to imply that Penelope was the most intelligent member of her family, although the compliment was backhanded, indeed.

But Penelope wasn't the only one singled out by the acerbic gossip columnist. Dark-haired Kate Sheffield was likened to a singed daffodil in her yellow dress, and Kate went on to marry Anthony Bridgerton, Colin's older brother and a viscount to boot!

So Penelope held out hope.

Well, not really. She knew Colin wasn't going to marry her, but at least he danced with her at every ball, and he made her laugh, and every now and then she made him laugh, and she knew that that would have to be enough.

And so Penelope's life continued. She had her third season, then her fourth. Her two older sisters, Prudence and Philippa, finally found husbands of their own and moved away. Mrs. Featherington held out hope that Penelope might still make a match, since it had taken both Prudence and Philippa five seasons to snare husbands, but Penelope knew that she was destined to remain a spinster. It wouldn't be fair to marry someone when she was still so desperately in love with Colin. And maybe, in the far reaches of her mind—in the farthest-back corner, tucked away behind the French verb conjugations she'd never mastered and the arithmetic she never used—she still held out a tiny shred of hope.

Until *that* day.

Even now, seven years later, she still referred to it as *that* day.

She'd gone to the Bridgerton household, as she frequently did, to take tea with Eloise and her mother and sisters. It was right before Eloise's brother Benedict had married Sophie, only he didn't know who she really was, and—well, that didn't signify, except that it may have been the one truly great secret in the last decade that Lady Whistledown had never managed to unearth.

Anyway, she was walking through the front hall, listening to her feet tap along the marble tile as she saw herself out. She was adjusting her pelisse and preparing to walk the short distance to her own home (just around the corner, really) when she heard voices. Male voices. Male Bridgerton voices.

It was the three elder Bridgerton brothers: Anthony, Benedict, and Colin. They were having one of those conversations that men have, the kind in which they grumble a lot and poke fun at each other. Penelope had always liked to watch the Bridgertons interact in this manner; they were such a *family*.

Penelope could see them through the open front door, but she couldn't hear what they were saying until she'd reached the threshold. And in a testament to the bad timing that had plagued her throughout her life, the first voice she heard was Colin's, and the words were not kind.

". . . and *I am certainly not going to marry Penelope Featherington!*"

"Oh!" The word slipped over her lips before she could even think, the squeal of it piercing the air like an off-key whistle.

The three Bridgerton men turned to face her with identical horrified faces, and Penelope knew that she had just entered into what would certainly be the most awful five minutes of her life.

She said nothing for what seemed like an eternity, and then, finally, with a dignity she never dreamed she possessed, she looked straight at Colin and said, "I never asked you to marry me."

His cheeks went from pink to red. He opened his mouth, but not a sound came out. It was, Penelope thought with wry satisfaction, probably the only time in his life he'd ever been at a loss for words.

"And I never—" She swallowed convulsively. "I never said to anyone that I wanted you to ask me."

"Penelope," Colin finally managed, "I'm so sorry."

"You have nothing to apologize for," she said.

"No," he insisted, "I do. I hurt your feelings, and—"

"You didn't know I was there."

"But nevertheless—"

"You are not going to marry me," she said, her voice sounding very strange and hollow to her ears. "There is nothing wrong with that. I am not going to marry your brother Benedict."

Benedict had clearly been trying not to look, but he snapped to attention at that.

Penelope fisted her hands at her sides. "It doesn't hurt his feelings when I announce that I am not going to marry him." She turned to Benedict, forcing her eyes directly on his. "Does it, Mr. Bridgerton?"

"Of course not," Benedict answered quickly.

"It's settled, then," she said tightly, amazed that, for once, *exactly* the right words were coming out of her mouth. "No feelings were hurt. Now, then, if you will excuse me, gentlemen, I should like to go home."

The three gentlemen immediately stood back to let her pass, and she would have made a clean escape, except that Colin suddenly blurted out, "Don't you have a maid?"

She shook her head. "I live just around the corner."

"I know, but—"

"I'll escort you," Anthony said smoothly.

"That's really not necessary, my lord."

"Humor me," he said, in a tone that told her quite clearly she hadn't any choice in the matter.

She nodded, and the two of them took off down the

street. After they had passed about three houses, Anthony said in a strangely respectful voice, "He didn't know you were there."

Penelope felt her lips tighten at the corners—not out of anger, just out of a weary sense of resignation. "I know," she replied. "He's not the sort to be cruel. I expect your mother has been hounding him to get married."

Anthony nodded. Lady Bridgerton's intentions to see each and every one of her eight offspring happily married were legendary.

"She likes me," Penelope said. "Your mother, that is. She can't see beyond that, I'm afraid. But the truth is, it doesn't matter so much if she likes Colin's bride."

"Well, I wouldn't say *that*," Anthony mused, sounding not so much like a highly feared and respected viscount and rather more like a well-behaved son. "I shouldn't like to be married to someone my mother didn't like." He shook his head in a gesture of great awe and respect. "She's a force of nature."

"Your mother or your wife?"

He considered that for about half a second. "Both."

They walked for a few moments, and then Penelope blurted out, "Colin should go away."

Anthony eyed her curiously. "I beg your pardon?"

"He should go away. Travel. He's not ready to marry,

and your mother won't be able to restrain herself from pressuring him. She means well. . . ." Penelope bit her lip in horror. She hoped the viscount didn't think she was actually criticizing Lady Bridgerton. As far as she was concerned, there was no greater lady in England.

"My mother always means well," Anthony said with an indulgent smile. "But maybe you're right. Perhaps he should get away. Colin does enjoy travel. Although he did just return from Wales."

"Did he?" Penelope murmured politely, as if she didn't know perfectly well that he'd been in Wales.

"Here we are," he said as he nodded his reply. "This is your house, is it not?"

"Yes. Thank you for accompanying me home."

"It was my pleasure, I assure you."

Penelope watched as he left, then she went inside and cried.

The very next day, the following account appeared in *Lady Whistledown's Society Papers*:

La, but such excitement yesterday on the front steps of Lady Bridgerton's residence on Bruton Street!

First, Penelope Featherington was seen in the company of not one, not two, but THREE Bridgerton brothers, surely a heretofore impossible feat for the poor girl, who is rather infamous for her wall-

flower ways. Sadly (but perhaps predictably) for Miss Featherington, when she finally departed, it was on the arm of the viscount, the only married man in the bunch.

If Miss Featherington were to somehow manage to drag a Bridgerton brother to the altar, it would surely mean the end of the world as we know it, and This Author, who freely admits she would not know heads from tails in such a world, would be forced to resign her post on the spot.

It seemed even Lady Whistledown understood the futility of Penelope's feelings for Colin.

The years drifted by, and somehow, without realizing it, Penelope ceased to be a debutante and found herself sitting with the chaperones, watching her younger sister Felicity—surely the only Featherington sister blessed with both natural beauty and charm—enjoying her own London seasons.

Colin developed a taste for travel and began to spend more and more time outside of London; it seemed that every few months he was off to some new destination. When he was in town, he always saved a dance and a smile for Penelope, and somehow she managed to pretend that nothing had ever happened, that he'd never declared his distaste for her on a public street, that her dreams had never been shattered.

And when he was in town, which wasn't often, they seemed to settle into an easy, if not terribly deep, friendship. Which was all an almost twenty-eight-year-old spinster could hope for, right?

Unrequited love was never easy, but at least Penelope Featherington was used to it.

Chapter 1

Matchmaking mamas are united in their glee—
Colin Bridgerton has returned from Greece!

For those gentle (and ignorant) readers who are
new to town this year, Mr. Bridgerton is third in
the legendary string of eight Bridgerton siblings
(hence the name Colin, beginning with C; he follows
Anthony and Benedict, and precedes Daphne,
Eloise, Francesca, Gregory, and Hyacinth).

Although Mr. Bridgerton holds no noble title
and is unlikely ever to do so (he is seventh in
line for the title of Viscount Bridgerton, behind the
two sons of the current viscount, his elder brother
Benedict, and his three sons) he is still considered
one of the prime catches of the season, due to his
fortune, his face, his form, and most of all, his

charm. It is difficult, however, to predict whether Mr. Bridgerton will succumb to matrimonial bliss this season; he is certainly of an age to marry (three-and-thirty), but he has never shown a decided interest in any lady of proper parentage, and to make matters even more complicated, he has an appalling tendency to leave London at the drop of a hat, bound for some exotic destination.

LADY WHISTLEDOWN'S SOCIETY PAPERS,
2 APRIL 1824

"Look at this!" Portia Featherington squealed. "Colin Bridgerton is back!"

Penelope looked up from her needlework. Her mother was clutching the latest edition of *Lady Whistledown's Society Papers* the way Penelope might clutch, say, a rope while hanging off a building. "I know," she murmured.

Portia frowned. She hated when someone—anyone—was aware of gossip before she was. "How did you get to *Whistledown* before I did? I told Briarly to set it aside for me and not to let anyone touch—"

"I didn't see it in *Whistledown*," Penelope interrupted, before her mother went off to castigate the poor, beleaguered butler. "Felicity told me. Yesterday afternoon. Hyacinth Bridgerton told her."

"Your sister spends a great deal of time over at the Bridgerton household."

"As do I," Penelope pointed out, wondering where this was leading.

Portia tapped her finger against the side of her chin, as she always did when she was plotting or scheming. "Colin Bridgerton is of an age to be looking for a wife."

Penelope managed to blink just before her eyes bugged right out of her head. "Colin Bridgerton is not going to marry Felicity!"

Portia gave a little shrug. "Stranger things have happened."

"Not that I've ever seen," Penelope muttered.

"Anthony Bridgerton married that Kate Sheffield girl, and she was even less popular than *you*."

That wasn't exactly true; Penelope rather thought they'd been on equally low rungs of the social ladder. But there seemed little point in telling this to her mother, who probably thought she'd complimented her third daughter by saying she'd not been the least popular girl that season.

Penelope felt her lips tightening. Her mother's "compliments" had a habit of landing rather like wasps.

"Do not think I mean to criticize," Portia said, suddenly all concern. "In truth, I am glad for your spinsterhood. I am alone in this world save for my daughters, and it's comforting to know that one of you shall be able to care for me in my older years."

Penelope had a vision of the future—the future as described by her mother—and she had a sudden urge to run out and marry the chimney sweep. She'd long since resigned herself to a life of eternal spinsterhood, but somehow she'd always pictured herself off in her own neat little terrace house. Or maybe a snug cottage by the sea.

But lately Portia had been peppering her conversations with references to her old age and how lucky she was that Penelope could care for her. Never mind that both Prudence and Philippa had married well-heeled men and possessed ample funds to see to their mother's every comfort. Or that Portia was moderately wealthy in her own right; when her family had settled money on her as a dowry, one-fourth had been set aside for her own personal account.

No, when Portia talked about being "cared for," she wasn't referring to money. What Portia wanted was a slave.

Penelope sighed. She was being overly harsh with her mother, if only in her own mind. She did that too often. Her mother loved her. She knew her mother loved her. And she loved her mother back.

It was just that sometimes she didn't much *like* her mother.

She hoped that didn't make her a bad person. But truly, her mother could try the patience of even the kindest, gentlest of daughters, and as Penelope was the first to admit, she could be a wee bit sarcastic at times.

"Why don't you think Colin would marry Felicity?" Portia asked.

Penelope looked up, startled. She'd thought they were done with that subject. She should have known better. Her mother was nothing if not tenacious. "Well," she said slowly, "to begin with, she's twelve years younger than he is."

"Pfft," Portia said, waving her hand dismissively. "That's nothing, and you know it."

Penelope frowned, then yelped as she accidentally stabbed her finger with her needle.

"Besides," Portia continued blithely, "he's"—she looked back down at *Whistledown* and scanned it for his exact age—"three-and-thirty! How is he meant to avoid a twelve-year difference between him and his wife? Surely you don't expect him to marry someone *your* age."

Penelope sucked on her abused finger even though she knew it was hopelessly uncouth to do so. But she needed to put something in her mouth to keep her from saying something horrible *and* horribly spiteful.

Everything her mother said was true. Many *ton* weddings—maybe even most of them—saw men marrying girls a dozen or more years their junior. But somehow the age gap between Colin and Felicity seemed even larger, perhaps because . . .

Penelope was unable to keep the disgust off her face. "She's like a sister to him. A little sister."

"Really, Penelope. I hardly think—"

"It's almost incestuous," Penelope muttered.

"What did you say?"

Penelope snatched up her needlework again. "Nothing."

"I'm sure you said something."

Penelope shook her head. "I did clear my throat. Perhaps you heard—"

"I heard you saying something. I'm sure of it!"

Penelope groaned. Her life loomed long and tedious ahead of her. "Mother," she said, with the patience of, if not a saint, at least a very devout nun, "Felicity is practically engaged to Mr. Albansdale."

Portia actually began rubbing her hands together. "She won't be engaged to him if she can catch Colin Bridgerton."

"Felicity would *die* before chasing after Colin."

"Of course not. She's a smart girl. Anyone can see that Colin Bridgerton is a better catch."

"But Felicity loves Mr. Albansdale!"

Portia deflated into her perfectly upholstered chair. "There is that."

"And," Penelope added with great feeling, "Mr. Albansdale is in possession of a perfectly respectable fortune."

Portia tapped her index finger against her cheek. "True. Not," she said sharply, "as respectable as a Bridgerton portion, but it's nothing to sneeze at, I suppose."

Penelope knew it was time to let it go, but she couldn't stop her mouth from opening one last time. "In all truth, Mother, he's a wonderful match for Felicity. We should be delighted for her."

"I know, I know," Portia grumbled. "It's just that I so wanted one of my daughters to marry a Bridgerton. What a coup! I would be the talk of London for weeks. Years, maybe."

Penelope stabbed her needle into the cushion beside her. It was a rather foolish way to vent her anger, but the alternative was to jump to her feet and yell, *What about me?* Portia seemed to think that once Felicity was wed, her hopes for a Bridgerton union were forever dashed. But Penelope was still unmarried—didn't that count for anything?

Was it so much to wish that her mother thought of her with the same pride she felt for her other three daughters? Penelope knew that Colin wasn't going to choose her as his bride, but shouldn't a mother be at least a little bit blind to her children's faults? It was obvious to Penelope that neither Prudence, Philippa, nor even Felicity had ever had a chance with a Bridgerton. Why did her mother seem to think their charms so exceeded Penelope's?

Very well, Penelope had to admit that Felicity enjoyed a popularity that exceeded that of her three older sisters combined. But Prudence and Philippa had never been Incomparables. They'd hovered on the perimeters of ballrooms just as much as Penelope had.

Except, of course, that they were married now. Penelope wouldn't have wanted to cleave herself unto either of their husbands, but at least they were wives.

Thankfully, however, Portia's mind had already moved on to greener pastures. "I must pay a call upon Violet," she was saying. "She'll be so relieved that Colin is back."

"I'm sure Lady Bridgerton will be delighted to see you," Penelope said.

"That poor woman," Portia said, her sigh dramatic. "She worries about him, you know—"

"I know."

"Truly, I think it is more than a mother should be expected to bear. He goes gallivanting about, the good Lord only knows where, to countries that are positively *heathen*—"

"I believe they practice Christianity in Greece," Penelope murmured, her eyes back down on her needlework.

"Don't be impertinent, Penelope Anne Featherington, and they're *Catholics*!" Portia shuddered on the word.

"They're not Catholics at all," Penelope replied, giving up on the needlework and setting it aside. "They're Greek Orthodox."

"Well, they're not Church of England," Portia said with a sniff.

"Seeing as how they're Greek, I don't think they're terribly worried about that."

Portia's eyes narrowed disapprovingly. "And how do you know about this Greek religion, anyway? No, don't tell me," she said with a dramatic flourish. "You read it somewhere."

Penelope just blinked as she tried to think of a suitable reply.

"I wish you wouldn't read so much," Portia sighed. "I probably could have married you off years ago if you had concentrated more on the social graces and less on . . . less on . . ."

Penelope had to ask. "Less on what?"

"I don't know. Whatever it is you do that has you staring into space and daydreaming so often."

"I'm just thinking," Penelope said quietly. "Sometimes I just like to stop and think."

"Stop what?" Portia wanted to know.

Penelope couldn't help but smile. Portia's query seemed to sum up all that was different between mother and daughter. "It's nothing, Mother," Penelope said. "Really."

Portia looked as if she wanted to say more, then thought the better of it. Or maybe she was just hungry. She did pluck a biscuit off the tea tray and pop it into her mouth.

Penelope started to reach out to take the last biscuit for herself, then decided to let her mother have it. She might as well keep her mother's mouth full. The last thing she wanted was to find herself in another conversation about Colin Bridgerton.

"Colin's back!"

Penelope looked up from her book—*A Brief History of Greece*—to see Eloise Bridgerton bursting into her room. As usual, Eloise had not been announced. The Featherington butler was so used to seeing her there that he treated her like a member of the family.

"Is he?" Penelope asked, managing to feign (in her opinion) rather realistic indifference. Of course, she did set *A Brief History of Greece* down behind *Mathilda*, the novel by S. R. Fielding that had been all the rage a year earlier. Everyone had a copy of *Mathilda* on their bedstand. And it was thick enough to hide *A Brief History of Greece*.

Eloise sat down in Penelope's desk chair. "Indeed, and he's very tanned. All that time in the sun, I suppose."

"He went to Greece, didn't he?"

Eloise shook her head. "He said the war there has worsened, and it was too dangerous. So he went to Cyprus instead."

"My, my," Penelope said with a smile. "Lady Whistledown got something wrong."

Eloise smiled that cheeky Bridgerton smile, and once again Penelope realized how lucky she was to have her as her closest friend. She and Eloise had been inseparable since the age of seventeen. They'd had their London seasons together, reached adulthood together, and, much to their mothers' dismay, had become spinsters together.

Eloise claimed that she hadn't met the right person. Penelope, of course, hadn't been asked.

"Did he enjoy Cyprus?" Penelope inquired.

Eloise sighed. "He said it was brilliant. How I should love to travel. It seems everyone has been somewhere but me."

"And me," Penelope reminded her.

"And you," Eloise agreed. "Thank goodness for you."

"Eloise!" Penelope exclaimed, throwing a pillow at her. But she thanked goodness for Eloise, too. Every day. Many women went through their entire lives without a close female friend, and here she had someone to whom she could tell anything. Well, almost anything. Penelope had never told her of her feelings for Colin, although she rather thought Eloise suspected the truth. Eloise was far too tactful to mention it, though, which only validated Penelope's certainty that Colin would never love her. If Eloise had thought, for even one moment, that Penelope actually had a chance at snaring Colin as a husband, she would have been plotting her matchmaking strategies with a ruthlessness that would have impressed any army general.

When it came right down to it, Eloise was a rather managing sort of person.

". . . and then he said that the water was so choppy that he actually cast up his accounts over the side of the boat, and—" Eloise scowled. "You're not listening to me."

"No," Penelope admitted. "Well, yes, actually, parts of it. I cannot believe Colin actually told you he vomited."

"Well, I *am* his sister."

"He'd be furious with you if he knew you'd told me."

Eloise waved off her protest. "He won't mind. You're like another sister to him."

Penelope smiled, but she sighed at the same time.

"Mother asked him—of course—whether he was planning to remain in town for the season," Eloise continued, "and—of course—he was terribly evasive, but then I decided to interrogate him myself—"

"Terribly smart of you," Penelope murmured.

Eloise threw the pillow back at her. "And I finally got him to admit to me that yes, he thinks he will stay for at least a few months. But he made me promise not to tell Mother."

"Now, that's not"—Penelope cleared her throat—"terribly intelligent of him. If your mother thinks his time here is limited, she will redouble her efforts to see him married. I should think that was what he wanted most to avoid."

"It does seem his usual aim in life," Eloise concurred.

"If he lulled her into thinking that there was no rush, perhaps she might not badger him quite so much."

"An interesting idea," Eloise said, "but probably more true in theory than in practice. My mother is so determined to see him wed that it matters not if she increases her efforts. Her regular efforts are enough to drive him mad as it is."

"Can one go doubly mad?" Penelope mused.

Eloise cocked her head. "I don't know," she said. "I don't think I should want to find out."

They both fell silent for a moment (a rare occurrence, indeed) and then Eloise quite suddenly jumped to her feet and said, "I must go."

Penelope smiled. People who didn't know Eloise very well thought she had a habit of changing the subject frequently (and abruptly), but Penelope knew that the truth was something else altogether. When Eloise had her mind set on something, she was completely unable to let it go. Which meant that if Eloise suddenly wanted to leave, it probably had to do with something they'd been talking about earlier in the afternoon, and—

"Colin is expected for tea," Eloise explained.

Penelope smiled. She loved being right.

"You should come," Eloise said.

Penelope shook her head. "He'll want it to be just family."

"You're probably right," Eloise said, nodding slightly. "Very well, then, I must be off. Terribly sorry to cut my visit so short, but I wanted to be sure that you knew Colin was home."

"*Whistledown*," Penelope reminded her.

"Right. Where does that woman get her information?" Eloise said, shaking her head in wonder. "I vow sometimes she knows so much about my family I wonder if I ought to be frightened."

"She can't go on forever," Penelope commented, getting up to see her friend out. "Someone will eventually figure out who she is, don't you think?"

"I don't know." Eloise put her hand on the doorknob, twisted, and pulled. "I used to think so. But it's been ten years. More, actually. If she were going to be caught, I think it would have happened already."

Penelope followed Eloise down the stairs. "Eventually she'll make a mistake. She has to. She's only human."

Eloise laughed. "And here I thought she was a minor god."

Penelope found herself grinning.

Eloise stopped and whirled around so suddenly that Penelope crashed right into her, nearly sending both of them tumbling down the last few steps on the staircase. "Do you know what?" Eloise demanded.

"I couldn't begin to speculate."

Eloise didn't even bother to pull a face. "I'd wager that she *has* made a mistake," she said.

"I beg your pardon?"

"You said it yourself. She—or it could be he, I suppose—has been writing the column for over a decade. No one could do that for so long without making a mistake. Do you know what I think?"

Penelope just spread her hands in an impatient gesture.

"I think the problem is that the rest of us are too stupid to notice her mistakes."

Penelope stared at her for a moment, then burst out laughing. "Oh, Eloise," she said, wiping tears from her eyes. "I do love you."

Eloise grinned. "And it's a good thing you do, spinster that I am. We shall have to set up a household together when we are thirty and truly crones."

Penelope caught hold of the idea like a lifeboat. "Do

you think we could?" she exclaimed. And then, in a hushed voice, after looking furtively up and down the hall, "Mother has begun to speak of her old age with alarming frequency."

"What's so alarming about that?"

"I'm in all of her visions, waiting on her hand and foot."

"Oh, dear."

"A milder expletive than had crossed my mind."

"Penelope!" But Eloise was grinning.

"I love my mother," Penelope said.

"I know you do," Eloise said, in a rather placating sort of voice.

"No, I really do."

The left corner of Eloise's mouth began to twitch. "I know you really do. Really."

"It's just that—"

Eloise put up a hand. "You don't need to say any more. I understand perfectly. I—Oh! Good day, Mrs. Featherington!"

"Eloise," Portia said, bustling down the hall. "I didn't realize you were here."

"I'm sneaky as always," Eloise said. "Cheeky, even."

Portia gave her an indulgent smile. "I heard your brother is back in town."

"Yes, we are all overjoyed."

"I'm sure you must be, especially your mother."

"Indeed. She is beside herself. I believe she is drawing up a list right now."

Portia's entire aspect perked up, as it did at the mention of anything that might be construed as gossip. "A list? What sort of list?"

"Oh, you know, the same list she has made for all of her adult children. Prospective spouses and all that."

"It makes me wonder," Penelope said in a dry voice, "what constitutes 'all that.' "

"Sometimes she includes one or two people who are hopelessly unsuitable so as to highlight the qualities of the *real* possibilities."

Portia laughed. "Perhaps she'll put you on Colin's list, Penelope!"

Penelope didn't laugh. Neither did Eloise. Portia didn't seem to notice.

"Well, I'd best be off," Eloise said, clearing her throat to cover a moment that was awkward to two of the three people in the hall. "Colin is expected for tea. Mother wants the entire family in attendance."

"Will you all fit?" Penelope asked. Lady Bridgerton's home was large, but the Bridgerton children, spouses, and grandchildren numbered twenty-one. It was a large brood, indeed.

"We're going to Bridgerton House," Eloise explained. Her mother had moved out of the Bridgertons' official London residence after her eldest son had married. Anthony, who had been viscount since the age of eighteen, had told Violet that she needn't go, but she had insisted that he and his wife needed their privacy. As a result, Anthony and Kate lived with their three children in Bridgerton House, while Violet lived with her unmarried children (with the exception of Colin, who kept his own lodgings) just a few blocks away at 5 Bruton Street. After a year or so of unsuccessful attempts to name Lady Bridgerton's new home, the family had taken to calling it simply Number Five.

"Do enjoy yourself," Portia said. "I must go and find Felicity. We are late for an appointment at the modiste."

Eloise watched Portia disappear up the stairs, then said to Penelope, "Your sister seems to spend a great deal of time at the modiste."

Penelope shrugged. "Felicity is going mad with all the fittings, but she's Mother's only hope for a truly grand match. I'm afraid she's convinced that Felicity will catch a duke if she's wearing the right gown."

"Isn't she practically engaged to Mr. Albansdale?"

"I imagine he'll make a formal offer next week. But

until then, Mother is keeping her options open." She rolled her eyes. "You'd best warn your brother to keep his distance."

"Gregory?" Eloise asked in disbelief. "He's not even out of university."

"Colin."

"*Colin?*" Eloise exploded with laughter. "Oh, that's rich."

"That's what I told her, but you know how she is once she gets an idea in her head."

Eloise chuckled. "Rather like me, I imagine."

"Tenacious to the end."

"Tenacity can be a very good thing," Eloise reminded her, "at the proper time."

"Right," Penelope returned with a sarcastic smile, "and at the improper time, it's an absolute nightmare."

Eloise laughed. "Cheer up, friend. At least she let you rid yourself of all those yellow frocks."

Penelope looked down at her morning dress, which was, if she did say so herself, a rather flattering shade of blue. "She stopped choosing my clothing once she finally realized I was officially on the shelf. A girl with no marriage prospects isn't worth the time and energy it takes her to offer fashion advice. She hasn't accompanied me to the modiste in over a year! Bliss!"

Eloise smiled at her friend, whose complexion

turned the loveliest peaches and cream whenever she wore cooler hues. "It was apparent to all, the moment you were allowed to choose your own clothing. Even Lady Whistledown commented upon it!"

"I hid that column from Mother," Penelope admitted. "I didn't want her feelings to be hurt."

Eloise blinked a few times before saying, "That was very kind of you, Penelope."

"I have my moments of charity and grace."

"One would think," Eloise said with a snort, "that a vital component of charity and grace is the ability not to draw attention to one's possession of them."

Penelope pursed her lips as she pushed Eloise toward the door. "Don't you need to go home?"

"I'm leaving! I'm leaving!"

And she left.

It was, Colin Bridgerton decided as he took a sip of some truly excellent brandy, rather nice to be back in England.

It was quite strange, actually, how he loved returning home just as much as he did the departure. In another few months—six at the most—he'd be itching to leave again, but for now, England in April was positively brilliant.

"It's good, isn't it?"

Colin looked up. His brother Anthony was leaning against the front of his massive mahogany desk, motioning to him with his own glass of brandy.

Colin nodded. "Hadn't realized how much I missed it until I returned. Ouzo has its charms, but this"—he lifted his glass—"is heaven."

Anthony smiled wryly. "And how long do you plan to remain this time?"

Colin wandered over to the window and pretended to look out. His eldest brother made little attempt to disguise his impatience with Colin's wanderlust. In truth, Colin really couldn't blame him. Occasionally, it was difficult to get letters home; he supposed that his family often had to wait a month or even two for word of his welfare. But while he knew that he would not relish being in their shoes—never knowing if a loved one was dead or alive, constantly waiting for the knock of the messenger at the front door—that just wasn't enough to keep his feet firmly planted in England.

Every now and then, he simply had to get *away*. There was no other way to describe it.

Away from the *ton,* who thought him a charming rogue and nothing else, away from England, which encouraged younger sons to enter the military or the clergy, neither of which suited his temperament. Even away from his family, who loved him unconditionally but had no clue that what he really wanted, deep down inside, was something to do.

His brother Anthony held the viscountcy, and with that came myriad responsibilities. He ran estates, managed the family's finances, and saw to the welfare of countless tenants and servants. Benedict, his elder by four years, had gained renown as an artist. He'd started with pencil and paper, but at the urging of his wife had moved on to oils. One of his landscapes now hung in the National Gallery.

Anthony would be forever remembered in family trees as the seventh Viscount Bridgerton. Benedict would live through his paintings, long after he left this earth.

But Colin had nothing. He managed the small property given to him by his family and he attended parties. He would never dream of claiming he didn't have fun, but sometimes he wanted something a little more than fun.

He wanted a purpose.

He wanted a legacy.

He wanted, if not to know then at least to hope, that when he was gone, he'd be memorialized in some manner other than in *Lady Whistledown's Society Papers.*

He sighed. No wonder he spent so much time traveling.

"Colin?" his brother prompted.

Colin turned to him and blinked. He was fairly certain Anthony had asked him a question, but somewhere in the meanderings of his mind, he'd forgotten what.

"Oh. Right." Colin cleared his throat. "I'll be here for the rest of the season, at least."

Anthony said nothing, but it was difficult to miss the satisfied expression on his face.

"If nothing else," Colin added, affixing his legendary crooked grin on his face, "someone has to spoil your children. I don't think Charlotte has nearly enough dolls."

"Only fifty," Anthony agreed in a deadpan voice. "The poor girl is horribly neglected."

"Her birthday is at the end of this month, is it not? I shall have to neglect her some more, I think."

"Speaking of birthdays," Anthony said, settling into the large chair behind his desk, "Mother's is a week from Sunday."

"Why do you think I hurried to return?"

Anthony raised a brow, and Colin had the distinct impression that he was trying to decide if Colin had truly rushed home for their mother's birthday, or if he was simply taking advantage of some very good timing.

"We're holding a party for her," Anthony said.

"She's letting you?" It was Colin's experience that women of a certain age did not enjoy birthday celebrations. And although his mother was still exceedingly lovely, she was definitely of a certain age.

"We were forced to resort to blackmail," Anthony admitted. "She agreed to the party or we revealed her true age."

Colin shouldn't have taken a sip of his brandy; he choked on it and just barely managed to avert spraying it all over his brother. "I should have liked to have seen *that.*"

Anthony offered a rather satisfied smile. "It was a brilliant maneuver on my part."

Colin finished the rest of his drink. "What, do you think, are the chances she won't use the party as an opportunity to find me a wife?"

"Very small."

"I thought so."

Anthony leaned back in his chair. "You *are* thirty-three now, Colin . . ."

Colin stared at him in disbelief. "God above, don't *you* start on me."

"I wouldn't dream of it. I was merely going to suggest that you keep your eyes open this season. You needn't actively look for a wife, but there's no harm in remaining at least amenable to the possibility."

Colin eyed the doorway, intending to pass through it very shortly. "I assure you I am not averse to the idea of marriage."

"I didn't think you were," Anthony demurred.

"I see little reason to rush, however."

"There's never a reason to rush," Anthony returned. "Well, rarely, anyway. Just humor Mother, will you?"

Colin hadn't realized he was still holding his empty glass until it slipped through his fingers and landed on the carpet with a loud thunk. "Good God," he whispered, "is she ill?"

"No!" Anthony said, his surprise making his voice loud and forceful. "She'll outlive us all, I'm sure of it."

"Then what is this about?"

Anthony sighed. "I just want to see you happy."

"I am happy," Colin insisted.

"Are you?"

"Hell, I'm the happiest man in London. Just read Lady Whistledown. She'll tell you so."

Anthony glanced down at the paper on his desk.

"Well, maybe not this column, but anything from last year. I've been called charming more times than

Lady Danbury has been called opinionated, and we both know what a feat *that* is."

"Charming doesn't necessarily equal happy," Anthony said softly.

"I don't have time for this," Colin muttered. The door had never looked so good.

"If you were truly happy," Anthony persisted, "you wouldn't keep leaving."

Colin paused with his hand on the doorknob. "Anthony, I *like* to travel."

"Constantly?"

"I must, or I wouldn't do it."

"That's an evasive sentence if ever I've heard one."

"And this"—Colin flashed his brother a wicked smile—"is an evasive maneuver."

"Colin!"

But he'd already left the room.

Chapter 2

It has always been fashionable among the ton to complain of ennui, but surely this year's crop of partygoers has raised boredom to an art form. One cannot take two steps at a society function these days without hearing the phrase "dreadfully dull," or "hopelessly banal." Indeed, This Author has even been informed that Cressida Twombley recently remarked that she was convinced that she might perish of eternal boredom if forced to attend one more off-key musicale.

(This Author must concur with Lady Twombley on that note; while this year's selection of debutantes are an amiable bunch, there is not a decent musician among them.)

If there is to be an antidote for the disease of tedium, surely it will be Sunday's fête at Bridgerton House. The entire family will gather, along with a hundred or so of their closest friends, to celebrate the dowager viscountess's birthday.

It is considered crass to mention a lady's age, and so This Author will not reveal which birthday Lady Bridgerton is celebrating.

But have no fear! This Author knows!

LADY WHISTLEDOWN'S SOCIETY PAPERS,
9 APRIL 1824

S pinsterhood was a word that tended to invoke either panic or pity, but Penelope was coming to realize that there were decided advantages to the unmarried state.

First of all, no one really expected the spinsters to dance at balls, which meant that Penelope was no longer forced to hover at the edge of the dance floor, looking this way and that, pretending that she didn't really want to dance. Now she could sit off to the side with the other spinsters and chaperones. She still wanted to dance, of course—she rather liked dancing, and she was actually quite good at it, not that anyone ever noticed—but it was much easier to feign disinterest the farther one got from the waltzing couples.

Second, the number of hours spent in dull conversation had been drastically reduced. Mrs. Featherington had officially given up hope that Penelope might ever snag a husband, and so she'd stopped thrusting her in the path of every third-tier eligible bachelor. Portia had never really thought Penelope had a prayer of attracting the attention of a first- or second-tier bachelor, which was probably true, but most of the third-tier bachelors were classified as such for a reason, and sadly, that reason was often personality, or lack thereof. Which, when combined with Penelope's shyness with strangers, didn't tend to promote sparkling conversation.

And finally, she could eat again. It was maddening, considering the amount of food generally on display at *ton* parties, but women on the hunt for husbands weren't supposed to exhibit anything more robust than a bird's appetite. This, Penelope thought gleefully (as she bit into what had to be the most heavenly éclair outside of France), had to be the best spinster perk of all.

"Good heavens," she moaned. If sin could take a solid form, surely it would be a pastry. Preferably one with chocolate.

"That good, eh?"

Penelope choked on the éclair, then coughed, sending a fine spray of pastry cream through the air. "Colin," she gasped, fervently praying the largest of the globs had missed his ear.

"Penelope." He smiled warmly. "It's good to see you."

"And you."

He rocked on his heels—once, twice, thrice—then said, "You look well."

"And you," she said, too preoccupied with trying to figure out where to set down her éclair to offer much variety to her conversation.

"That's a nice dress," he said, motioning to her green silk gown.

She smiled ruefully, explaining, "It's not yellow."

"So it's not." He grinned, and the ice was broken. It was strange, because one would think her tongue would be tied the tightest around the man she loved, but there was something about Colin that set everyone at ease.

Maybe, Penelope had thought on more than one occasion, part of the reason she loved him was that he made her feel comfortable with herself.

"Eloise tells me you had a splendid time in Cyprus," she said.

He grinned. "Couldn't resist the birthplace of Aphrodite, after all."

Penelope found herself smiling as well. His good humor was infectious, even if the last thing she wanted to do was take part in a discussion of the goddess of love. "Was it as sunny as everyone says?" she asked. "No, forget I asked. I can see from your face that it was."

"I did acquire a bit of a tan," he said with a nod. "My mother nearly fainted when she saw me."

"From delight, I'm sure," Penelope said emphatically. "She misses you terribly when you're gone."

He leaned in. "Come, now, Penelope, surely you're not going to start in on me? Between my mother, Anthony, Eloise, and Daphne, I'm liable to perish of guilt."

"Not Benedict?" she couldn't help quipping.

He shot her a slightly smirky look. "He's out of town."

"Ah, well, that explains his silence."

His narrowed eyes matched his crossed arms to perfection. "You've always been cheeky, did you know that?"

"I hide it well," she said modestly.

"It's easy to see," he said in a dry voice, "why you are such good friends with my sister."

"I'm assuming you intended that as a compliment?"

"I'm fairly certain I'd be endangering my health if I'd intended it any other way."

Penelope was standing there hoping she'd think of a witty rejoinder when she heard a strange, wet, splattish sound. She looked down to discover that a large yellowish blob of pastry cream had slid from her half-eaten éclair and landed on the pristine wooden floor. She looked back up to find Colin's oh-so-green eyes dancing with laughter, even as his mouth fought for a serious expression.

"Well, now, that's embarrassing," Penelope said, deciding that the only way to avoid dying of mortification was to state the painfully obvious.

"I suggest," Colin said, raising one brow into a perfectly debonair arch, "that we flee the scene."

Penelope looked down at the empty carcass of the éclair still in her hand. Colin answered her with a nod toward a nearby potted plant.

"No!" she said, her eyes growing wide.

He leaned in closer. "I dare you."

Her eyes darted from the éclair to the plant and back to Colin's face. "I couldn't," she said.

"As far as naughty things go, this one is fairly mild," he pointed out.

It was a dare, and Penelope was usually immune to such childish ploys, but Colin's half-smile was difficult to resist. "Very well," she said, squaring her shoulders and dropping the pastry onto the soil. She took a step back, examined her handiwork, looked around to see if anyone besides Colin was watching her, then leaned down and rotated the pot so that a leafy branch covered the evidence.

"I didn't think you'd do it," Colin said.

"As you said, it's not terribly naughty."

"No, but it is my mother's favorite potted palm."

"Colin!" Penelope whirled around, fully intending to sink her hand right back into the plant to retrieve the éclair. "How could you let me—Wait a second." She straightened, her eyes narrowed. "This isn't a palm."

He was all innocence. "It's not?"

"It's a miniature orange tree."

He blinked. "Is it, now?"

She scowled at him. Or at least she hoped it was a scowl. It was difficult to scowl at Colin Bridgerton. Even his mother had once remarked that it was nearly impossible to reprimand him.

He would just smile and look contrite and say something funny, and you just couldn't stay angry with him. You simply couldn't do it.

"You were trying to make me feel guilty," Penelope said.

"Anyone could confuse a palm with an orange tree."

She fought the urge to roll her eyes. "Except for the oranges."

He chewed on his lower lip, his eyes thoughtful. "Yes, hmmm, one would think they'd be a bit of a giveaway."

"You're a terrible liar, did you know that?"

He straightened, tugging slightly at his waistcoat as he lifted his chin. "Actually, I'm an excellent liar. But what I'm really good at is appearing appropriately sheepish and adorable after I'm caught."

What, Penelope wondered, was she meant to say to *that*? Because surely there was no one more adorably sheepish (sheepishly adorable?) than Colin Bridgerton with his hands clasped behind his back, his eyes flitting along the ceiling, and his lips puckered into an innocent whistle.

"When you were a child," Penelope asked, abruptly changing the subject, "were you ever punished?"

Colin immediately straightened to attention. "I beg your pardon?"

"Were you ever punished as a child?" she repeated. "Are you ever punished now?"

Colin just stared at her, wondering if she had any

idea what she was asking. Probably not. "Errr . . ." he said, mostly because he hadn't anything else to say.

She let out a vaguely patronizing sigh. "I thought not."

If he were a less indulgent man, and if this were anyone but Penelope Featherington, whom he knew did not possess a malicious bone in her body, he might take offense. But he was an uncommonly easygoing fellow, and this *was* Penelope Featherington, who had been a faithful friend to his sister for God knows how many years, so instead of adopting a hard, cynical stare (which, admittedly, was an expression at which he'd never excelled), he merely smiled and murmured, "Your point being?"

"Do not think I mean to criticize your parents," she said with an expression that was innocent and sly at the same time. "I would never dream of implying that you were spoiled in any way."

He nodded graciously.

"It's just that"—she leaned in, as if imparting a grave secret—"I rather think you could get away with murder if you so chose."

He coughed—not to clear his throat and not because he wasn't feeling well, but rather because he was so damned startled. Penelope was such a funny character. No, that wasn't quite right. She was . . . *surprising*.

Yes, that seemed to sum her up. Very few people really knew her; she had certainly never developed a reputation as a sterling conversationalist. He was fairly certain she'd made it through three-hour parties without ever venturing beyond words of a single syllable.

But when Penelope was in the company of someone with whom she felt comfortable—and Colin realized that he was probably privileged to count himself among that number—she had a dry wit, a sly smile, and evidence of a very intelligent mind, indeed.

He wasn't surprised that she'd never attracted any serious suitors for her hand; she wasn't a beauty by any stretch, although upon close examination she was more attractive than he'd remembered her to be. Her brown hair had a touch of red to it, highlighted nicely by the flickering candles. And her skin was quite lovely— that perfect peaches-and-cream complexion that ladies were always slathering their faces with arsenic to achieve.

But Penelope's attractiveness wasn't the sort that men usually noticed. And her normally shy and occasionally even stuttering demeanor didn't exactly showcase her personality.

Still, it was too bad about her lack of popularity. She would have made someone a perfectly good wife.

"So you're saying," he mused, steering his mind

back to the matter at hand, "that I should consider a life of crime?"

"Nothing of the sort," she replied, a demure smile on her face. "Just that I rather suspect you could talk your way out of anything." And then, unexpectedly, her mien grew serious, and she quietly said, "I envy that."

Colin surprised himself by holding out his hand and saying, "Penelope Featherington, I think you should dance with me."

And then Penelope surprised *him* by laughing and saying, "That's very sweet of you to ask, but you don't have to dance with me any longer."

His pride felt oddly pricked. "What the devil do you mean by that?"

She shrugged. "It's official now. I'm a spinster. There's no longer a reason to dance with me just so that I don't feel left out."

"That's not why I danced with you," he protested, but he knew that it was exactly the reason. And half the time he'd only remembered to ask because his mother had poked him—*hard*—in the back and reminded him.

She gave him a faintly pitying look, which galled him, because he'd never thought to be pitied by Penelope Featherington.

"If you think," he said, feeling his spine grow stiff,

"that I'm going to allow you to wiggle out of a dance with me *now*, you're quite delusional."

"You don't have to dance with me just to prove you don't mind doing it," she said.

"I *want* to dance with you," he fairly growled.

"Very well," she said, after what seemed to be a ridiculously long pause. "It would surely be churlish for me to refuse."

"It was probably churlish of you to doubt my intentions," he said as he took her arm, "but I'm willing to forgive you if you can forgive yourself."

She stumbled, which made him smile.

"I do believe I'll manage," she choked out.

"Excellent." He offered her a bland smile. "I'd hate to think of you living with the guilt."

The music was just beginning, so Penelope took his hand and curtsied as they began the minuet. It was difficult to talk during the dance, which gave Penelope a few moments to catch her breath and gather her thoughts.

Perhaps she'd been a bit too harsh with Colin. She shouldn't have scolded him for asking her to dance, when the truth was, those dances were among her most cherished memories. Did it really matter if he'd only done it out of pity? It would have been worse if he'd never asked her at all.

She grimaced. Worse still, did this mean she had to apologize?

"Was something wrong with that éclair?" Colin inquired the next time they stepped toward each other.

A full ten seconds passed before they were close enough again for her to say, "I beg your pardon?"

"You look as if you've swallowed something vile," he said, loudly this time, for he'd clearly lost patience with waiting for the dance to allow them to speak.

Several people looked over, then stepped discreetly away, as if Penelope might actually be sick right there on the ballroom floor.

"Do you need to shout it to the entire world?" Penelope hissed.

"You know," he said thoughtfully, bending into an elegant bow as the music drew to a close, "that was the loudest whisper I've ever heard."

He was insufferable, but Penelope wasn't going to say so, because it would only make her sound like a character in a very bad romantic novel. She'd read one just the other day in which the heroine used the word (or one of its synonyms) on every other page.

"Thank you for the dance," she said, once they'd reached the perimeter of the room. She almost added, *You can now tell your mother that you've fulfilled your obligations,* but immediately regretted her impulse.

Colin hadn't done anything to deserve such sarcasm. It wasn't his fault that men only danced with her when forced to by their mothers. He'd always at least smiled and laughed while doing his duty, which was more than she could say for the rest of the male population.

He nodded politely and murmured his own thanks. They were just about to part ways when they heard a loud female voice bark out, "Mr. Bridgerton!"

They both froze. It was a voice they both knew. It was a voice everyone knew.

"Save me," Colin groaned.

Penelope looked over her shoulder to see the infamous Lady Danbury pushing her way through the crowd, wincing when her ever-present cane landed on the foot of some hapless young lady. "Maybe she means a different Mr. Bridgerton?" Penelope suggested. "There are quite a few of you, after all, and it's possible—"

"I'll give you ten pounds if you don't leave my side," Colin blurted out.

Penelope choked on air. "Don't be silly, I—"

"Twenty."

"Done!" she said with a smile, not because she particularly needed the money but rather because it was strangely enjoyable to be extorting it from Colin. "Lady Danbury!" she called out, hurrying to the elderly lady's side. "How nice to see you."

"Nobody ever thinks it's nice to see me," Lady Danbury said sharply, "except maybe my nephew, and half the time I'm not even sure about him. But I thank you for lying all the same."

Colin said nothing, but she still turned in his direction and swatted his leg with her cane. "Good choice dancing with this one," she said. "I've always liked her. More brains than the rest of her family put together."

Penelope opened her mouth to defend at least her younger sister, when Lady Danbury barked out, "Ha!" after barely a second's pause, adding, "I noticed neither of you contradicted me."

"It is always a delight to see you, Lady Danbury," Colin said, giving her just the sort of smile he might have directed at an opera singer.

"Glib, this one is," Lady Danbury said to Penelope. "You'll have to watch out for him."

"It is rarely necessary that I do so," Penelope said, "as he is most often out of the country."

"See!" Lady Danbury crowed again. "I told you she was bright."

"You'll notice," Colin said smoothly, "that I did not contradict you."

The old lady smiled approvingly. "So you didn't. You're getting smart in your old age, Mr. Bridgerton."

"It has occasionally been remarked that I possessed a small modicum of intelligence in my youth, as well."

"Hmmph. The important word in that sentence being *small,* of course."

Colin looked at Penelope through narrowed eyes. She appeared to be choking on laughter.

"We women must look out for one another," Lady Danbury said to no one in particular, "since it is clear that no one else will do so."

Colin decided it was definitely time to go. "I think I see my mother."

"Escape is impossible," Lady Danbury crowed. "Don't bother to attempt it, and besides, I know for a fact you don't see your mother. She's attending to some brainless twit who tore the hem off her dress." She turned to Penelope, who was now exerting such effort to control her laughter that her eyes were glistening with unshed tears. "How much did he pay you not to leave him alone with me?"

Penelope quite simply exploded. "I beg your pardon," she gasped, clasping a hand over her horrified mouth.

"Oh, no, go right ahead," Colin said expansively. "You've been such a help already."

"You don't have to give me the twenty pounds," she said.

"I wasn't planning to."

"Only twenty pounds?" Lady Danbury asked. "Hmmph. I would have thought I'd be worth at least twenty-five."

Colin shrugged. "I'm a third son. Perpetually short of funds, I'm afraid."

"Ha! You're as plump in the pocket as at least three earls," Lady Danbury said. "Well, maybe not earls," she added, after a bit of thought. "But a few viscounts, and most barons, to be sure."

Colin smiled blandly. "Isn't it considered impolite to talk about money in mixed company?"

Lady Danbury let out a noise that was either a wheeze or a giggle—Colin wasn't sure which—then said, "It's always impolite to talk about money, mixed company or no, but when one is my age, one can do almost anything one pleases."

"I do wonder," Penelope mused, "what one *can't* do at your age."

Lady Danbury turned to her. "I beg your pardon?"

"You said that one could do *almost* anything one pleases."

Lady Danbury stared at her in disbelief, then cracked a smile. Colin realized he was smiling as well.

"I like her," Lady D said to him, pointing at Penelope as if she were some sort of statue for sale. "Did I tell you I like her?"

"I believe you did," he murmured.

Lady Danbury turned to Penelope and said, her face a mask of utter seriousness, "I do believe I couldn't get away with murder, but that might be all."

All at once, both Penelope and Colin burst out laughing.

"Eh?" Lady Danbury said. "What's so funny?"

"Nothing," Penelope gasped. As for Colin, he couldn't even manage that much.

"It's not nothing," Lady D persisted. "And I shall remain here and pester you all night until you tell me what it is. Trust me when I tell you that that is *not* your desired course of action."

Penelope wiped a tear from her eye. "I just got through telling him," she said, motioning with her head toward Colin, "that he probably could get away with murder."

"Did you, now?" Lady Danbury mused, tapping her cane lightly against the floor the way someone else might scratch her chin while pondering a deep question. "Do you know, but I think you might be right. A more charming man I don't think London has ever seen."

Colin raised a brow. "Now, why don't I think you meant that as a compliment, Lady Danbury?"

"Of course it's a compliment, you dunderhead."

Colin turned to Penelope. "As opposed to *that,* which was clearly a compliment."

Lady Danbury beamed. "I declare," she said (or in all truth, declared), "this is the most fun I've had all season."

"Happy to oblige," Colin said with an easy smile.

"It's been an especially dull year, don't you think?" Lady Danbury asked Penelope.

Penelope nodded. "Last year was a bit tedious as well."

"But not as bad as this year," Lady D persisted.

"Don't ask me," Colin said affably. "I've been out of the country."

"Hmmph. I suppose you're going to say that your absence is the reason we've all been so bored."

"I would never dream of it," Colin said with a disarming smile. "But clearly, if the thought has crossed your mind, it must have some merit."

"Hmmph. Whatever the case, I'm bored."

Colin looked over at Penelope, who appeared to be holding herself very, very still—presumably to stave off laughter.

"Haywood!" Lady Danbury suddenly called out,

waving over a middle-aged gentleman. "Wouldn't you agree with me?"

A vaguely panicked expression drifted across Lord Haywood's face, and then, when it became clear that he could not escape, he said, "I try to make a policy of *always* agreeing with you."

Lady Danbury turned to Penelope and said, "Is it my imagination, or are men getting more sensible?"

Penelope's only answer was a noncommittal shrug. Colin decided she was a wise girl, indeed.

Haywood cleared his throat, his blue eyes blinking fast and furious in his rather fleshy face. "Er, what, precisely, am I agreeing to?"

"That the season is boring," Penelope supplied helpfully.

"Ah, Miss Featherington," Haywood said in a blustery sort of voice. "Didn't see you there."

Colin stole just enough of a glance at Penelope to see her lips straighten into a small, frustrated smile. "Right here next to you," she muttered.

"So you are," Haywood said jovially, "and yes, the season is dreadfully boring."

"Did someone say the season is dull?"

Colin glanced to his right. Another man and two ladies had just joined the group and were avidly expressing their agreement.

"Tedious," one of them murmured. "Appallingly tedious."

"I have never attended a more banal round of parties," one of the ladies announced with an affected sigh.

"I shall have to inform my mother," Colin said tightly. He was among the most easygoing of men, but really, there were some insults he could not let pass.

"Oh, not this gathering," the woman hastened to add. "This ball is truly the only shining light in an otherwise dark and dismal string of gatherings. Why, I was just saying to—"

"Stop now," Lady Danbury ordered, "before you choke on your foot."

The lady quickly silenced herself.

"It's odd," Penelope murmured.

"Oh, Miss Featherington," said the lady who'd previously been going on about dark and dismal gatherings. "Didn't see you there."

"What's odd?" Colin asked, before anyone else could tell Penelope how unremarkable they found her.

She gave him a small, grateful smile before explaining herself. "It's odd how the *ton* seems to entertain themselves by pointing out how unentertained they are."

"I beg your pardon?" Haywood said, looking confused.

Penelope shrugged. "I think the lot of you are having a jolly good time talking about how bored you are, that's all."

Her comment was met with silence. Lord Haywood continued to look confused, and one of the two ladies must have had a speck of dust in her eye, because she couldn't seem to do anything but blink.

Colin couldn't help but smile. He hadn't thought Penelope's statement was such a terribly complicated concept.

"The only interesting thing to do is read *Whistledown,*" said the nonblinking lady, as if Penelope had never even spoken.

The gentleman next to her murmured his assent.

And then Lady Danbury began to smile.

Colin grew alarmed. The old lady had a look in her eye. A frightening look.

"I have an idea," she said.

Someone gasped. Someone else groaned.

"A brilliant idea."

"Not that any of your ideas are anything but," Colin murmured in his most affable voice.

Lady Danbury shushed him with a wave of her hand. "How many great mysteries are there in life, really?"

No one answered, so Colin guessed, "Forty-two?"

She didn't even bother to scowl at him. "I am telling you all here and now. . . ."

Everyone leaned in. Even Colin. It was impossible not to indulge the drama of the moment.

"You are all my witnesses. . . ."

Colin thought he heard Penelope mutter, "Get *on* with it."

"One thousand pounds," Lady Danbury said.

The crowd surrounding her grew.

"One thousand pounds," she repeated, her voice growing in volume. Really, she would have been a natural on the stage. "One thousand pounds . . ."

It seemed the entire ballroom had hushed into reverent silence.

". . . to the person who unmasks Lady Whistledown!"

Chapter 3

This Author would be remiss if it was not mentioned that the most talked-about moment at last night's birthday ball at Bridgerton House was not the rousing toast to Lady Bridgerton (age not to be revealed) but rather Lady Danbury's impertinent offer of one thousand pounds to whomever unmasks . . .

Me.

Do your worst, ladies and gentlemen of the ton. You haven't a prayer of solving this mystery.

LADY WHISTLEDOWN'S SOCIETY PAPERS,
12 APRIL 1824

Precisely three minutes were required for news of Lady Danbury's outrageous dare to spread throughout the ballroom. Penelope knew this to be true because she happened to be facing a large (and, according to Kate Bridgerton, extremely precise) grandfather clock when Lady Danbury made her announcement. At the words, "One thousand pounds to the person who unmasks Lady Whistledown," the clock read forty-four minutes past ten. The long hand had advanced no farther than forty-seven when Nigel Berbrooke stumbled into the rapidly growing circle of people surrounding Lady Danbury and proclaimed her latest scheme "scrumbly good fun!"

And if Nigel had heard about it, that meant everyone had, because Penelope's brother-in-law was not known for his intelligence, his attention span, or his listening ability.

Nor, Penelope thought wryly, for his vocabulary. Scrumbly, indeed.

"And who do you think Lady Whistledown is?" Lady Danbury asked Nigel.

"No earthly idea," he admitted. "Ain't me, that's all I know!"

"I think we all know that," Lady D replied.

"Who do you think it is?" Penelope asked Colin.

He offered her a one-shouldered shrug. "I've been out of town too often to speculate."

"Don't be silly," Penelope said. "Your cumulative time in London certainly adds up to enough parties and routs to form a few theories."

But he just shook his head. "I really couldn't say."

Penelope stared at him for a moment longer than was necessary, or, in all honesty, socially acceptable. There was something odd in Colin's eyes. Something fleeting and elusive. The *ton* often thought him nothing more than a devil-may-care charmer, but he was far more intelligent than he let on, and she'd have bet her life that he had a few suspicions.

But for some reason, he wasn't willing to share them with her.

"Who do you think it is?" Colin asked, avoiding her question with one of his own. "You've been out in society just about as long as Lady Whistledown. Surely you must have thought about it."

Penelope looked about the ballroom, her eyes resting on this person and that, before finally returning to the small crowd around her. "I think it could very well be Lady Danbury," she replied. "Wouldn't that be a clever joke on everyone?"

Colin looked over at the elderly lady, who was having a grand old time talking up her latest scheme. She was thumping her cane on the ground, chattering animatedly, and smiling like a cat with cream, fish, and an entire roast turkey. "It makes sense," he said thoughtfully, "in a rather perverse sort of way."

Penelope felt the corners of her mouth twist. "She's nothing if not perverse."

She watched Colin watching Lady D for another few seconds, then quietly said, "But you don't think it's her."

Colin slowly turned his head to face her, raising one brow in silent question.

"I can tell by the expression on your face," Penelope explained.

He grinned, that loose easy grin he so often used in public. "And here I thought I was inscrutable."

"Afraid not," she replied. "Not to me, anyway."

Colin sighed. "I fear it will never be my destiny to be a dark, brooding hero."

"You may well find yourself *someone's* hero," Penelope allowed. "There's time for you yet. But dark and brooding?" She smiled. "Not very likely."

"Too bad for me," he said jauntily, giving her another one of his well-known smiles—this one the lopsided, boyish one. "The dark, brooding types get all the women."

Penelope coughed discreetly, a bit surprised he'd be speaking of such things with her, not to mention the fact that Colin Bridgerton had never had trouble attracting women. He was grinning at her, awaiting a response, and she was trying to decide whether the correct reaction was polite maidenly outrage or a laugh and an I'm-such-a-good-sport sort of chuckle, when Eloise quite literally skidded to a halt in front of them.

"Did you hear the news?" Eloise asked breathlessly.

"Were you *running*?" Penelope returned. Truly a remarkable feat in such a crowded ballroom.

"Lady Danbury has offered one thousand pounds to whomever unmasks Lady Whistledown!"

"We know," Colin said in that vaguely superior tone exclusive to older brothers.

Eloise let out a disappointed sigh. "You do?"

Colin motioned to Lady Danbury, who was still a scant few yards away. "We were right here when it happened."

Eloise looked annoyed in the extreme, and Penelope knew exactly what she was thinking (and would most probably relate to her the following afternoon). It was one thing to miss an important moment. It was another entirely to discover that one's brother had seen the entire thing.

"Well, people are already talking about it," Eloise

said. "Gushing, really. I haven't been witness to such excitement in years."

Colin turned to Penelope and murmured, "This is why I so often choose to leave the country."

Penelope tried not to smile.

"I know you're talking about me and I don't care," Eloise continued, barely pausing to take a breath. "I tell you, the *ton* has gone mad. Everyone—and I mean everyone—is speculating on her identity, although the shrewdest ones won't say a word. Don't want others to win on their hunch, don't you know."

"I think," Colin announced, "that I am not so in need of a thousand pounds that I care to worry about this."

"It's a lot of money," Penelope said thoughtfully.

He turned to her in disbelief. "Don't tell me you're going to join in this ridiculous game."

She cocked her head to the side, lifting her chin in what she hoped was an enigmatic—or if not enigmatic, at the very least slightly mysterious—manner. "I am not so well heeled that I can ignore the offer of one thousand pounds," she said.

"Perhaps if we work together . . ." Eloise suggested.

"God save me," was Colin's reply.

Eloise ignored him, saying to Penelope, "We could split the money."

Penelope opened her mouth to reply, but Lady Danbury's cane suddenly came into view, waving wildly through the air. Colin had to take a quick step to the side just to avoid getting his ear clipped off.

"Miss Featherington!" Lady D boomed. "You haven't told me who *you* suspect."

"No, Penelope," Colin said, a rather smirky smile on his face, "you haven't."

Penelope's first instinct was to mumble something under her breath and hope that Lady Danbury's age had left her hard enough of hearing that she would assume that any lack of understanding was the fault of her own ears and not Penelope's lips. But even without glancing to her side, she could feel Colin's presence, sense his quirky, cocky grin egging her on, and she found herself standing a little straighter, with her chin perched just a little higher than usual.

He made her more confident, more daring. He made her more . . . herself. Or at least the herself she wished she could be.

"Actually," Penelope said, looking Lady Danbury *almost* in the eye, "I think it's you."

A collective gasp echoed around them.

And for the first time in her life, Penelope Featherington found herself at the very center of attention.

Lady Danbury stared at her, her pale blue eyes

shrewd and assessing. And then the most amazing thing happened. Her lips began to twitch at the corners. Then they widened until Penelope realized she was not just smiling, but positively grinning.

"I like you, Penelope Featherington," Lady Danbury said, tapping her right on the toe with her cane. "I wager half the ballroom is of the same notion, but no one else has the mettle to tell me so."

"I really don't, either," Penelope admitted, grunting slightly as Colin elbowed her in the ribs.

"Obviously," Lady Danbury said with a strange light in her eyes, "you do."

Penelope didn't know what to say to this. She looked at Colin, who was smiling at her encouragingly, then she looked back to Lady Danbury, who looked almost . . . maternal.

Which had to be the strangest thing of all. Penelope rather doubted that Lady Danbury had given maternal looks to her own children.

"Isn't it nice," the older lady said, leaning in so that only Penelope could hear her words, "to discover that we're not exactly what we thought we were?"

And then she walked away, leaving Penelope wondering if maybe she wasn't quite what she'd thought she was.

Maybe—just maybe—she was something a little bit more.

The next day was a Monday, which meant that Penelope took tea with the Bridgerton ladies at Number Five. She didn't know when, precisely, she'd fallen into that habit, but it had been so for close to a decade, and if she didn't show up on a Monday afternoon, she rather thought Lady Bridgerton would send someone over to fetch her.

Penelope rather enjoyed the Bridgerton custom of tea and biscuits in the afternoon. It wasn't a widespread ritual; indeed, Penelope knew of no one else who made a daily habit of it. But Lady Bridgerton insisted that she simply could not last from luncheon to supper, especially not when they were observing town hours and eating so late at night. And thus, every afternoon at four, she and any number of her children (and often a friend or two) met in the informal upstairs drawing room for a snack.

There was drizzle in the air, even though it was a fairly warm day, so Penelope took her black parasol with her for the short walk over to Number Five. It was a route she'd followed hundreds of times before, a few houses down to the corner of Mount and Davies Street, then along the edge of Berkeley Square to Bruton Street. But she was in an odd mood that day, a little bit lighthearted and maybe even a little bit childish, so she decided to cut across the northern corner of the Berkeley Square green for no other reason than she liked the squishy sound her boots made on the wet grass.

It was Lady Danbury's fault. It had to be. She'd been positively giddy since their encounter the night before.

"Not. What. I. Thought. I. Was," she sang to herself as she walked, adding a word every time the soles of her boots sank into the ground. "Something more. Something more."

She reached a particularly wet patch and moved like a skater on the grass, singing (softly, of course; she hadn't changed so much from the night before that she actually wanted someone to hear her singing in public), "Something moooore," as she slid forward.

Which was, of course (since it was fairly well established—in her own mind, at least—that she had the worst timing in the history of civilization), right when she heard a male voice call out her name.

She skidded to a halt and gave fervent thanks that she caught her balance at the very last moment instead of landing on her bottom on the wet and messy grass.

It was, of course, *him*.

"Colin!" she said in a slightly embarrassed voice,

holding still as she waited for him to reach her side. "What a surprise."

He looked like he was trying not to smile. "Were you dancing?"

"Dancing?" she echoed.

"It looked like you were dancing."

"Oh. No." She swallowed guiltily, because even though she wasn't technically lying, it felt as if she were. "Of course not."

His eyes crinkled slightly at the corners. "Pity, then. I would have felt compelled to partner you, and I've never danced in Berkeley Square."

If he'd said the same to her just two days earlier, she would have laughed at his joke and let him be the witty and charming one. But she must have heard Lady Danbury's voice at the back of her head again, because she suddenly decided she didn't want to be the same old Penelope Featherington.

She decided to join in the fun.

She smiled a smile she didn't think she'd even known how to smile. It was wicked and she was mysterious, and she knew it wasn't all in her head because Colin's eyes widened markedly as she murmured, "That's a shame. It's rather enjoyable."

"Penelope Featherington," he drawled, "I thought you said you weren't dancing."

She shrugged. "I lied."

"If that's the case," he said, "then surely this must be my dance."

Penelope's insides suddenly felt very queer. This was why she shouldn't let whispers from Lady Danbury go to her head. She might manage daring and charm for a fleeting moment, but she had no idea how to follow through.

Unlike Colin, obviously, who was grinning devilishly as he held his arms out in perfect waltz position.

"Colin," she gasped, "we're in Berkeley Square!"

"I know. I just finished telling you I've never danced here, don't you recall?"

"But—"

Colin crossed his arms. "Tsk. Tsk. You can't issue a dare like that and then try to weasel out of it. Besides, dancing in Berkeley Square seems like the sort of thing a person ought to do at least once in his life, wouldn't you agree?"

"Anyone might see," she whispered urgently.

He shrugged, trying to hide the fact that he was rather entertained by her reaction. "I don't care. Do you?"

Her cheeks grew pink, then red, and it seemed to take her a great deal of effort to form the words, "People will think you are courting me."

He watched her closely, not understanding why she was disturbed. Who cared if people thought they were courting? The rumor would soon be proven false, and they'd have a good laugh at society's expense. It was on the tip of his tongue to say, *Hang society,* but he held silent. There was something lurking deep in the brown depths of her eyes, some emotion he couldn't even begin to identify.

An emotion he suspected he'd never even felt.

And he realized that the last thing he wanted to do was hurt Penelope Featherington. She was his sister's best friend, and moreover, she was, plain and simple, a very nice girl.

He frowned. He supposed he shouldn't be calling her a girl anymore. At eight-and-twenty she was no more a girl than he was still a boy at three-and-thirty.

Finally, with great care and what he hoped was a good dose of sensitivity, he asked, "Is there a reason why we should worry if people think we are courting?"

She closed her eyes, and for a moment Colin actually thought she might be in pain. When she opened them, her gaze was almost bittersweet. "It would be very funny, actually," she said. "At first."

He said nothing, just waited for her to continue.

"But eventually it would become apparent that we are not actually courting, and it would . . ." She stopped, swallowed, and Colin realized that she was not as composed on the inside as she hoped to appear.

"It would be assumed," she continued, "that you were the one to break things off, because—well, it just would be."

He didn't argue with her. He knew that her words were true.

She let out a sad-sounding exhale. "I don't want to subject myself to that. Even Lady Whistledown would probably write about it. How could she not? It would be far too juicy a piece of gossip for her to resist."

"I'm sorry, Penelope," Colin said. He wasn't sure what he was apologizing for, but it still seemed like the right thing to say.

She acknowledged him with a tiny nod. "I know I shouldn't care what other people say, but I do."

He found himself turning slightly away as he considered her words. Or maybe he was considering the tone of her voice. Or maybe both.

He'd always thought of himself as somewhat above society. Not really outside of it, precisely, since he certainly moved within it and usually enjoyed himself quite a bit. But he'd always assumed that his happiness did not depend upon the opinions of others.

But maybe he wasn't thinking about this the right way. It was easy to assume that you didn't care about the opinions of others when those opinions were consistently favorable. Would he be so quick to dismiss the rest of society if they treated him the way they treated Penelope?

She'd never been ostracized, never been made the subject of scandal. She just hadn't been . . . popular.

Oh, people were polite, and the Bridgertons had all befriended her, but most of Colin's memories of Penelope involved her standing at the perimeter of a ballroom, trying to look anywhere but at the dancing couples, clearly pretending that she really didn't want to dance. That was usually when he went over and asked her himself. She always looked grateful for the request, but also a little bit embarrassed, because they both knew he was doing it at least a little bit because he felt sorry for her.

Colin tried to put himself in her shoes. It wasn't easy. He'd always been popular; his friends had looked up to him at school and the women had flocked to his side when he'd entered society. And as much as he could say he didn't care what people thought, when it came right down to it . . .

He rather liked being liked.

Suddenly he didn't know what to say. Which was strange, because he *always* knew what to say. In fact, he was somewhat famous for always knowing what to say. It was, he reflected, probably one of the reasons he was so well liked.

But he sensed that Penelope's feelings depended on his next words, and at some point in the last ten minutes, her feelings had become very important to him.

"You're right," he finally said, deciding that it was always a good idea to tell someone she was correct. "It was very insensitive of me. Perhaps we should start anew?"

She blinked. "I beg your pardon?"

He waved his hand about, as if the motion could explain everything. "Make a fresh start."

She looked quite adorably confused, which confused *him,* since he'd never thought Penelope the least bit adorable.

"But we've known each other for twelve years," she said.

"Has it really been that long?" He searched his brain, but for the life of him, he couldn't recall the event of their first meeting. "Never mind that. I meant just for this afternoon, you ninny."

She smiled, clearly in spite of herself, and he knew that calling her a ninny had been the exact right thing to do, although in all truth he had no idea why.

"Here we go," he said slowly, drawing his words out with a long flourish of his arm. "You are walking across

Berkeley Square, and you spy me in the distance. I call out your name, and you reply by saying . . ."

Penelope caught her lower lip between her teeth, trying, for some unknown reason, to contain her smile. What magical star had Colin been born under, that he *always* knew what to say? He was the pied piper, leaving nothing but happy hearts and smiling faces in his wake. Penelope would have bet money—far more than the thousand pounds Lady Danbury had offered up—that she was not the only woman in London desperately in love with the third Bridgerton.

He dipped his head to the side and then righted it in a prompting sort of motion.

"I would reply . . ." Penelope said slowly. "I would reply . . ."

Colin waited two seconds, then said, "Really, any words will do."

Penelope had planned to fix a bright grin on her face, but she discovered that the smile on her lips was quite genuine. "Colin!" she said, trying to sound as if she'd just been surprised by his arrival. "What are you doing about?"

"Excellent reply," he said.

She shook her finger at him. "You're breaking out of character."

"Yes, yes, of course. Apologies." He paused, blinked

twice, then said, "Here we are. How about this: Much the same as you, I imagine. Heading to Number Five for tea."

Penelope found herself falling into the rhythm of the conversation. "You sound as if you're just going for a visit. Don't you live there?"

He grimaced. "Hopefully just for the next week. A fortnight at most. I'm trying to find a new place to live. I had to give up the lease on my old set of rooms when I left for Cyprus, and I haven't found a suitable replacement yet. I had a bit of business down on Piccadilly and thought I'd walk back."

"In the rain?"

He shrugged. "It wasn't raining when I left earlier this morning. And even now it's just drizzle."

Just drizzle, Penelope thought. Drizzle that clung to his obscenely long eyelashes, framing eyes of such perfect green that more than one young lady had been moved to write (extremely bad) poetry about them. Even Penelope, levelheaded as she liked to think herself, had spent many a night in bed, staring at the ceiling and seeing nothing but those eyes.

Just drizzle, indeed.

"Penelope?"

She snapped to attention. "Right. Yes. I'm going to your mother's for tea as well. I do so every Monday.

And often on other days, too," she admitted. "When there's, er, nothing interesting occurring at my house."

"No need to sound so guilty about it. My mother's a lovely woman. If she wants you over for tea, you should go."

Penelope had a bad habit of trying to hear between the lines of people's conversations, and she had a suspicion that Colin was really saying that he didn't blame her if she wanted to escape her own mother from time to time.

Which somehow, unaccountably, made her feel a little sad.

He rocked on his heels for a moment, then said, "Well, I shouldn't keep you out here in the rain."

She smiled, since they'd been standing outside for at least fifteen minutes. Still, if he wanted to continue with the ruse, she would do so as well. "I'm the one with the parasol," she pointed out.

His lips curved slightly. "So you are. But still, I wouldn't be much of a gentleman if I didn't steer you toward a more hospitable environment. Speaking of which . . ." He frowned, looking around.

"Speaking of what?"

"Of being a gentleman. I believe we're supposed to see to the welfare of ladies."

"And?"

He crossed his arms. "Shouldn't you have a maid with you?"

"I live just around the corner," she said, a little bit deflated that he didn't remember that. She and her sister were best friends with two of his sisters, after all. He'd even walked her home once or twice. "On Mount Street," she added, when his frown did not dissipate.

He squinted slightly, looking in the direction of Mount Street, although she had no idea what he hoped to accomplish by doing so.

"Oh, for heaven's sake, Colin. It's just near the corner of Davies Street. It can't be more than a five-minute walk to your mother's. Four, if I'm feeling exceptionally sprightly."

"I was just looking to see if there were any darkened or recessed spots." He turned back to face her. "Where a criminal might lurk."

"In *Mayfair*?"

"In Mayfair," he said grimly. "I really think you ought to have a maid accompany you when you journey to and fro. I should hate for something to happen to you."

She was oddly touched by his concern, even though she knew he would have extended equal thoughtfulness to just about every female of his acquaintance. That was simply the sort of man he was.

"I can assure you that I observe all of the usual proprieties when I am traveling longer distances," she said. "But truly, this is so close. Just a few blocks, really. Even my mother doesn't mind."

Colin's jaw suddenly looked quite stiff.

"Not to mention," Penelope added, "that I am eight-and-twenty."

"What has that to do with anything? I am three-and-thirty, if you care to know."

She knew that, of course, since she knew almost everything about him. "Colin," she said, a slightly annoyed whine creeping into her voice.

"Penelope," he replied, in exactly the same tone.

She let out a long exhale before saying, "I am quite firmly on the shelf, Colin. I needn't worry about all of the rules that plagued me when I was seventeen."

"I hardly think—"

One of Penelope's hands planted itself on her hip. "Ask your sister if you don't believe me."

He suddenly looked more serious than she had ever seen him. "I make it a point not to ask my sister on matters that relate to common sense."

"Colin!" Penelope exclaimed. "That's a terrible thing to say."

"I didn't say I don't love her. I didn't even say I don't like her. I adore Eloise, as you well know. However—"

"Anything that begins with *however* has got to be bad," Penelope muttered.

"Eloise," he said with uncharacteristic high-handedness, "should be married by now."

Now, *that* was really too much, especially in that tone of voice. "Some might say," Penelope returned with a self-righteous little tilt of her chin, "that you should be married by now, too."

"Oh, pl—"

"You are, as you so proudly informed me, three-and-thirty."

His expression was slightly amused, but with that pale tinge of irritation which told her he would not remain amused for long. "Penelope, don't even—"

"Ancient!" she chirped.

He swore under his breath, which surprised her, since she didn't think she'd ever heard him do so in the presence of a lady. She probably should have taken it as a warning, but she was too riled up. She supposed the old saying was true—courage spawned more courage.

Or maybe it was more that recklessness emboldened more recklessness, because she just looked at him archly and said, "Weren't both of your older brothers married by the age of thirty?"

To her surprise, Colin merely smiled and crossed his arms as he leaned one shoulder against the tree they were standing beneath. "My brothers and I are very different men."

It was, Penelope realized, a very telling statement, because so many members of the *ton,* including the fabled Lady Whistledown, made so much of the fact that the Bridgerton brothers looked so alike. Some had even gone so far as to call them interchangeable. Penelope hadn't thought any of them were bothered by this—in fact, she'd assumed they'd all felt flattered by the comparison, since they seemed to like each other so well. But maybe she was wrong.

Or maybe she'd never looked closely enough.

Which was rather strange, because she felt as if she'd spent half her life watching Colin Bridgerton.

One thing she did know, however, and should have remembered, was that if Colin had any sort of a temper, he had never chosen to let her see it. Surely she'd flattered herself when she thought that her little quip about his brothers marrying before they turned thirty might set him off.

No, his method of attack was a lazy smile, a well-timed joke. If Colin ever lost his temper . . .

Penelope shook her head slightly, unable even to fathom it. Colin would never lose his temper. At least not in front of her. He'd have to be really, truly—no, *profoundly*—upset to lose his temper. And that kind of fury could only be sparked by someone you really, truly, *profoundly* cared about.

Colin liked her well enough—maybe even better than he liked most people—but he didn't *care*. Not that way.

"Perhaps we should just agree to disagree," she finally said.

"On what?"

"Er . . ." She couldn't remember. "Er, on what a spinster may or may not do?"

He seemed amused by her hesitation. "That would probably require that I defer to my younger sister's judgment in some capacity, which would be, as I'm sure you can imagine, very difficult for me."

"But you don't mind deferring to *my* judgment?"

His smile was lazy and wicked. "Not if you promise not to tell another living soul."

He didn't mean it, of course. And she knew he knew she knew he didn't mean it. But that was his way. Humor and a smile could smooth any path. And blast him, it worked, because she heard herself sighing and felt herself smiling, and before she knew it she was saying, "Enough! Let us be on our way to your mother's."

Colin grinned. "Do you think she'll have biscuits?"

Penelope rolled her eyes. "I *know* she'll have biscuits."

"Good," he said, taking off at a lope and half dragging her with him. "I do love my family, but I really just go for the food."

Chapter 4

It is difficult to imagine that there is any news from the Bridgerton ball other than Lady Danbury's determination to discern the identity of This Author, but the following items should be duly noted:

Mr. Geoffrey Albansdale was seen dancing with Miss Felicity Featherington.

Miss Felicity Featherington was also seen dancing with Mr. Lucas Hotchkiss.

Mr. Lucas Hotchkiss was also seen dancing with Miss Hyacinth Bridgerton.

Miss Hyacinth Bridgerton was also seen dancing with Viscount Burwick.

Viscount Burwick was also seen dancing with Miss Jane Hotchkiss.

Miss Jane Hotchkiss was also seen dancing with Mr. Colin Bridgerton.

Mr. Colin Bridgerton was also seen dancing with Miss Penelope Featherington.

And to round out this incestuous little ring-around-the-rosy, Miss Penelope Featherington was seen speaking with Mr. Geoffrey Albansdale. (It would have been too perfect if she'd actually danced with him, don't you agree, Dear Reader?)

LADY WHISTLEDOWN'S SOCIETY PAPERS,
12 APRIL 1824

When Penelope and Colin entered the drawing room, Eloise and Hyacinth were already sipping tea, along with both of the Ladies Bridgerton. Violet, the dowager, was seated in front of a tea service, and Kate, her daughter-in-law and the wife of Anthony, the current viscount, was attempting, without much success, to control her two-year-old daughter Charlotte.

"Look who I bumped into in Berkeley Square," Colin said.

"Penelope," Lady Bridgerton said with a warm smile, "do sit down. The tea is still nice and hot, and Cook made her famous butter biscuits."

Colin made a beeline for the food, barely pausing to acknowledge his sisters.

Penelope followed Lady Bridgerton's wave to a nearby chair and took a seat.

"Biscuits are good," Hyacinth said, thrusting a plate in her direction.

"Hyacinth," Lady Bridgerton said in a vaguely disapproving voice, "do try to speak in complete sentences."

Hyacinth looked at her mother with a surprised expression. "Biscuits. Are. Good." She cocked her head to the side. "Noun. Verb. Adjective."

"Hyacinth."

Penelope could see that Lady Bridgerton was trying to look stern as she scolded her daughter, but she wasn't quite succeeding.

"Noun. Verb. Adjective," Colin said, wiping a crumb from his grinning face. "Sentence. Is. Correct."

"If you're barely literate," Kate retorted, reaching for a biscuit. "These *are* good," she said to Penelope, a sheepish smile crossing her face. "This one's my fourth."

"I love you, Colin," Hyacinth said, ignoring Kate completely.

"Of course you do," he murmured.

"I myself," Eloise said archly, "prefer to place articles before my nouns in my own writings."

Hyacinth snorted. "Your *writings?*" she echoed.

"I write many letters," Eloise said with a sniff. "And I keep a journal, which I assure you is a very beneficial habit."

"It does keep one disciplined," Penelope put in, taking her cup and saucer from Lady Bridgerton's outstretched hands.

"Do you keep a journal?" Kate asked, not really looking at her, since she had just jumped up from her chair to grasp her daughter before the two-year-old climbed on a side table.

"I'm afraid not," Penelope said with a shake of her head. "It requires far too much discipline for me."

"I don't think it is always necessary to put an article before a noun," Hyacinth persisted, completely unable, as always, to let her side of the argument go.

Unfortunately for the rest of the assemblage, Eloise was equally tenacious. "You may leave off the article if you are referring to your noun in a general sense," she said, pursing her lips in a rather supercilious manner, "but in this case, as you were referring to *specific* biscuits . . ."

Penelope wasn't positive, but she thought she heard Lady Bridgerton groan.

". . . then specifically," Eloise said with an arch of her brows, "you are incorrect."

Hyacinth turned to Penelope. "I am positive she did not use *specifically* correctly in that last sentence."

Penelope reached for another butter biscuit. "I refuse to enter the conversation."

"Coward," Colin murmured.

"No, just hungry." Penelope turned to Kate. "These *are* good."

Kate nodded her agreement. "I have heard rumors," she said to Penelope, "that your sister may become betrothed."

Penelope blinked in surprise. She hadn't thought that Felicity's connection to Mr. Albansdale was public knowledge. "Er, where have you heard rumors?"

"Eloise, of course," Kate said matter-of-factly. "She always knows everything."

"And what I don't know," Eloise said with an easy grin, "Hyacinth usually does. It's very convenient."

"Are you certain that neither one of you is Lady Whistledown?" Colin joked.

"Colin!" Lady Bridgerton exclaimed. "How could you even think such a thing?"

He shrugged. "They're certainly both smart enough to carry off such a feat."

Eloise and Hyacinth beamed.

Even Lady Bridgerton couldn't quite dismiss the

compliment. "Yes, well," she hemmed, "Hyacinth is much too young, and Eloise . . ." She looked over at Eloise, who was watching her with a most amused expression. "Well, Eloise is not Lady Whistledown. I'm sure of it."

Eloise looked at Colin. "I'm not Lady Whistledown."

"That's too bad," he replied. "You'd be filthy rich by now, I imagine."

"You know," Penelope said thoughtfully, "that might be a good way to discern her identity."

Five pairs of eyes turned in her direction.

"She has to be someone who has more money than she ought to have," Penelope explained.

"A good point," Hyacinth said, "except that I haven't a clue how much money people ought to have."

"Neither do I, of course," Penelope replied. "But most of the time one has a *general* idea." At Hyacinth's blank stare, she added, "For example, if I suddenly went out and bought myself a diamond parure, that would be very suspect."

Kate nudged Penelope with her elbow. "Bought any diamond parures lately, eh? I could use a thousand pounds."

Penelope let her eyes roll up for a second before replying, because as the current Viscountess Bridgerton,

Kate most certainly did not need a thousand pounds. "I can assure you," she said, "I don't own a single diamond. Not even a ring."

Kate let out an "euf" of mock disgruntlement. "Well, you're no help, then."

"It's not so much the money," Hyacinth announced. "It's the glory."

Lady Bridgerton coughed on her tea. "I'm sorry, Hyacinth," she said, "but *what* did you just say?"

"Think of the accolades one would receive for having finally caught Lady Whistledown," Hyacinth said. "It would be glorious."

"Are you saying," Colin asked, a deceptively bland expression on his face, "that you don't care about the money?"

"I would never say *that*," Hyacinth said with a cheeky grin.

It occurred to Penelope that of all the Bridgertons, Hyacinth and Colin were the most alike. It was probably a good thing Colin was so often out of the country. If he and Hyacinth ever joined forces in earnest, they could probably take over the world.

"Hyacinth," Lady Bridgerton said firmly, "you are *not* to make the search for Lady Whistledown your life's work."

"But—"

"I'm not saying you cannot ponder the problem and ask a few questions," Lady Bridgerton hastened to add, holding up one hand to ward off further interruptions. "Good gracious, I would hope that after nearly forty years of motherhood I would know better than to try to stop you when you have your mind quite so set on something, nonsense as it may be."

Penelope brought her teacup to her mouth to cover her smile.

"It's just that you have been known to be rather"— Lady Bridgerton delicately cleared her throat—"single-minded at times . . ."

"Mother!"

Lady Bridgerton continued as if Hyacinth had never spoken. ". . . and I do not want you to forget that your primary focus at this time must be to look for a husband."

Hyacinth uttered the word "Mother" again, but this time it was more of a groan than a protest.

Penelope stole a glance at Eloise, who had her eyes fixed on the ceiling and was clearly trying not to break out in a grin. Eloise had endured years of relentless matchmaking at her mother's hands and did not mind in the least that she seemed to have given up and moved on to Hyacinth.

In truth, Penelope was surprised that Lady Bridgerton seemed to have finally accepted Eloise's unmarried state. She had never hidden the fact that her greatest aim in life was to see all eight of her children happily married. And she'd succeeded with four. First Daphne had married Simon and become the Duchess of Hastings. The following year Anthony had married Kate. There had been a bit of a lull after that, but both Benedict and Francesca had married within a year of each other, Benedict to Sophie, and Francesca to the Scottish Earl of Kilmartin.

Francesca, unfortunately, had been widowed only two years after her marriage. She now divided her time between her late husband's family in Scotland and her own in London. When in town, however, she insisted upon living at Kilmartin House instead of at Bridgerton House or Number Five. Penelope didn't blame her. If she were a widow, she'd want to enjoy all of her independence, too.

Hyacinth generally bore her mother's matchmaking with good humor since, as she had told Penelope, it wasn't as if she didn't want to get married eventually. Might as well let her mother do all the work and then she could choose a husband when the right one presented himself.

And it was with this good humor that she stood,

kissed her mother on the cheek, and dutifully promised that her main focus in life was to look for a husband—all the while directing a cheeky, sneaky smile at her brother and sister. She was barely back in her seat when she said to the crowd at large, "So, do you think she'll be caught?"

"Are we still discussing that Whistledown woman?" Lady Bridgerton groaned.

"Have you not heard Eloise's theory, then?" Penelope asked.

All eyes turned to Penelope, then to Eloise.

"Er, what *is* my theory?" Eloise asked.

"It was just, oh, I don't know, maybe a week ago," Penelope said. "We were talking about Lady Whistledown, and I said that I didn't see how she could possibly go on forever, that eventually she would have to make a mistake. Then Eloise said she wasn't so sure, that it had been over ten years and if she were going to make a mistake, wouldn't she have already done so? Then I said, no, she was only human. Eventually she would have to slip up, because no one could go on forever, and—"

"Oh, I remember now!" Eloise cut in. "We were at your house, in your room. I had the most brilliant idea! I said to Penelope that I would wager that Lady

Whistledown has already made a mistake, and it's just *we* were too stupid to have noticed it."

"Not very complimentary for us, I must say," Colin murmured.

"Well, I did intend *we* to mean all of society, not just us Bridgertons," Eloise demurred.

"So maybe," Hyacinth mused, "all I need to do to catch Lady Whistledown is peruse back issues of her column."

Lady Bridgerton's eyes filled with a mild panic. "Hyacinth Bridgerton, I don't like the look on your face."

Hyacinth smiled and shrugged. "I could have a great deal of fun with one thousand pounds."

"God help us all," was her mother's reply.

"Penelope," Colin said quite suddenly, "you never did finish telling us about Felicity. Is it true that she is to be engaged?"

Penelope gulped down the tea she'd been in the process of sipping. Colin had a way of looking at a person, his green eyes so focused and intent that you felt as if you must be the only two people in the universe. Unfortunately for Penelope, it also seemed to have a way of reducing her to a stammering imbecile. If they were in the midst of conversation, she could generally hold her own, but when he surprised her like that, turning his attention onto her just when she'd convinced herself she blended in perfectly with the wallpaper, she was completely and utterly lost.

"Er, yes, it is quite possible," she said. "Mr. Albansdale has been hinting at his intentions. But if he does decide to propose, I imagine he will travel to East Anglia to ask my uncle for her hand."

"Your uncle?" Kate asked.

"My uncle Geoffrey. He lives near Norwich. He's our closest male relative, although truth be told, we don't see him very often. But Mr. Albansdale is rather traditional. I don't think he would feel comfortable asking my mother."

"I hope he asks Felicity as well," Eloise said. "I've often thought it foolish that a man asks a woman's father for her hand before he asks her. The father doesn't have to live with him."

"This attitude," Colin said with an amused smile that was only partly hidden by his teacup, "may explain why you are as yet unmarried."

Lady Bridgerton gave her son a stern glare and said his name disapprovingly.

"Oh, no, Mother," Eloise said, "I don't mind. I'm perfectly comfortable as an old maid." She gave Colin a rather superior look. "I'd much rather be a spinster than be married to a bore. As," she added with a flourish, "would Penelope!"

Startled by Eloise's hand waving rather suddenly in her direction, Penelope straightened her spine and said, "Er, yes. Of course."

But Penelope had a feeling she wasn't quite as firm in her convictions as her friend. Unlike Eloise, she hadn't refused six offers of marriage. She hadn't refused any; she hadn't received even a one.

She'd told herself that she wouldn't have accepted in any case, since her heart belonged to Colin. But was that really the truth, or was she just trying to make herself feel better for having been such a resounding failure on the marriage mart?

If someone asked her to marry him tomorrow— someone perfectly kind and acceptable, whom she might never love but would in all probability like very well—would she say yes?

Probably.

And this made her melancholy, because admitting this to herself meant she'd really, truly given up hope on Colin. It meant she wasn't as true to her principles as she'd hoped she was. It meant she was willing to settle on a less-than-perfect husband in order to have a home and family of her own.

It wasn't anything that hundreds of women didn't do every year, but it was something that she'd never thought she'd do herself.

"You look very serious all of a sudden," Colin said to her.

Penelope jerked out of her musings. "Me? Oh. No, no. I just lost myself in my thoughts, that's all."

Colin acknowledged her statement with a brief nod before reaching for another biscuit. "Have we anything more substantial?" he asked, wrinkling his nose.

"If I'd known you were coming," his mother said in a dry voice, "I would have doubled the food."

He stood and walked to the bellpull. "I'll ring for more." After giving it a yank, he turned back and asked, "Did you hear about Penelope's Lady Whistledown theory?"

"No, I haven't," Lady Bridgerton replied.

"It's very clever, actually," Colin said, stopping to ask a maid for sandwiches before finishing with, "She thinks it's Lady Danbury."

"Ooooh." Hyacinth was visibly impressed. "That's very cunning, Penelope."

Penelope nodded her head to the side in thanks.

"And just the sort of thing Lady Danbury would do," Hyacinth added.

"The column or the challenge?" Kate asked, catching hold of the sash on Charlotte's frock before the little girl could scramble out of reach.

"Both," Hyacinth said.

"And," Eloise put in, "Penelope told her so. Right to her face."

Hyacinth's mouth dropped open, and it was obvious to Penelope that she'd just gone up—way up—in Hyacinth's estimation.

"I should have liked to have seen that!" Lady Bridgerton said with a wide, proud smile. "Frankly, I'm surprised that didn't show up in this morning's *Whistledown*."

"I hardly think Lady Whistledown would comment upon individual people's theories as to her identity," Penelope said.

"Why not?" Hyacinth asked. "It would be an excellent way for her to set out a few red herrings. For example"—she held her hand out toward her sister in a most dramatic pose—"say I thought it was Eloise."

"It is not Eloise!" Lady Bridgerton protested.

"It's not me," Eloise said with a grin.

"But say I *thought* it was," Hyacinth said in an extremely beleaguered voice. "And that I said so publicly."

"Which you would never do," her mother said sternly.

"Which I would never do," Hyacinth parroted. "But just to be academic, let us pretend that I did. And say that Eloise really was Lady Whistledown. Which she's not," she hastened to add before her mother could interrupt again.

Lady Bridgerton held up her hands in silent defeat.

"What better way to fool the masses," Hyacinth continued, "than to make fun of me in her column?"

"Of course, if Lady Whistledown really *were* Eloise . . ." Penelope mused.

"She's not!" Lady Bridgerton burst out.

Penelope couldn't help but laugh. "But if she were . . ."

"You know," Eloise said, "now I *really* wish I were."

"What a joke you'd be having on us all," Penelope continued. "Of course, then on Wednesday you couldn't run a column making fun of Hyacinth for thinking you are Lady Whistledown, because then we'd all know it had to be you."

"Unless it was *you*." Kate laughed, looking at Penelope. "*That* would be a devious trick."

"Let me see if I have it straight," Eloise said with a laugh. "Penelope is Lady Whistledown, and she is going to run a column on Wednesday making fun of Hyacinth's theory that *I'm* Lady Whistledown just to trick you into thinking that I really *am* Lady Whistledown, because Hyacinth suggested that that would be a cunning ruse."

"I am utterly lost," Colin said to no one in particular.

"Unless *Colin* were really Lady Whistledown . . ." Hyacinth said with a devilish gleam in her eye.

"Stop!" Lady Bridgerton said. "I beg you."

By then everyone was laughing too hard for Hyacinth to continue, anyway.

"The possibilities are endless," Hyacinth said, wiping a tear from her eye.

"Perhaps we should all simply look to the left," Colin suggested as he sat back down. "Who knows, that person may very well be our infamous Lady Whistledown."

Everyone looked left, with the exception of Eloise, who looked right . . . right to Colin. "Were you trying to tell me something," she asked with an amused smile, "when you sat down to my right?"

"Not at all," he murmured, reaching for the biscuit plate and then stopping when he remembered it was empty.

But he didn't quite meet Eloise's eyes when he said so.

If anyone other than Penelope had noticed his evasiveness, they were unable to question him on it, because that was when the sandwiches arrived, and he was useless for conversation after that.

Chapter 5

It has come to This Author's attention that Lady Blackwood turned her ankle earlier this week whilst chasing down a delivery boy for This Humble Newssheet.

One thousand pounds is certainly a great deal of money, but Lady Blackwood is hardly in need of funds, and moreover, the situation is growing absurd. Surely Londoners have better things to do with their time than chase down poor, hapless delivery boys in a fruitless attempt to uncover the identity of This Author.

Or maybe not.

This Author has chronicled the activities of the ton for over a decade now and has found no

evidence that they do indeed have anything better
to do with their time.

LADY WHISTLEDOWN'S SOCIETY PAPERS,
14 APRIL 1824

Two days later Penelope found herself once again cutting across Berkeley Square, on her way to Number Five to see Eloise. This time, however, it was late morning, and it was sunny, and she did not bump into Colin along the way.

Penelope wasn't sure if that was a bad thing or not.

She and Eloise had made plans the week before to go shopping, but they'd decided to meet at Number Five so that they could head out together and forgo the accompaniment of their maids. It was a perfect sort of day, far more like June than April, and Penelope was looking forward to the short walk up to Oxford Street.

But when she arrived at Eloise's house, she was met with a puzzled expression on the butler's face.

"Miss Featherington," he said, blinking several times in rapid succession before locating a few more words. "I don't believe Miss Eloise is here at present."

Penelope's lips parted in surprise. "Where did she go? We made our plans over a week ago."

Wickham shook his head. "I do not know. But she departed with her mother and Miss Hyacinth two hours earlier."

"I see." Penelope frowned, trying to decide what to do. "May I wait, then? Perhaps she was merely delayed. It's not like Eloise to forget an appointment."

He nodded graciously and showed her upstairs to the informal drawing room, promising to bring a plate of refreshments and handing her the latest edition of *Whistledown* to read while she bided her time.

Penelope had already read it, of course; it was delivered quite early in the morning, and she made a habit of perusing the column at breakfast. With so little to occupy her mind, she wandered over to the window and peered out over the Mayfair streetscape. But there wasn't much new to see; it was the same buildings she'd seen a thousand times before, even the same people walking along the street.

Maybe it was because she was pondering the sameness of her life that she noticed the one object new to her vista: a bound book lying open on the table. Even from several feet away she could see that it was filled not with the printed word, but rather with neat hand-written lines.

She inched toward it and glanced down without actually touching the pages. It appeared to be a journal of sorts, and in the middle of the right-hand side there was a heading that was set apart from the rest of the text by a bit of space above and below:

22 February 1824
Troodos Mountains, Cyprus

One of her hands flew to her mouth. Colin had written this! He'd said just the other day that he'd visited Cyprus instead of Greece. She had no idea that he kept a journal.

She lifted a foot to take a step back, but her body didn't budge. She shouldn't read this, she told herself. This was Colin's private journal. She really ought to move away.

"Away," she muttered, looking down at her recalcitrant feet. "Away."

Her feet didn't move.

But maybe she wasn't quite so in the wrong. After all, was she really invading his privacy if she read only what she could see without turning a page? He *had* left it lying open on the table, for all the world to see.

But then again, Colin had every reason to think that no one would stumble across his journal if he dashed out for a few moments. Presumably, he was aware that his mother and sisters had departed for the morning.

Most guests were shown to the formal drawing room on the ground floor; as far as Penelope knew, she and Felicity were the only non-Bridgertons who were taken straight up to the informal drawing room. And since Colin wasn't expecting her (or, more likely, hadn't thought of her one way or another), he wouldn't have thought there was any danger in leaving his journal behind while he ran an errand.

On the other hand, he *had* left it lying open.

Open, for heaven's sake! If there were any valuable secrets in that journal, surely Colin would have taken greater care to secret it when he left the room. He wasn't stupid, after all.

Penelope leaned forward.

Oh, bother. She couldn't read the writing from that distance. The heading had been legible since it was surrounded by so much white space, but the rest was a bit too close together to make out from far away.

Somehow she'd thought she wouldn't feel so guilty if she didn't have to step any closer to the book to read it. Never mind, of course, that she'd already crossed the room to get to where she was at that moment.

She tapped her finger against the side of her jaw, right near her ear. That was a good point. She had crossed the room some time ago, which surely meant that she'd already committed the biggest sin she was likely to that day. One little step was nothing compared to the length of the room.

She inched forward, decided that only counted as half a step, then inched forward again and looked down, beginning her reading right in the middle of a sentence.

in England. Here the sand ripples between tan and white, and the consistency is so fine that it slides over a bare foot like a whisper of silk. The water is a blue unimaginable in England, aquamarine with the glint of the sun, deep cobalt when the clouds take the sky. And it is warm—surprisingly, astoundingly warm, like a bath that was heated perhaps a half an hour earlier. The waves are gentle, and they lap up on the shore with a soft rush of foam, tickling the skin and turning the perfect sand into a squishy delight that slips and slides along the toes until another wave arrives to clean up the mess.

It is easy to see why this is said to be the birthplace of Aphrodite. With every step I almost expect to see her as in Botticelli's painting, rising from the ocean, perfectly balanced on a giant shell, her long titian hair streaming around her.

If ever a perfect woman was born, surely this would be the place. I am in paradise. And yet . . .

And yet with every warm breeze and cloudless sky I am reminded that this is not my home, that I was born to live my life elsewhere. This does not quell the desire—no, the compulsion!—to travel, to see, to meet. But it does feed a strange longing to touch a dew-dampened lawn, or feel a cool mist on one's face, or even to remember the joy of a perfect day after a week of rain.

The people here can't know that joy. Their days are always perfect. Can one appreciate perfection when it is a constant in one's life?

22 February 1824
Troodos Mountains, Cyprus

It is remarkable that I am cold. It is, of course, February, and as an Englishman I'm quite used to a February chill (as well as that of any month with an R in its name), but I am not in England. I am in Cyprus, in the heart of the Mediterranean, and just two days ago I was in Paphos, on the southwest coast of the island, where the sun is strong and the ocean salty and warm. Here, one can see the peak

*of Mount Olympus, still capped with snow so white
one is temporarily blinded when the sun glints off
of it.*

*The climb to this altitude was treacherous, with
danger lurking around more than one corner. The
road is rudimentary, and along the way we met*

Penelope let out a soft grunt of protest when she
realized that the page ended in the middle of a sentence. Who had he met? What had happened? *What
danger?*

She stared down at the journal, absolutely *dying* to
flip the page and see what happened next. But when
she'd started reading, she had managed to justify it by
telling herself she wasn't really invading Colin's privacy; he'd left the book open, after all. She was only
looking at what he had left exposed.

Turning the page, however, was something else altogether.

She reached out, then yanked her hand back. This
wasn't right. She couldn't read his journal. Well, not
beyond what she'd already read.

On the other hand, it was clear that these were words
worth reading. It was a crime for Colin to keep them
for himself. Words should be celebrated, shared. They
should be—

"Oh, for God's sake," she muttered to herself. She reached for the edge of the page.

"What are you doing?"

Penelope whirled around. "Colin!"

"Indeed," he snapped.

Penelope lurched back. She'd never heard him use such a tone. She hadn't even thought him capable of it.

He strode across the room, grabbed the journal, and snapped it shut. "What are you doing here?" he demanded.

"Waiting for Eloise," she managed to get out, her mouth suddenly quite dry.

"In the upstairs drawing room?"

"Wickham always takes me here. Your mother told him to treat me like family. I . . . uh . . . he . . . uh . . ." She realized that she was wringing her hands together and willed herself to stop. "It's the same with my sister Felicity. Because she and Hyacinth are such good friends. I—I'm sorry. I thought you knew."

He threw the leather-bound book carelessly onto a nearby chair and crossed his arms. "And do you make a habit of reading the personal letters of others?"

"No, of course not. But it was open and—" She gulped, recognizing how awful the excuse sounded the second the words left her lips. "It's a public room," she mumbled, somehow feeling like she had to finish her defense. "Maybe you should have taken it with you."

"Where I went," he ground out, still visibly furious with her, "one doesn't ordinarily take a book."

"It's not very big," she said, wondering why why *why* she was still talking when she was so clearly in the wrong.

"For the love of God," he exploded. "Do you *want* me to say the word *chamberpot* in your presence?"

Penelope felt her cheeks blush deep red. "I'd better go," she said. "Please tell Eloise—"

"*I'll* go," Colin practically snarled. "I'm moving out this afternoon, anyway. Might as well leave now, since you've so obviously taken over the house."

Penelope had never thought that words could cause physical pain, but right then she would have sworn that she'd taken a knife to the heart. She hadn't realized until that very moment just how much it meant to her that Lady Bridgerton had opened her home to her.

Or how much it would hurt to know that Colin resented her presence there.

"Why do you have to make it so difficult to apologize?" she burst out, dogging his heels as he crossed the room to gather the rest of his things.

"And why, pray tell, should I make it easy?" he returned. He didn't face her as he said it; he didn't even break his stride.

"Because it would be the nice thing to do," she ground out.

That got his attention. He whirled around, his eyes flashing so furiously that Penelope stumbled back a step. Colin was the nice one, the easygoing one. He didn't lose his temper.

Until now.

"Because it would be the nice thing to do?" he thundered. "Is that what you were thinking when you read my journal? That it would be a nice thing to read someone's private papers?"

"No, Colin, I—"

"There is nothing you can say—" he said, jabbing her in the shoulder with his index finger.

"Colin! You—"

He turned around to gather his belongings, rudely giving her his back while he spoke. "Not a thing that could justify your behavior."

"No, of course not, but—"

"OW!"

Penelope felt the blood drain from her face. Colin's yell was one of real pain. His name escaped her lips in a panicked whisper and she rushed to his side. "What's—Oh, my heavens!"

Blood was gushing from a wound on the palm of his hand.

Never terribly articulate in a crisis, Penelope managed to say, "Oh! Oh! The carpet!" before leaping forward with a piece of writing paper that had been lying on a nearby table and sliding it under his hand to catch the blood before it ruined the priceless carpet below.

"Ever the attentive nurse," Colin said in a shaky voice.

"Well, you're not going to die," she explained, "and the carpet—"

"It's all right," he assured her. "I was trying to make a joke."

Penelope looked up at his face. Tight white lines were etched in the skin around his mouth, and he looked very pale. "I think you'd better sit down," she said.

He nodded grimly and sagged into a chair.

Penelope's stomach did a rather seasickish sway. She'd never been terribly good with blood. "Maybe I'd better sit down, too," she mumbled, sinking onto the low table opposite him.

"Are you going to be all right?" he asked.

She nodded, swallowing against a tiny wave of nausea. "We need to find something to wrap this," she said, grimacing as she looked down at the ridiculous setup below. The paper wasn't absorbent, and the blood was rolling precariously along its surface, with Penelope desperately trying to keep it from dripping over the side.

"I have a handkerchief in my pocket," he said.

She carefully set the paper down and retrieved the handkerchief from his breast pocket, trying not to notice the warm beat of his heart as her fingers fumbled for the creamy white scrap of cloth. "Does it hurt?" she asked as she wrapped it around his hand. "No, don't answer that. Of course it hurts."

He managed a very wobbly smile. "It hurts."

She peered down at the gash, forcing herself to look at it closely even though the blood made her stomach turn. "I don't think you'll need stitches."

"Do you know much about wounds?"

She shook her head. "Nothing. But it doesn't look too bad. Except for . . . ah, all the blood."

"Feels worse than it looks," he joked.

Her eyes flew to his face in horror.

"Another joke," he reassured her. "Well, not really. It *does* feel worse than it looks, but I assure you it's bearable."

"I'm sorry," she said, increasing pressure on the wound to staunch the flow of blood. "This is all my fault."

"That I sliced open my hand?"

"If you hadn't been so angry . . ."

He just shook his head, closing his eyes briefly against the pain. "Don't be silly, Penelope. If I hadn't gotten angry with you, I would have gotten angry with someone else some other time."

"And you'd of course have a letter opener by your side when that happened," she murmured, looking up at him through her lashes as she bent over his hand.

When his eyes met hers, they were filled with humor and maybe just a touch of admiration.

And something else she'd never thought to see— vulnerability, hesitancy, and even insecurity. He didn't know how good his writing was, she realized with amazement. He had no idea, and he was actually embarrassed that she'd seen it.

"Colin," Penelope said, instinctively pressing harder on his wound as she leaned in, "I must tell you. You—"

She broke off when she heard the sharp, even clatter of footsteps coming down the hall. "That will be Wickham," she said, glancing toward the door. "He insisted upon bringing me a small meal. Can you keep the pressure on this for now?"

Colin nodded. "I don't want him to know I've hurt myself. He'll only tell Mother, and then I'll never hear the end of it."

"Well, here, then." She stood and tossed him his journal. "Pretend you're reading this."

Colin barely had time to open it and lay it across his injured hand before the butler entered with a large tray.

"Wickham!" Penelope said, jumping to her feet and turning to face him as if she hadn't already known he was coming. "As usual you've brought far more than I could possibly eat. Luckily, Mr. Bridgerton has been keeping me company. I'm certain that with his help, I'll be able to do justice to your meal."

Wickham nodded and removed the covers from the serving dishes. It was a cold repast—pieces of meat, cheese, and fruit, accompanied by a tall pitcher of lemonade.

Penelope smiled brightly. "I hope you didn't think I could eat all of this myself."

"Lady Bridgerton and her daughters are expected soon. I thought they might be hungry as well."

"Won't be any left after I'm through with it," Colin said with a jovial smile.

Wickham bowed slightly in his direction. "If I'd known you were here, Mr. Bridgerton, I would have trebled the portions. Would you like me to fix you a plate?"

"No, no," Colin said, waving his uninjured hand. "I'll get up just as soon as I . . . ah . . . finish reading this chapter."

The butler said, "Let me know if you require further assistance," and exited the room.

"Aaaaaahhh," Colin groaned, the moment he heard Wickham's steps disappear down the hall. "Damn—I mean, dash it—it hurts."

Penelope plucked a napkin off the tray. "Here, let's replace that handkerchief." She peeled it away from his skin, keeping her eyes on the cloth rather than the wound. For some reason that didn't seem to bother her stomach quite as much. "I'm afraid your handkerchief is ruined."

Colin just closed his eyes and shook his head. Penelope was smart enough to interpret the action to mean, *I don't care.* And she was sensible enough not to say anything further on the subject. Nothing worse than a female who chattered forever about nothing.

He'd always liked Penelope, but how was it he'd never realized how intelligent she was up till now? Oh, he supposed if someone had asked him, he would have said she was bright, but he'd certainly never taken the time to think about it.

It was becoming clear to him, however, that she was very intelligent, indeed. And he thought he remembered his sister once telling him that she was an avid reader.

And probably a discriminating one as well.

"I think the bleeding is slowing down," she was saying as she wrapped the fresh napkin around his hand. "In fact, I'm sure it is, if only because I don't feel quite so sick every time I look at the wound."

He wished that she hadn't read his journal, but now that she *had* . . .

"Ah, Penelope," he began, startled by the hesitancy in his own voice.

She looked up. "I'm sorry. Am I pressing too hard?"

For a moment Colin did nothing but blink. How was it possible he'd never noticed how big her eyes were? He'd known they were brown, of course, and . . . No, come to think of it, if he were to be honest with himself, he would have to admit that if asked earlier this morning, he'd not have been able to identify the color of her eyes.

But somehow he knew that he'd never forget again.

She eased up on the pressure. "Is this all right?"

He nodded. "Thank you. I would do it myself, but it's my right hand, and—"

"Say no more. It's the very least I can do, after . . . after . . ." Her eyes slid slightly to the side, and he knew she was about to apologize another time.

"Penelope," he began again.

"No, wait!" she cried out, her dark eyes flashing with . . . could it be passion? Certainly not the brand of passion with which he was most familiar. But there were other sorts, weren't there? Passion for learning. Passion for . . . literature?

"I must tell you this," she said urgently. "I know it was unforgivably intrusive of me to look at your journal. I was just . . . bored . . . and waiting . . . and I had nothing to do, and then I saw the book and I was curious."

He opened his mouth to interrupt her, to tell her that what was done was done, but the words were rushing from her mouth, and he found himself oddly compelled to listen.

"I should have stepped away the moment I realized what it was," she continued, "but as soon as I read one sentence I had to read another! Colin, it was wonderful! It was just like I was there. I could feel the water—I knew exactly the temperature. It was so clever of you to describe it the way you did. Everyone knows exactly what a bath feels like a half an hour after it has been filled."

For a moment Colin could do nothing but stare at her. He'd never seen Penelope quite so animated, and it was strange and . . . good, really, that all that excitement was over his journal.

"You—you liked it?" he finally asked.

"Liked it? Colin, I loved it! I—"

"Ow!"

In her excitement, she'd started squeezing his hand a bit too hard. "Oh, sorry," she said perfunctorily. "Colin, I really must know. What was the danger? I couldn't bear to be left hanging like that."

"It was nothing," he said modestly. "The page you read really wasn't a very exciting passage."

"No, it was mostly description," she agreed, "but the description was very compelling and evocative. I could see everything. But it wasn't—oh, dear, how do I explain this?"

Colin discovered that he was very impatient for her to figure out what she was trying to say.

"Sometimes," she finally continued, "when one reads a passage of description, it's rather . . . oh, I don't know . . . detached. Clinical, even. You brought the island to life. Other people might call the water warm, but you related it to something we all know and understand. It made me feel as if I were there, dipping my toe in right alongside you."

Colin smiled, ridiculously pleased by her praise.

"Oh! And I don't want to forget—there was another brilliant thing I wanted to mention."

Now he knew he must be grinning like an idiot. Brilliant brilliant brilliant. What a *good* word.

Penelope leaned in slightly as she said, "You also showed the reader how *you* relate to the scene and how it affects you. It becomes more than mere description because we see how you react to it."

Colin knew he was fishing for compliments, but he didn't much care as he asked, "What do you mean?"

"Well, if you look at—May I see the journal to refresh my memory?"

"Of course," he murmured, handing it to her. "Wait, let me find the correct page again."

Once he had done so, she scanned his lines until she found the section she was looking for. "Here we are. Look at this part about how you are reminded that England is your home."

"It's funny how travel can do that to a person."

"Do what to a person?" she asked, her eyes wide with interest.

"Make one appreciate home," he said softly.

Her eyes met his, and they were serious, inquisitive. "And yet you still like to go away."

He nodded. "I can't help it. It's like a disease."

She laughed, and it sounded unexpectedly musical.

"Don't be ridiculous," she said. "A disease is harmful. It's clear that your travels feed your soul." She looked down to his hand, carefully peeling the napkin back to inspect his wound. "It's almost better," she said.

"Almost," he agreed. In truth, he suspected the bleeding had stopped altogether, but he was reluctant to let the conversation end. And he knew that the moment she was done caring for him, she would go.

He didn't think she wanted to go, but he somehow knew that she would. She'd think it was the proper thing to do, and she'd probably also think it was what he wanted.

Nothing, he was surprised to realize, could be further from the truth.

And nothing could have scared him more.

Chapter 6

Everyone has secrets.
Especially me.
LADY WHISTLEDOWN'S SOCIETY PAPERS,
14 APRIL 1824

"I wish I'd known you kept a journal," Penelope said, reapplying pressure to his palm.

"Why?"

"I'm not sure," she said with a shrug. "It's always interesting to find out that there is more to someone than meets the eye, don't you think?"

Colin didn't say anything for several moments,

and then, quite suddenly, he blurted out, "You really liked it?"

She looked amused. He was horrified. Here he was, considered one of the most popular and sophisticated men of the *ton*, and he'd been reduced to a bashful schoolboy, hanging on Penelope Featherington's every word, just for a single scrap of praise.

Penelope Featherington, for God's sake.

Not that there was anything wrong with Penelope, of course, he hastened to remind himself. Just that she was . . . well . . . Penelope.

"Of course I liked it," she said with a soft smile. "I just finished telling you so."

"What was the first thing that struck you about it?" he asked, deciding that he might as well act like a complete fool, since he was already more than halfway there.

She smiled wickedly. "Actually, the first thing that struck me was that your penmanship was quite a bit neater than I would have guessed."

He frowned. "What does that mean?"

"I have difficulty seeing you bent over a desk, practicing your flicks," she replied, her lips tightening at the corners to suppress a smile.

If ever there were a time for righteous indignation,

this was clearly it. "I'll have you know I spent many an hour in the nursery schoolroom, bent over a desk, as you so delicately put it."

"I'm sure," she murmured.

"Hmmmph."

She looked down, clearly trying not to smile.

"I'm quite good with my flicks," he added. It was just a game now, but somehow it was rather fun to play the part of the petulant schoolboy.

"Obviously," she replied. "I especially liked them on the H's. Very well done. Quite . . . flicky of you."

"Indeed."

She matched his straight face perfectly. "Indeed."

His gaze slid from hers, and for a moment he felt quite unaccountably shy. "I'm glad you liked the journal," he said.

"It was lovely," she said in a soft, faraway kind of voice. "Very lovely, and . . ." She looked away, blushing. "You're going to think I'm silly."

"Never," he promised.

"Well, I think one of the reasons I enjoyed it so much is that I could somehow feel that *you'd* enjoyed writing it."

Colin was silent for a long moment. It hadn't ever occurred to him that he enjoyed his writing; it was just something he *did*.

He did it because he couldn't imagine not doing it. How could he travel to foreign lands and not keep a record of what he saw, what he experienced, and perhaps most importantly, what he felt?

But when he thought back, he realized that he felt a strange rush of satisfaction whenever he wrote a phrase that was exactly right, a sentence that was particularly true. He distinctly remembered the moment he'd written the passage Penelope had read. He'd been sitting on the beach at dusk, the sun still warm on his skin, the sand somehow rough and smooth at the same time under his bare feet. It had been a heavenly moment—full of that warm, lazy feeling one can truly only experience in the dead of summer (or on the perfect beaches of the Mediterranean), and he'd been trying to think of the exact right way to describe the water.

He'd sat there for ages—surely a full half an hour—his pen poised above the paper of his journal, waiting for inspiration. And then suddenly he'd realized the temperature was precisely that of slightly old bathwater, and his face had broken into a wide, delighted smile.

Yes, he enjoyed writing. Funny how he'd never realized it before.

"It's good to have something in your life," Penelope said quietly. "Something satisfying—that will fill the hours with a sense of purpose." She crossed her hands in her lap and looked down, seemingly engrossed by her knuckles. "I've never understood the supposed joys of a lazy life."

Colin wanted to touch his fingers to her chin, to see her eyes when he asked her—*And what do you do to fill your hours with a sense of purpose?* But he didn't. It would be far too forward, and it would mean admitting to himself just how interested he was in her answer.

So he asked the question, and he kept his own hands still.

"Nothing, really," she replied, still examining her fingernails. Then, after a pause, she looked up quite suddenly, her chin rising so quickly it almost made him dizzy. "I like to read," she said. "I read quite a bit, actually. And I do a bit of embroidery now and then, but I'm not very good at it. I wish there were more, but, well . . ."

"What?" Colin prodded.

Penelope shook her head. "It's nothing. You should be grateful for your travels. I'm quite envious of you."

There was a long silence, not awkward, but strange nonetheless, and finally Colin said brusquely, "It's not enough."

The tone of his voice seemed so out of place in the

conversation that Penelope could do nothing but stare. "What do you mean?" she finally asked.

He shrugged carelessly. "A man can't travel forever; to do so would take all the fun out of it."

She laughed, then looked at him and realized he was serious. "I'm sorry," she said. "I didn't mean to be rude."

"You weren't rude," he said, taking a swig of his lemonade. It sloshed on the table when he set the glass down; clearly, he was unused to using his left hand. "Two of the best parts of travel," he explained, wiping his mouth with one of the clean napkins, "are the leaving and the coming home, and besides, I'd miss my family too much were I to go off indefinitely."

Penelope had no reply—at least nothing that wouldn't sound like platitudes, so she just waited for him to continue.

For a moment he didn't say anything, then he scoffed and shut his journal with a resounding thud. "These don't count. They're just for me."

"They don't have to be," she said softly.

If he heard her, he made no indication. "It's all very well and good to keep a journal while you're traveling," he continued, "but once I'm home I still have nothing to do."

"I find that difficult to believe."

He didn't say anything, just reached for a piece of cheese off the tray. She watched him while he ate, and then, after he'd washed it down with more lemonade, his entire demeanor changed. He seemed more alert, more on edge as he asked, "Have you read *Whistledown* lately?"

Penelope blinked at the sudden change of subject. "Yes, of course, why? Doesn't everyone read it?"

He waved off her question. "Have you noticed how she describes me?"

"Er, it's almost always favorable, isn't it?"

His hand began to wave again—rather dismissively, in her opinion. "Yes, yes, that's not the point," he said in a distracted voice.

"You might think it more the point," Penelope replied testily, "if you'd ever been likened to an overripe citrus fruit."

He winced, and he opened and closed his mouth twice before finally saying, "If it makes you feel better, I didn't remember that she'd called you that until just now." He stopped, thought for a moment, then added, "In fact, I still don't remember it."

"It's all right," she said, putting on her best I'm-a-good-sport face. "I assure you, I'm quite beyond it. And I've always had a fondness for oranges and lemons."

He started to say something again, then stopped, then looked at her rather directly and said, "I hope what I'm about to say isn't abominably insensitive or insulting, given that when all is said and done, I've very little to complain about."

The implication being, Penelope realized, that perhaps *she* did.

"But I'm telling you," he continued, his eyes clear and earnest, "because I think maybe you'll understand."

It was a compliment. A strange, uncommon one, but a compliment nonetheless. Penelope wanted nothing more than to lay her hand across his, but of course she could not, so she just nodded and said, "You can tell me anything, Colin."

"My brothers—" he began. "They're—" He stopped, staring rather blankly toward the window before finally turning back to her and saying, "They're very accomplished. Anthony is the viscount, and God knows I wouldn't want that responsibility, but he has a purpose. Our entire heritage is in his hands."

"More than that, I should think," Penelope said softly.

He looked at her, question in his eyes.

"I think your brother feels responsible for your entire family," she said. "I imagine it's a heavy burden."

Colin tried to keep his face impassive, but he'd never been an accomplished stoic, and he must have shown his dismay on his face, because Penelope practically rose from her seat as she rushed to add, "Not that I think he minds it! It's part of who he is."

"Exactly!" Colin exclaimed, as if he'd just discovered something that was actually important. As opposed to this . . . this . . . this inane discussion about his life. He had nothing to complain about. He *knew* he had nothing to complain about, and yet . . .

"Did you know Benedict paints?" he found himself asking.

"Of course," she replied. "Everyone knows he paints. He has a painting in the National Gallery. And I believe they are planning to hang another soon. Another landscape."

"Really?"

She nodded. "Eloise told me."

He slumped again. "Then it must be true. I can't believe no one mentioned it to me."

"You *have* been away," she reminded him.

"What I'm trying to say," he continued, "is that they both have a purpose to their lives. I have nothing."

"That can't be true," she said.

"I should think I would be in a position to know."

Penelope sat back, startled by the sharp tone of his voice.

"I know what people think of me," he began, and although Penelope had told herself that she was going to remain silent, to allow him to speak his mind fully, she couldn't help but interrupt.

"Everyone likes you," she rushed to say. "They adore you."

"I know," he groaned, looking anguished and sheepish at the same time. "But . . ." He raked a hand through his hair. "God, how to say this without sounding a complete ass?"

Penelope's eyes widened.

"I'm sick of being thought an empty-headed charmer," he finally blurted out.

"Don't be silly," she said, faster than immediately, if that were possible.

"Penelope—"

"No one thinks you're stupid," she said.

"How would—"

"Because I've been stuck here in London for more years than anyone should have to," she said sharply. "I may not be the most popular woman in town, but after ten years, I've heard more than my fair share of gossip and lies and foolish opinions, and I have never—not once—heard someone refer to you as stupid."

He stared at her for a moment, a bit startled by her passionate defense. "I didn't mean *stupid,* precisely," he said in a soft, and he hoped humble, voice. "More . . . without substance. Even Lady Whistledown refers to me as a charmer."

"What's wrong with that?"

"Nothing," he replied testily, "if she didn't do it every other day."

"She only *publishes* every other day."

"My point exactly," he shot back. "If she thought there was anything to me other than my so-called legendary charm, don't you think she would have said so by now?"

Penelope was quiet for a long moment, then she said, "Does it really matter what Lady Whistledown thinks?"

He slumped forward, smacking his hands against his knees, then yelping with pain when he (belatedly) remembered his injury. "You're missing the point," he said, wincing as he reapplied pressure to his palm. "I couldn't care less about Lady Whistledown. But whether we like it or not, she represents the rest of society."

"I would imagine that there are quite a few people who would take exception to that statement."

He raised one brow. "Including yourself?"

"Actually, I think Lady Whistledown is rather astute," she said, folding her hands primly in her lap.

"The woman called you an overripe melon!"

Two splotches of red burned in her cheeks. "An overripe citrus fruit," she ground out. "I assure you there is a very big difference."

Colin decided then and there that the female mind was a strange and incomprehensible organ—one which no man should even attempt to understand. There wasn't a woman alive who could go from point A to B without stopping at C, D, X, and 12 along the way.

"Penelope," he finally said, staring at her in disbelief, "the woman insulted you. How can you defend her?"

"She said nothing more than the truth," she replied, crossing her arms over her chest. "She's been rather kind, actually, since my mother started allowing me to pick out my own clothing."

Colin groaned. "Surely we were talking about something else at some point. Tell me we didn't *intend* to discuss your wardrobe."

Penelope's eyes narrowed. "I believe we were discussing your dissatisfaction with life as the most popular man in London."

Her voice rose on the last four words, and Colin realized he'd been scolded. Soundly.

Which he found extraordinarily irritating. "I don't know why I thought you'd understand," he bit off, hating the childish tinge in his voice but completely unable to edit it out.

"I'm sorry," she said, "but it's a little difficult for me to sit here and listen to you complain that your life is nothing."

"I didn't say that."

"You most certainly did!"

"I said I *have* nothing," he corrected, trying not to wince as he realized how stupid that sounded.

"You have more than anyone I know," she said, jabbing him in the shoulder. "But if you don't realize that, then maybe you are correct—your life is nothing."

"It's too hard to explain," he said in a petulant mutter.

"If you want a new direction for your life," she said, "then for heaven's sake, just pick something out and do it. The world is your oyster, Colin. You're young, wealthy, and you're a *man*." Penelope's voice turned bitter, resentful. "You can do anything you want."

He scowled, which didn't surprise her. When people were convinced they had problems, the last thing they wanted to hear was a simple, straightforward solution.

"It's not that simple," he said.

"It's exactly that simple." She stared at him for the

longest moment, wondering, perhaps for the first time in her life, just who he was.

She'd thought she knew everything about him, but she hadn't known that he kept a journal.

She hadn't known that he possessed a temper.

She hadn't known that he felt dissatisfied with his life.

And she certainly hadn't known that he was petulant and spoiled enough to feel that dissatisfaction, when heaven knew he didn't deserve to. What right did he have to feel unhappy with his life? How dare he complain, especially to her?

She stood, smoothing out her skirts in an awkward, defensive gesture. "Next time you want to complain about the trials and tribulations of universal adoration, try being an on-the-shelf spinster for a day. See how that feels and then let me know what you want to complain about."

And then, while Colin was still sprawled on the sofa, gaping at her as if she were some bizarre creature with three heads, twelve fingers, and a tail, she swept out of the room.

It was, she thought as she descended the outer steps to Bruton Street, quite the most splendid exit of her existence.

It was really too bad, then, that the man she'd been

leaving was the only one in whose company she'd ever wanted to remain.

Colin felt like hell all day.

His hand hurt like the devil, despite the brandy he'd sloshed both on his skin and into his mouth. The estate agent who'd handled the lease for the snug little terrace house he'd found in Bloomsbury had informed him that the previous tenant was having difficulties and Colin wouldn't be able to move in today as planned—would next week be acceptable?

And to top it off, he suspected that he might have done irreparable harm to his friendship with Penelope.

Which made him feel worst of all, since (A) he rather valued his friendship with Penelope and (B) he hadn't realized how much he valued his friendship with Penelope, which (C) made him feel slightly panicked.

Penelope was a constant in his life. His sister's friend—the one who was always at the fringes of the party; nearby, but not truly a part of things.

But the world seemed to be shifting. He'd only been back in England for a fortnight, but already Penelope had changed. Or maybe he'd changed. Or maybe she hadn't changed but the way he saw her had changed.

She mattered. He didn't know how else to put it.

And after ten years of her just being . . . *there*, it was rather bizarre for her to matter quite so much.

He didn't like that they'd parted ways that afternoon on such awkward terms. He couldn't remember feeling awkward with Penelope, ever—no, that wasn't true. There was that time . . . dear God, how many years ago was it? Six? Seven? His mother had been pestering him about getting married, which was nothing new, except this time she'd suggested Penelope as a potential bride, which *was* new, and Colin just hadn't been in the mood to deal with his mother's matchmaking in his usual manner, which was to tease her back.

And then she just hadn't stopped. She'd talked about Penelope all day and night, it seemed, until Colin finally fled the country. Nothing drastic—just a short jaunt to Wales. But really, what had his mother been thinking?

When he'd returned, his mother had wanted to speak with him, of course—except this time it had been because his sister Daphne was with child again and she had wanted to make a family announcement. But how was he to have known that? So he had not been looking forward to the visit, since he was sure it would involve a great deal of completely unveiled hints about marriage. Then he had run into his brothers, and they'd started tormenting him about the very same subject, as only brothers can do, and the next thing he knew, he announced, in a very loud voice, that he was not going to marry Penelope Featherington!

Except somehow Penelope had been standing right there in the doorway, her hand to her mouth, her eyes wide with pain and embarrassment and probably a dozen other unpleasant emotions that he'd been too ashamed to delve into.

It had been one of the most awful moments of his life. One, in fact, that he made an effort not to remember. He didn't think Penelope had ever fancied him—at least not any more than other ladies fancied him—but he'd embarrassed her. To single her out for such an announcement . . .

It had been unforgivable.

He'd apologized, of course, and she'd accepted, but he'd never quite forgiven himself.

And now he'd gone and insulted her again. Not in as direct a manner, of course, but he should have thought a bit longer and harder before complaining about his life.

Hell, it had sounded stupid, even to him. What did he have to complain about?

Nothing.

And yet there was still this nagging emptiness. A

longing, really, for something he couldn't define. He was jealous of his brothers, for God's sake, for having found their passions, their legacies.

The only mark Colin had left on the world was in the pages of *Lady Whistledown's Society Papers*.

What a joke.

But all things were relative, weren't they? And compared to Penelope, he had little to complain about.

Which probably meant that he should have kept his thoughts to himself. He didn't like to think of her as an on-the-shelf spinster, but he supposed that was exactly what she was. And it wasn't a position of much reverence in British society.

In fact, it was a situation about which many people would complain. Bitterly.

Penelope had never once presented herself as anything less than a stoic—perhaps not content with her lot, but at least accepting of it.

And who knows? Maybe Penelope had hopes and dreams of a life beyond the one she shared with her mother and sister in their small home on Mount Street. Maybe she had plans and goals of her own but kept them to herself under a veil of dignity and good humor.

Maybe there was more to her than there seemed.

Maybe, he thought with a sigh, she deserved an

apology. He wasn't precisely certain what he needed to apologize for; he wasn't certain there *was* a precise thing that needed it.

But the situation needed *something*.

Aw, hell. Now he was going to have to attend the Smythe-Smith musicale this evening. It was a painful, discordant, annual event; just when one was sure that all the Smythe-Smith daughters had grown up, some new cousin rose to take her place, each more tone deaf than the last.

But that was where Penelope was going to be that evening, and that meant that was where Colin would have to be as well.

Chapter 7

Colin Bridgerton had quite the bevy of young ladies at his side at the Smythe-Smith musicale Wednesday night, all fawning over his injured hand.

This Author does not know how the injury was sustained—indeed, Mr. Bridgerton has been rather annoyingly tight-lipped about it. Speaking of annoyances, the man in question seemed rather irritated by all of the attention. Indeed, This Author overheard him tell his brother Anthony that he wished he'd left the (unrepeatable word) bandage at home.

LADY WHISTLEDOWN'S SOCIETY PAPERS,
16 APRIL 1824

Why why why did she do this to herself?

Year after year the invitation arrived by messenger, and year after year Penelope swore she would never, as God was her witness, ever attend another Smythe-Smith musicale.

And yet year after year she found herself seated in the Smythe-Smith music room, desperately trying not to cringe (at least not visibly) as the latest generation of Smythe-Smith girls butchered poor Mr. Mozart in musical effigy.

It was painful. Horribly, awfully, hideously painful. Truly, there was no other way to describe it.

Even more perplexing was that Penelope always seemed to end up in the front row, or close to it, which was beyond excruciating. And not just on the ears. Every few years, there would be one Smythe-Smith girl who seemed aware that she was taking part in what could only be termed a crime against auditory law. While the other girls attacked their violins and pianofortes with oblivious vigor, this odd one out played with a pained expression on her face—an expression Penelope knew well.

It was the face one put on when one wanted to be anywhere but where one was. You could try to hide it, but it always came out in the corners of the mouth, which were held tight and taut. And the eyes, of course, which floated either above or below everyone else's line of vision.

Heaven knew Penelope's face had been cursed with that same expression many a time.

Maybe that was why she never quite managed to stay home on a Smythe-Smith night. Someone had to smile encouragingly and pretend to enjoy the music.

Besides, it wasn't as if she were forced to come and listen more than once per year, anyway.

Still, one couldn't help but think that there must be a fortune to be made in discreet earplugs.

The quartet of girls were warming up—a jumble of discordant notes and scales that only promised to worsen once they began to play in earnest. Penelope had taken a seat in the center of the second row, much to her sister Felicity's dismay.

"There are two perfectly good seats in the back corner," Felicity hissed in her ear.

"It's too late now," Penelope returned, settling down on the lightly cushioned chair.

"God help me," Felicity groaned.

Penelope picked up her program and began leafing through it. "If we don't sit here, someone else will," she said.

"Precisely my desire!"

Penelope leaned in so that only her sister could hear

her murmured words. "We can be counted on to smile and be polite. Imagine if someone like Cressida Twombley sat here and snickered all the way through."

Felicity looked around. "I don't think Cressida Twombley would be caught dead here."

Penelope chose to ignore the statement. "The last thing they need is someone seated right in front who likes to make unkind remarks. Those poor girls would be mortified."

"They're going to be mortified anyway," Felicity grumbled.

"No, they won't," Penelope said. "At least not that one, that one, or that one," she said, pointing to the two on violins and the one at the piano. But that one"—she motioned discreetly to the girl sitting with a cello between her knees—"is already miserable. The least we can do is not to make it worse by allowing someone catty and cruel to sit here."

"She's only going to be eviscerated later this week by Lady Whistledown," Felicity muttered.

Penelope opened her mouth to say more, but at that exact moment she realized that the person who had just occupied the seat on her other side was Eloise.

"Eloise," Penelope said with obvious delight. "I thought you were planning to stay home."

Eloise grimaced, her skin taking on a decidedly

green pallor. "I can't explain it, but I can't seem to stay away. It's rather like a carriage accident. You just can't *not* look."

"Or listen," Felicity said, "as the case may be."

Penelope smiled. She couldn't help it.

"Did I hear you talking about Lady Whistledown when I arrived?" Eloise asked.

"I told Penelope," Felicity said, leaning rather inelegantly across her sister to speak to Eloise, "that they're going to be destroyed by Lady W later this week."

"I don't know," Eloise said thoughtfully. "She doesn't pick on the Smythe-Smith girls every year. I'm not sure why."

"I know why," cackled a voice from behind.

Eloise, Penelope, and Felicity all twisted in their seats, then lurched backward as Lady Danbury's cane came perilously close to their faces.

"Lady Danbury," Penelope gulped, unable to resist the urge to touch her nose—if only to reassure herself that it was still there.

"I have that Lady Whistledown figured out," Lady Danbury said.

"You do?" Felicity asked.

"She's soft at heart," the old lady continued. "You see that one"—she poked her cane in the direction of

the cellist, nearly piercing Eloise's ear in the process—
"right over there?"

"Yes," Eloise said, rubbing her ear, "although I don't
think I'm going to be able to hear her."

"Probably a blessing," Lady Danbury said before
turning back to the subject at hand. "You can thank
me later."

"You were saying something about the cellist?" Penelope said swiftly, before Eloise said something entirely inappropriate.

"Of course I was. Look at her," Lady Danbury said.
"She's miserable. And well she should be. She's clearly
the only one who has a clue as to how dreadful they are.
The other three don't have the musical sense of a gnat."

Penelope gave her younger sister a rather smug
glance.

"You mark my words," Lady Danbury said. "Lady
Whistledown won't have a thing to say about this musicale. She won't want to hurt that one's feelings. The
rest of them—"

Felicity, Penelope, and Eloise all ducked as the cane
came swinging by.

"Bah. She couldn't care less for the rest of them."

"It's an interesting theory," Penelope said.

Lady Danbury sat back contentedly in her chair.
"Yes, it is. Isn't it?"

Penelope nodded. "I think you're right."

"Hmmph. I usually am."

Still twisted in her seat, Penelope turned first to Felicity, then to Eloise, and said, "It's the same reason why I keep coming to these infernal musicales year after year."

"To see Lady Danbury?" Eloise asked, blinking with confusion.

"No. Because of girls like her." Penelope pointed at the cellist. "Because I know exactly how she feels."

"Don't be silly, Penelope," Felicity said. "You've never played piano in public, and even if you did, you're quite accomplished."

Penelope turned to her sister. "It's not about the music, Felicity."

Then the oddest thing happened to Lady Danbury. Her face changed. Completely, utterly, astoundingly changed. Her eyes grew misty, wistful. And her lips, which were usually slightly pinched and sarcastic at the corners, softened. "I was that girl, too, Miss Featherington," she said, so quietly that both Eloise and Felicity were forced to lean forward, Eloise with an, "I beg your pardon," and Felicity with a considerably less polite, "What?"

But Lady Danbury only had eyes for Penelope. "It's why I attend, year after year," the older lady said. "Just like you."

And for a moment Penelope felt the oddest sense of connection to the older woman. Which was mad, because they had nothing in common aside from gender—not age, not status, nothing. And yet it was almost as if the countess had somehow chosen her—for what purpose Penelope could never guess. But she seemed determined to light a fire under Penelope's well-ordered and often boring life.

And Penelope couldn't help but think that it was somehow working.

Isn't it nice to discover that we're not exactly what we thought we were?

Lady Danbury's words from the other night still echoed in Penelope's head. Almost like a litany.

Almost like a dare.

"Do you know what I think, Miss Featherington?" Lady Danbury asked, her tone deceptively mild.

"I couldn't possibly begin to guess," Penelope said with great honesty—and respect—in her voice.

"I think *you* could be Lady Whistledown."

Felicity and Eloise gasped.

Penelope's lips parted with surprise. No one had ever even thought to accuse her of such before. It was unbelievable . . . unthinkable . . . and . . .

Rather flattering, actually.

Penelope felt her mouth sliding into a sly smile, and

she leaned forward, as if getting ready to impart news of great import.

Lady Danbury leaned forward.

Felicity and Eloise leaned forward.

"Do you know what *I* think, Lady Danbury?" Penelope asked, in a compellingly soft voice.

"Well," Lady D said, a wicked gleam in her eye, "I would tell you that I am breathless with anticipation, but you've already told me once before that you think that *I* am Lady Whistledown."

"Are you?"

Lady Danbury smiled archly. "Maybe I am."

Felicity and Eloise gasped again, louder this time.

Penelope's stomach lurched.

"Are you admitting it?" Eloise whispered.

"Of course I'm not admitting it," Lady Danbury barked, straightening her spine and thumping her cane against the floor with enough force to momentarily stop the four amateur musicians in their warm-up. "Even if it were true—and I'm not saying whether or not it is— would I be fool enough to admit it?"

"Then why did you say—"

"Because, you ninnyhead, I'm trying to make a point."

She then proceeded to fall silent until Penelope was forced to ask, "Which is?"

Lady Danbury gave them all an extremely exasperated look. "That *anyone* could be Lady Whistledown," she exclaimed, thumping her cane on the floor with renewed vigor. "Anyone at all."

"Well, except *me*," Felicity put in. "I'm quite certain it's not me."

Lady Danbury didn't even honor Felicity with a glance. "Let me tell you something," she said.

"As if we could stop you," Penelope said, so sweetly that it came out like a compliment. And truth be told, it *was* a compliment. She admired Lady Danbury a great deal. She admired anyone who knew how to speak her mind in public.

Lady Danbury chuckled. "There's more to you than meets the eye, Penelope Featherington."

"It's true," Felicity said with a grin. "She can be rather cruel, for example. Nobody would believe it, but when we were young—"

Penelope elbowed her in the ribs.

"See?" Felicity said.

"What I was going to say," Lady Danbury continued, "was that the *ton* is going about my challenge all wrong."

"How do you suggest we go about it, then?" Eloise asked.

Lady Danbury waved her hand dismissively in Eloise's face. "I have to explain what people are doing wrong first," she said. "They keep looking toward the obvious people. People like your mother," she said, turning to Penelope and Felicity.

"Mother?" they both echoed.

"Oh, please," Lady Danbury scoffed. "A bigger busybody this town has never seen. She's exactly the sort of person everyone suspects."

Penelope had no idea what to say to that. Her mother *was* a notorious gossip, but it was difficult to imagine her as Lady Whistledown.

"Which is why," Lady Danbury continued, a shrewd look in her eye, "it can't be her."

"Well, *that*," Penelope said with a touch of sarcasm, "and the fact that Felicity and I could tell you for certain that it's not her."

"Pish. If your mother were Lady Whistledown, she'd have figured out a way to keep it from you."

"My mother?" Felicity said doubtfully. "I don't think so."

"What I am trying to *say*," Lady Danbury ground out, "prior to all of these infernal *interruptions*—"

Penelope thought she heard Eloise snort.

"—was that if Lady Whistledown were someone *obvious*, she'd have been found out by now, don't you think?"

Silence, until it became clear some response was required, then all three of them nodded with appropriate thoughtfulness and vigor.

"She must be someone that nobody suspects," Lady Danbury said. "She has to be."

Penelope found herself nodding again. Lady Danbury did make sense, in a strange sort of way.

"Which is why," the older lady continued triumphantly, "I am not a likely candidate!"

Penelope blinked, not quite following the logic. "I beg your pardon?"

"Oh, *please.*" Lady Danbury gave Penelope quite the most disdainful glance. "Do you think you're the first person to suspect me?"

Penelope just shook her head. "I still think it's you."

That earned her a measure of respect. Lady Danbury nodded approvingly as she said, "You're cheekier than you look."

Felicity leaned forward and said in a rather conspiratorial voice, "It's true."

Penelope swatted her sister's hand. "Felicity!"

"I think the musicale is starting," Eloise said.

"Heaven help us all," Lady Danbury announced. "I don't know why I—Mr. Bridgerton!"

Penelope had turned to face the small stage area, but

she whipped back around to see Colin making his way along the row to the empty seat beside Lady Danbury, apologizing good-naturedly as he bumped into people's knees.

His apologies, of course, were accompanied by one of his lethal smiles, and no fewer than three ladies positively melted in their seats as a result.

Penelope frowned. It was disgusting.

"Penelope," Felicity whispered. "Did you just growl?"

"Colin," Eloise said. "I didn't know you were coming."

He shrugged, his face alight with a lopsided grin. "Changed my mind at the last moment. I've always been a great lover of music, after all."

"Which would explain your presence here," Eloise said in an exceptionally dry voice.

Colin acknowledged her statement with nothing more than an arch of his brow before turning to Penelope and saying, "Good evening, Miss Featherington." He nodded at Felicity with another, "Miss Featherington."

It took Penelope a moment to find her voice. They had parted most awkwardly that afternoon, and now here he was with a friendly smile. "Good evening, Mr. Bridgerton," she finally managed.

"Does anyone know what is on the program tonight?" he asked, looking terribly interested.

Penelope had to admire that. Colin had a way of looking at you as if nothing in the world could be more interesting than your next sentence. It was a talent, that. Especially now, when they all knew that he couldn't possibly care one way or another what the Smythe-Smith girls chose to play that evening.

"I believe it's Mozart," Felicity said. "They almost always choose Mozart."

"Lovely," Colin replied, leaning back in his chair as if he'd just finished an excellent meal. "I'm a great fan of Mr. Mozart."

"In that case," Lady Danbury cackled, elbowing him in the ribs, "you might want to make your escape while the possibility still exists."

"Don't be silly," he said. "I'm sure the girls will do their best."

"Oh, there's no question of them doing their best," Eloise said ominously.

"Shhh," Penelope said. "I think they're ready to begin."

Not, she admitted to herself, that she was especially eager to listen to the Smythe-Smith version of *Eine Kleine Nachtmusik*. But she felt profoundly ill-at-ease with Colin. She wasn't sure what to say to him—except that whatever it was she *should* say definitely shouldn't be said in front of Eloise, Felicity, and most of all Lady Danbury.

A butler came around and snuffed out a few candles to signal that the girls were ready to begin. Penelope braced herself, swallowed in such a way as to clog her inner ear canals (it didn't work), and then the torture began.

And went on . . . and on . . . and on.

Penelope wasn't certain what was more agonizing—the music or the knowledge that Colin was sitting right behind her. The back of her neck prickled with awareness, and she found herself fidgeting like mad, her fingers tapping relentlessly on the dark blue velvet of her skirts.

When the Smythe-Smith quartet was finally done, three of the girls were beaming at the polite applause, and the fourth—the cellist—looked as if she wanted to crawl under a rock.

Penelope sighed. At least she, in all of her unsuccessful seasons, hadn't ever been forced to parade her deficiencies before all the *ton* like these girls had. She'd always been allowed to melt into the shadows, to hover quietly at the perimeter of the room, watching the other girls take their turns on the dance floor. Oh, her mother dragged her here and there, trying to place her in the path of some eligible gentleman or another, but that was nothing—nothing!—like what the Smythe-Smith girls were forced to endure.

Although, in all honesty, three out of the four seemed blissfully unaware of their musical ineptitude. Penelope just smiled and clapped. She certainly wasn't going to burst their collective bubble.

And if Lady Danbury's theory was correct, Lady Whistledown wasn't going to write a word about the musicale.

The applause petered out rather quickly, and soon everyone was milling about, making polite conversation with their neighbors and eyeing the sparsely laid refreshment table at the back of the room.

"Lemonade," Penelope murmured to herself. Perfect. She was dreadfully hot—really, what had she been thinking, wearing velvet on such a warm night?—and a cool beverage would be just the thing to make her feel better. Not to mention that Colin was trapped in conversation with Lady Danbury, so it was the ideal time to make her escape.

But as soon as Penelope had her glass in hand, she heard Colin's achingly familiar voice behind her, murmuring her name.

She turned around, and before she had any idea what she was doing, she said, "I'm sorry."

"You are?"

"Yes," she assured him. "At least I think I am."

His eyes crinkled slightly at the corners. "The conversation grows more intriguing by the second."

"Colin—"

He held out his arm. "Take a turn with me around the room, will you?"

"I don't think—"

He moved his arm closer to her—just by an inch or so, but the message was clear. "Please," he said.

She nodded and set her lemonade down. "Very well."

They walked in silence for almost a minute, then Colin said, "I would like to apologize to you."

"I was the one who stormed out of the room," Penelope pointed out.

He tilted his head slightly, and she could see an indulgent smile playing across his lips. "I'd hardly call it 'storming,' " he said.

Penelope frowned. She probably shouldn't have left in such a huff, but now that she had, she was oddly proud of it. It wasn't every day that a woman such as herself got to make such a dramatic exit.

"Well, I shouldn't have been so rude," she muttered, by now not really meaning it.

He arched a brow, then obviously decided not to

pursue the matter. "I would like to apologize," he said, "for being such a whiny little brat."

Penelope actually tripped over her feet.

He helped her regain her balance, then said, "I am aware that I have many, many things in my life for which I should be grateful. For which I *am* grateful," he corrected, his mouth not quite smiling but certainly sheepish. "It was unforgivably rude to complain to you."

"No," she said, "I have spent all evening thinking about what you said, and while I . . ." She swallowed, then licked her lips, which had gone quite dry. She'd spent all day trying to think of the right words, and she'd thought that she'd found them, but now that he was here, at her side, she couldn't think of a deuced thing.

"Do you need another glass of lemonade?" Colin asked politely.

She shook her head. "You have every right to your feelings," she blurted out. "They may not be what I would feel, were I in your shoes, but you have every right to them. But—"

She broke off, and Colin found himself rather desperate to know what she'd planned to say. "But what, Penelope?" he urged.

"It's nothing."

"It's not nothing to me." His hand was on her arm, and so he squeezed slightly, to let her know that he meant what he said.

For the longest time, he didn't think she was actually going to respond, and then, just when he thought his face would crack from the smile he held so carefully on his lips—they were in public, after all, and it wouldn't do to invite comment and speculation by appearing urgent and disturbed—she sighed.

It was a lovely sound, strangely comforting, soft, and wise. And it made him want to look at her more closely, to see into her mind, to hear the rhythms of her soul.

"Colin," Penelope said quietly, "if you feel frustrated by your current situation, you should do something to change it. It's really that simple."

"That's what I do," he said with a careless shrug of his outside shoulder. "My mother accuses me of picking up and leaving the country completely on a whim, but the truth is—"

"You do it when you're feeling frustrated," she finished for him.

He nodded. She understood him. He wasn't sure how it had happened, or even that it made any sense, but Penelope Featherington understood him.

"I think you should publish your journals," she said.

"I couldn't."

"Why not?"

He stopped in his tracks, letting go of her arm. He didn't really have an answer, other than the odd pounding in his heart. "Who would want to read them?" he finally asked.

"I would," she said frankly. "Eloise, Felicity . . ." she added, ticking off names on her fingers. "Your mother, Lady Whistledown, I'm sure," she added with a mischievous smile. "She does write about you rather a lot."

Her good humor was infectious, and Colin couldn't quite suppress his smile. "Penelope, it doesn't count if the only people who buy the book are the people I know."

"Why not?" Her lips twitched. "You know a lot of people. Why, if you only count Bridgertons—"

He grabbed her hand. He didn't know why, but he grabbed her hand. "Penelope, stop."

She just laughed. "I think Eloise told me that you have piles and piles of cousins as well, and—"

"Enough," he warned. But he was grinning as he said it.

Penelope stared down at her hand in his, then said, "Lots of people will want to read about your travels. Maybe at first it will only be because you're a well-known figure in London, but it won't take long before everyone realizes what a good writer you are. And then they'll be clamoring for more."

"I don't want to be a success because of the Bridgerton name," he said.

She dropped his hand and planted hers on her hips. "Are you even *listening* to me? I just told you that—"

"What are you two talking about?"

Eloise. Looking very, very curious.

"Nothing," they both muttered at the same time.

Eloise snorted. "Don't insult me. It's not nothing. Penelope looked as if she might start breathing fire at any moment."

"Your brother is just being obtuse," Penelope said.

"Well, that is nothing new," Eloise said.

"Wait a moment!" Colin exclaimed.

"But what," Eloise probed, ignoring him entirely, "is he being obtuse about?"

"It's a private matter," Colin ground out.

"Which makes it all the more interesting," Eloise said. She looked to Penelope expectantly.

"I'm sorry," Penelope said. "I really can't say."

"I can't believe it!" Eloise cried out. "You're not going to tell me."

"No," Penelope replied, feeling rather oddly satisfied with herself, "I'm not."

"I can't believe it," Eloise said again, turning to her brother. "I can't believe it."

His lips quirked into the barest of smiles. "Believe it."

"You're keeping secrets from me."

He raised his brows. "Did you think I told you everything?"

"Of course not." She scowled. "But I thought Penelope did."

"But this isn't my secret to tell," Penelope said. "It's Colin's."

"I think the planet has shifted on its axis," Eloise grumbled. "Or perhaps England has crashed into France. All I know is this is not the same world I inhabited just this morning."

Penelope couldn't help it. She giggled.

"And you're laughing at me!" Eloise added.

"No, I'm not," Penelope said, laughing. "Really, I'm not."

"Do you know what you need?" Colin asked.

"Me?" Eloise queried.

He nodded. "A husband."

"You're as bad as Mother!"

"I could be a lot worse if I really put my mind to it."

"Of that I have no doubt," Eloise shot back.

"Stop, stop!" Penelope said, truly laughing in earnest now.

They both looked at her expectantly, as if to say, *Now what?*

"I'm so glad I came tonight," Penelope said, the words tumbling unbidden from her lips. "I can't remember a nicer evening. Truly, I can't."

Several hours later, as Colin was lying in bed, staring up at the ceiling in the bedroom of his new flat in Bloomsbury, it occurred to him that he felt the exact same way.

Chapter 8

Colin Bridgerton and Penelope Featherington were seen in conversation at the Smythe-Smith musicale, although no one seems to know what exactly they were discussing. This Author would venture to guess that their conversation centered upon This Author's identity, since that was what everyone else seemed to be talking about before, after, and (rather rudely, in This Author's esteemed opinion) during the performance.

In other news, Honoria Smythe-Smith's violin was damaged when Lady Danbury accidentally knocked it off a table while waving her cane.

Lady Danbury insisted upon replacing the instrument, but then declared that as it is not her habit to buy anything but the best, Honoria will have a Ruggieri violin, imported from Cremona, Italy.

It is This Author's understanding that, when one factors in manufacture and shipping time, along with a lengthy waiting list, it takes six months for a Ruggieri violin to reach our shores.

LADY WHISTLEDOWN'S SOCIETY PAPERS,
16 APRIL 1824

There are moments in a woman's life when her heart flips in her chest, when the world suddenly seems uncommonly pink and perfect, when a symphony can be heard in the tinkle of a doorbell.

Penelope Featherington had just such a moment two days after the Smythe-Smith musicale.

All it took was a knock on her bedroom door, followed by her butler's voice, informing her:

"Mr. Colin Bridgerton is here to see you."

Penelope tumbled right off the bed.

Briarly, who had butlered for the Featherington family long enough so that he did not even so much as bat an eyelash at Penelope's clumsiness, murmured, "Shall I tell him you are not in?"

"No!" Penelope nearly shrieked, stumbling to her

feet. "I mean, no," she added in a more reasonable voice. "But I will require ten minutes to prepare myself." She glanced in the mirror and winced at her disheveled appearance. "Fifteen."

"As you wish, Miss Penelope."

"Oh, and make certain to prepare a tray of food. Mr. Bridgerton is sure to be hungry. He's always hungry."

The butler nodded again.

Penelope stood stock-still as Briarly disappeared out the door, then, completely unable to contain herself, danced from foot to foot, emitting a strange squealing sort of noise—one that she was convinced—or at least hoped—had never before crossed her lips.

Then again, she couldn't remember the last time a gentleman had called upon her, much less the one with whom she'd been desperately in love for almost half of her life.

"Settle down," she said, spreading her fingers and pressing her flattened palms out in much the same motion she might make if she were trying to placate a small, unruly crowd. "You must remain calm. Calm," she repeated, as if that would actually do the trick. "Calm."

But inside, her heart was dancing.

She took a few deep breaths, walked over to her dressing table, and picked up her hairbrush. It would only take a few minutes to repin her hair; surely Colin wasn't going to flee if she kept him waiting for a short while. He'd expect her to take a bit of time to ready herself, wouldn't he?

But still, she found herself fixing her hair in record time, and by the time she stepped through the sitting room door, a mere five minutes had passed since the butler's announcement.

"That was quick," Colin said with a quirky grin. He'd been standing by the window, peering out at Mount Street.

"Oh, was it?" Penelope said, hoping that the heat she felt on her skin wasn't translating into a blush. A woman was supposed to keep a gentleman waiting, although not too long. Still, it made no sense to hold to such silly behavior with Colin, of all people. He would never be interested in her in a romantic fashion, and besides, they were friends.

Friends. It seemed like such an odd concept, and yet that was exactly what they were. They'd always been friendly acquaintances, but since his return from Cyprus, they'd become friends in truth.

It was magical.

Even if he never loved her—and she rather thought he never would—this was better than what they'd had before.

"To what do I owe the pleasure?" she asked, taking a seat on her mother's slightly faded yellow damask sofa.

Colin sat across from her in a rather uncomfortable straight-backed chair. He leaned forward, resting his hands on his knees, and Penelope knew instantly that something was wrong. It simply wasn't the pose a gentleman adopted for a regular social call. He looked too distraught, too intense.

"It's rather serious," he said, his face grim.

Penelope nearly rose to her feet. "Has something happened? Is someone ill?"

"No, no, nothing like that." He paused, let out a long breath, then raked his hand through his already mussed-up hair. "It's about Eloise."

"What is it?"

"I don't know how to say this. I—Do you have anything to eat?"

Penelope was ready to wring his neck. "For heaven's sake, Colin!"

"Sorry," he muttered. "I haven't eaten all day."

"A first, I'm sure," Penelope said impatiently. "I already told Briarly to fix a tray. Now, will you just tell me what is wrong, or do you plan to wait until I expire of impatience?"

"I think she's Lady Whistledown," he blurted out.

Penelope's mouth fell open. She wasn't sure what she'd expected him to say, but it wasn't this.

"Penelope, did you hear me?"

"Eloise?" she asked, even though she knew exactly who he was talking about.

He nodded.

"She can't be."

He stood and began to pace, too full of nervous energy to sit still. "Why not?"

"Because . . . because . . ." Because *why*? "Because there is no way she could have done that for ten years without my knowing."

His expression went from disturbed to disdainful in an instant. "I hardly think you're privy to everything that Eloise does."

"Of course not," Penelope replied, giving him a rather irritated look, "but I can tell you with absolute certainty that there is no way Eloise could keep a secret of that magnitude from me for over ten years. She's simply not capable of it."

"Penelope, she's the nosiest person I know."

"Well, that much is true," Penelope agreed. "Except for my mother, I suppose. But that's hardly enough to convict her."

Colin stopped his pacing and planted his hands on his hips. "She is always writing things down."

"Why would you think that?"

He held up his hand, rubbing his thumb briskly against his fingertips. "Inkstains. Constantly."

"Lots of people use pen and ink." Penelope motioned broadly at Colin. "You write in journals. I am certain you've had your share of ink on your fingers."

"Yes, but I don't *disappear* when I write in my journals."

Penelope felt her pulse quicken. "What do you mean?" she asked, her voice growing breathless.

"I mean that she locks herself in her room for hours on end, and it's after those periods that her fingers are covered with ink."

Penelope didn't say anything for an agonizingly long moment. Colin's "evidence" was damning, indeed, especially when combined with Eloise's well-known and well-documented penchant for nosiness.

But she wasn't Lady Whistledown. She couldn't be. Penelope would bet her life on it.

Finally Penelope just crossed her arms and, in a tone of voice that probably would have been more at home on an exceedingly stubborn six-year-old, said, "It's not her. It's not."

Colin sat back down, looking defeated. "I wish I could share your certainty."

"Colin, you need to—"

"Where the hell is the food?" he grumbled.

She should have been shocked, but somehow his lack of manners amused her. "I'm sure Briarly will be here shortly."

He sprawled into a chair. "I'm hungry."

"Yes," Penelope said, lips twitching, "I surmised as much."

He sighed, weary and worried. "If she's Lady Whistledown, it'll be a disaster. A pure, unmitigated disaster."

"It wouldn't be that bad," Penelope said carefully. "Not that I think she's Lady Whistledown, because I don't! But truly, if she were, would it be so very dreadful? I rather like Lady Whistledown myself."

"Yes, Penelope," Colin said rather sharply, "it would be so very dreadful. She'd be ruined."

"I don't think she'd be *ruined.* . . ."

"Of course she'd be ruined. Do you have any idea how many people that woman has insulted over the years?"

"I didn't realize you hated Lady Whistledown so much," Penelope said.

"I don't hate her," Colin said impatiently. "It doesn't matter if I hate her. Everyone else hates her."

"I don't think that's true. They all buy her paper."

"Of course they buy her paper! Everyone buys her bloody paper."

"Colin!"

"Sorry," he muttered, but it didn't really sound like he meant it.

Penelope nodded her acceptance of his apology.

"Whoever that Lady Whistledown is," Colin said, shaking his finger at her with such vehemence that she actually lurched backward, "when she is unmasked, she will not be able to show her face in London."

Penelope delicately cleared her throat. "I didn't realize you cared so much about the opinions of society."

"I don't," he retorted. "Well, not much, at least. Anyone who tells you they don't care at all is a liar and a hypocrite."

Penelope rather thought he was correct, but she was surprised he'd admitted it. It seemed men always liked to pretend that they were wholly self-contained, completely unaffected by the whims and opinions of society.

Colin leaned forward, his green eyes burning with intensity. "This isn't about me, Penelope, it's about Eloise. And if she is cast out of society, she will be crushed." He sat back, but his entire body radiated tension. "Not to mention what it would do to my mother."

Penelope let out a long breath. "I really think you're getting upset over nothing," she said.

"I hope you're right," he replied, closing his eyes. He wasn't sure when he'd started to suspect that his sister might be Lady Whistledown. Probably after Lady Danbury had issued her now famous challenge. Unlike most of London, Colin had never been terribly interested in Lady Whistledown's true identity. The column was entertaining, and he certainly read it along with everyone else, but to his mind, Lady Whistledown was simply . . . Lady Whistledown, and that was all she needed to be.

But Lady Danbury's dare had started him thinking, and like the rest of the Bridgertons, once he got hold of an idea, he was fundamentally incapable of letting it go. Somehow it had occurred to him that Eloise had the perfect temperament and skills to write such a column, and then, before he could convince himself that he was crazy, he'd seen the ink spots on her fingers. Since then he'd gone nearly mad, unable to think about anything but the possibility that Eloise had a secret life.

He didn't know which irritated him more—that Eloise might be Lady Whistledown, or that she had managed to hide it from him for over a decade.

How galling, to be hoodwinked by one's sister. He liked to think himself smarter than that.

But he needed to focus on the present. Because if his suspicions were correct, how on earth were they going to deal with the scandal when she was discovered?

And she *would* be discovered. With all of London lusting after the thousand-pound prize, Lady Whistledown didn't stand a chance.

"Colin! Colin!"

He opened his eyes, wondering how long Penelope had been calling his name.

"I really think you should stop worrying about Eloise," she said. "There are hundreds and hundreds of people in London. Lady Whistledown could be any one of them. Heavens, with your eye for detail"—she waggled her fingers to remind him of Eloise's ink-stained fingertips—"*you* could be Lady Whistledown."

He shot her a rather condescending look. "Except for the small detail of my having been out of the country half the time."

Penelope chose to ignore his sarcasm. "You're certainly a good enough writer to carry it off."

Colin had intended to say something droll and slightly gruff, dismissing her rather weak arguments, but the truth was he was so secretly delighted about her "good writer" compliment that all he could do was sit there with a loopy smile on his face.

"Are you all right?" Penelope asked.

"Perfectly fine," he replied, snapping to attention and trying to adopt a more sober mien. "Why would you ask?"

"Because you suddenly looked quite ill. Dizzy, actually."

"I'm fine," he repeated, probably a little louder than was necessary. "I'm just thinking about the scandal."

She let out a beleaguered sigh, which irritated him, because he didn't see that she had any reason to feel so impatient with him. "What scandal?" she asked.

"The scandal that is going to erupt when she is discovered," he ground out.

"She's not Lady Whistledown!" she insisted.

Colin suddenly sat up straight, his eyes alight with a new idea. "Do you know," he said in a rather intense sort of voice, "but I don't think it matters if she is Lady Whistledown or not."

Penelope stared at him blankly for a full three seconds before looking about the room, muttering, "Where's the food? I must be light-headed. Haven't you spent the last ten minutes positively going *mad* over the possibility that she is?"

As if on cue, Briarly entered the room with a heavily laden tray. Penelope and Colin watched in silence as the butler laid out the meal. "Would you like me to fix your plates?" he inquired.

"No, that's quite all right," Penelope said quickly. "We can manage for ourselves."

Briarly nodded and, as soon as he'd laid the flatware and filled the two glasses with lemonade, left the room.

"Listen to me," Colin said, jumping to his feet and moving the door so that it almost rested against the doorframe (but remained technically open, should anyone quibble about proprieties).

"Don't you want something to eat?" Penelope inquired, holding aloft a plate that she'd filled with various small snacks.

He snatched a piece of cheese, ate it in two rather indelicate bites, then continued, "Even if Eloise isn't Lady Whistledown—and mind you, I still think she is—it doesn't matter. Because if *I* suspect that she's Lady Whistledown, then surely someone else will as well."

"Your point being?"

Colin realized that his arms were reaching forward, and he stopped himself before he reached out to shake her shoulders. "It doesn't matter! Don't you see? If someone points his finger at her, she'll be ruined."

"But not," Penelope said, appearing to require a great deal of effort to unclench her teeth, "if she's not Lady Whistledown!"

"How could she prove it?" Colin returned, jumping to his feet. "Once a rumor is started, the damage is done. It develops a life of its own."

"Colin, you ceased to make sense five minutes ago."

"No, hear me out." He whirled to face her, and he was seized by a feeling of such intensity that he couldn't have ripped his eyes from hers if the house were falling down around them. "Suppose I told everyone that I had seduced you."

Penelope grew very, very still.

"You would be ruined forever," he continued, crouching down near the edge of the sofa so that they were more on the same level. "It wouldn't matter that we had never even kissed. *That*, my dear Penelope, is the power of the word."

She looked oddly frozen. And at the same time flushed. "I . . . I don't know what to say," she stammered.

And then the most bizarre thing happened. He realized that he didn't know what to say, either. Because he'd forgotten about rumors and the power of the word and all of that rot, and the only thing he could think of was the part about the kissing, and—

And—

And—

Good God in heaven, he wanted to kiss Penelope Featherington.

Penelope Featherington!

He might as well have said he wanted to kiss his sister.

Except—he stole a glance at her; she looked uncommonly fetching, and he wondered how he hadn't noticed that earlier that afternoon—she wasn't his sister.

She definitely wasn't his sister.

"Colin?" His name was a mere whisper on her lips, her eyes were quite adorably blinking and befuddled, and how was it he'd never noticed what an intriguing shade of brown they were? Almost gold near the pupil. He'd never seen anything like it, and yet it wasn't as if he hadn't seen her a hundred times before.

He stood—suddenly, drunkenly. Best if they weren't quite on the same latitude. Harder to see her eyes from up here.

She stood, too.

Damn it.

"Colin?" she asked, her voice barely audible. "Could I ask you a favor?"

Call it male intuition, call it insanity, but a very insistent voice inside of him was screaming that whatever she wanted *had* to be a very bad idea.

He was, however, an idiot.

He had to be, because he felt his lips part and then

he heard a voice that sounded an awful lot like his own say, "Of course."

Her lips puckered, and for a moment he thought she was trying to kiss him, but then he realized that she was just bringing them together to form a word.

"Would—"

Just a word. Nothing but a word beginning with *W*. *W* always looked like a kiss.

"Would you kiss me?"

Chapter 9

Every week there seems to be one invitation that is coveted above all others, and this week's prize must surely go to the Countess of Macclesfield, who is hosting a grand ball on Monday night. Lady Macclesfield is not a frequent hostess here in London, but she is very popular, as is her husband, and it is expected that a great many bachelors plan to attend, including Mr. Colin Bridgerton (assuming he does not collapse from exhaustion after four days with the ten Bridgerton grandchildren), Viscount Burwick, and Mr. Michael Anstruther-Wetherby.

This Author anticipates that a great many young and unmarried ladies will choose to attend as well, following the publication of this column.

LADY WHISTLEDOWN'S SOCIETY PAPERS,
16 APRIL 1824

H is life as he knew it was over.

"What?" he asked, aware that he was blinking rapidly.

Her face turned a deeper shade of crimson than he'd thought humanly possible, and she turned away. "Never mind," she mumbled. "Forget I said anything."

Colin thought that a *very* good idea.

But then, just when he'd thought that his world might resume its normal course (or at least that he'd be able to pretend it had), she whirled back around, her eyes alight with a passionate fire that astonished him.

"No, I'm not going to forget it," she cried out. "I've spent my life forgetting things, not saying them, never telling anyone what I really want."

Colin tried to say something, but it was clear to him that his throat had begun to close. Any minute now he'd be dead. He was sure of it.

"It won't mean a thing," she said. "I promise you, it won't mean anything, and I'd never expect anything from you because of it, but I could die tomorrow, and—"

"*What?*"

Her eyes looked huge, and meltingly dark, and pleading, and . . .

He could feel his resolve melting away.

"I'm eight-and-twenty," she said, her voice soft and sad. "I'm an old maid, and I've never been kissed."

"Gah . . . gah . . . gah . . ." He knew he knew how to speak; he was fairly certain he'd been perfectly articulate just minutes earlier. But now he didn't seem able to form a word.

And Penelope kept talking, her cheeks delightfully pink, and her lips moving so quickly that he couldn't help but wonder what they'd feel like on his skin. On his neck, on his shoulder, on his . . . other places.

"I'm going to be an old maid at nine-and-twenty," she said, "and I'll be an old maid at thirty. I could die tomorrow, and—"

"You're not going to die tomorrow!" he somehow managed to get out.

"But I could! I could, and it would kill me, because—"

"You'd already be dead," he said, thinking his voice sounded rather strange and disembodied.

"I don't want to die without ever having been kissed," she finally finished.

Colin could think of a hundred reasons why kissing Penelope Featherington was a very bad idea, the number one being that he actually *wanted* to kiss her.

He opened his mouth, hoping that a sound would emerge and that it might actually be intelligible speech, but there was nothing, just the sound of breath on his lips.

And then Penelope did the one thing that could break his resolve in an instant. She looked up at him, deeply into his eyes, and uttered one, simple word.

"Please."

He was lost. There was something heartbreaking in the way she was gazing at him, as if she might die if he didn't kiss her. Not from heartbreak, not from embarrassment—it was almost as if she needed him for nourishment, to feed her soul, to fill her heart.

And Colin couldn't remember anyone else ever needing him with such fervor.

It humbled him.

It made him want her with an intensity that nearly buckled his knees. He looked at her, and somehow he didn't see the woman he'd seen so many times before. She was different. She glowed. She was a siren, a goddess, and he wondered how on earth no one had ever noticed this before.

"Colin?" she whispered.

He took a step forward—barely a half a foot, but it was close enough so that when he touched her chin and tipped her face up, her lips were mere inches from his.

Their breath mingled, and the air grew hot and heavy. Penelope was trembling—he could feel that under his fingers—but he wasn't so sure that he wasn't trembling, too.

He assumed he'd say something flip and droll, like the devil-may-care fellow he was reputed to be. *Anything for you,* perhaps, or maybe, *Every woman deserves at least one kiss.* But as he closed the bare distance between them, he realized that there were no words that could capture the intensity of the moment.

No words for the passion. No words for the need.

No words for the sheer epiphany of the moment.

And so, on an otherwise unremarkable Friday afternoon, in the heart of Mayfair, in a quiet drawing room on Mount Street, Colin Bridgerton kissed Penelope Featherington.

And it was glorious.

His lips touched hers softly at first, not because he was trying to be gentle, although if he'd had the presence of mind to think about such things, it probably would have occurred to him that this was her first kiss, and it ought to be reverent and beautiful and all the things a girl dreams about as she's lying in bed at night.

But in all truth, none of that was on Colin's mind. In fact, he was thinking of quite little. His kiss was soft and gentle because he was still so surprised that he was kissing her. He'd known her for years, had never even thought about touching his lips to hers. And now he couldn't have let her go if the fires of hell were licking his toes. He could barely believe what he was doing—or that he wanted to do it so damned much.

It wasn't the sort of a kiss one initiates because one is overcome with passion or emotion or anger or desire. It was a slower thing, a learning experience—for Colin just as much as for Penelope.

And he was learning that everything he thought he'd known about kissing was rubbish.

Everything else had been mere lips and tongue and softly murmured but meaningless words.

This was a kiss.

There was something in the friction, the way he could hear and feel her breath at the same time. Something in the way she held perfectly still, and yet he could feel her heart pounding through her skin.

There was something in the fact that he knew it was *her.*

Colin moved his lips slightly to the left, until he was nipping the corner of her mouth, softly tickling the very spot where her lips joined. His tongue dipped and traced, learning the contours of her mouth, tasting the sweet-salty essence of her.

This was more than a kiss.

His hands, which had been lightly splayed against her back, grew rigid, more tense as they pressed into the fabric of her dress. He could feel the heat of her under his fingertips, seeping up through the muslin, swirling in the delicate muscles of her back.

He drew her to him, pulling her closer, closer, until their bodies were pressed together. He could feel her, the entire length of her, and it set him on fire. He was growing hard, and he wanted her—dear God, how he wanted her.

His mouth grew more insistent, and his tongue darted forward, nudging her until her lips parted. He swallowed her soft moan of acquiescence, then pushed forward to taste her. She was sweet and a little tart from the lemonade, and she was clearly as intoxicating as fine brandy, because Colin was starting to doubt his ability to remain on his feet.

He moved his hands along the length of her—slowly, so as not to frighten her. She was soft, curvy, and lush, just as he'd always thought a woman should be. Her hips flared, and her bottom was perfect, and her breasts . . . good God, her breasts felt good pressing against his chest. His palms itched to cup them, but he forced his hands to remain where they were (rather enjoyably on her derrière, so it really wasn't that much of a sacrifice.) Beside the fact that he really shouldn't be groping a gently bred lady's breasts in the middle of her drawing room, he had a rather painful suspicion that if he touched her in that way, he would lose himself completely.

"Penelope, Penelope," he murmured, wondering why her name tasted so good on his lips. He was ravenous for her, heady and drugged by passion, and he wanted desperately for her to feel the same way. She felt perfect in his arms, but thus far, she had made no reaction. Oh, she had swayed in his arms and opened her mouth to welcome his sweet invasion, but other than that, she had done nothing.

And yet, from the pant of her breath and the beat of her heart, he knew that she was aroused.

He pulled back, just a few inches so that he could touch her chin and tilt her face up toward his. Her eyelids fluttered open, revealing eyes that were dazed with passion, perfectly matching her lips, which were lightly parted, completely soft, and thoroughly swollen from his kisses.

She was beautiful. Utterly, completely, soul-stirringly beautiful. He didn't know how he hadn't noticed it all these years.

Was the world populated with blind men, or merely stupid ones?

"You can kiss me, too," he whispered, leaning his forehead lightly against hers.

She did nothing but blink.

"A kiss," he murmured, lowering his lips to hers again, although just for a fleeting moment, "is for two people."

Her hand stirred at his back. "What do I do?" she whispered.

"Whatever you want to do."

Slowly, tentatively, she lifted one of her hands to his face. Her fingers trailed lightly over his cheek, skimming along the line of his jaw until they fell away.

"Thank you," she whispered.

Thank you?

He went still.

It was *exactly* the wrong thing to say. He didn't want to be thanked for his kiss.

It made him feel guilty.

And shallow.

As if it had been something done out of pity. And the worst part was he knew that if all this had come to pass only a few months earlier, it *would* have been out of pity.

What the hell did that say about him?

"Don't thank me," he said gruffly, shoving himself backward until they were no longer touching.

"But—"

"I said *don't*," he repeated harshly, turning away as if he couldn't bear the sight of her, when the truth was that he couldn't quite bear himself.

And the damnedest thing was—he wasn't sure why. This desperate, gnawing feeling—was it guilt? Because he shouldn't have kissed her? Because he shouldn't have liked it?

"Colin," she said, "don't be angry with yourself."

"I'm not," he snapped.

"I asked you to kiss me. I practically forced you—"

Now, there was a surefire way to make a man feel manly. "You didn't force me," he bit off.

"No, but—"

"For the love of God, Penelope, *enough*!"

She drew back, her eyes wide. "I'm sorry," she whispered.

He looked down at her hands. They were shaking. He closed his eyes in agony. Why why *why* was he being such an ass?

"Penelope . . ." he began.

"No, it's all right," she said, her words rushed. "You don't have to say anything."

"No, I should."

"I really wish you wouldn't."

And now she looked so quietly dignified. Which

made him feel even worse. She was standing there, her hands clasped demurely in front of her, her eyes downward—not quite on the floor, but not on his face.

She thought he'd kissed her out of pity.

And he was a knave because a small part of him wanted her to think that. Because if she thought it, then maybe he could convince himself that it was true, that it was just pity, that it couldn't possibly be more.

"I should go," he said, the words quiet, and yet still too loud in the silent room.

She didn't try to stop him.

He motioned to the door. "I should go," he said again, even as his feet refused to move.

She nodded.

"I didn't—" he started to say, and then, horrified by the words that had nearly come out of his mouth, he actually did head toward the door.

But Penelope called out—of *course* she called out—"You didn't what?"

And he didn't know what to say, because what he'd started to say was, *I didn't kiss you out of pity.* If he wanted her to know that, if he wanted to convince himself of that, then that could only mean that he craved her good opinion, which could only mean—

"I have to go," he blurted out, desperate now, as if leaving the room might be the only way to keep his thoughts from traveling down such a dangerous road. He crossed the remaining distance to the door, waiting for her to say something, to call out his name.

But she didn't.

And he left.

And he'd never hated himself more.

Colin was in an exceedingly bad mood before the footman showed up at his front door with a summons from his mother. Afterward, he was beyond repair.

Bloody hell. She was going to start in on him again about getting married. Her summonses were *always* about getting married. And he really wasn't in the mood for it right now.

But she was his mother. And he loved her. And that meant he couldn't very well ignore her. So with considerable grumbling and a fair bit of cursing while he was at it, he yanked on his boots and coat, and headed out the door.

He was living in Bloomsbury, not the most fashionable section of town for a member of the aristocracy, although Bedford Square, where he had taken out a lease on a small but elegant terrace house, was certainly an upscale and respectable address.

Colin rather liked living in Bloomsbury, where his neighbors were doctors and lawyers and scholars and people who actually *did* things other than attend party after party. He wasn't ready to trade in his heritage for a life in trade—it was rather good to be a Bridgerton, after all—but there was something stimulating about watching professional men going about their daily business, the lawyers heading east to the Inns of the Court, the doctors northwest to Portland Place.

It would have been easy enough to drive his curricle across town; it had only been brought back to the mews an hour ago upon his return from the Featheringtons'. But Colin was feeling a bit in need of some fresh air, not to mention perverse enough to take the slowest means possible to Number Five.

If his mother intended to deliver another lecture on the virtues of marriage, followed by a lengthy dissertation on the attributes of each and every eligible miss in London, she could bloody well wait for him.

Colin closed his eyes and groaned. His mood must be worse than even he had thought if he was cursing in relation to his mother, whom he (and all the Bridgertons, really) held in the highest esteem and affection.

It was Penelope's fault.

No, it was Eloise's fault, he thought, grinding his teeth. Better to blame a sibling.

No—he slumped back into his desk chair, groaning—it was his fault. If he was in a bad mood, if he was ready to yank someone's head off with his bare hands, it was his fault and his fault alone.

He shouldn't have kissed Penelope. It didn't matter that he'd *wanted* to kiss her, even though he hadn't even *realized* that he wanted to until right before she'd mentioned it. He still shouldn't have kissed her.

Although, when he really thought about it, he wasn't quite sure *why* he shouldn't have kissed her.

He stood, then trudged to the window and let his forehead rest against the pane. Bedford Square was quiet, with only a few men walking along the pavement. Laborers, they looked to be, probably working on the new museum being built just to the east. (It was why Colin had taken a house on the west side of the square; the construction could get very noisy.)

His gaze traveled north, to the statue of Charles James Fox. Now, there was a man with a purpose. Led the Whigs for years. He hadn't always been very well liked, if some of the older members of the *ton* were to be believed, but Colin was coming to think that perhaps being well liked was overrated. Heaven knew that no one was better liked than he was, and look at him now, frustrated and malcontent, grumpy and ready to lash out at anyone who crossed his path.

He sighed, planting one hand on the window frame and pushing himself back to an upright position. He'd better get going, especially if he was planning to walk all the way to Mayfair. Although, in truth, it really wasn't that far. Probably not more than thirty minutes if he kept his pace brisk (and he always did), less if the pavements weren't littered with slow people. It was longer than most members of the *ton* cared to be outside in London unless they were shopping or fashionably strolling in the park, but Colin felt the need to clear his head. And if the air in London wasn't particularly fresh, well, it would still have to do.

His luck that day being what it was, however, by the time he reached the intersection of Oxford and Regent Streets, the first splats of raindrops began to dance against his face. By the time he was turning off Hanover Square onto St. George Street, it was pouring in earnest. And he was just close enough to Bruton Street that it would have been really ridiculous to have tried to hail a hackney to take him the rest of the way.

So he walked on.

After the first minute or so of annoyance, however, the rain began to feel oddly good. It was warm enough out that it didn't chill him to the bone, and the fat, wet sting of it almost felt like a penance.

And he felt like maybe that was what he deserved.

The door to his mother's house opened before Colin's foot had even found the top step; Wickham must have been waiting for him.

"Might I suggest a towel?" the butler intoned, handing him a large white cloth.

Colin took it, wondering how on earth Wickham had had time to get a towel. He couldn't have known that Colin would be fool enough to walk in the rain.

Not for the first time it occurred to Colin that butlers must be possessed of strange, mystical powers. Perhaps it was a job requirement.

Colin used the towel to dry his hair, causing great consternation to Wickham, who was terribly proper and surely expected Colin to retire to a private room for at least a half an hour to mend his appearance.

"Where's my mother?" Colin asked.

Wickham's lips tightened, and he looked pointedly down at Colin's feet, which were now creating small puddles. "She is in her office," he replied, "but she is speaking with your sister."

"Which sister?" Colin asked, keeping a sunny smile on his face, just to annoy Wickham, who had surely been trying to annoy him by omitting his sister's name.

As if you could simply say "your sister" to a Bridgerton and expect him to know who you were talking about.

"Francesca."

"Ah, yes. She's returning to Scotland soon, isn't she?"

"Tomorrow."

Colin handed the towel back to Wickham, who regarded it as he might a large insect. "I won't bother her, then. Just let her know I'm here when she's done with Francesca."

Wickham nodded. "Would you care to change your clothes, Mr. Bridgerton? I believe we have some of your brother Gregory's garments upstairs in his bedchamber."

Colin found himself smiling. Gregory was finishing up his final term at Cambridge. He was eleven years younger than Colin, and it was difficult to believe they could actually share clothing, but he supposed it was time to accept that his little brother had finally grown up.

"That's an excellent idea," Colin said. He gave his sodden sleeve a rueful glance. "I'll leave these here to be cleaned and fetch them later."

Wickham nodded again, murmured, "As you wish," and disappeared down the hall to parts unknown.

Colin took the steps two at a time up to the family quarters. As he sloshed down the hall, he heard the sound of a door opening. Turning around, he saw that it was Eloise.

Not the person he wanted to see. She immediately brought back all the memories of his afternoon with Penelope. Their conversation. The kiss.

Especially the kiss.

And even worse, the guilt he'd felt afterward.

The guilt he still felt.

"Colin," Eloise said brightly, "I didn't realize you— what did you do, *walk*?"

He shrugged. "I like the rain."

She eyed him curiously, her head cocking to the side as it always did when she was puzzling through something. "You're in a rather odd mood today."

"I'm soaking wet, Eloise."

"No need to snap at me about it," she said with a sniff. "I didn't force you to walk across town in the rain."

"It wasn't raining when I left," he felt rather compelled to say. There was something about a sibling that brought out the eight-year-old in a body.

"I'm sure the sky was gray," she returned.

Clearly, she had a bit of the eight-year-old in her as well.

"May we continue this discussion when I'm dry?" he asked, his voice deliberately impatient.

"Of course," she said expansively, all accommodation. "I'll wait for you right here."

Colin took his time while he changed into Gregory's clothes, taking more care with his cravat than he had in years. Finally, when he was convinced that Eloise must be grinding her teeth, he reentered the hall.

"I heard you went to see Penelope today," she said without preamble.

Wrong thing to say.

"Where did you hear that?" he asked carefully. He knew that his sister and Penelope were close, but surely Penelope wouldn't have told Eloise about *that*.

"Felicity told Hyacinth."

"And Hyacinth told you."

"Of course."

"Something," Colin muttered, "has got to be done about all the gossip in this town."

"I hardly think this counts as gossip, Colin," Eloise said. "It's not as if you're *interested* in Penelope."

If she had been talking about any other woman, Colin would have expected her to give him a sidelong glance, followed by a coy, *Are you?*

But this was Penelope, and even though Eloise was her very best friend, and thus her finest champion, even she couldn't imagine that a man of Colin's reputation and popularity would be interested in a woman of Penelope's reputation and (lack of) popularity.

Colin's mood shifted from bad to foul.

"Anyway," Eloise continued, completely oblivious to the thunderstorm that was brewing in her normally sunny and jovial brother, "Felicity told Hyacinth that Briarly told her that you'd visited. I was just wondering what it was about."

"It's none of your business," Colin said briskly, hoping she'd leave it at that, but not really believing she would. He took a step toward the stairwell, though, always optimistic.

"It's about my birthday, isn't it?" Eloise guessed, dashing in front of him with such suddenness that his toe crashed into her slipper. She winced, but Colin didn't feel particularly sympathetic.

"No, it's not about your birthday," he snapped. "Your birthday isn't even until—"

He stopped. Ah, hell.

"Until next week," he grumbled.

She smiled slyly. Then, as if her brain had just realized it had taken a wrong turn, her lips parted with dismay as she mentally backed up and headed in another direction. "So," she continued, moving slightly so that she better blocked his path, "if you didn't go over there to discuss my birthday—and there's nothing you could say now that would convince me you did—why *did* you go see Penelope?"

"Is nothing private in this world?"

"Not in *this* family."

Colin decided that his best bet was to adopt his usual sunny persona, even though he didn't feel the least bit charitable toward her at the moment, and so he slapped on the smoothest and easiest of his smiles, quirked his head to the side, and asked, "Do I hear Mother calling my name?"

"I didn't hear a thing," Eloise said pertly, "and what is wrong with you? You look very odd."

"I'm fine."

"You're not fine. You look as if you've been to the dentist."

His voice descended into a mutter. "It's always nice to receive compliments from family."

"If you can't trust your family to be honest with you," she volleyed, "who *can* you trust?"

He leaned fluidly back against the wall, crossing his arms. "I prefer flattery to honesty."

"No, you don't."

Dear God, he wanted to smack her. He hadn't done that since he was twelve. And he'd been horsewhipped for it. The only time he could recall his father laying a hand on him.

"What I want," Colin returned, arching one brow, "is an immediate cessation of this conversation."

"What you want," Eloise needled, "is for me to stop

asking you why you went to see Penelope Feathering-ton, but I think we both know *that* isn't likely to occur."

And that was when he knew it. Knew it deep in his bones, from his head to his toes, his heart to his mind that his sister was Lady Whistledown. All of the pieces fit. There was no one more stubborn and bullheaded, no one who could—or would—take the time to get to the bottom of every last piece of gossip and innuendo.

When Eloise wanted something, she didn't stop until she had it firmly in her grasp. It wasn't about money, or greed, or material goods. With her it was about knowl-edge. She liked knowing things, and she'd needle and needle and needle until you'd told her exactly what she wanted to hear.

It was a miracle no one had found her out sooner.

Out of nowhere he said, "I need to talk to you." He grabbed her arm and hauled her into the nearest room, which happened to be her own.

"Colin!" she shrieked, trying unsuccessfully to shake him off. "What are you doing?"

He slammed the door shut, let go of her, and crossed his arms, his stance wide, his expression menacing.

"Colin?" she repeated, her voice dubious.

"I know what you've been up to."

"What I've been—"

And then, damn her, she started laughing.

"Eloise!" he boomed. "I'm talking to you!"

"Clearly," she just barely managed to get out.

He held his ground, glaring at her.

She was looking away, nearly doubled over with laughter. Finally, she said, "What are you—"

But then she looked at him again and even though she'd tried to keep her mouth shut, she exploded again.

If she'd been drinking something, Colin thought without a trace of humor, it would have come out her nose. "What the hell is the matter with you?" he snapped.

That finally got her attention. He didn't know whether it was his tone of voice or maybe his use of profanity, but she sobered in an instant.

"My word," she said softly, "you're serious."

"Do I look like I'm joking?"

"No," Eloise said. "Although you did at first. I'm sorry, Colin, but it's just not like you to be glowering and yelling and all that. You looked rather like Anthony."

"You—"

"Actually," she said, giving him a look that was not nearly as wary as it should have been, "you looked more like yourself, trying to imitate Anthony."

He was going to kill her. Right here in her room, in his mother's house, he was going to commit sororicide.

"Colin?" she asked hesitantly, as if she'd just finally noticed that he had long since passed angry on his way to furious.

"Sit. Down." He jerked his head toward a chair. "Now."

"Are you all right?"

"SIT DOWN!" he roared.

And she did. With alacrity.

"I can't remember the last time you raised your voice," she whispered.

"I can't remember the last time I had cause to."

"What's wrong?"

He decided he might as well just come out and say it. "Colin?"

"I know you're Lady Whistledown."

"Whaaaaat?"

"There's no use denying it. I've seen—"

Eloise jumped to her feet. "Except that it's not true!"

Suddenly he no longer felt quite so angry. Instead he felt tired, old. "Eloise, I've seen the proof."

"What proof?" she asked, her voice rising with disbelief. "How can there be proof of something that isn't true?"

He grabbed one of her hands. "Look at your fingers."

She did so. "What about them?"

"Inkstains."

Her mouth fell open. "From *that* you've deduced that I'm Lady Whistledown?"

"Why are they there, then?"

"You've never used a quill?"

"Eloise . . ." There was a great deal of warning in his voice.

"I don't have to tell you why I have inkstains on my fingers."

He said her name again.

"I don't," she protested. "I owe you no—oh, very well, fine." She crossed her arms mutinously. "I write letters."

He shot her an extremely disbelieving look.

"I do!" she protested. "Every day. Sometimes two in a day when Francesca is away. I'm quite a loyal correspondent. You should know. I've written enough letters with *your* name on the envelope, although I doubt half of them ever reached you."

"Letters?" he asked, his voice full of doubt . . . and derision. "For God's sake, Eloise, do you really think that will wash? Who the devil are you writing so many letters to?"

She blushed. Really, truly, deeply blushed. "It's none of your business."

He would have been intrigued by her reaction if

he still weren't so sure that she was lying about being Lady Whistledown. "For God's sake, Eloise," he bit off, "who is going to believe that you're writing letters every day? I certainly don't."

She glared at him, her dark gray eyes flashing with fury. "I don't care what you think," she said in a very low voice. "No, that's not true. I am *furious* that you don't believe me."

"You're not giving me much to believe in," he said wearily.

She stood, walked over to him, and poked him in the chest. Hard. "You are my brother," she spat out. "You should believe me unquestioningly. Love me unconditionally. That's what it means to be family."

"Eloise," he said, her name coming out really as nothing more than a sigh.

"Don't try to make excuses now."

"I wasn't."

"That's even worse!" She stalked to the door. "You should be on your hands and knees, begging me for forgiveness."

He hadn't thought he had it in him to smile, but somehow that did it for him. "Now, that doesn't really seem in keeping with my character, does it?"

She opened her mouth to say something, but the sound that came out was not precisely English.

All she managed was something along the lines of, "Oooooooooh," in an extremely irate voice, and then she stormed out, slamming the door behind her.

Colin slouched into a chair, wondering when she'd realize that she'd left him in her own bedchamber.

The irony was, he reflected, possibly the only bright spot in an otherwise miserable day.

Chapter 10

Dear Reader—

It is with a surprisingly sentimental heart that I write these words. After eleven years of chronicling the lives and times of the beau monde, This Author is putting down her pen.

Although Lady Danbury's challenge was surely the catalyst for the retirement, in truth the blame cannot be placed (entirely) upon that countess's shoulders. The column has grown wearisome of late, less fulfilling to write, and perhaps less entertaining to read. This Author needs a change. It is not so difficult to fathom. Eleven years is a long time.

And in truth, the recent renewal of interest in This Author's identity has grown disturbing.

Friends are turning against friends, brothers against sisters, all in the futile attempt to solve an unsolvable secret. Furthermore, the sleuthing of the ton has grown downright dangerous. Last week it was Lady Blackwood's twisted ankle, this week's injury apparently belongs to Hyacinth Bridgerton, who was slightly hurt at Saturday's soirée held at the London home of Lord and Lady Riverdale. (It has not escaped This Author's notice that Lord Riverdale is Lady Danbury's nephew.) Miss Hyacinth must have suspected someone in attendance, because she sustained her injuries while falling into the library after the door was opened while she had her ear pressed up to the wood.

Listening at doors, chasing down delivery boys—and these are only the tidbits that have reached This Author's ears! What has London Society come to? This Author assures you, Dear Reader, that she never once listened at a door in all eleven years of her career. All gossip in this column was come by fairly, with no tools or tricks other than keen eyes and ears.

I bid you au revoir, London! It has been a pleasure to serve you.

LADY WHISTLEDOWN'S SOCIETY PAPERS,
19 APRIL 1824

I t was, not surprisingly, the talk of the Macclesfield ball.

"Lady Whistledown has retired!"

"Can you believe it?"

"What will I read with my breakfast?"

"How will I know what happened if I miss a party?"

"We'll never find out who she is now!"

"Lady Whistledown has retired!"

One woman fainted, nearly cracking her head against the side of a table as she slumped gracelessly to the floor. Apparently, she had not read that morning's column and thus heard the news for the first time right there at the Macclesfield ball. She was revived by smelling salts but then quickly swooned again.

"She's a faker," Hyacinth Bridgerton muttered to Felicity Featherington as they stood in a small group with the Dowager Lady Bridgerton and Penelope. Penelope was officially attending as Felicity's chaperone due to their mother's decision to remain home with an upset stomach.

"The first faint was real," Hyacinth explained. "Anyone could tell that by the clumsy way she fell. But this . . ." Her hand flicked toward the lady on the floor with a gesture of disgust. "No one swoons like a ballet dancer. Not even ballet dancers."

Penelope had overheard the entire conversation, as

Hyacinth was directly to her left, and so she murmured, "Have you ever swooned?" all the while keeping her eyes on the unfortunate woman, who was now coming awake with a delicate fluttering of eyelashes as the smelling salts were once again wafted under her nose.

"Absolutely not!" Hyacinth replied, with no small measure of pride. "Swoons are for the tenderhearted and foolish," she added. "And if Lady Whistledown were still writing, mark my words, she would say the exact same thing in her next column."

"Alas, there are no words to mark anymore," Felicity answered with a sad sigh.

Lady Bridgerton agreed. "It's the end of an era," she said. "I feel quite bereft without her."

"Well, it's not as if we've had to go more than eighteen hours without her yet," Penelope felt compelled to point out. "We did receive a column this morning. What is there yet to feel bereft about?"

"It's the principle of it," Lady Bridgerton said with a sigh. "If this were an ordinary Monday, I would know that I'd receive a new report on Wednesday. But now . . ."

Felicity actually sniffled. "Now we're lost," she said.

Penelope turned to her sister in disbelief. "Surely you're being a little melodramatic."

Felicity's overblown shrug was worthy of the stage. "Am I? *Am I?*"

Hyacinth gave her a sympathetic pat on the back. "I don't think you are, Felicity. I feel precisely the same way."

"It's only a gossip column," Penelope said, looking around for any sign of sanity in her companions. Surely they realized that the world was not drawing to a close just because Lady Whistledown had decided to end her career.

"You're right, of course," said Lady Bridgerton, jutting her chin out and pursing her lips in a manner that was probably supposed to convey an air of practicality. "Thank you for being the voice of reason for our little party." But then she seemed to deflate slightly, and she said, "But I must admit, I'd grown rather used to having her around. Whoever she is."

Penelope decided it was well past time to change the topic. "Where is Eloise this evening?"

"Ill, I'm afraid. A headache," Lady Bridgerton said, small frowns of worry creasing her otherwise unlined face. "She hasn't been feeling the thing for almost a week now. I'm starting to grow concerned about her."

Penelope had been staring rather aimlessly at a sconce on the wall, but her attention was immediately brought back to Lady Bridgerton. "It's nothing serious, I hope?"

"It's nothing serious," Hyacinth answered, before her mother could even open her mouth. "Eloise never gets sick."

"Which is precisely why I'm worried," Lady Bridgerton said. "She hasn't been eating very well."

"That's not true," Hyacinth said. "Just this afternoon Wickham brought up a very heavy tray. Scones and eggs and I think I smelled gammon steak." She gave an arch look to no one in particular. "And when Eloise left the tray out in the hall it was completely empty."

Hyacinth Bridgerton, Penelope decided, had a surprisingly good eye for detail.

"She's been in a bad mood," Hyacinth continued, "since she quarreled with Colin."

"She quarreled with Colin?" Penelope asked, an awful feeling beginning to roil her stomach. "When?"

"Sometime last week," Hyacinth said.

WHEN? Penelope wanted to scream, but surely it would look odd if she demanded an exact day. Was it Friday? Was it?

Penelope would always remember that her first, and most probably only, kiss had occurred on a Friday.

She was strange that way. She always remembered the days of the week.

She'd met Colin on a Monday.

She'd kissed him on a Friday.

Twelve years later.

She sighed. It seemed fairly pathetic.

"Is something wrong, Penelope?" Lady Bridgerton asked.

Penelope looked at Eloise's mother. Her blue eyes were kind and filled with concern, and there was something about the way she tilted her head to the side that made Penelope want to cry.

She was getting far too emotional these days. Crying over the tilt of a head.

"I'm fine," she said, hoping that her smile looked true. "I'm just worried about Eloise."

Hyacinth snorted.

Penelope decided she needed to make her escape. All these Bridgertons—well, two of them, anyway—were making her think of Colin.

Which wasn't anything she hadn't been doing nearly every minute of the day for the past three days. But at least that had been in private where she could sigh and moan and grumble to her heart's content.

But this must have been her lucky night, because just then she heard Lady Danbury barking her name.

(What was her world coming to, that she considered herself lucky to be trapped in a corner with London's most acerbic tongue?)

But Lady Danbury would provide the perfect excuse to leave her current little quartet of ladies, and besides, she was coming to realize that in a very odd way, she rather liked Lady Danbury.

"Miss Featherington! Miss Featherington!"

Felicity instantly took a step away. "I think she means you," she whispered urgently.

"Of course she means me," Penelope said, with just a touch of hauteur. "I consider Lady Danbury a cherished friend."

Felicity's eyes bugged out. "You do?"

"Miss Featherington!" Lady Danbury said, thumping her cane an inch away from Penelope's foot as soon as she reached her side. "Not you," she said to Felicity, even though Felicity had done nothing more than smile politely as the countess had approached. "You," she said to Penelope.

"Er, good evening, Lady Danbury," Penelope said, which she considered an admirable number of words under the circumstances.

"I have been looking for you all evening," Lady D announced.

Penelope found that a trifle surprising. "You have?"

"Yes. I want to talk with you about that Whistledown woman's last column."

"Me?"

"Yes, you," Lady Danbury grumbled. "I'd be happy to talk with someone else if you could find me a body with more than half a brain."

Penelope choked on the beginnings of laughter as she motioned to her companions. "Er, I assure you that Lady Bridgerton—"

Lady Bridgerton was furiously shaking her head.

"She's too busy trying to get that oversized brood of hers married off," Lady Danbury announced. "Can't be expected to know how to conduct a decent conversation these days."

Penelope stole a frantic glance over at Lady Bridgerton to see if she was upset by the insult—after all, she had been trying to marry off her oversized brood for a decade now. But Lady Bridgerton didn't look the least bit upset. In fact, she appeared to be stifling laughter.

Stifling laughter and inching away, taking Hyacinth and Felicity with her.

Sneaky little traitors.

Ah, well, Penelope shouldn't complain. She'd wanted an escape from the Bridgertons, hadn't she? But she didn't particularly enjoy having Felicity and Hyacinth think they'd somehow pulled one over on her.

"They're gone now," Lady Danbury cackled, "and a good thing it is, too. Those two gels haven't an intelligent thing to say between them."

"Oh, now, that isn't true," Penelope felt compelled to protest. "Felicity and Hyacinth are both very bright."

"I never said they weren't smart," Lady D replied acidly, "just that they haven't an intelligent thing to say. But don't worry," she added, giving Penelope a reassuring—reassuring? whoever heard of Lady Danbury being reassuring?—pat on the arm. "It's not their fault that their conversation is useless. They'll grow out of it. People are like fine wines. If they start off good, they only get better with age."

Penelope had actually been glancing slightly to the right of Lady Danbury's face, peering over her shoulder at a man who she thought might be Colin (but wasn't), but this brought her attention right back to where the countess wanted it.

"Fine wines?" Penelope echoed.

"Hmmph. And here I thought you weren't listening."

"No, of course I was listening." Penelope felt her

lips tugging into something that wasn't quite a smile. "I was just . . . distracted."

"Looking for that Bridgerton boy, no doubt."

Penelope gasped.

"Oh, don't look so shocked. It's written all over your face. I'm just surprised he hasn't noticed."

"I imagine he has," Penelope mumbled.

"Has he? Hmmph." Lady Danbury frowned, the corners of her mouth spilling into long vertical wrinkles on either side of her chin. "Doesn't speak well of him that he hasn't done anything about it."

Penelope's heart ached. There was something oddly sweet about the old lady's faith in her, as if men like Colin fell in love with women like Penelope on a regular basis. Penelope had had to beg him to kiss her, for heaven's sake. And look how that had ended up. He'd left the house in a fit of temper and they hadn't spoken for three days.

"Well, don't worry over him," Lady Danbury said quite suddenly. "We'll find you someone else."

Penelope delicately cleared her throat. "Lady Danbury, have you made me your *project*?"

The old lady beamed, her smile a bright and glowing streak in her wrinkled face. "Of course! I'm surprised it has taken you so long to figure it out."

"But why?" Penelope asked, truly unable to fathom it.

Lady Danbury sighed. The sound wasn't sad—more wistful, really. "Would you mind if we sat down for a spell? These old bones aren't what they used to be."

"Of course," Penelope said quickly, feeling terrible that she'd never once considered Lady Danbury's age as they stood there in the stuffy ballroom. But the countess was so vibrant; it was difficult to imagine her ailing or weak.

"Here we are," Penelope said, taking her arm and leading her to a nearby chair. Once Lady Danbury was settled, Penelope took a seat beside her. "Are you more comfortable now? Would you like something to drink?"

Lady Danbury nodded gratefully, and Penelope signaled to a footman to bring them two glasses of lemonade, since she didn't want to leave the countess while she was looking so pale.

"I'm not as young as I used to be," Lady Danbury told her once the footman had hied off to the refreshment table.

"None of us are," Penelope replied. It could have been a flip comment, but it was spoken with wry warmth, and somehow Penelope thought that Lady Danbury would appreciate the sentiment.

She was right. Lady D chuckled and sent Penelope an appreciative glance before saying, "The older I get, the more I realize that most of the people in this world are fools."

"You're only just figuring that out now?" Penelope asked, not to mock, but rather because, given Lady Danbury's usual demeanor, it was difficult to believe that she hadn't reached that conclusion years ago.

Lady Danbury laughed heartily. "No, sometimes I think I knew that before I was born. What I'm realizing now is that it's time I did something about it."

"What do you mean?"

"I couldn't care less what happens to the fools of this world, but the people like you"—lacking a handkerchief, she dabbed at her eyes with her fingers—"well, I'd like to see you settled."

For several seconds, Penelope did nothing but stare at her. "Lady Danbury," she said carefully, "I very much appreciate the gesture . . . and the sentiment . . . but you must know that I am not your responsibility."

"Of course I know that," Lady Danbury scoffed. "Have no fear, I feel no responsibility to you. If I did, this wouldn't be half so much fun."

Penelope knew she sounded the veriest ninny, but all she could think to say was, "I don't understand."

Lady Danbury held silent while the footmen returned with their lemonade, then began speaking once she had taken several small sips. "I like you, Miss

Featherington. I don't like a lot of people. It's as simple as that. And I want to see you happy."

"But I am happy," Penelope said, more out of reflex than anything else.

Lady Danbury raised one arrogant brow—an expression that she did to perfection. "Are you?" she murmured.

Was she? What did it mean, that she had to stop and think about the answer? She wasn't *unhappy*, of that she was sure. She had wonderful friends, a true confidante in her younger sister Felicity, and if her mother and older sisters weren't women she'd have chosen as close friends—well, she still loved them. And she knew they loved her.

Hers wasn't such a bad lot. Her life lacked drama and excitement, but she was content.

But contentment wasn't the same thing as happiness, and she felt a sharp, stabbing pain in her chest as she realized that she could not answer Lady Danbury's softly worded question in the affirmative.

"I've raised my family," Lady Danbury said. "Four children, and they all married well. I even found a bride for my nephew, who, truth be told"—she leaned in and whispered the last three words, giving Penelope the impression that she was about to divulge a state secret—"I like better than my own children."

Penelope couldn't help but smile. Lady Danbury looked so furtive, so naughty. It was rather cute, actually.

"It may surprise you," Lady Danbury continued, "but by nature I'm a bit of a meddler."

Penelope kept her expression scrupulously even.

"I find myself at loose ends," Lady Danbury said, holding up her hands as if in surrender. "I'd like to see one last person happily settled before I go."

"Don't talk that way, Lady Danbury," Penelope said, impulsively reaching out and taking her hand. She gave it a little squeeze. "You'll outlive us all, I am certain."

"Pfffft, don't be silly." Lady Danbury's tone was dismissive, but she made no move to remove her hand from Penelope's grasp. "I'm not being depressive," she added. "I'm just realistic. I've passed seventy years of age, and I'm not going to tell you how many years ago that was. I haven't much time left in this world, and that doesn't bother me one bit."

Penelope hoped she would be able to face her own mortality with the same equanimity.

"But I like you, Miss Featherington. You remind me of myself. You're not afraid to speak your mind."

Penelope could only look at her in shock. She'd spent the last ten years of her life never quite saying what she wanted to say. With people she knew well she was open and honest and even sometimes a little funny, but among strangers her tongue was quite firmly tied.

She remembered a masquerade ball she'd once attended. She'd attended many masquerade balls, actually, but this one had been unique because she'd actually found a costume—nothing special, just a gown styled as if from the 1600s—in which she'd truly felt her identity was hidden. It had probably been the mask. It was overly large and covered almost all of her face.

She had felt transformed. Suddenly free of the burden of being Penelope Featherington, she felt a new personality coming to the fore. It wasn't as if she had been putting on false airs; rather, it was more like her true self—the one she didn't know how to show to anyone she didn't know well—had finally broken loose.

She'd laughed; she'd joked. She'd even flirted.

And she'd sworn that the following night, when the costumes were all put away and she was once again attired in her finest evening dress, she'd remember how to be herself.

But it hadn't happened. She'd arrived at the ball and she'd nodded and smiled politely and once again found herself standing near the perimeter of the room, quite literally a wallflower.

It seemed that being Penelope Featherington meant

something. Her lot had been cast years ago, during that first awful season when her mother had insisted she make her debut even though Penelope had begged otherwise. The pudgy girl. The awkward girl. The one always dressed in colors that didn't suit her. It didn't matter that she'd slimmed and grown graceful and finally thrown out all of her yellow dresses. In this world—the world of London society and the *ton*—she would always be the same old Penelope Featherington.

It was her own fault just as much as anyone else's. A vicious circle, really. Every time Penelope stepped into a ballroom, and she saw all those people who had known her for so long, she felt herself folding up inside, turning into the shy, awkward girl of years gone past, rather than the self-assured woman she liked to think she'd become—at least in her heart.

"Miss Featherington?" came Lady Danbury's soft—and surprisingly gentle—voice. "Is something wrong?"

Penelope knew she took longer than she should have to reply, but somehow she needed a few seconds to find her voice. "I don't think I know how to speak my mind," she finally said, turning to look at Lady Danbury only as she uttered the final words of the sentence. "I never know what to say to people."

"You know what to say to *me*."

"You're different."

Lady Danbury threw her head back and laughed. "If ever there was an understatement . . . Oh, Penelope—I hope you don't mind if I call you by your given name—if you can speak your mind to me, you can speak it to anyone. Half the grown men in this room run cowering into corners the minute they see me coming."

"They just don't know you," Penelope said, patting her on the hand.

"And they don't know *you*, either," Lady Danbury quite pointedly replied.

"No," Penelope said, a touch of resignation in her voice, "they don't."

"I'd say that it was their loss, but that would be rather cavalier of me," Lady Danbury said. "Not to them, but to you, because as often as I call them all fools—and I do call them fools often, as I'm sure you know—some of them are actually rather decent people, and it's a crime they haven't gotten to know you. I— Hmmm . . . I wonder what is going on."

Penelope found herself unaccountably sitting up a little straighter. She asked Lady Danbury, "What do you mean?" but it was clear that something was afoot. People were whispering and motioning to the small dais where the musicians were seated.

"You there!" Lady Danbury said, poking her cane into the hip of a nearby gentleman. "What is going on?"

"Cressida Twombley wants to make some sort of announcement," he said, then quickly stepped away, presumably to avoid any further conversation with Lady Danbury or her cane.

"I hate Cressida Twombley," Penelope muttered.

Lady Danbury choked on a bit of laughter. "And you say you don't know how to speak your mind. Don't keep me in suspense. Why do you detest her so?"

Penelope shrugged. "She's always behaved quite badly toward me."

Lady Danbury nodded knowingly. "All bullies have a favorite victim."

"It's not so bad now," Penelope said. "But back when we were both out—when she was still Cressida Cowper—she never could resist the chance to torment me. And people . . . well . . ." She shook her head. "Never mind."

"No, please," Lady Danbury said, "do go on."

Penelope sighed. "It's nothing, really. Just that I've noticed that people don't often rush to another's defense. Cressida was popular—at least with a certain set—and she was rather frightening to the other girls our age. No one dared go against her. Well, almost no one."

That got Lady Danbury's attention, and she smiled. "Who was your champion, Penelope?"

"Champions, actually," Penelope replied. "The Bridgertons always came to my aid. Anthony Bridgerton once gave her the cut direct and took me in to dinner, and"—her voice rose with remembered excitement—"he really shouldn't have done so. It was a formal dinner party, and he was supposed to escort in some marchioness, I think." She sighed, treasuring the memory. "It was lovely."

"He's a good man, that Anthony Bridgerton."

Penelope nodded. "His wife told me that that was the day she fell in love with him. When she saw him being my hero."

Lady Danbury smiled. "And has the younger Mr. Bridgerton ever rushed to your aid?"

"Colin, you mean?" Penelope didn't even wait for Lady Danbury's nod before adding, "Of course, although never with quite so much drama. But I must say, as nice as it is that the Bridgertons are so supportive. . . ."

"What is it, Penelope?" Lady Danbury asked.

Penelope sighed again. It seemed a night for sighs. "I just wish they didn't have to defend me so often. You'd think I could defend myself. Or at least comport myself in such a manner so that no defending was necessary."

Lady Danbury patted her hand. "I think you get on a great deal better than you think you do. And as for that Cressida Twombley . . ." Lady Danbury's face soured with distaste. "Well, she got her just desserts, if you ask me. Although," she added sharply, "people don't ask me as often as they should."

Penelope could not quite suppress a little snort of laughter.

"Look where she is now," Lady Danbury said sharply. "Widowed and without even a fortune to show for it. She married that old lecher Horace Twombley and it turned out he'd managed to fool everyone into thinking he had money. Now she has nothing but fading good looks."

Honesty compelled Penelope to say, "She is still quite attractive."

"Hmmph. If you like flashy women." Lady Danbury's eyes narrowed. "There is something far too obvious about that woman."

Penelope looked toward the dais, where Cressida was waiting, standing there with a surprising amount of patience while the ballroom quieted down. "I wonder what she is going to say."

"Nothing that could possibly interest me," Lady Danbury retorted. "I—Oh." She stopped, and her lips curved into the oddest of expressions, a little bit frown, a little bit smile.

"What is it?" Penelope asked. She craned her neck

to try to see Lady Danbury's line of vision, but a rather portly gentleman was blocking her way.

"Your Mr. Bridgerton is approaching," Lady Danbury said, the smile edging out the frown. "And he looks quite determined."

Penelope immediately twisted her head around.

"For the love of God, girl, don't look!" Lady Danbury exclaimed, jamming her elbow into Penelope's upper arm. "He'll know you're interested."

"I don't think there's much of a chance he hasn't figured that out already," Penelope mumbled.

And then there he was, standing splendidly in front of her, looking like some handsome god, deigning to grace earth with his presence. "Lady Danbury," he said, executing a smooth and graceful bow. "Miss Featherington."

"Mr. Bridgerton," Lady Danbury said, "how nice to see you."

Colin looked to Penelope.

"Mr. Bridgerton," she murmured, not knowing what else to say. What *did* one say to a man one had recently kissed? Penelope certainly had no experience in that area. Not to mention the added complication of his storming out of the house once they were through.

"I'd hoped . . ." Colin began, then stopped and

frowned, looking up toward the dais. "What is everyone looking at?"

"Cressida Twombley has some sort of announcement," Lady Danbury said.

Colin's face slid into a vaguely annoyed frown. "Can't imagine what she has to say that I'd want to listen to," he muttered.

Penelope couldn't help but grin. Cressida Twombley was considered a leader in society, or at least she had been when she'd been young and unmarried, but the Bridgertons had never liked her, and somehow that had always made Penelope feel a little better.

Just then a trumpet blared, and the room fell silent as everyone turned their attention to the Earl of Macclesfield, who was standing on the dais next to Cressida, looking vaguely uncomfortable with all the attention.

Penelope smiled. She'd been told the earl had once been a terrible rake, but now he was a rather scholarly sort, devoted to his family. He was still handsome enough to be a rake, though. Almost as handsome as Colin.

But only almost. Penelope knew she was biased, but it was difficult to imagine any creature quite as magnetically good-looking as Colin when he was smiling.

"Good evening," the earl said loudly.

"Good evening to you!" came a drunken shout from the back of the room.

The earl gave a good-natured nod, a tolerant half-smile playing along his lips. "My, er, esteemed guest here"—he motioned to Cressida—"would like to make an announcement. So if you would all give your attention to the lady beside me, I give you Lady Twombley."

A low ripple of whispers spread across the room as Cressida stepped forward, nodding regally at the crowd. She waited for the room to fall into stark silence, and then she said, "Ladies and gentleman, thank you so much for taking time out of your festivities to lend me your attention."

"Hurry up with it!" someone shouted, probably the same person who had yelled good evening to the earl.

Cressida ignored the interruption. "I have come to the conclusion that I can no longer continue the deception that has ruled my life for the last eleven years."

The ballroom was rocked with the low buzz of whispers. Everyone knew what she was going to say, and yet no one could believe it was actually true.

"Therefore," Cressida continued, her voice growing in volume, "I have decided to reveal my secret.

"Ladies and gentleman, *I am Lady Whistledown*."

Chapter 11

C olin couldn't remember the last time he'd entered a ballroom with quite so much apprehension.

The last few days had not been among his best. He'd been in a bad mood, which had only been worsened by the fact that he was rather renowned for his good humor, which meant that everyone had felt compelled to comment on his foul disposition.

There was nothing worse for a bad mood than being subjected to constant queries of, "Why are you in such a bad mood?"

His family had stopped asking after he'd actually snarled—snarled!—at Hyacinth when she'd asked him to accompany her to the theater the following week.

Colin hadn't even been aware that he knew how to snarl.

He was going to have to apologize to Hyacinth, which was going to be a chore, since Hyacinth never accepted apologies gracefully—at least not those that came from fellow Bridgertons.

But Hyacinth was the least of his problems. Colin groaned. His sister wasn't the only person who deserved his apology.

And that was why his heart was beating with this strange, nervous, and completely unprecedented rapidity as he entered the Macclesfield ballroom. Penelope would be here. He knew she'd be here because she always attended the major balls, even if she was now most often doing so as her sister's chaperone.

There was something quite humbling in feeling nervous about seeing Penelope. Penelope was . . . Penelope. It was almost as if she'd always been there, smiling politely at the perimeter of a ballroom. And he'd taken her for granted, in a way. Some things didn't change, and Penelope was one of them.

Except she *had* changed.

Colin didn't know when it had happened, or even if anyone other than himself had noticed it, but Penelope Featherington was not the same woman he used to know.

Or maybe she was, and *he* had changed.

Which made him feel even worse, because if that

was the case, then Penelope had been interesting and lovely and kissable years ago, and he hadn't the maturity to notice.

No, better to think that Penelope had changed. Colin had never been a great fan of self-flagellation.

Whatever the case, he needed to make his apology, and he needed to do it soon. He had to apologize for the kiss, because she was a lady and he was (most of the time, at least) a gentleman. And he had to apologize for behaving like a raving idiot afterward, because it was simply the right thing to do.

God only knew what Penelope thought he thought of her now.

It wasn't difficult to find her once he entered the ballroom. He didn't bother to look among the dancing couples (which angered him—why didn't the other men think to ask her to dance?). Rather, he focused his attention along the walls, and sure enough, there she was, seated on a long bench next to—oh, *God*—Lady Danbury.

Well, there was nothing else to do but walk right up. The way Penelope and the old busybody were clutching each other's hands, he couldn't expect Lady Danbury to disappear anytime soon.

When he reached the pair of ladies, he turned first to Lady Danbury and swept into an elegant bow. "Lady

Danbury," he said, before turning his attention to Penelope. "Miss Featherington."

"Mr. Bridgerton," Lady Danbury said, with a surprising lack of sharpness in her voice, "how nice to see you."

He nodded, then looked to Penelope, wondering what she was thinking, and whether he'd be able to see it in her eyes.

But whatever she was thinking—or feeling—it was hidden under a rather thick layer of nervousness. Or maybe the nervousness was all she was feeling. He couldn't really blame her. The way he'd stormed out of her drawing room without an explanation . . . she had to feel confused. And it was his experience that confusion invariably led to apprehension.

"Mr. Bridgerton," she finally murmured, her entire bearing scrupulously polite.

He cleared his throat. How to extract her from Lady Danbury's clutches? He'd really rather not humble himself in front of the nosy old countess.

"I'd hoped . . ." he began, intending to say that he'd hoped to have a private word with Penelope. Lady Danbury would be ferociously curious, but there was really no other course of action, and it would probably do her good to be left in the dark for once.

But just as his lips were forming his query, he realized that something strange was afoot in the Macclesfield ballroom. People were whispering and pointing toward the small orchestra, whose members had recently laid their instruments down. Furthermore, neither Penelope nor Lady Danbury were paying him the least attention.

"What is everyone looking at?" Colin asked.

Lady Danbury didn't even bother looking back at him as she replied, "Cressida Twombley has some sort of announcement."

How annoying. He'd never liked Cressida. She'd been mean and petty when she was Cressida Cowper, and she was meaner and pettier as Cressida Twombley. But she was beautiful, and she was intelligent, in a rather cruel sort of way, and so she was still considered a leader in certain society circles.

"Can't imagine what she has to say that I'd want to listen to," Colin muttered.

He spied Penelope trying to stifle a smile and flashed her an I-caught-you sort of look. But it was the sort of I-caught-you look that also said And-I-agree-completely.

"Good evening!" came the loud voice of the Earl of Macclesfield.

"Good evening to you!" replied some drunken fool in the back. Colin twisted to see who it was, but the crowd had grown too thick.

The earl spoke some more, then Cressida opened her mouth, at which point Colin ceased paying attention. Whatever Cressida had to say, it wasn't going to help him solve his main problem: figuring out exactly how he was going to apologize to Penelope. He'd tried rehearsing the words in his mind, but they never sounded quite right, and so he was hoping his famously glib tongue would lead him in the right direction when the time came. Surely she'd understand—

"Whistledown!"

Colin only caught the last word of Cressida's monologue, but there was no way he could have missed the massive collective indrawn breath that swept the ballroom.

Followed by the flurry of harsh, urgent whispers one generally only hears after someone is caught in a very embarrassing, very public compromising position.

"What?" he blurted out, turning to Penelope, who'd gone white as a sheet. "What did she say?"

But Penelope was speechless.

He looked to Lady Danbury, but the old lady had her hand over her mouth and looked as if she might possibly swoon.

Which was somewhat alarming, as Colin would have bet large sums of money that Lady Danbury had never once swooned in all of her seventy-odd years.

"What?" he demanded again, hoping one of them would break free of her stupor.

"It can't be true," Lady Danbury finally whispered, her mouth slack even as she spoke the words. "I don't believe it."

"*What?*"

She pointed toward Cressida, her extended index finger quivering in the flickering candlelight. "That lady is not Lady Whistledown."

Colin's head snapped back and forth. To Cressida. To Lady Danbury. To Cressida. To Penelope. "*She's* Lady Whistledown?" he finally blurted out.

"So she says," Lady Danbury replied, doubt written all over her face.

Colin tended to agree with her. Cressida Twombley was the last person he'd have pegged as Lady Whistledown. She was smart; there was no denying that. But she wasn't clever, and she wasn't terribly witty unless she was poking fun at others. Lady Whistledown had a rather cutting sense of humor, but with the exception of her infamous comments on fashion, she never seemed to pick on the less popular members of society.

When all was said and done, Colin had to say that Lady Whistledown had rather good taste in people.

"I can't believe this," Lady Danbury said with a loud snort of disgust. "If I'd dreamed *this* would happen, I would never have made that beastly challenge."

"This is horrible," Penelope whispered.

Her voice was quavering, and it made Colin uneasy. "Are you all right?" he asked.

She shook her head. "No, I don't think I am. I feel rather ill, actually."

"Do you want to leave?"

Penelope shook her head again. "But I'll sit right here, if you don't mind."

"Of course," he said, keeping a concerned eye on her. She was still terribly pale.

"Oh, for the love of . . ." Lady Danbury blasphemed, which took Colin by surprise, but then she actually swore, which he thought might very well have tilted the planet on its axis.

"Lady Danbury?" he asked, gaping.

"She's coming this way," she muttered, jerking her head to the right. "I should have known I'd not escape."

Colin looked to his left. Cressida was trying to make her way through the crowd, presumably to confront Lady Danbury and collect her prize. She was, naturally, being accosted at every turn by fellow partygo-ers. She seemed to be reveling in the attention—no big surprise there; Cressida had always reveled in attention—but she also seemed rather determined to reach Lady Danbury's side.

"There's no way to avoid her, I'm afraid," Colin said to Lady Danbury.

"I know," she grumbled. "I've been trying to avoid her for years, and I've never succeeded. I thought I was so clever." She looked to Colin, shaking her head with disgust. "I thought it would be such fun to rout out Lady Whistledown."

"Er, well, it was fun," Colin said, not really mean-ing it.

Lady Danbury jabbed him in the leg with her cane. "It's not the least bit fun, you foolish boy. Now look what I have to do!" She waved the cane toward Cres-sida, who was drawing ever closer. "I never dreamed I'd have to deal with the likes of *her*."

"Lady Danbury," Cressida said, swishing to a stop in front of her. "How nice to see you."

Lady Danbury had never been known for her pleas-antries, but even she outdid herself by skipping any pretense of a greeting before snapping, "I suppose you're here to try to collect your money."

Cressida cocked her head to the side in a very pretty,

very practiced manner. "You did say you would give a thousand pounds to whomever unmasked Lady Whistledown." She shrugged, lifting her hands in the air and then twisting them gracefully until her palms were up in a gesture of false humility. "You never stipulated that I couldn't unmask myself."

Lady Danbury rose to her feet, narrowed her eyes, and said, "I don't believe it's you."

Colin liked to think that he was rather suave and unflappable, but even he gasped at that.

Cressida's blue eyes blazed with fury, but she quickly regained control of her emotions and said, "I would be shocked if you did not behave with a degree of skepticism, Lady Danbury. After all, it is not your way to be trusting and gentle."

Lady Danbury smiled. Well, perhaps not a smile, but her lips did move. "I shall take that as a compliment," she said, "and allow you to tell me that you meant it as such."

Colin watched the stalemate with interest—and with a growing sense of alarm—until Lady Danbury turned quite suddenly to Penelope, who had risen to her feet mere seconds after she had.

"What do you think, Miss Featherington?" Lady Danbury asked.

Penelope visibly started, her entire body jerking

slightly as she stammered, "What . . . I . . . I beg your pardon?"

"What do you think?" Lady Danbury persisted. "Is Lady Twombley Lady Whistledown?"

"I—I'm sure I don't know."

"Oh, come, now, Miss Featherington." Lady Danbury planted her hands on her hips and looked at Penelope with an expression that bordered on exasperation. "Surely you have an opinion on the matter."

Colin felt himself stepping forward. Lady Danbury had no right to speak to Penelope in such a manner. And furthermore, he didn't like the expression on Penelope's face. She looked trapped, like a fox in a hunt, her eyes darting to him with a panic he'd never seen there before.

He'd seen Penelope uncomfortable, and he'd seen her pained, but he'd never seen her truly panicked. And then it occurred to him—she hated being the center of attention. She might poke fun at her status as a wallflower and a spinster, and she'd probably have liked a little more attention from society, but this kind of attention . . . with everyone staring at her and awaiting the merest word from her lips . . .

She was miserable.

"Miss Featherington," Colin said smoothly, moving to her side, "you look unwell. Would you like to leave?"

"Yes," she said, but then something strange happened.

She changed. He didn't know how else to describe it. She simply changed. Right there, in the Macclesfield ballroom, by his side, Penelope Featherington became someone else.

Her spine stiffened, and he could swear the heat from her body increased, and she said, "No. No, I have something to say."

Lady Danbury smiled.

Penelope looked straight at the old countess and said, "I don't think she's Lady Whistledown. I think she's lying."

Colin instinctively pulled Penelope a little closer to his side. Cressida looked as if she might go for her throat.

"I've always liked Lady Whistledown," Penelope said, her chin rising until her bearing was almost regal. She looked to Cressida, and their eyes caught as she added, "And it would break my heart if she turned out to be someone like Lady Twombley."

Colin took her hand and squeezed it. He couldn't help himself.

"Well said, Miss Featherington!" Lady Danbury exclaimed, clapping her hands together in delight. "That is exactly what I was thinking, but I couldn't find the words." She turned to Colin with a smile. "She's very clever, you know."

"I know," he replied, a strange, new pride brimming within him.

"Most people don't notice it," Lady Danbury said, twisting so that her words were directed to—and probably only heard by—Colin.

"I know," he murmured, "but I do." He had to smile at Lady Danbury's behavior, which he was certain was chosen in part to annoy the devil out of Cressida, who did *not* like to be ignored.

"I will not be insulted by that . . . by that *nothing*!" Cressida fumed. She turned to Penelope with a seething glare and hissed, "I demand an apology."

Penelope just nodded slowly and said, "That is your prerogative."

And then she said nothing more.

Colin had to physically wipe the smile from his face.

Cressida clearly wanted to say more (and perhaps commit an act of violence while she was at it), but she held back, presumably because it was obvious that Penelope was among friends. She had always been renowned for her poise, however, and thus Colin was not surprised when she composed herself, turned to Lady Danbury, and said, "What do you plan to do about the thousand pounds?"

Lady Danbury looked at her for the longest second Colin had ever endured, then she turned to *him*—dear God, the last thing he wanted to do was get involved in this disaster—and asked, "And what do you think, Mr. Bridgerton? Is our Lady Twombley telling the truth?"

Colin gave her a practiced smile. "You must be mad if you think I'm going to offer an opinion."

"You're a surprisingly wise man, Mr. Bridgerton," Lady Danbury said approvingly.

He nodded modestly, then ruined the effect by saying, "I pride myself on it." But what the hell—it wasn't every day a man was called wise by Lady Danbury.

Most of her adjectives, after all, were of the decidedly negative variety.

Cressida didn't even bother to bat her eyelashes at him; as Colin had already reflected, she wasn't stupid, just mean, and after a dozen years out in society, she had to know that he didn't much like her and certainly wasn't about to fall prey to her charms. Instead, she looked squarely at Lady Danbury and kept her voice evenly modulated as she asked, "What shall we do now, my lady?"

Lady Danbury's lips pursed together until she almost appeared mouthless, then she said, "I need proof."

Cressida blinked. "I beg your pardon?"

"Proof!" Lady Danbury's cane slammed against the floor with remarkable force. "Which letter of the word did you not understand? I'm not handing over a king's ransom without proof."

"One thousand pounds is hardly a king's ransom," Cressida said, her expression growing petulant.

Lady Danbury's eyes narrowed. "Then why are you so keen to get it?"

Cressida was silent for a moment, but there was a tightness in everything about her—her stance, her posture, the line of her jaw. Everyone knew that her husband had left her in bad financial straits, but this was the first time anyone had hinted as such to her face.

"Get me proof," Lady Danbury said, "and I'll give you the money."

"Are you saying," Cressida said (and even as he despised her, Colin was forced to admire her ability to keep her voice even), "that my word is not good enough?"

"That's precisely what I'm saying," Lady Danbury barked. "Good God, girl, you don't get to be my age without being allowed to insult anyone you please."

Colin thought he heard Penelope choking, but when he stole a glance at her, there she was at his side, avidly watching the exchange. Her brown eyes were huge and luminous in her face, and she'd regained most of the color she'd lost when Cressida had made her unexpected announcement. In fact, now Penelope looked positively intrigued by the goings-on.

"Fine," Cressida said, her voice low and deadly. "I will bring you proof in a fortnight's time."

"What sort of proof?" Colin asked, then mentally kicked himself. The last thing he wanted to do was embroil himself in this mess, but his curiosity had gotten the better of him.

Cressida turned to him, her face remarkably placid considering the insult she'd just been dealt by Lady Danbury—before countless witnesses. "You shall know it when I deliver it," she told him archly. And then she held out her arm, waiting for one of her minions to take it and lead her away.

Which was really quite amazing, because a young man (a besotted fool, from all appearances) materialized at her side as if she'd conjured him by the mere tilt of her arm. A moment later they were gone.

"Well," Lady Danbury said, after everyone had stood in reflective—or maybe stunned—silence for nearly a minute. "That was unpleasant."

"I've never liked her," Colin said, to no one in particular. A small crowd had gathered around them, so his words were heard by more than Penelope and Lady Danbury, but he didn't much care.

"Colin!"

He turned to see Hyacinth skidding through the crowd, dragging along Felicity Featherington as she barreled to his side.

"What did she say?" Hyacinth asked breathlessly. "We tried to get here sooner, but it's been such a crush."

"She said exactly what you would have expected her to say," he replied.

Hyacinth pulled a face. "Men are never good for gossip. I want exact words."

"It's very interesting," Penelope said suddenly.

Something about the thoughtful tone of her voice demanded attention, and in seconds the entire crowd had quieted.

"Speak up," Lady Danbury instructed. "We're all listening."

Colin expected such a demand to make Penelope uncomfortable, but whatever silent infusion of confidence she'd experienced a few minutes earlier was still with her, because she stood straight and proud as she said, "Why would someone reveal herself as Lady Whistledown?"

"For the money, of course," Hyacinth said.

Penelope shook her head. "Yes, but you'd think that Lady Whistledown would be quite wealthy by now. We've all been paying for her paper for years."

"By God, she's right!" Lady Danbury exclaimed.

"Perhaps Cressida merely sought attention," Colin suggested. It wasn't such an unbelievable hypothesis; Cressida had spent the bulk of her adult life trying to place herself at the center of attention.

"I'd thought of that," Penelope allowed, "but does she really want *this* sort of attention? Lady Whistledown has insulted quite a few people over the years."

"No one who means anything to me," Colin joked. Then, when it became obvious that his companions required an explanation, he added, "Haven't you all noticed that Lady Whistledown only insults the people who need insulting?"

Penelope cleared her throat delicately. "I have been referred to as an overripe citrus fruit."

He waved off her concern. "Except for the bits about fashion, of course."

Penelope must have decided not to pursue the matter any further, because all she did was give Colin a long, assessing stare before turning back to Lady Danbury and saying, "Lady Whistledown has no motive to reveal herself. Cressida obviously does."

Lady Danbury beamed, then all at once her face scrunched into a frown. "I suppose I'll have to give her the fortnight to come up with her 'proof.' Fair play and all that."

"I, for one, will be very interested to see what she

comes up with," Hyacinth put in. She turned to Penelope and added, "I say, you're very clever, did you know that?"

Penelope blushed modestly, then she turned to her sister and said, "We must be going, Felicity."

"So soon?" Felicity asked, and to his horror, Colin realized that he'd mouthed the very same words.

"Mother wanted us home early," Penelope said.

Felicity looked truly perplexed. "She did?"

"She did," Penelope said emphatically. "And besides that, I am not feeling well."

Felicity nodded glumly. "I shall instruct a footman to see that our carriage is brought around."

"No, you stay," Penelope said, placing a hand on her sister's arm. "I will see to it."

"I will see to it," Colin announced. Really, what was the use of being a gentleman when ladies insisted upon doing things for themselves?

And then, before he even realized what he was doing, he'd facilitated Penelope's departure, and she left the scene without his ever having apologized to her.

He supposed he should have deemed the evening a failure for that reason alone, but in all truth, he couldn't quite bring himself to do so.

After all, he'd spent the better part of five minutes holding her hand.

Chapter 12

It wasn't until Colin woke up the following morning that he realized he still hadn't apologized to Penelope. Strictly speaking, it probably was no longer necessary that he do so; even though they'd barely spoken at the Macclesfield ball the night before, they seemed to have forged an unspoken truce. Still, Colin didn't think he'd feel comfortable in his own skin until he spoke the words, "I'm sorry."

It was the right thing to do.

He was a gentleman, after all.

And besides, he rather fancied seeing her that morning.

He'd gone to Number Five for breakfast with his family, but he wanted to head straight for home after seeing Penelope, so he hopped in his carriage for the trip to the Featherington home on Mount Street, even though the distance was short enough to make him feel utterly lazy for doing so.

He smiled contentedly and lay back against the squabs, watching the lovely springtime scene roll by his window. It was one of those perfect sorts of days when everything simply felt right. The sun was shining, he felt remarkably energized, he'd had an excellent morning meal . . .

Life really didn't get better than this.

And he was going over to see Penelope.

Colin chose not to analyze why he was so eager to see her; that was the sort of thing an unmarried man of three-and-thirty didn't generally care to think about. Instead he simply enjoyed the day—the sun, the air, even the three neat townhouses he passed on Mount Street before spying Penelope's front door. There was nothing remotely different or original about any of them, but it was such a perfect morning that they seemed unusually charming butted up next to each other, tall and thin, and stately with their gray Portland stone.

It was a wonderful day, warm and serene, sunny and tranquil . . .

Except that just as he started to rise from his seat, a short flurry of movement across the street caught his eye.

Penelope.

She was standing on the corner of Mount and Penter streets—the far corner, the one that would be not be visible to anyone looking out a window in the Featherington home. And she was climbing into a hired hack.

Interesting.

Colin frowned, mentally smacking himself on the forehead. It wasn't *interesting*. What the hell was he thinking? It wasn't interesting at all. It might have been interesting, had she been, say, a *man*. Or it might have been interesting if the conveyance into which she'd just entered had been one from the Featherington mews and not some scruffy hired hack.

But no, this was Penelope, who was certainly not a man, and she was entering a carriage by herself, presumably heading to some completely unsuitable location, because if she were doing anything proper and normal, she'd be in a Featherington conveyance. Or better yet, with one of her sisters or a maid, or anyone, just not, damn it, by herself.

This wasn't interesting, it was idiotic.

"Fool woman," he muttered, hopping down from his carriage with every intention of dashing toward the hack, wrenching the door open, and dragging her out. But just as his right foot left the confines of his carriage, he was struck by the same madness that led him to wander the world.

Curiosity.

Several choice curses were grumbled under his breath, all of them self-directed. He couldn't help it. It was so unlike Penelope to be taking off by herself in a hired hack; he *had* to know where she was going.

And so, instead of forcibly shaking some sense into her, he directed his driver to follow the hack, and they rolled north toward the busy thoroughfare of Oxford Street, where, Colin reflected, surely Penelope intended to do a bit of shopping. There could be any number of reasons she wasn't using the Featherington carriage. Perhaps it was damaged, or one of their horses had taken ill, or Penelope was buying someone a gift and wanted to keep it a secret.

No, that wasn't right. Penelope would never embark on a shopping expedition by herself. She would take a maid, or one of her sisters, or even one of *his* sisters. To stroll along Oxford Street by herself was to invite gossip. A woman alone was practically an advertisement for the next *Whistledown* column.

Or used to be, he supposed. It was hard to get used to a life without *Whistledown*. He hadn't realized how accustomed he'd been to seeing it at his breakfast table whenever he was in town.

And speaking of Lady Whistledown, he was even more certain than ever that she was none other than his sister Eloise. He'd gone over to Number Five for breakfast with the express purpose of questioning her, only to be informed that she was still feeling poorly and would not be joining the family that morning.

It had not escaped Colin's notice, however, that a rather hefty tray of food had been sent up to Eloise's room. Whatever ailed his sister, it had not affected her appetite.

He hadn't made any mention of his suspicions at the breakfast table; truly, he saw no reason to upset his mother, who would surely be horrified at the thought. It was difficult to believe, however, that Eloise—whose love of discussing scandal was eclipsed only by her thrill at discovering it—would miss the opportunity to gossip about Cressida Twombley's revelation of the night before.

Unless *Eloise* was Lady Whistledown, in which case she'd be up in her room, plotting her next step.

The pieces all fit. It would have been depressing if Colin hadn't felt so oddly thrilled at having found her out.

After they rolled along for a few minutes, he poked his head outside to make sure his driver had not lost sight of Penelope's carriage. There she was, right in front of him. Or at least he thought it was her. Most hired hacks looked the same, so he was going to have to trust and hope that he was following the right one. But as he looked out, he realized that they'd traveled much farther east than he would have anticipated. In fact, they were just now passing Soho Street, which meant they were nearly to Tottenham Court Road, which meant—

Dear God, was Penelope taking the carriage to his house? Bedford Square was practically right around the corner.

A delicious thrill shot up his spine, because he couldn't imagine what she was doing in this part of town if not to see him; who else would a woman like Penelope know in Bloomsbury? He couldn't imagine that her mother allowed her to associate with people who actually worked for a living, and Colin's neighbors, though certainly well enough born, were not of the aristocracy and rarely even of the gentry. And they all plodded off to work each day, doctoring and lawyering, or—

Colin frowned. Hard. They'd just rolled past Tottenham Court Road. What the devil was she doing this far east? He supposed her driver might not know his way around town very well and thought to take Bloomsbury Street up to Bedford Square, even though it was a bit out of the way, but—

He heard something very strange and realized it was the sound of his teeth grinding together. They'd just passed Bloomsbury Street and were presently veering right onto High Holborn.

Devil take it, they were nearly in the City. What in God's name was Penelope planning to do in the City? It was no place for a woman. Hell, he hardly ever went there himself. The world of the *ton* was farther west, in the hallowed buildings of St. James's and Mayfair. Not here in the City, with its narrow, twisting, medieval roads and rather dangerous proximity to the tenements of the East End.

Colin's jaw dropped progressively lower as they rolled on . . . and on . . . and on . . . until he realized they were turning down Shoe Lane. He craned his head out the window. He'd only been here once before, at the age of nine when his tutor had dragged him and Benedict off to show them where the Great Fire of London had started in 1666. Colin remembered feeling vaguely disappointed when he'd learned that the culprit was a mere baker who'd not dampened the ashes in his oven properly. A fire like that should have had arson or intrigue in its origin.

A fire like that was nothing compared to the feelings coming to a boil in his chest. Penelope had better have a *damned* good reason for coming out here by herself. She shouldn't be going *anywhere* unaccompanied, much less the City.

Then, just when Colin was convinced that Penelope was going to travel all the way to the Dover coast, the carriages crossed Fleet Street and ground to a halt. Colin held still, waiting to see what Penelope was up to even though every fiber of his being was screaming to leap out of the carriage and tackle her right there on the pavement.

Call it intuition, call it madness, but somehow he knew that if he accosted Penelope right away, he would never learn of her true purpose here near Fleet Street.

Once she was far enough away so that he could alight unnoticed, he jumped down from the carriage and followed her south toward some church that looked decidedly like a wedding cake.

"For God's sake," Colin muttered, completely unaware of blasphemy or puns, "now is not the time to find religion, Penelope."

She disappeared into the church, and his legs ate up the pavement after her, slowing only when he reached the front door. He didn't want to surprise her too quickly. Not before he found out what exactly she was doing there. His earlier words notwithstanding, he did not for one moment think that Penelope had suddenly developed a desire to extend her churchgoing habits to midweek visits.

He slipped quietly into the church, keeping his footsteps as soft as he could. Penelope was walking down the center aisle, her left hand tapping along each pew, almost as if she were . . .

Counting?

Colin frowned as she picked her pew, then scooted in until she was in the middle. She sat utterly still for a moment, then reached into her reticule and pulled out an envelope. Her head moved the teeniest bit to the left, then to the right, and Colin could easily picture her face, her dark eyes darting in either direction as she checked the room for other people. He was safe from her gaze at the back, so far in the shadows that he was practically pressed up against the wall. And besides, she seemed intent upon remaining still and quiet in her movements; she certainly hadn't moved her head far enough to see him behind her.

Bibles and prayer books were tucked in little pockets on the backs of the pews, and Colin watched as Penelope surreptitiously slid the envelope behind one. Then she stood and edged her way out toward the center aisle.

And that was when Colin made his move.

Stepping out of the shadows, he strode purposefully toward her, taking grim satisfaction in the horror on her face when she saw him.

"Col—Col—" she gasped.

"That would be Colin," he drawled, grasping her arm just above the elbow. His touch was light, but his grip was firm, and there was no way she could think that she might make an escape.

Smart girl that she was, she didn't even try.

But smart girl that she was, she did attempt a play at innocence.

"Colin!" she finally managed to get out. "What a . . . what a . . ."

"Surprise?"

She gulped. "Yes."

"I'm sure it is."

Her eyes darted to the door, to the nave, everywhere but to the pew where she'd hidden her envelope. "I've—I've never seen you here before."

"I've never been."

Penelope's mouth moved several times before her next words emerged. "It's quite appropriate, actually, that you'd be here, actually, because, actually . . . uh . . . do you know the story of St. Bride's?"

He raised one brow. "Is that where we are?"

Penelope was clearly trying for a smile, but the result was more of the openmouthed idiot sort of look. Normally this would have amused him, but he was still angry with her for taking off on her own, not giving a care to her safety and welfare.

But most of all, he was furious that she had a secret.

Not so much that she'd *kept* a secret. Secrets were meant to be kept, and he couldn't blame her for that. Irrational as it was, he absolutely could not tolerate the fact that she *had* a secret. She was Penelope. She was supposed to be an open book. He knew her. He'd always known her.

And now it seemed he'd never known her.

"Yes," she finally replied, her voice squeaking on the word. "It's one of Wren's churches, actually, you know, the ones he did after the Great Fire, they're all over the City, and actually it's my favorite. I do so love the steeple. Don't you think it looks like a wedding cake?"

She was babbling. It was never a good sign when someone babbled. It generally meant they were hiding something. It was already obvious that Penelope was making an attempt at concealment, but the uncharacteristic rapidity of her words told him that her secret was exceedingly large, indeed.

He stared at her for a very long time, drawn out over many seconds just to torture her, then finally asked, "Is that why you think it's appropriate that I'm here?"

Her face went blank.

"The wedding cake . . ." he prompted.

"Oh!" she squealed, her skin flushing a deep, guilty red. "No! Not at all! It's just that—What I meant to say was that this is the church for writers. And publishers. I think. About the publishers, that is."

She was flailing and she knew she was flailing. He could see it in her eyes, on her face, in the very way her hands twisted as she spoke. But she kept trying, kept attempting to keep up the pretense, and so he did nothing but give her a sardonic stare as she continued with, "But I'm sure about the writers." And then, with a flourish that might have been triumphant if she hadn't ruined it with a nervous swallow, "And you're a writer!"

"So you're saying this is my church?"

"Er . . ." Her eyes darted to her left. "Yes."

"Excellent."

She gulped. "It is?"

"Oh, yes," he said, with a smooth casualness to his words that was intended to terrify her.

Her eyes darted to her left again . . . toward the pew where she'd hidden her correspondence. She'd been so good until now, keeping her attention off of her incriminating evidence. He'd almost been proud of her for it.

"My church," he repeated. "What a lovely notion."

Her eyes grew round, scared. "I'm afraid I don't catch your meaning."

He tapped his finger to his jaw, then held out his hand in a thoughtful manner. "I believe I'm developing a taste for prayer."

"Prayer?" she echoed weakly. "You?"

"Oh, yes."

"I . . . well . . . I . . . I . . ."

"Yes?" he queried, beginning to enjoy this in a sick sort of way. He'd never been the angry, brooding type. Clearly, he hadn't known what he was missing. There was something rather pleasing in making her squirm. "Penelope?" he continued. "Did you have something to say?"

She swallowed. "No."

"Good." He smiled blandly. "Then I believe I require a few moments for myself."

"I'm sorry?"

He stepped to his right. "I'm in a church. I believe I want to pray."

She stepped to her left. "I beg your pardon?"

He cocked his head very slightly to the side in question. "I said that I want to pray. It wasn't a terribly complicated sentiment."

He could tell that she was straining hard not to rise

to his bait. She was trying to smile, but her jaw was tense, and he'd wager that her teeth were going to grind themselves to powder within minutes.

"I didn't think you were a particularly religious person," she said.

"I'm not." He waited for her to react, then added, "I intend to pray for *you*."

She swallowed uncontrollably. "Me?" she squeaked.

"Because," he began, unable to prevent his voice from rising in volume, "by the time I'm done, prayer is the only thing that is going to save you!"

And with that he brushed her aside and strode to where she'd hidden the envelope.

"Colin!" she yelled, running frantically after him. "No!"

He yanked the envelope out from behind the prayer book but didn't yet look at it. "Do you want to tell me what this is?" he demanded. "Before I look myself, do you want to tell me?"

"No," she said, her voice breaking on the word.

His heart breaking at the expression in her eyes.

"Please," she begged him. "Please give it to me." And then, when he did nothing but stare at her with hard, angry eyes, she whispered, "It's mine. It's a secret."

"A secret worth your welfare?" he nearly roared. "Worth your life?"

"What are you talking about?"

"Do you have any idea how dangerous it is for a woman alone in the City? Alone anywhere?"

All she said was, "Colin, please." She reached for the envelope, still held out of her reach.

And suddenly he didn't know what he was doing. This wasn't him. This insane fury, this anger—it couldn't be his.

And yet it was.

But the troubling part was . . . it was Penelope who had made him thus. And what had she done? Traveled across London by herself? He was rather irritated at her for her lack of concern for her own safety, but that paled in comparison to the fury he felt at her keeping of secrets.

His anger was entirely unwarranted. He had no right to expect that Penelope share her secrets with him. They had no commitments to each other, nothing beyond a rather nice friendship and a single, albeit disturbingly moving, kiss. He certainly wouldn't have shared his journals with her if she hadn't stumbled upon them herself.

"Colin," she whispered. "Please . . . don't."

She'd seen his secret writings. Why shouldn't he see hers? Did she have a lover? Was all that nonsense about never having been kissed exactly that—nonsense?

Dear God, was this fire burning in his belly . . . *jealousy?*

"Colin," she said again, choking now. She placed her hand on his, trying to prevent him from opening the envelope. Not with strength, for she could never match him on that, just with her presence.

But there was no way . . . no way he could have stopped himself at that point. He would have died before surrendering that envelope to her unopened.

He tore it open.

Penelope let out a strangled cry and ran from the church.

Colin read the words.

And then he sank to the pew, bloodless, breathless.

"Oh, my God," he whispered. *"Oh, my God."*

By the time Penelope reached the outer steps to St. Bride's Church, she was hysterical. Or at least as hysterical as she'd ever been. Her breath was coming in short, sharp gasps, tears pricked her eyes, and her heart felt . . .

Well, her heart felt as if it wanted to throw up, if such a thing were possible.

How could he have done this? He'd followed her. *Followed her!* Why would Colin follow her? What would he have to gain? Why would he—

She suddenly looked around.

"Oh, damn!" she wailed, not caring if anyone heard her. The hack had left. She'd given specific instructions to the driver to wait for her, that she'd only be a minute, but he was nowhere in sight.

Another transgression she could lay at Colin's door. He'd delayed her inside the church, and now the hack had left, and she was stuck here on the steps of St. Bride's Church, in the middle of the City of London, so far from her home in Mayfair that she might as well have been in France. People were staring at her and any minute now she was sure to be accosted, because who had ever seen a gently bred lady alone in the City, much less one who was so clearly on the verge of a nervous attack?

Why why *why* had she been so foolish as to think that he was the perfect man? She'd spent half her life worshiping someone who wasn't even real. Because the Colin she knew—no, the Colin she'd *thought* she'd known—clearly didn't exist. And whoever this man was, she wasn't even sure she liked him. The man she'd loved so faithfully over the years never would have behaved like this. He wouldn't have followed her—Oh, very well, he would have, but only to assure himself of her safety. But he wouldn't have been so cruel, and he certainly wouldn't have opened her private correspondence.

She had read two pages of his journal, that was true, but they hadn't been in a sealed envelope!

She sank onto the steps and sat down, the stone cool even through the fabric of her dress. There was little she could do now besides sit here and wait for Colin. Only a fool would take off on foot by herself so far from home. She supposed she could hail a hack on Fleet Street, but what if they were all occupied, and besides, was there really any point in running from Colin? He knew where she lived, and unless she decided to run to the Orkney Islands, she wasn't likely to escape a confrontation.

She sighed. Colin would probably find her in the Orkneys, seasoned traveler that he was. And she didn't even want to *go* to the Orkneys.

She choked back a sob. Now she wasn't even making sense. Why was she fixated on the Orkney Islands?

And then there was Colin's voice behind her, clipped and so very cold. "Get up," was all he said.

She did, not because he'd ordered her to (or at least that was what she told herself), and not because she was afraid of him, but rather because she couldn't sit on the steps of St. Bride's forever, and even if she wanted nothing more than to hide herself from Colin for the next six months, at the moment he was her only safe means home.

He jerked his head toward the street. "Into the carriage."

She went, climbing up as she heard Colin give the driver her address and then instruct him to "take the long way."

Oh, God.

They'd been moving a good thirty seconds before he handed her the single sheet of paper that had been folded into the envelope she'd left in the church. "I believe this is yours," he said.

She gulped and looked down, not that she needed to. She already had the words memorized. She'd written and rewritten them so many times the previous night, she didn't think they'd ever escape her memory.

There is nothing I despise more than a gentleman who thinks it amusing to give a lady a condescending pat on the hand as he murmurs, "It is a woman's prerogative to change her mind." And indeed, because I feel one should always support one's words with one's actions, I endeavor to keep my opinions and decisions steadfast and true.

Which is why, Gentle Reader, when I wrote my

column of 19 April, I truly intended it to be my last. However, events entirely beyond my control (or indeed beyond my approval) force me to put my pen to paper one last time.

Ladies and Gentleman, This Author is NOT Lady Cressida Twombley. She is nothing more than a scheming imposter, and it would break my heart to see my years of hard work attributed to one such as her.

LADY WHISTLEDOWN'S SOCIETY PAPERS,
21 APRIL 1824

Penelope refolded the paper with great precision, using the time to try to compose herself and figure out what on earth she was supposed to say at a moment like that. Finally, she attempted a smile, didn't quite meet his eyes, and joked, "Did you guess?"

He didn't say anything, so she was forced to look up. She immediately wished she hadn't. Colin looked completely unlike himself. The easy smile that always tugged at his lips, the good humor forever lurking in his eyes—they were all gone, replaced by harsh lines and cold, pure ice.

The man she knew, the man she'd loved for so very long—she didn't know who he was anymore.

"I'll take that as a no," she said shakily.

"Do you know what I am trying to do right now?" he asked, his voice startling and loud against the rhythmic clip-clop of the horses' hooves.

She opened her mouth to say no, but one look at his face told her he didn't desire an answer, so she held her tongue.

"I am trying to decide what, precisely, I am most angry with you about," he said. "Because there are so many things—so very *many* things—that I am finding it extraordinarily difficult to focus upon just one."

It was on the tip of Penelope's tongue to suggest something—her deception was a likely place to start—but on second thought, now seemed an excellent time to hold her counsel.

"First of all," he said, the terribly even tone of his voice suggesting that he was trying *very* hard to keep his temper in check (and this was, in and of itself, rather disturbing, as she hadn't been aware that Colin even possessed a temper), "I cannot believe you were stupid enough to venture into the City by yourself, and in a hired hack, no less!"

"I could hardly go by myself in one of our own carriages," Penelope blurted out before she remembered that she'd meant to remain silent.

His head moved about an inch to the left. She didn't know what that meant, but she couldn't imagine it was good, especially since it almost seemed as if his neck were tightening as it twisted. "I beg your pardon?" he asked, his voice still that awful blend of satin and steel.

Well, now she *had* to answer, didn't she? "Er, it's nothing," she said, hoping the evasion would reduce his attention on the rest of her reply. "Just that I'm not allowed to go out by myself."

"I am aware of that," he bit off. "There's a damned good reason for it, too."

"So if I wanted to go out by myself," she continued, choosing to ignore the second part of his reply, "I couldn't very well use one of our carriages. None of our drivers would agree to take me here."

"Your drivers," he snapped, "are clearly men of impeccable wisdom and sense."

Penelope said nothing.

"Do you have any idea what could have happened to you?" he demanded, his sharp mask of control beginning to crack.

"Er, very little, actually," she said, gulping on the sentence. "I've come here before, and—"

"*What?*" His hand closed over her upper arm with painful force. "What did you just say?"

Repeating it seemed almost dangerous to her health, so Penelope just stared at him, hoping that maybe she could break through the wild anger in his eyes and find the man she knew and loved so dearly.

"It's only when I need to leave an urgent message for my publisher," she explained. "I send a coded message, then he knows to pick up my note here."

"And speaking of which," Colin said roughly, snatching the folded paper back from her hands, "what the *hell* is this?"

Penelope stared at him in confusion. "I would have thought it was obvious. I'm—"

"Yes, of course, you're bloody Lady Whistledown, and you've probably been laughing at me for weeks as I insisted it was Eloise." His face twisted as he spoke, nearly breaking her heart.

"No!" she cried out. "No, Colin, never. I would never laugh at you!"

But his face told her clearly that he did not believe her. There was humiliation in his emerald eyes, something she'd never seen there, something she'd never expected to see. He was a Bridgerton. He was popular, confident, self-possessed. Nothing could embarrass him. No one could humiliate him.

Except, apparently, her.

"I couldn't tell you," she whispered, desperately trying to make that awful look in his eyes go away. "Surely you knew I couldn't tell you."

He was silent for an agonizingly long moment, and then, as if she'd never spoken, never tried to explain herself, he lifted the incriminating sheet of paper into the air and shook it, completely disregarding her impassioned outcry. "This is stupidity," he said. "Have you lost your mind?"

"I don't know what you mean."

"You had a perfectly good escape, just waiting for you. Cressida Twombley was willing to take the blame for you."

And then suddenly his hands were on her shoulders, and he was holding her so tightly she could barely breathe.

"Why couldn't you just let it die, Penelope?" His voice was urgent, his eyes blazing. It was the most feeling she'd ever seen in him, and it broke her heart that it was directed toward her in anger. And in shame.

"I couldn't let her do it," she whispered. "I couldn't let her be me."

Chapter 13

"*Why the hell not?*"

Penelope could do nothing but stare for several seconds. "Because . . . because . . ." she flailed, wondering how she was supposed to explain this. Her heart was breaking, her most terrifying—and exhilarating—secret had been shattered, and he thought she had the presence of mind to *explain* herself?

"I realize she's quite possibly the biggest bitch . . ." Penelope gasped.

". . . that England has produced in this generation at least, but for God's sake, Penelope"—he raked his hand through his hair, then fixed a hard stare on her face—"she was going to take the blame—"

"The credit," Penelope interrupted testily.

"The blame," he continued. "Do you have any idea

what will happen to you if people find out who you really are?"

The corners of her lips tightened with impatience . . . and irritation at being so obviously condescended to. "I've had over a decade to ruminate the possibility."

His eyes narrowed. "Are you being sarcastic?"

"Not at all," she shot back. "Do you really think I haven't spent a good portion of the last ten years of my life contemplating what would happen if I were found out? I'd be a blind idiot if I hadn't."

He grabbed her by the shoulders, holding tight even as the carriage bumped over uneven cobbles. "You will be ruined, Penelope. Ruined! Do you understand what I am saying?"

"If I did not," she replied, "I assure you I would now, after your lengthy dissertations on the subject when you were accusing Eloise of being Lady Whistledown."

He scowled, obviously annoyed at having his errors thrown in his face. "People will stop talking to you," he continued. "They will cut you dead—"

"People never talked to me," she snapped. "Half the time they didn't even know I was there. How do you think I was able to keep up the ruse for so long in the first place? I was invisible, Colin. No one saw me, no one talked to me. I just stood and listened, *and no one noticed.*"

"That's not true." But his eyes slid from hers as he said it.

"Oh, it *is* true, and you know it. You only deny it," she said, jabbing him in the arm, "because you feel guilty."

"I do not!"

"Oh, *please*," she scoffed. "Everything you do, you do out of guilt."

"Pen—"

"That involves me, at least," she corrected. Her breath was rushing through her throat, and her skin was pricking with heat, and for once, her soul was on fire. "Do you think I don't know how your family pities me? Do you think it escapes my notice that anytime you or your brothers happen to be at the same party as me, you ask me to dance?"

"We're polite," he ground out, "and we *like* you."

"*And* you feel sorry for me. You like Felicity but I don't see you dancing with her every time your paths cross."

He let go of her quite suddenly and crossed his arms. "Well, I don't like her as well as I do you."

She blinked, knocked rather neatly off her verbal stride. Trust him to go and *compliment* her in the middle of an argument. Nothing could have disarmed her more.

"And," he continued with a rather arch and superior lifting of his chin, "you have not addressed my original point."

"Which was?"

"That Lady Whistledown will ruin you!"

"For God's sake," she muttered, "you talk as if she were a separate person."

"Well, excuse me if I still have difficulty reconciling the woman in front of me with the harridan writing the column."

"Colin!"

"Insulted?" he mocked.

"Yes! I've worked very hard on that column." She clenched her fists around the thin fabric of her mint-green morning dress, oblivious to the wrinkled spirals she was creating. She had to do something with her hands or she'd quite possibly explode with the nervous energy and anger coursing through her veins. Her only other option seemed to be crossing her arms, and she refused to give in to such an obvious show of petulance. Besides, he was crossing his arms, and one of them needed to act older than six.

"I wouldn't dream of denigrating what you've done," he said condescendingly.

"Of course you would," she interrupted.

"No, I wouldn't."

"Then what do you think you're doing?"

"Being an adult!" he answered, his voice growing loud and impatient. "One of us has to be."

"Don't you dare speak to me of adult behavior!" she exploded. "You, who run at the very hint of responsibility."

"And what the hell does that mean?" he bit off.

"I thought it was rather obvious."

He drew back. "I can't believe you're speaking to me like this."

"You can't believe I'm doing it," she taunted, "or that I possess the nerve to do so?"

He just stared at her, obviously surprised by her question.

"There's more to me than you think, Colin," she said. And then, in a quieter tone of voice, she added, "There's more to me than *I* used to think."

He said nothing for several moments, and then, as if he just couldn't drag himself away from the topic, he asked, practically between his teeth, "What did you mean when you said I run from responsibility?"

She pursed her lips, then relaxed as she let out what she hoped would be a calming exhale. "Why do you think you travel so much?"

"Because I like it," he replied, his tone clipped.

"And because you're bored out of your mind here in England."

"And that makes me a child because . . . ?"

"Because you're not willing to grow up and do something adult that would keep you in one place."

"Like what?"

Her hands came up in an I-should-think-it-was-obvious sort of gesture. "Like get married."

"Is that a proposal?" he mocked, one corner of his mouth rising into a rather insolent smile.

She could feel her cheeks flushing deep and hot, but she forced herself to continue. "You know it's not, and don't try to change the subject by being deliberately cruel." She waited for him to say something, perhaps an apology. His silence was an insult, and so she let out a snort and said, "For heaven's sake, Colin, you're three-and-thirty."

"And you're eight-and-twenty," he pointed out, and not in a particularly kind tone of voice.

It felt like a punch in the belly, but she was too riled up to retreat into her familiar shell. "Unlike you," she said with low precision, "I don't have the luxury of asking someone. And unlike *you*," she added, her intention now solely to induce the guilt she'd accused him of just minutes earlier, "I don't have a massive pool of prospective suitors, so I've never had the luxury of saying no."

His lips tightened. "And you think that your unveiling as Lady Whistledown is going to increase the number of your suitors?"

"Are you *trying* to be insulting?" she ground out.

"I'm trying to be realistic! Something which you seem to have completely lost sight of."

"I never said I was planning to unveil myself as Lady Whistledown."

He snatched the envelope with the final column in it back up off the cushioned bench. "Then what is this about?"

She grabbed it back, yanking the paper from the envelope. "I beg your pardon," she said, every syllable heavy with sarcasm. "I must have missed the sentence proclaiming my identity."

"You think this swan song of yours will do anything to dampen the frenzy of interest in Lady Whistledown's identity? Oh, excuse me"—he placed one insolent hand over his heart—"perhaps I should have said *your* identity. After all, I don't want to deny you your *credit*."

"Now you're just being ugly," she said, a little voice at the back of her brain wondering why she wasn't crying by now. This was Colin, and she'd loved him forever, and he was acting as if he hated her. Was there anything else in the world more worthy of tears?

Or maybe that wasn't it at all. Maybe all this sadness building up inside of her was for the death of a dream. Her dream of him. She'd built up the perfect image of him in her mind, and with every word he spat in her face, it was becoming more and more obvious that her dream was quite simply wrong.

"I'm making a point," he said, snatching the paper back from her hands. "Look at this. It might as well be an invitation for further investigation. You're mocking society, daring them to uncover you."

"That's not at all what I'm doing!"

"It may not be your intention, but it is certainly the end result."

He probably had something of a point there, but she was loath to give him credit for it. "It's a chance I'll have to take," she replied, crossing her arms and looking pointedly away from him. "I've gone eleven years without detection. I don't see why I'm in need of undue worry now."

His breath left him in a short punch of exasperation. "Do you have any concept of money? Any idea how many people would like Lady Danbury's thousand pounds?"

"I have more of a concept of money than you do,"

she replied, bristling at the insult. "And besides, Lady Danbury's reward doesn't make my secret any more vulnerable."

"It makes everyone else more determined, and that makes you more vulnerable. Not to mention," he added with a wry twist to his lips, "as my youngest sister pointed out, there is the glory."

"Hyacinth?" she asked.

He nodded grimly, setting the paper down on the bench beside him. "And if Hyacinth thinks the glory at having uncovered your identity is enviable, then you can be sure she's not the only one. It may very well be why Cressida is pursuing her stupid ruse."

"Cressida's doing it for the money," Penelope grumbled. "I'm sure of it."

"Fine. It doesn't matter why she's doing it. All that matters is that she is, and once you dispose of her with your idiocy"—he slammed his hand against the paper, causing Penelope to wince as a loud crinkle filled the air—"someone else will take her place."

"This is nothing I don't already know," she said, mostly because she couldn't bear to give him the last word.

"Then for the love of God, woman," he burst out,

"let Cressida get away with her scheme. She's the answer to your prayers."

Her eyes snapped up to his. "You don't know my prayers."

Something in her tone hit Colin squarely in the chest. She hadn't changed his mind, hadn't even budged it, but he couldn't seem to find the right words to fill the moment. He looked at her, then he looked out the window, his mind absently focusing on the dome of St. Paul's Cathedral.

"We really are taking the long way home," he murmured.

She didn't say anything. He didn't blame her. It had been a stupid non sequitur, words to fill the silence and nothing else.

"If you let Cressida—" he began.

"Stop," she implored him. "Please, don't say any more. I can't let her do it."

"Have you really thought about what you'd gain?"

She looked at him sharply. "Do you think I've been able to think of anything else these past few days?"

He tried another tactic. "Does it truly matter that people know you were Lady Whistledown? *You* know that you were clever and fooled us all. Can't that be enough?"

"You're not listening to me!" Her mouth remained frozen open, in an odd incredulous oval, as if she couldn't quite believe that he didn't understand what she was saying. "I don't need for people to know it was me. I just need for them to know it wasn't *her*."

"But clearly you don't mind if people think someone else is Lady Whistledown," he insisted. "After all, you've been accusing Lady Danbury for weeks."

"I had to accuse *someone*," she explained. "Lady Danbury asked me point-blank who I thought it was, and I couldn't very well say myself. Besides, it wouldn't be so very bad if people thought it was Lady Danbury. At least I like Lady Danbury."

"Penelope—"

"How would you feel if your journals were published with Nigel Berbrooke as the author?" she demanded.

"Nigel Berbrooke can barely string two sentences together," he said with a derisive snort. "I hardly think anyone would believe he could have written my journals." As an afterthought, he gave her a little nod as an apology, since Berbrooke was, after all, married to her sister.

"Try to imagine it," she ground out. "Or substitute whomever you think is similar to Cressida."

"Penelope," he sighed, "I'm not you. You can't compare the two. Besides, if I were to publish my journals, they would hardly ruin me in the eyes of society."

She deflated in her seat, sighing loudly, and he knew that his point had been well made. "Good," he announced, "then it is decided. We will tear this up—" He reached for the sheet of paper.

"No!" she cried out, practically leaping from her seat. "Don't!"

"But you just said—"

"I said nothing!" she shrilled. "All I did was sigh."

"Oh, for God's sake, Penelope," he said testily. "You clearly agreed with—"

She gaped at his audacity. "When did I give you leave to interpret my sighs?"

He looked at the incriminating paper, still held in his hands, and wondered what on earth he was meant to do with it at this moment.

"And *anyway*," she continued, her eyes flashing with an anger and fire that made her almost beautiful, "it isn't as if I don't have every last word memorized. You can destroy that paper, but you can't destroy me."

"I'd like to," he muttered.

"*What* did you say?"

"Whistledown," he ground out. "I'd like to destroy Whistledown. You, I'm happy to leave as is."

"But I *am* Whistledown."

"God help us all."

And then something within her simply snapped. All her rage, all her frustration, every last negative feeling she'd kept bottled up inside over the years broke forth, all directed at Colin, who, of all the *ton*, was probably the least deserving of it.

"Why are you so angry with me?" she burst out. "What have I done that is so repellent? Been cleverer than you? Kept a secret? Had a good laugh at the expense of society?"

"Penelope, you—"

"No," she said forcefully. "You be quiet. It's my turn to speak."

His jaw went slack as he stared at her, shock and disbelief crowding in his eyes.

"I am proud of what I've done," she managed to say, her voice shaking with emotion. "I don't care what you say. I don't care what anyone says. No one can take that from me."

"I'm not trying—"

"I don't need for people to know the truth," she said, jumping on top of his ill-timed protest. "But I will be *damned* if I allow Cressida Twombley, the very person who . . . who . . ." Her entire body was trembling now, as memory after memory swept over her, all of them bad.

Cressida, renowned for her grace and carriage, tripping and spilling punch on Penelope's gown that first year—the only one her mother had allowed her to buy that wasn't yellow or orange.

Cressida, sweetly begging young bachelors to ask Penelope to dance, her requests made with such volume and fervor that Penelope could only be mortified by them.

Cressida, saying before a crowd how worried she was about Penelope's appearance. "It's just not *healthful* to weigh more than ten stone at our age," she'd cooed.

Penelope never knew whether Cressida had been able to hide her smirk following her barb. She'd fled the room, blinded by tears, unable to ignore the way her hips jiggled as she ran away.

Cressida had always known exactly where to stick her sword, and she'd known how to twist her bayonet. It didn't matter that Eloise remained Penelope's champion or that Lady Bridgerton always tried to bolster her confidence. Penelope had cried herself to sleep more times than she could remember, always due to some well-placed barb from Cressida Cowper Twombley.

She'd let Cressida get away with so much in the past,

all because she hadn't the courage to stand up for herself. But she couldn't let Cressida have *this*. Not her secret life, not the one little corner of her soul that was strong and proud and completely without fear.

Penelope might not know how to defend herself, but by God, Lady Whistledown did.

"Penelope?" Colin asked cautiously.

She looked at him blankly, taking several seconds to remember that it was 1824, not 1814, and she was here in a carriage with Colin Bridgerton, not cowering in the corner of a ballroom, trying to escape Cressida Cowper.

"Are you all right?" he asked.

She nodded. Or at least she tried to.

He opened his mouth to say something, then paused, his lips remaining parted for several seconds. Finally, he just placed his hand on hers, saying, "We'll talk about this later?"

This time she did manage a short nod. And truly, she just wanted the entire awful afternoon to be over, but there was one thing she couldn't quite let go of yet.

"Cressida wasn't ruined," she said quietly.

He turned to her, a slight veil of confusion descending over his eyes. "I beg your pardon?"

Her voice rose slightly in volume. "Cressida said she was Lady Whistledown, and she wasn't ruined."

"That's because no one believed her," Colin replied. "And besides," he added without thinking, "she's . . . different."

She turned to him slowly. Very slowly, with steadfast eyes. "Different how?"

Something akin to panic began to pound in Colin's chest. He'd known he wasn't saying the right words even as they'd spilled from his lips. How could one little sentence, one little word be so very wrong?

She's different.

They both knew what he'd meant. Cressida was popular, Cressida was beautiful, Cressida could carry it all off with aplomb.

Penelope, on the other hand . . .

She was Penelope. Penelope Featherington. And she hadn't the clout nor the connections to save her from ruin. The Bridgertons could stand behind her and offer support, but even they wouldn't be able prevent her downfall. Any other scandal might have been manageable, but Lady Whistledown had, at one time or another, insulted almost every person of consequence in the British Isles. Once people were over their surprise, that was when the unkind remarks would begin.

Penelope wouldn't be praised for being clever or witty or daring.

She'd be called mean, and petty, and jealous.

Colin knew the *ton* well. He knew how his peers acted. The aristocracy was capable of individual greatness, but collectively they tended to sink to the lowest common denominator.

Which was very low, indeed.

"I see," Penelope said into the silence.

"No," he said quickly, "you don't. I—"

"No, Colin," she said, sounding almost painfully wise, "I do. I suppose I'd just always hoped *you* were different."

His eyes caught hers, and somehow his hands were on her shoulders, gripping her with such intensity that she couldn't possibly look away. He didn't say anything, letting his eyes ask his questions.

"I thought you believed in me," she said, "that you saw beyond the ugly duckling."

Her face was so familiar to him; he'd seen it a thousand times before, and yet until these past few weeks, he couldn't have said he truly knew it. Would he have remembered that she had a small birthmark near her left earlobe? Had he ever noticed the warm glow to her skin? Or that her brown eyes had flecks of gold in them, right near the pupil?

How had he danced with her so many times and

never noticed that her mouth was full and wide and made for kissing?

She licked her lips when she was nervous. He'd seen her do that just the other day. Surely she'd done that at some point in the dozen years of their acquaintance, and yet it was only now that the mere sight of her tongue made his body clench with need.

"You're not ugly," he told her, his voice low and urgent.

Her eyes widened.

And he whispered, "You're beautiful."

"No," she said, the word barely more than a breath. "Don't say things you don't mean."

His fingers dug into her shoulders. "You're beautiful," he repeated. "I don't know how . . . I don't know when . . ." He touched her lips, feeling her hot breath on his fingertips. "But you are," he whispered.

He leaned forward and kissed her, slowly, reverently, no longer quite so surprised that this was happening, that he wanted her so badly. The shock was gone, replaced by a simple, primitive need to claim her, to brand her, to mark her as his.

His?

He pulled back and looked at her for a moment, his eyes searching her face.

Why not?

"What is it?" she whispered.

"You *are* beautiful," he said, shaking his head in confusion. "I don't know why nobody else sees it."

Something warm and lovely began to spread in Penelope's chest. She couldn't quite explain it; it was almost as if someone had heated her blood. It started in her heart and then slowly swept through her arms, her belly, down to the tips of her toes.

It made her light-headed. It made her content.

It made her whole.

She wasn't beautiful. She knew she wasn't beautiful, she knew she'd never be more than passably attractive, and that was only on her good days. But he thought she was beautiful, and when he looked at her . . .

She *felt* beautiful. And she'd never felt that way before.

He kissed her again, his lips hungrier this time, nibbling, caressing, waking her body, rousing her soul. Her belly had begun to tingle, and her skin felt hot and needy where his hands touched her through the thin green fabric of her dress.

And never once did she think, *This is wrong*. This kiss was everything she'd been brought up to fear and avoid, but she knew—body, mind, and soul—that nothing in her life had ever been so right. She had been born for this man, and she'd spent so many years trying to accept the fact that he had been born for someone else.

To be proven wrong was the most exquisite pleasure imaginable.

She wanted him, she wanted this, she wanted the way he made her feel.

She wanted to be beautiful, even if it was only in one man's eyes.

They were, she thought dreamily as he laid her down on the plush cushion of the carriage bench, the only eyes that mattered.

She loved him. She had always loved him. Even now, when he was so angry with her that she barely recognized him, when he was so angry with her that she wasn't even sure she *liked* him, she loved him.

And she wanted to be his.

The first time he had kissed her, she had accepted his advances with a passive delight, but this time she was determined to be an active partner. She still couldn't quite believe that she was here, with him, and she certainly wasn't ready to let herself dream that he might ever be kissing her on a regular basis.

This might never happen again. She might never again feel the exquisite weight of him pressing against her, or the scandalous tickle of his tongue against hers.

She had one chance. One chance to make a memory that would have to last a lifetime. One chance to reach for bliss.

Tomorrow would be awful, knowing that he would find some other woman with whom to laugh and joke and even marry, but today . . .

Today was hers.

And by God, she was going to make this a kiss to remember.

She reached up and touched his hair. She was hesitant at first—just because she was determined to be an active, willing partner didn't mean she had a clue what she was doing. His lips were slowly easing all the reason and intelligence from her mind, but still, she couldn't quite help noticing that his hair felt exactly like Eloise's, which she had brushed countless times during their years of friendship. And heaven help her . . .

She giggled.

That got his attention, and he lifted his head, his lips touched by an amused smile. "I beg your pardon?" he queried.

She shook her head, trying to fight off her smile, knowing she was losing the battle.

"Oh, no, you must," he insisted. "I couldn't possibly continue without knowing the reason for the giggle."

She felt her cheeks burning, which struck her as ridiculously ill-timed. Here she was, completely misbehaving in the back of a carriage, and it was only *now* that she had the decency to blush?

"Tell me," he murmured, nibbling at her ear.

She shook her head.

His lips found the exact point where her pulse beat in her throat. "Tell me."

All she did—all she could do—was moan, arching her neck to give him greater access.

Her dress, which she hadn't even realized had been partially unbuttoned, slid down until her collarbone was exposed, and she watched with giddy fascination as his lips traced the line of it, until his entire face was nuzzled perilously close to her bosom.

"Will you tell me?" he whispered, grazing her skin with his teeth.

"Tell you what?" she gasped.

His lips were wicked, moving lower, then lower still. "Why you were laughing?"

For several seconds Penelope couldn't even remember what he was talking about.

His hand cupped her breast through her dress. "I'll torment you until you tell me," he threatened.

Penelope's answer was an arch of her back, settling her breast even more firmly in his grasp.

She liked his torment.

"I see," he murmured, simultaneously sliding her bodice down and moving his hand so that his palm grazed her nipple. "Then perhaps I'll"—his hand stilled, then lifted—"stop."

"No," she moaned.

"Then tell me."

She stared at her breast, mesmerized by the sight of it, bare and open to his gaze.

"Tell me," he whispered, blowing softly so that his breath brushed across her.

Something clenched inside Penelope, deep inside of her, in places that were never talked about.

"Colin, please," she begged.

He smiled, slow and lazy, satisfied and still somehow hungry. "Please what?" he asked.

"Touch me," she whispered.

His index finger slid along her shoulder. "Here?"

She shook her head frantically.

He trailed down the column of her neck. "Am I getting closer?" he murmured.

She nodded, her eyes never leaving her breast.

He found her nipple again, his fingers tracing slow, tantalizing spirals around it, then on it, and all the while she watched, her body growing tighter and tighter.

And all she could hear was her breath, hot and heavy from her lips.

Then—

"Colin!" His name flew from her mouth in a strangled gasp. Surely he couldn't—

His lips closed around her, and before she'd even felt more than the heat of him, she bucked off the bench in surprise, her hips pressing shamelessly against his, then settling back down as he ground against her, holding her immobile as he pleasured her.

"Oh, Colin, Colin," she gasped, her hands flying around to his back, pressing desperately into his muscles, wanting nothing other than to hold him and keep him and never let him go.

He yanked at his shirt, pulling it free from the waist of his breeches, and she followed his cue by slipping her hands under the fabric and running them along the hot skin of his back. She'd never touched a man this way; she'd never touched *anyone* like this, except maybe herself, and even then, it wasn't like she could easily reach her own back.

He groaned when she touched him, then tensed when her fingers skimmed along his skin. Her heart leaped. He liked this; he liked the way she was touching him. She hadn't the least clue what to do with herself, but he liked it just the same.

"You're perfect," he whispered against her skin, his lips blazing a trail back up to the underside of her chin.

His mouth claimed hers again, this time with increased fervor, and his hands slid underneath to cup her derriere, squeezing and kneading and pressing her up against his arousal.

"My God, I want you," he gasped, grinding his hips down. "I want to strip you bare and sink into you and never let you go."

Penelope groaned with desire, unable to believe how much pleasure she could feel from mere words. He made her feel wicked, naughty, and oh-so-desirable.

And she never wanted it to end.

"Oh, Penelope," he was groaning, his lips and hands growing more frantic. "Oh, Penelope. Oh, Penelope, oh—" He lifted his head. Very abruptly.

"Oh, God."

"What is it?" she asked, trying to lift the back of her head from the cushion.

"We've stopped."

It took her a moment to recognize the import of this. If they'd stopped, that meant they'd most likely reached their destination, which was . . .

Her home.

"Oh, God!" She started yanking at the bodice of her gown with frantic motions. "Can't we just ask the driver to keep going?"

She'd already proven herself a complete wanton. There seemed little harm at this point in adding "shameless" to her list of behaviors.

He grabbed the bodice for her and hauled it into place. "What is the possibility your mother won't have noticed my carriage in front of your house yet?"

"Fairly good, actually," she said, "but Briarly will have done."

"Your butler will recognize my carriage?" he asked in disbelief.

She nodded. "You came the other day. He always remembers things like that."

His lips twisted in a grimly determined manner. "Very well, then," he said. "Make yourself presentable."

"I can race up to my room," Penelope said. "No one will see me."

"I doubt that," he said ominously, tucking in his shirt and smoothing his hair.

"No, I assure you—"

"And I assure you," he said, leaping on top of her words. "You will be seen." He licked his fingers, then ran them through his hair. "Do I look presentable?"

"Yes," she lied. In truth, he looked rather flushed, with swollen lips, and hair that didn't remotely adhere to a current style.

"Good." He hopped down from the carriage and held his hand out to her.

"You're coming in as well?" she asked.

He looked at her as if she'd suddenly gone daft. "Of course."

She didn't move, too perplexed by his actions to give her legs the orders to step down. There was certainly no reason he had to accompany her inside. Propriety didn't really demand it, and—

"For God's sake, Penelope," he said, grabbing her hand and yanking her down. "Are you going to marry me or not?"

Chapter 14

S he hit the pavement.

Penelope was—in her opinion, at least—a bit more graceful than most people gave her credit for. She was a good dancer, could play the piano with her fingers arched perfectly, and could usually navigate a crowded room without bumping into an uncommon amount of people or furniture.

But when Colin made his rather matter-of-fact proposal, her foot—at the time halfway out of the carriage—found only air, her left hip found the curb, and her head found Colin's toes.

"Good God, Penelope," he exclaimed, crouching down. "Are you all right?"

"Just fine," she managed to get out, searching for

the hole in the ground that must have just opened up, so that she could crawl into it and die.

"Are you certain?"

"It's nothing, really," she replied, holding her cheek, which she was certain now sported a perfect imprint of the top of Colin's boot. "Just a bit surprised, that is all."

"Why?"

"Why?" she echoed.

"Yes, why?"

She blinked. Once, twice, then again. "Er, well, it might have to do with your mentioning marriage."

He yanked her unceremoniously to her feet, nearly dislocating her shoulder in the process. "Well, what did you think I would say?"

She stared at him in disbelief. Was he mad? "Not *that*," she finally replied.

"I'm not a complete boor," he muttered.

She brushed dust and pebbles off her sleeves. "I never said you were, I just—"

"I can assure you," he continued, now looking mortally offended, "that I do not behave as I did with a woman of your background without rendering a marriage proposal."

Penelope's mouth fell open, leaving her feeling rather like an owl.

"Don't you have a reply?" he demanded.

"I'm still trying to figure out what you said," she admitted.

He planted his hands on his hips and stared at her with a decided lack of indulgence.

"You must admit," she said, her chin dipping until she was regarding him rather dubiously through her lashes, "it did sound rather like you've, er—how did you say it—rendered marriage proposals before."

He scowled at her. "Of course I haven't. Now take my arm before it starts to rain."

She looked up at the clear blue sky.

"At the rate you're going," he said impatiently, "we'll be here for days."

"I . . . well . . ." She cleared her throat. "Surely you can forgive me my lack of composure in the face of such tremendous surprise."

"Now who's speaking in circles?" he muttered.

"I beg your pardon."

His hand tightened on her arm. "Let's just get going."

"Colin!" she nearly shrieked, tripping over her feet as she stumbled up the stairs. "Are you sure—"

"No time like the present," he said, almost jauntily. He seemed quite pleased with himself, which puzzled her, because she would have bet her entire fortune— and as Lady Whistledown, she'd amassed quite a fortune—that he had not intended to ask her to marry him until the moment his carriage had ground to a halt in front her house.

Perhaps not even until the words had left his lips.

He turned to her. "Do I need to knock?"

"No, I—"

He knocked anyway, or rather banged, if one wanted to be particular about it.

"Briarly," Penelope said through an attempted smile as the butler opened the door to receive them.

"Miss Penelope," he murmured, one brow rising in surprise. He nodded at Colin. "Mr. Bridgerton."

"Is Mrs. Featherington at home?" Colin asked brusquely.

"Yes, but—"

"Excellent." Colin barged in, pulling Penelope along with him. "Where is she?"

"In the drawing room, but I should tell you—"

But Colin was already halfway down the hall, Penelope one step behind him. (Not that she could be anywhere else, seeing as how his hand was wrapped rather tightly around her upper arm.)

"Mr. Bridgerton!" the butler yelled out, sounding slightly panicked.

Penelope twisted, even as her feet continued to follow Colin. Briarly never panicked. About anything. If he didn't think she and Colin ought to enter the drawing room, he had to have a very good reason.

Maybe even—

Oh, *no.*

Penelope dug in her heels, skidding along the hardwood floor as Colin dragged her along by the arm. "Colin," she said, gulping on the first syllable. "Colin!"

"What?" he asked, not breaking his stride.

"I really think—Aaack!" Her skidding heels hit the edge of the runner carpet, sending her flying forward.

He caught her neatly and set her on her feet. "What is it?"

She glanced nervously at the door to the drawing room. It was slightly ajar, but maybe there was enough noise inside so that her mother hadn't yet heard them approaching.

"Penelope . . ." Colin prompted impatiently.

"Er . . ." There was still time to escape, wasn't there? She looked frantically about, not that she was likely to find a solution to her problems anywhere in the hall.

"Penelope," Colin said, now tapping his foot, "what the devil is the matter?"

She looked back to Briarly, who simply shrugged his

shoulders. "This really might not be the best time to speak to my mother."

He raised one brow, looking rather like the butler had just seconds earlier. "You're not planning to refuse me, are you?"

"No, of course not," she said hastily, even though she hadn't truly accepted the fact that he even intended to offer for her.

"Then this is an excellent time," he stated, his tone inviting no further protest.

"But it's—"

"What?"

Tuesday, she thought miserably. And it was just past noon, which meant—

"Let's go," Colin said, striding forward, and before she could stop him, he pushed open the door.

Colin's first thought upon stepping into the drawing room was that the day, while certainly not proceeding in any manner he might have anticipated when he'd risen from bed that morning, was turning out to be a most excellent endeavor. Marriage to Penelope was an eminently sensible idea, and surprisingly appealing as well, if their recent encounter in the carriage was any indication.

His second thought was that he'd just entered his worst nightmare.

Because Penelope's mother was not alone in the drawing room. Every last Featherington, current and former, was there, along with assorted spouses and even a cat.

It was the most frightening assemblage of people Colin had ever witnessed. Penelope's family was . . . well . . . except for Felicity (whom he'd always held in some suspicion; how could one truly trust anyone who was such good friends with Hyacinth?), her family was . . . well . . .

He couldn't think of a good word for it. Certainly nothing complimentary (although he'd like to think he could have avoided an outright insult), and really, was there a word that effectively combined slightly dim, overly talkative, rather meddlesome, excruciatingly dull, and—and one couldn't forget this, not with Robert Huxley a recent addition to the clan—uncommonly loud.

So Colin just smiled. His great, big, friendly, slightly mischievous smile. It almost always worked, and today was no exception. The Featheringtons all smiled right back at him, and—thank God—said nothing.

At least not right away.

"Colin," Mrs. Featherington said with visible surprise. "How nice of you to bring Penelope home for our family meeting."

"Your family meeting?" he echoed. He looked to Penelope, who was standing next to him, looking rather ill.

"Every Tuesday," she said, smiling weakly. "Didn't I mention it?"

"No," he replied, even though it was obvious her question had been for the benefit of their audience. "No, you didn't mention it."

"Bridgerton!" bellowed Robert Huxley, who was married to Penelope's eldest sister Prudence.

"Huxley," Colin returned, taking a discreet step back. Best to protect his eardrums in case Penelope's brother-in-law decided to leave his post near the window.

Thankfully, Huxley stayed put, but Penelope's other brother-in-law, the well-meaning but vacant-minded Nigel Berbrooke, did cross the room, greeting Colin with a hearty slap on the back. "Wasn't expecting you," Berbrooke said jovially.

"No," Colin murmured, "I wouldn't think so."

"Just family, after all," Berbrooke said, "and you're not family. Not my family, at least."

"Not yet, anyway," Colin murmured, stealing a glance at Penelope. She was blushing.

Then he looked back at Mrs. Featherington, who looked as if she might faint from excitement. Colin groaned through his smile. He hadn't meant for her to hear his comment about possibly joining the family. For some reason he'd wanted to retain an element of surprise before he asked for Penelope's hand. If Portia Featherington knew his intentions ahead of time, she'd likely twist the whole thing around (in her mind, at least) so that she had somehow orchestrated the match herself.

And for some reason, Colin found that exceedingly distasteful.

"I hope I'm not intruding," he said to Mrs. Featherington.

"No, of course not," she said quickly. "We are delighted to have you here, at a *family* gathering." But she looked rather odd, not precisely undecided about his presence there, but certainly unsure of what her next move should be. She was chewing on her lower lip, and then she darted a furtive glance at Felicity, of all people.

Colin turned to Felicity. She was looking at Penelope, a small secret smile fixed to her face. Penelope was glaring at her mother, her mouth twisted into an irritated grimace.

Colin's gaze went from Featherington to Featherington to Featherington. Something was clearly sim-

322 • JULIA QUINN

mering under the surface here and if he weren't trying to figure out (A) how to avoid being trapped into conversation with Penelope's relations while (B) somehow managing to issue a proposal of marriage at the same time—well, he'd be rather curious as to what was causing all the secret, underhanded glances being tossed back and forth between the Featherington women.

Mrs. Featherington cast one last glance at Felicity, did a little gesture that Colin could have sworn meant, *Sit up straight,* then fixed her attention on Colin. "Won't you sit down?" she asked, smiling widely and patting the seat next to her on the sofa.

"Of course," he murmured, because there was really no getting out of it now. He still had to ask for Penelope's hand in marriage, and even if he didn't particularly want to do it in front of every last Featherington (and their two inane spouses), he was stuck here, at least until a polite opportunity to make his escape presented itself.

He turned and offered his arm to the woman he intended to make his bride. "Penelope?"

"Er, yes, of course," she stammered, placing her hand at the crook of his elbow.

"Oh, yes," Mrs. Featherington said, as if she'd completely forgotten about her daughter's presence. "Terribly sorry, Penelope. Didn't see you. Won't you please go and ask Cook to increase our order? We'll surely need more food with Mr. Bridgerton here."

"Of course," Penelope said, the corners of her lips quivering.

"Can't she ring for it?" Colin asked loudly.

"What?" Mrs. Featherington said distractedly. "Well, I suppose she could, but it would take longer, and Penelope doesn't mind, do you?"

Penelope gave her head a little shake.

"I mind," Colin said.

Mrs. Featherington let out a little "Oh" of surprise, then said, "Very well. Penelope, er, why don't you sit right there?" She motioned to a chair that was not quite situated to be a part of the inner conversation circle.

Felicity, who was seated directly across from her mother, jumped up. "Penelope, please take my seat."

"No," Mrs. Featherington said firmly. "You have been feeling under the weather, Felicity. You need to sit."

Colin thought Felicity looked the picture of perfect health, but she sat back down.

"Penelope," Prudence said loudly, from over by the window. "I need to speak with you."

Penelope glanced helplessly from Colin to Prudence to Felicity to her mother.

Colin yanked her in closer. "I need to speak with her as well," he said smoothly.

"Right, well, I suppose there is room for both of you," Mrs. Featherington said, scooting over on the sofa.

Colin was caught between the good manners that had been drummed into his head since birth and the overwhelming urge to strangle the woman who would someday be his mother-in-law. He had no idea why she was treating Penelope like some sort of lesser-favored stepchild, but really, it had to stop.

"What brings you this way?" yelled Robert Huxley.

Colin touched his ears—he couldn't help himself—then said, "I was—"

"Oh, goodness," fluttered Mrs. Featherington, "we do not mean to interrogate our guest, do we?"

Colin hadn't really thought Huxley's question constituted an interrogation, but he didn't really want to insult Mrs. Featherington by saying so, so he merely nodded and said something completely meaningless like, "Yes, well, of course."

"Of course what?" asked Philippa.

Philippa was married to Nigel Berbrooke, and Colin had always thought it was a rather good match, indeed.

"I'm sorry?" he queried.

"You said, 'Of course,' " Philippa said. "Of course what?"

"I don't know," Colin said.

"Oh. Well, then, why did you—"

"Philippa," Mrs. Featherington said loudly, "perhaps you should fetch the food, since Penelope has forgotten to ring for it."

"Oh, I'm sorry," Penelope said quickly, starting to rise to her feet.

"Don't worry," Colin said through a smooth smile, grabbing hold of her hand and yanking her back down. "Your mother said Prudence could go."

"Philippa," Penelope said.

"What about Philippa?"

"She said Philippa could go, not Prudence."

He wondered what had happened to her brain, because somewhere between his carriage and this sofa, it had clearly disappeared. "Does it matter?" he asked.

"No, not really, but—"

"Felicity," Mrs. Featherington interrupted, "why don't you tell Mr. Bridgerton about your watercolors?"

For the life of him, Colin couldn't imagine a less interesting topic (except, maybe, for Philippa's watercolors), but he nonetheless turned to the youngest Featherington with a friendly smile and asked, "And how are your watercolors?"

But Felicity, bless her heart, gave him a rather friendly smile herself and said nothing but, "I imagine they're fine, thank you."

Mrs. Featherington looked as if she'd just swallowed a live eel, then exclaimed, "Felicity!"

"Yes?" Felicity said sweetly.

"You didn't tell him that you'd won an award." She turned to Colin. "Felicity's watercolors are very unique." She turned back to Felicity. "Do tell Mr. Bridgerton about your award."

"Oh, I don't imagine he is interested in that."

"Of course he is," Mrs. Featherington ground out.

Normally, Colin would have chimed in with, *Of course I am,* since he was, after all, an exceedingly affable fellow, but doing so would have validated Mrs. Featherington's statement and, perhaps more critically, ruined Felicity's good fun.

And Felicity appeared to be having a *lot* of fun. "Philippa," she said, "weren't you going to go after the food?"

"Oh, right," Philippa replied. "Forgot all about it. I do that a lot. Come along, Nigel. You can keep me company."

"Right-o!" Nigel beamed. And then he and Philippa left the room, giggling all the way.

Colin reaffirmed his conviction that the Berbrooke-Featherington match had been a good one, indeed.

"I think I shall go out to the garden," Prudence suddenly announced, taking hold of her husband's arm. "Penelope, why don't you come with me?"

Penelope opened her mouth a few seconds before she figured out what to say, leaving her looking a little bit like a confused fish (but in Colin's opinion a rather fetching fish, if such a thing were possible). Finally, her chin took on a resolute mien, and she said, "I don't think so, Prudence."

"Penelope!" Mrs. Featherington exclaimed.

"I need you to show me something," Prudence ground out.

"I really think I'm needed here," Penelope replied. "I can join you later this afternoon, if you like."

"I need you *now.*"

Penelope looked to her sister in surprise, clearly not expecting quite so much resistance. "I'm sorry, Prudence," she reiterated. "I believe I'm needed here."

"Nonsense," Mrs. Featherington said breezily. "Felicity and I can keep Mr. Bridgerton company."

Felicity jumped to her feet. "Oh, no!" she exclaimed, her eyes round and innocent. "I forgot something."

"What," Mrs. Featherington asked between her teeth, "could you possibly have forgotten?"

"Uhh . . . my watercolors." She turned to Colin with a sweet, mischievous smile. "You did want to see them, didn't you?"

"Of course," he murmured, deciding he very much liked Penelope's younger sister. "Seeing as how they are so unique."

"One might say they are uniquely ordinary," Felicity said with an overly earnest nod.

"Penelope," Mrs. Featherington said, obviously trying to hide her annoyance, "would you be so kind as to fetch Felicity's watercolors?"

"Penelope doesn't know where they are," Felicity said quickly.

"Why don't you tell her?"

"For God's sake," Colin finally exploded, "let Felicity go. I need a private moment with you, anyway."

Silence reigned. It was the first time Colin Bridgerton had ever lost his temper in public. Beside him, Colin heard Penelope let out a little gasp, but when he glanced at her, she was hiding a tiny smile behind her hand.

And that made him feel ridiculously good.

"A private moment?" Mrs. Featherington echoed, her hand fluttering to her chest. She glanced over at

Prudence and Robert, who were still standing by the window. They immediately left the room, although not without a fair bit of grumbling on Prudence's part.

"Penelope," Mrs. Featherington said, "perhaps you should accompany Felicity."

"Penelope will remain," Colin ground out.

"Penelope?" Mrs. Featherington asked doubtfully.

"Yes," he said slowly, in case she still didn't understand his meaning, "Penelope."

"But—"

Colin gave her such a glare that she actually drew back and folded her hands in her lap.

"I'm gone!" Felicity chirped, sailing out of the room. But before she closed the door behind her, Colin saw her give a quick wink to Penelope.

And Penelope smiled, love for her younger sister shining clearly in her eyes.

Colin relaxed. He hadn't realized just how tense Penelope's misery was making him. And she was definitely miserable. Good God, he couldn't wait to remove her from the bosom of her ridiculous family.

Mrs. Featherington's lips spread into a feeble attempt at a smile. She looked from Colin to Penelope and back again, and then finally said, "You desired a word?"

"Yes," he replied, eager to get this done with. "I

would be honored if you would grant me your daughter's hand in marriage."

For a moment Mrs. Featherington made no reaction. Then her eyes grew round, her mouth grew round, her body—well, her body was already round—and she clapped her hands together, unable to say anything other than, "Oh! Oh!"

And then, "Felicity! Felicity!"

Felicity?

Portia Featherington jumped to her feet, ran to the door and actually screamed like a fishwife. "Felicity! Felicity!"

"Oh, Mother," Penelope moaned, closing her eyes.

"Why are you summoning Felicity?" Colin asked, rising to his feet.

Mrs. Featherington turned to him quizzically. "Don't you want to marry Felicity?"

Colin actually thought he might be sick. "No, for God's sake, I don't want to marry Felicity," he snapped. "If I'd wanted to marry Felicity, I'd hardly have sent her upstairs for her bloody watercolors, would I?"

Mrs. Featherington swallowed uncomfortably. "Mr. Bridgerton," she said, wringing her hands together. "I don't understand."

He stared at her in horror, which then turned to disgust. "Penelope," he said, grabbing her hand and yanking her until she was pressed close to his side. "I want to marry Penelope."

"Penelope?" Mrs. Featherington echoed. "But—"

"But what?" he interrupted, his voice pure menace.

"But—but—"

"It's all right, Colin," Penelope said hastily. "I—"

"No, it is not all right," he exploded. "I've never given any indication I'm the least bit interested in Felicity."

Felicity appeared in the doorway, clapped her hand over her mouth, and quickly disappeared, wisely shutting the door behind her.

"Yes," Penelope said placatingly, shooting a quick look at her mother, "but Felicity is unmarried, and—"

"So are you," he pointed out.

"I know, but I'm old, and—"

"And Felicity is an *infant*," he spat. "Good God, marrying her would be like marrying Hyacinth."

"Er, except for the incest," Penelope said.

He gave her an extremely unamused look.

"Right," she said, mostly to fill the silence. "It's just a terrible misunderstanding, isn't it?"

No one said anything. Penelope looked at Colin pleadingly. "Isn't it?"

"It certainly is," he muttered.

She turned to her mother. "Mama?"

"Penelope?" she murmured, and Penelope knew that her mother wasn't asking her a question; rather, she was still expressing her disbelief that Colin would want to marry her.

And oh, but it hurt so much. You'd think she'd be used to it by now.

"I would like to marry Mr. Bridgerton," Penelope said, trying to summon up as much quiet dignity as she could manage. "He asked me, and I said yes."

"Well, of course you would say yes," her mother retorted. "You'd have to be an idiot to say no."

"Mrs. Featherington," Colin said tightly, "I suggest you begin treating my future wife with a bit more respect."

"Colin, it's not necessary," Penelope said, placing her hand on his arm, but the truth was—her heart was soaring. He might not love her, but he cared about her. No man could defend a woman with such fierce protectiveness without caring for her a little.

"It *is* necessary," he returned. "For God's sake, Penelope, I arrived with you. I made it abundantly clear that I required your presence in the room, and I practically shoved Felicity out the door to fetch her watercolors. Why on earth would anyone think I wanted Felicity?"

Mrs. Featherington opened and closed her mouth

several times before finally saying, "I love Penelope, of course, but—"

"But do you know her?" Colin shot back. "She's lovely and intelligent and has a fine sense of humor. Who wouldn't want to marry a woman like that?"

Penelope would have melted to the floor if she weren't already holding on to his hand. "Thank you," she whispered, not caring if her mother heard her, not even really caring if Colin heard her. Somehow she needed to say the words for herself.

Not what she thought she was.

Lady Danbury's face swam before her eyes, her expression warm and just a little bit cunning.

Something more. Maybe Penelope was something more, and maybe Colin was the only other person to realize that as well.

It made her love him all the more.

Her mother cleared her throat, then stepped forward and gave Penelope a hug. It was, at first, a hesitant embrace on both of their parts, but then Portia tightened her arms around her thirdborn daughter, and with a choked cry, Penelope found herself returning the hug in equal measure.

"I do love you, Penelope," Portia said, "and I am very pleased for you." She drew back and wiped a tear from her eye. "I shall be lonely without you, of course, since I'd assumed we would grow old together, but this is what's best for you, and that, I suppose, is what being a mother is all about."

Penelope let out a loud sniffle, then blindly reached for Colin's handkerchief, which he had already pulled from his pocket and was holding in front of her.

"You'll learn someday," Portia said, patting her on the arm. She turned to Colin and said, "We are delighted to welcome you to the family."

He nodded, not terribly warmly, but Penelope thought he made a rather nice effort considering how angry he'd been just moments earlier.

Penelope smiled and squeezed his hand, aware that she was about to embark upon the adventure of her life.

Chapter 15

"You know," Eloise said, three days after Colin and Penelope made their surprise announcement, "it's really a pity that Lady Whistledown has retired, because this would have been the coup of the decade."

"Certainly from Lady Whistledown's viewpoint," Penelope murmured, lifting her teacup to her lips and keeping her eyes trained on the wall clock in Lady Bridgerton's informal drawing room. Better not to look at Eloise directly. She had a way of noticing secrets in a person's eyes.

It was funny. Penelope had gone years without worrying that Eloise would discover the truth about Lady Whistledown. At least, not worrying overmuch. But now that Colin knew, it somehow felt as if her secret were floating about in the air, like particles of dust just waiting to form into a cloud of knowledge.

Maybe the Bridgertons were like dominoes. Once one found out, it was only a matter of time before they all fell.

"What do you mean?" Eloise asked, breaking into Penelope's nervous thoughts.

"If I recall correctly," Penelope said, very carefully, "she once wrote that she would have to retire if I ever married a Bridgerton."

Eloise's eyes bugged out. "She did?"

"Or something like that," Penelope said.

"You're joking," Eloise said, making a "pffft" sort of sound as she waved her hand dismissively. "She would never have been that cruel."

Penelope coughed, not really thinking that she could end the topic by faking a biscuit crumb in her throat, but trying nonetheless.

"No, really," Eloise persisted. "What did she say?"

"I don't recall, precisely."

"Try."

Penelope stalled by setting her cup down and reaching for another biscuit. They were alone for tea, which was odd. But Lady Bridgerton had dragged Colin off on some errand regarding the upcoming wedding—set for only a month hence!—and Hyacinth was off shopping with Felicity, who had, upon hearing Penelope's news, thrown her arms around her sister and shrieked her delight until Penelope's ears had gone numb.

As far as sisterly moments went, it had been something wonderful.

"Well," Penelope said, chewing on a bite of biscuit, "I believe she said that if I married a Bridgerton, it would be the end of the world as she knew it, and as she wouldn't be able to make heads or tails of such a world, she would have to retire immediately."

Eloise stared at her for a moment. "That's not a precise recollection?"

"One doesn't forget things like that," Penelope demurred.

"Hmmmph." Eloise's nose wrinkled with disdain. "Well, that was rather horrid of her, I must say. Now I doubly wish she were still writing, because she would have to eat an entire gaggle of crow."

"Do crows gather in gaggles?"

"I don't know," Eloise replied promptly, "but they should."

"You're a very good friend, Eloise," Penelope said quietly.

"Yes," Eloise said with an affected sigh, "I know. The very best."

Penelope smiled. Eloise's breezy reply made it clear

that she wasn't in the mood for emotion or nostalgia. Which was fine. There was a time and a place for everything. Penelope had said what she wanted to say, and she knew that Eloise returned the sentiment, even if she preferred to joke and tease at that moment.

"I must confess, though," Eloise said, reaching for another biscuit, "you and Colin did surprise me."

"We surprised me as well," Penelope admitted wryly.

"Not that I'm not delighted," Eloise hastened to add. "There is no one I'd rather have as a sister. Well, aside from the ones I already have, of course. And if I'd ever dreamed the two of you were inclined in that direction, I'm sure I would have meddled horribly."

"I know," Penelope said, laughter forcing her lips up at the corners.

"Yes, well"—Eloise waved the comment away—"I'm not known for minding my own business."

"What's that on your fingers?" Penelope asked, leaning forward for a better look.

"What? That? Oh, nothing." But she settled her hands in her lap nonetheless.

"It's not nothing," Penelope said. "Let me see. It looks like ink."

"Well, of course it does. It *is* ink."

"Then why didn't you say so when I asked?"

"Because," Eloise said pertly, "it's none of your business."

Penelope drew back in shock at Eloise's sharp tone. "I'm terribly sorry," she said stiffly. "I had no idea it was such a sensitive subject."

"Oh, it's not," Eloise said quickly. "Don't be silly. It's just that I'm clumsy and I can't write without getting ink all over my fingers. I suppose I could wear gloves, but then *they'd* be stained, and I'd be forever replacing them, and I can assure you that I have no wish to spend my entire allowance—meager as it is— on gloves."

Penelope stared at her through her lengthy explanation, then asked, "What were you writing?"

"Nothing," Eloise said dismissively. "Just letters."

Penelope could tell from Eloise's brisk tone that she didn't particularly want to subject the topic to further exploration, but she was being so uncharacteristically evasive that Penelope couldn't resist asking, "To whom?"

"The letters?"

"Yes," Penelope replied, even though she thought that was rather obvious.

"Oh, no one."

"Well, unless they're a diary, they're not to *no one*," Penelope said, impatience adding a short tinge to her voice.

Eloise gave her a vaguely affronted look. "You're rather nosy today."

"Only because you're being so evasive."

"They're just to Francesca," Eloise said with a little snort.

"Well, then, why didn't you say so?"

Eloise crossed her arms. "Perhaps I didn't appreciate your questioning me."

Penelope's mouth fell open. She couldn't remember the last time she and Eloise had had anything even remotely approaching a row. "Eloise," she said, her shock showing in her voice, "what is wrong?"

"Nothing is wrong."

"I know that's not true."

Eloise said nothing, just pursed her lips and glanced toward the window, a clear attempt to end the conversation.

"Are you angry with me?" Penelope persisted.

"Why would I be angry with you?"

"I don't know, but it's clear that you are."

Eloise let out a little sigh. "I'm not angry."

"Well, you're *some*thing."

"I'm just . . . I'm just . . ." She shook her head.

"I don't know what I am. Restless, I suppose. Out of sorts."

Penelope was silent as she digested that, then said quietly, "Is there anything I can do?"

"No." Eloise smiled wryly. "If there were, you can be sure I'd have already asked it of you."

Penelope felt something that was almost a laugh rising within her. How like Eloise to make such a comment.

"I suppose it's . . ." Eloise began, her chin lifting in thought. "No, never mind."

"No," Penelope said, reaching out and taking her friend's hand. "Tell me."

Eloise pulled her hand free and looked away. "You'll think I'm silly."

"Maybe," Penelope said with a smile, "but you'll still be my very closest friend."

"Oh, Penelope, but I'm not," Eloise said sadly. "I'm not worthy of it."

"Eloise, don't talk such madness. I'd have gone right-out insane trying to navigate London and society and the *ton* without you."

Eloise smiled. "We did have fun, didn't we?"

"Well, yes, when I was with you," Penelope admitted. "The rest of the time I was bloody miserable."

"Penelope! I don't believe I've ever heard you curse before."

Penelope gave her a sheepish smile. "It slipped out. And besides, I couldn't possibly think of a better adjective to describe life for a wallflower among the *ton*."

Eloise let out an unexpected chuckle. "Now, that's a book I would like to read: *A Wallflower Among the Ton*."

"Not unless you're given to tragedies."

"Oh, come, now, it couldn't be a tragedy. It would have to be a romance. You're getting your happy ending, after all."

Penelope smiled. As strange as it was, she *was* getting her happy ending. Colin had been a lovely and attentive fiancé, at least for the three days that he'd been playing that role. And it couldn't have been particularly easy; they'd been subject to more speculation and scrutiny than Penelope could have imagined.

She wasn't surprised, though; when she (as Lady Whistledown) had written that the world would end as she knew it if a Featherington married a Bridgerton, she rather thought she'd been echoing a prevalent sentiment.

To say that the *ton* had been shocked by Penelope's engagement would have been an understatement, indeed.

But much as Penelope liked to anticipate and reflect upon her upcoming marriage, she was still a bit disturbed about Eloise's strange mood. "Eloise," she said seriously, "I want you to tell me what has you so upset."

Eloise sighed. "I'd hoped you'd forgotten about it."

"I've learned tenacity from the master," Penelope commented.

That made Eloise smile, but only for a moment. "I feel so disloyal," she said.

"What have you done?"

"Oh, nothing." She patted her heart. "It's all inside. I—" She stopped, looked to the side, her eyes settling on the fringed corner of the carpet, but Penelope suspected that she didn't see much of anything. At least nothing beyond what was rumbling about in her mind.

"I'm so happy for you," Eloise said, the words tumbling forth in odd bursts, punctuated by awkward pauses. "And I honestly think I can really, truly say that I'm not jealous. But at the same time . . ."

Penelope waited for Eloise to collect her thoughts. Or maybe she was collecting her courage.

"At the same time," she said, so softly that Penelope could barely hear her, "I suppose I always thought you'd be a spinster right along with me. I've chosen this life. I know that I have. I could have married."

"I know," Penelope said quietly.

"But I never did, because it never seemed right, and I didn't want to settle for anything less than what my brothers and sister have. And now Colin, too," she said, motioning toward Penelope.

Penelope didn't mention that Colin had never said he loved her. It didn't seem like the right time, or, frankly, the sort of thing she cared to share. Besides, even if he didn't love her, she still thought he cared about her, and that was enough.

"I would never have wanted you *not* to marry," Eloise explained, "I just never thought you would." She closed her eyes, looking quite agonized. "That came out all wrong. I've insulted you terribly."

"No, you haven't," Penelope said, meaning it. "I never thought I would marry, either."

Eloise nodded sadly. "And somehow, it made it all . . . all right. I was almost twenty-eight and unmarried, and you were already twenty-eight and unmarried, and we'd always have each other. But now you have Colin."

"I still have you, too. At least I hope I do."

"Of course you do," Eloise said fervently. "But it won't be the same. You must cleave unto your husband. Or at least that's what they all say," she added with a slightly mischievous spark in her eyes. "Colin will come first, and that is how it should be. And frankly," she added, her smile growing a bit sly, "I'd have to kill you if he didn't. He *is* my favorite brother, after all. It really wouldn't do for him to have a disloyal wife."

Penelope laughed out loud at that.

"Do you hate me?" Eloise asked.

Penelope shook her head. "No," she said softly. "If anything I love you all the more, because I know how difficult it must have been to be honest with me about this."

"I'm so glad you said that," Eloise said with a loud, dramatic sigh. "I was terrified you'd say that the only solution would be for me to find myself a husband as well."

The thought had crossed Penelope's mind, but she shook her head and said, "Of course not."

"Good. Because my mother has been saying it constantly."

Penelope smiled wryly. "I'd be surprised if she hadn't."

"Good afternoon, ladies!"

The two women looked up to see Colin entering the room. Penelope's heart did a little flip upon seeing him, and she found herself oddly out of breath. Her heart had been doing little flips for years whenever he walked into a room, but it was somehow different now, more intense.

Perhaps because she *knew.*

Knew what it was like to be with him, to be wanted by him.

To know that he would be her husband.

Her heart flipped again.

Colin let out a loud groan. "You ate all the food?"

"There was only one small plate of biscuits," Eloise said in their defense.

"That's not what I was led to believe," Colin grumbled.

Penelope and Eloise shared a glance, then both burst out laughing.

"What?" Colin demanded, leaning down to press a quick, dutiful kiss on Penelope's cheek.

"You sounded so sinister," Eloise explained. "It's just food."

"It's never just food," Colin said, plopping down in a chair.

Penelope was still wondering when her cheek would stop tingling.

"So," he said, taking a half-eaten biscuit off of Eloise's plate, "what were you two talking about?"

"Lady Whistledown," Eloise said promptly.

Penelope choked on her tea.

"Were you?" Colin said softly, but Penelope detected a definite edge in his voice.

"Yes," Eloise said. "I was telling Penelope that it is really too bad she's retired, since your engagement would have been quite the most newsworthy piece of gossip we've had all year."

"Interesting how that works out," Colin murmured.

"Mmmm," Eloise agreed, "and she surely would have devoted an entire column just to your engagement ball tomorrow night."

Penelope did not lower her teacup from her mouth.

"Do you want some more?" Eloise asked her.

Penelope nodded and handed her the cup, although she very much missed having it in front of her face as a shield. She knew that Eloise had blurted out Lady Whistledown's name because she did not want Colin to know that she had mixed feelings about his marriage, but still, Penelope fervently wished that Eloise had said anything else in reply to Colin's question.

"Why don't you ring for more food?" Eloise asked Colin.

"Already did so," he answered. "Wickham intercepted me in the hall and asked if I was hungry." He popped the last bite of Eloise's biscuit into his mouth. "Wise man, that Wickham."

"Where did you go today, Colin?" Penelope asked, eager to get the topic firmly off of Lady Whistledown.

He gave his head a beleaguered shake. "Devil if I know. Mother dragged me from shop to shop."

"Aren't you thirty-three years old?" Eloise inquired sweetly.

He answered her with a scowl.

"Just thought you'd be beyond the age of having Mother drag you about, that's all," she murmured.

"Mother will be dragging all of us about when we're doddering old fools, and you know it," he replied. "Besides, she's so delighted to see me married, I really can't bring myself to spoil her fun."

Penelope sighed. This had to be why she loved the man. Anyone who treated his mother so well would surely be an excellent husband.

"And how are your wedding preparations coming along?" Colin asked Penelope.

She hadn't meant to pull a face, but she did, anyway. "I have never been so exhausted in all my life," she admitted.

He reached over and grabbed a large crumb off of her plate. "We should elope."

"Oh, could we *really?*" Penelope asked, the words flying from her lips in an unsummoned rush.

He blinked. "Actually, I was joking, mostly, although it does seem a prime idea."

"I shall arrange for a ladder," Eloise said, clapping her hands together, "so that you might climb to her room and steal her away."

"There's a tree," Penelope said. "Colin will have no difficulty with it."

"Good God," he said, "you're not serious, are you?"

"No," she sighed. "But I could be. If you were."

"I can't be. Do you know what it would do to my mother?" He rolled his eyes. "Not to mention yours."

Penelope groaned. "I know."

"She'd hunt me down and kill me," Colin said.

"Mine or yours?"

"Both. They'd join forces." He craned his neck toward the door. "*Where* is the food?"

"You just got here, Colin," Eloise said. "Give them time."

"And here I thought Wickham a sorcerer," he grumbled, "able to conjure food with the snap of his hand."

"Here you are, sir!" came Wickham's voice as he sailed into the room with a large tray.

"See?" Colin said, raising his brows first at Eloise and then at Penelope. "I told you so."

"Why," Penelope asked, "do I sense that I will be hearing those words from your lips far too many times in my future?"

"Most likely because you will," Colin replied. "You'll soon learn"—he shot her an extremely cheeky grin—"that I am almost always right."

"Oh, *please*," Eloise groaned.

"I may have to side with Eloise on this one," Penelope said.

"Against your husband?" He placed a hand on his heart (while the other one reached for a sandwich). "I'm wounded."

"You're not my husband yet."

Colin turned to Eloise. "The kitten has claws."

Eloise raised her brows. "You didn't realize that before you proposed?"

"Of course I did," he said, taking a bite of his sandwich. "I just didn't think she'd use them on me."

And then he looked at her with such a hot, masterful expression that Penelope's bones went straight to water.

"Well," Eloise announced, rising quite suddenly to her feet, "I think I shall allow you two soon-to-be-newlyweds a moment or two of privacy."

"How positively forward-thinking of you," Colin murmured.

Eloise looked to him with a peevish twist to her mouth. "Anything for you, dear brother. Or rather," she added, her expression growing arch, "anything for Penelope."

Colin stood and turned to his betrothed, "I seem to be slipping down the pecking order."

Penelope just smiled behind her teacup and said, "I am making it my policy never to get in the middle of a Bridgerton spat."

"Oh ho!" Eloise chortled. "You'll not be able to keep to that one, I'm afraid, Mrs. Soon-to-be-Bridgerton. Besides," she added with a wicked grin, "if you think this is a spat, I can't wait until you see us in full form."

"You mean I haven't?" Penelope asked.

Both Eloise and Colin shook their heads in a way that made her extremely fearful.

Oh, dear.

"Is there something I should know?" Penelope asked.

Colin grinned rather wolfishly. "It's too late now."

Penelope gave Eloise a helpless glance, but all she did was laugh as she left the room, closing the door firmly behind her.

"Now, *that* was nice of Eloise," Colin murmured.

"What?" Penelope asked innocently.

His eyes gleamed. "The door."

"The door? Oh!" she yelped. "The door."

Colin smiled, moving over to the sofa beside her. There was something rather delightful about Penelope on a rainy afternoon. He'd hardly seen her since they'd become engaged—wedding plans had a way of doing that to a couple—and yet she'd not been out of his thoughts, even as he slept.

Funny how that happened. He'd spent years not really ever thinking about her unless she was standing in front of his face, and now she had permeated his every last thought.

His every last desire.

How had this happened?

When had it happened?

And did it really matter? Maybe the only important thing was that he wanted her and she was—or at least she would be—his. Once he put his ring on her finger, the hows, whys, and whens would become irrelevant, provided that this madness he felt never went away.

He touched his finger to her chin, tipping her face up to the light. Her eyes shone with anticipation, and her lips—dear God, how was it possible that the men of London had never noticed how perfect they were?

He smiled. This was a permanent madness. And he couldn't have been more pleased.

Colin had never been opposed to marriage. He'd simply been opposed to a dull marriage. He wasn't picky; he just wanted passion and friendship and intellectual conversation and a good laugh every now and then. A wife from whom he wouldn't want to stray.

Amazingly, he seemed to have found that in Penelope.

All he needed to do now was make sure her Big Secret remained just that. A secret.

Because he didn't think he could bear the pain he'd see in her eyes if she were cast out of society.

"Colin?" she whispered, her breath quivering across her lips, making him *really* want to kiss her.

He leaned in. "Hmmm?"

"You were so quiet."

"Just thinking."

"About what?"

He gave her an indulgent smile. "You really have been spending too much time with my sister."

"What does that mean?" she asked, her lips twitching in such a way that he knew she'd never feel any compunction at poking fun at him. She would keep him on his toes, this woman.

"You seem," he said, "to have developed a certain penchant for persistence."

"Tenacity?"

"That, too."

"But that's a good thing."

Their lips were still mere inches apart, but the urge to continue the teasing conversation was too strong. "When you're persistently avowing your obedience for your husband," he murmured, "that's a good thing."

"Oh, really?"

His chin dipped into the barest hint of a nod. "And when you're tenaciously holding on to my shoulders when I'm kissing you, that's a good thing as well."

Her dark eyes widened so delightfully that he had to add, "Don't you think?"

And then she surprised him.

"Like this?" she asked, placing her hands on his shoulders. Her tone was daring, her eyes pure flirtation.

Lord, he loved that she surprised him.

"That's a start," he said. "You might have to"—he moved one of his hands to cover hers, pressing her fingers into his skin—"hold me a little more tenaciously."

"I see," she murmured. "So what you're saying is that I should never let go?"

He thought about that for a moment. "Yes," he answered, realizing that there was a deeper meaning in her words, whether she'd intended it or not. "That's exactly what I'm saying."

And then words were simply not enough. He brought

his lips to hers, remaining gentle for barely a second before his hunger overtook him. He kissed her with a passion he hadn't even known he possessed. It wasn't about desire—or at least it wasn't *just* about desire.

It was about need.

It was about a strange sensation, hot and fierce inside of him, urging him to lay claim to her, to somehow brand her as his.

He wanted her desperately, and he had absolutely no idea how he could possibly make it through an entire month before the wedding.

"Colin?" Penelope gasped, just as he was easing her down onto her back on the sofa.

He was kissing her jaw, and then her neck, and his lips were far too busy for anything other than a low, "Mmm?"

"We're—Oh!"

He smiled, even as he nipped her earlobe gently with his teeth. If she could finish a sentence, then he clearly wasn't befuddling her as much as he ought.

"You were saying?" he murmured, then kissed her deeply on the mouth, just to torture her.

He lifted his lips off hers just long enough for her to say, "I just—" and then he kissed her again, reeling with pleasure when she groaned with desire.

"I'm sorry," he said, scooting his hands under the hem of her dress and then using them to do all sorts of wicked things to her calves, "you were saying?"

"I was?" she asked, her eyes glazed.

He moved his hands higher, until they were tickling the back of her knee. "You were saying *something*," he said, pressing his hips against her because he honestly thought he would burst into flame at that very moment if he did not. "I think," he whispered, sliding his hand over the soft skin of her thigh, "that you were going to say that you wanted me to touch you *here*."

She gasped, then groaned, then somehow managed to say, "I don't think that was what I was going to say."

He grinned against her neck. "Are you sure?"

She nodded.

"So then you want me to stop?"

She shook her head. Frantically.

He could take her now, he realized. He could make love to her right there on his mother's sofa and not only would she let him, she would enjoy herself in every way a woman should.

It wouldn't be a conquest, it wouldn't even be seduction.

It would be more than that. Maybe even . . .

Love.

Colin froze.

"Colin?" she whispered, opening her eyes.

Love?

It wasn't possible.

"Colin?"

Or maybe it was.

"Is something wrong?"

It wasn't that he feared love, or didn't believe in it. He just hadn't . . . expected it.

He'd always thought love would hit a man like a thunderbolt, that one day you'd be loitering about at some party, bored to tears, and then you'd see a woman, and you'd know instantly that your life would be changed forever. That was what had happened to his brother Benedict, and heaven knew that he and his wife Sophie were blissfully happy rusticating away in the country.

But this thing with Penelope . . . it had crept up on him. The change had been slow, almost lethargic, and if it was love, well . . .

If it was love, wouldn't he *know*?

He watched her closely, curiously, thinking that maybe he'd find his answer in her eyes, or the sweep of her hair, or the way the bodice of her gown hung slightly crookedly. Maybe if he watched her long enough, he'd know.

"Colin?" she whispered, starting to sound slightly anxious.

He kissed her again, this time with a fierce determination. If this was love, wouldn't it become obvious when they kissed?

But if his mind and body were working separately, then the kiss was clearly in league with his body, because while his mind's confusion remained just as blurry as ever, his body's need was brought into sharper focus.

Hell, now he was in pain. And he really couldn't do anything about it here in his mother's drawing room, even if Penelope would have been a willing participant.

He pulled back, letting his hand slip down her leg toward the edge of her skirt. "We can't do this here."

"I know," she said, sounding so sad that his hand stilled on her knee, and he almost lost his resolve to do the right thing and mind the dictates of propriety.

He thought hard and fast. It was possible that he could make love to her and no one would walk in on them. Heaven knew that in his current state, it would be an embarrassingly fast endeavor, anyway.

"When is the wedding?" he growled.

"A month."

"What would it take to change that to a fortnight?"

She thought about that for a moment. "Bribery or blackmail. Maybe both. Our mothers will not be easily swayed."

He groaned, letting his hips sink against hers for

one delicious moment before heaving himself off. He couldn't take her now. She was going to be his wife. There would be plenty of time for midday tumbles on illicit sofas, but he owed it to her to use a bed for the first time, at least.

"Colin?" she asked, straightening her dress and smoothing her hair, even though there was no way she was going to make the latter look anything even approaching presentable without a mirror, hairbrush, and maybe even a maid. "Is something wrong?"

"I want you," he whispered.

She looked up at him, startled.

"I just wanted you to know that," he said. "I didn't want you to think I stopped because you didn't please me."

"Oh." She looked as if she wanted to say something; she looked almost absurdly happy at his words. "Thank you for saying that."

He took her hand and squeezed.

"Do I look a mess?" she asked.

He nodded. "But you're *my* mess," he whispered.

And he was very glad for that.

Chapter 16

As Colin liked to walk, and in fact frequently did so to clear his mind, it was no surprise that he spent much of the next day traversing Bloomsbury . . . and Fitzrovia . . . and Marylebone . . . and in fact several other London neighborhoods, until he looked up and realized that he was standing in the heart of Mayfair, in Grosvenor Square, to be precise, outside of Hastings House, town home of the Dukes of Hastings, the latest of whom happened to be married to his sister Daphne.

It had been a while since they'd had a conversation, anything above the usual family chitchat, that was. Of all his siblings, Daphne was the closest in age to him, and they'd always shared a rather special bond, even though they didn't see each other as much as they used to, what with Colin's frequent travels and Daphne's busy family life.

Hastings House was one of those enormous mansions that one could find scattered throughout Mayfair and St. James's. Large and square and constructed of elegant Portland stone, it was thoroughly imposing in its ducal splendor.

Which made it all the more amusing, Colin thought with a wry grin, that his sister was the current duchess. He couldn't imagine anyone less haughty or imposing. In fact, Daphne had had difficulty finding a husband when she'd been out on the marriage mart, precisely because she *was* so friendly and easy to be with. Gentlemen had tended to think of her as their friend and not as a prospective bride.

But all that had changed when she'd met Simon Bassett, Duke of Hastings, and now she was a respectable society matron with four children, aged ten, nine, eight, and seven. It still sometimes seemed odd to Colin that his sister was a mother, of all things, while he still lived the free and unfettered life of a bachelor. With only one year between them, he and Daphne had always passed through the various stages of life together. Even when she'd married, things hadn't seemed so very different; she and Simon attended the same parties he did and had many of the same interests and pursuits.

But then she'd started reproducing, and while Colin was always delighted to welcome a new niece or nephew into his life, each arrival had brought home the fact that Daphne had moved on in a way he had not.

But, he thought, smiling as Penelope's face drifted through his mind, he supposed all that would soon change.

Children. It was a rather nice thought, actually.

He hadn't consciously meant to visit Daphne, but now that he was here, he figured he might as well stop by and say hello, so he marched up the steps and gave the big brass knocker a sturdy clanking. Jeffries, the butler, opened the door almost immediately.

"Mr. Bridgerton," he said. "Your sister was not expecting you."

"No, I decided to surprise her. Is she at home?"

"I shall see," the butler said with a nod, even though they both knew that Daphne would never refuse to see a member of her family.

Colin waited in the drawing room while Jeffries informed Daphne of his presence, wandering idly about, feeling too restless to sit or even stand in one place. After a few minutes, Daphne appeared in the doorway, looking slightly disheveled but happy as always.

And why shouldn't she be? Colin wondered. All she'd ever wanted in life was to be a wife and mother, and it seemed that reality had more than surpassed her dreams.

"Hello there, sister," he said with a sloppy smile as he crossed the room to give her a quick hug. "You've got . . ." He motioned to his shoulder.

She looked down at her own shoulder, then smiled sheepishly as she saw the large dark gray smudge on the pale pink fabric of her dress. "Charcoal," she explained ruefully. "I've been trying to teach Caroline to draw."

"You?" Colin asked doubtfully.

"I know, I know," she said. "She really couldn't have picked a worse tutor, but she only decided yesterday that she loves art, so I'm all she's got on such short notice."

"You should pack her off to see Benedict," Colin suggested. "I'm sure he'd be happy to give her a lesson or two."

"The thought had already crossed my mind, but I'm sure she'll have moved on to some other pursuit by the time I can make the arrangements." She motioned to a sofa. "Sit. You look rather like a caged cat over there, pacing as you are."

He sat, even though he felt uncommonly fidgety.

"And before you ask," Daphne said, "I already told Jeffries to see to food. Will sandwiches be enough?"

"Could you hear my stomach grumbling from across the room?"

"From across town, I'm afraid." She laughed. "Did you know that whenever it thunders, David says that it's your stomach?"

"Oh, good God," Colin muttered, but he was chuckling all the while. His nephew was a rather clever little fellow.

Daphne smiled broadly as she settled down against the sofa cushions, folding her hands elegantly in her lap. "What brings you by, Colin? Not that you need a reason, of course. It's always lovely to see you."

He shrugged. "Just passing by."

"Did you visit Anthony and Kate?" she asked. Bridgerton House, where their eldest brother lived with his family, was just across the square from Hastings House. "Benedict and Sophie are already there with the children, helping to prepare for your engagement ball tonight."

He shook his head. "No, you're my chosen victim, I'm afraid."

She smiled again, but this time it was a softer expression, tempered by a fair dose of curiosity. "Is something wrong?"

"No, of course not," he said quickly. "Why would you ask that?"

"I don't know." She cocked her head to the side. "You seem odd, that's all."

"Just tired."

She nodded knowingly. "Wedding plans, I'm sure."

"Yes," he said, jumping on the excuse, although for the life of him, he wasn't even sure what it was he was trying to hide from her.

"Well, remember that whatever you're going through," she said with a peevish twist to her lips, "it's a thousand times worse for Penelope. It's always worse for women. Trust me."

"For weddings or for everything?" he asked mildly.

"Everything," she said promptly. "I know you men think you're actually in charge, but—"

"I wouldn't dream of thinking we're actually in charge," Colin said, and not entirely sarcastically.

Her face pinched into a peevish expression. "Women have far more to do than men. *Especially* with weddings. With all the fittings I'm sure Penelope has had for her wedding gown, she probably feels like a pincushion."

"I suggested eloping," Colin said conversationally, "and I think she rather hoped I was serious."

Daphne chuckled. "I'm so glad you're marrying her, Colin."

He nodded, not planning to say anything, and then somehow, he was saying her name. "Daff—"

"Yes?"

He opened his mouth, and then—"Never mind."

"Oh, no, you don't," she said. "Now you really have my curiosity piqued."

He drummed his fingers against the sofa. "Do you suppose the food might arrive soon?"

"Are you even hungry or are you merely trying to change the subject?"

"I'm always hungry."

She was silent for several seconds. "Colin," she finally asked, her voice soft and carefully gentle, "what were you going to say?"

He jumped to his feet, too restless to remain still, and began to pace. He stopped, turned to her, looked at her concerned face. "It's nothing," he started to say, except it wasn't nothing, and—

"How does one know?" he blurted out, not even aware that he hadn't completed his question until she replied, "How does one know what?"

He stopped in front of the window. It looked like it might rain. He'd have to borrow a carriage from Daphne unless he wanted to get soaked on the long walk home. Yet, he didn't know why he was even thinking about precipitation, because what he really wanted to know was—

"How does one know *what*, Colin?" Daphne repeated.

He turned around and just let the words break free. "How do you know if it's love?"

For a moment she just stared at him, her large brown eyes wide with surprise, her lips parted and utterly still.

"Forget I asked," he muttered.

"No!" she exclaimed, jumping to her feet. "I'm *glad* you asked. Very glad. I'm just . . . surprised, I must say."

He closed his eyes, thoroughly disgusted with himself. "I can't believe I just asked you that."

"No, Colin, don't be silly. It's really rather . . . sweet that you asked. And I can't even begin to tell you how flattered I am that you would come to me when—"

"Daphne . . ." he said warningly. She had a way of wandering off the topic, and he really wasn't in the right frame of mind to follow her errant thoughts.

Impulsively, she reached out and hugged him; then, her hands still on his shoulders, she said, "I don't know."

"I beg your pardon?"

She gave her head a little shake. "I don't know how you know it's love. I think it's different for everyone."

"How did you know?"

She chewed on her lower lip for several seconds before replying, "I don't know."

"*What?*"

She shrugged helplessly. "I don't remember. It's been so long. I just . . . *knew.*"

"So what you're saying," he said, leaning against the windowsill and crossing his arms, "is that if one doesn't know one's in love, then one probably isn't."

"Yes," she said firmly. "No! No, that's not what I mean at all."

"Then what do you mean?"

"I don't know," she said weakly.

He stared at her. "And how long have you been married?" he muttered.

"Colin, don't tease. I'm trying to be helpful."

"And I appreciate the attempt, but truly, Daphne, you—"

"I know, I know," she interrupted. "I'm useless. But listen to me. Do you like Penelope?" Then she gasped in horror. "We are talking about Penelope, aren't we?"

"Of course we are," he snapped.

She let out a relieved sigh. "Good, because if we weren't, then I can assure you I would have had no advice whatsoever."

"I'll go," he said abruptly.

"No, don't," she pleaded, placing her hand on his arm. "Stay, Colin, please."

He looked at her, sighing, feeling defeated. "I feel like an ass."

"Colin," she said, guiding him to the sofa and pushing him down until he sat, "listen to me. Love grows and changes every day. And it isn't like some thunderbolt from the sky, instantly transforming you into a different man. I know Benedict says it was that way for him, and that's just lovely, but you know, Benedict is *not* normal."

Colin very much wanted to take that bait, but he just couldn't summon the energy.

"It wasn't like that for me," Daphne said, "and I don't think it was like that for Simon, although truthfully, I don't think I've ever asked."

"You should."

She paused while her mouth was forming a word, leaving her looking like a surprised bird. "Why?"

He shrugged. "So you can tell me."

"What, do you think it's different for men?"

"Everything else is."

She grimaced. "I'm beginning to develop a fair dose of pity for Penelope."

"Oh, absolutely you should," he agreed. "I'll make a dreadful husband, to be sure."

"You will not," she said, batting his arm. "Why on earth would you say that? You would never be unfaithful to her."

"No," he agreed. He was quiet for a moment, and

when he finally spoke again, his voice was soft. "But I might not love her the way she deserves."

"But you *might*." She threw up her hands in a gesture of exasperation. "For heaven's sake, Colin, just the fact that you're sitting here asking your *sister* about love probably means you're more than halfway there."

"Do you think?"

"If I didn't *think* so," she said, "I wouldn't have *said* so." She sighed. "Stop thinking so hard, Colin. You'll find marriage a lot easier if you simply allow it to be."

He eyed her suspiciously. "When did you grow so philosophical?"

"When you came by to see me and forced the issue," she said promptly. "You're marrying the right person. Stop worrying so much."

"I'm not worrying," he said automatically, but of course he *was* worrying, so he didn't even bother to defend himself when Daphne shot him an extremely sarcastic look. But it wasn't as if he were worrying whether Penelope was the right woman. He was certain of that.

And he wasn't worried about whether his marriage would be a good one. He was certain of that, as well.

No, he was worrying about stupid things. About whether or not he loved her, not because it would be the end of the world if he did (or the end of the world if he didn't), but because he found it extremely unsettling not to know exactly what it was he was feeling.

"Colin?"

He looked over at his sister, who was regarding him with a rather bemused expression. He stood, intending to leave before he embarrassed himself beyond repair, then leaned down and kissed her cheek. "Thank you," he said.

She narrowed her eyes. "I can't tell if you're serious or are teasing me for being an utter lack of help."

"You *were* an utter lack of help," he said, "but it's an honest thank-you, nonetheless."

"Points for effort?"

"Something like that."

"Are you going over to Bridgerton House now?" she asked.

"Why, so I may embarrass myself with Anthony next?"

"Or Benedict," she said. "He's there, too."

The thing about large families was, there was never a lack of opportunity to make a fool of oneself with a sibling. "No," he said with a small, wry smile, "I think I'll walk home."

"Walk?" she echoed, gaping.

He squinted toward the window. "Do you think it might rain?"

"Take my carriage, Colin," she insisted, "and please wait for the sandwiches. There is sure to be a mountain of them, and if you leave before they arrive, I know I'll eat half, and then I'll hate myself for the rest of the day."

He nodded and sat back down, and was glad he did. He'd always been partial to smoked salmon. In fact, he took a plate with him in the carriage, staring out the window the whole way home at the pouring rain.

When the Bridgertons threw a party, they did it right.

And when the Bridgertons threw an engagement ball . . . well, had Lady Whistledown still been writing, it would have taken at least three columns to chronicle the event.

Even this engagement ball, thrown together at the last minute (due to the fact that neither Lady Bridgerton nor Mrs. Featherington were willing to allow their children the possibility of changing their minds during a long engagement), easily qualified as *the* party of the season.

Although part of that, Penelope thought wryly, had little to do with the party itself and everything to do with the continued speculation over why on earth Colin Bridgerton would choose a nobody like Penelope Featherington to be his wife. It hadn't even been this

bad when Anthony Bridgerton had married Kate Sheffield, who, like Penelope, had never been considered
a diamond of the first water. But at least Kate hadn't
been *old*. Penelope couldn't even begin to count the
number of times she'd heard the word *spinster* whispered behind her back during the past few days.

But while the gossip was a bit tedious, it didn't really
bother her, because she was still floating along on the
cloud of her own bliss. A woman couldn't spend her
entire adult life in love with one man and then not
be almost stupid with happiness after he asked her to
marry him.

Even if she couldn't quite figure out how it had all
happened.

It *had* happened. That was all that mattered.

And Colin was everything anyone could dream of in
a fiancé. He stuck to her side like glue the entire evening, and Penelope didn't even think he was doing it to
protect her from gossip. In all truth, he seemed rather
oblivious to the talk.

It was almost as if . . . Penelope smiled dreamily. It
was almost as if Colin were remaining by her side because he wanted to be there.

"Did you see Cressida Twombley?" Eloise whispered in her ear while Colin was off dancing with his
mother. "She's green with envy."

"That's just her dress," Penelope said with an impressively straight face.

Eloise laughed. "Oh, I wish Lady Whistledown were writing. She would *skewer* her."

"I think Lady Whistledown is supposed to *be* her," Penelope said carefully.

"Oh, pish and tosh. I don't believe for one moment that Cressida is Lady Whistledown, and I can't believe that you do, either."

"Probably not," Penelope allowed. She knew that her secret would be better protected if she claimed to believe Cressida's story, but anyone who knew her would have found that so out of character that it would have been quite suspicious indeed.

"Cressida just wanted the money," Eloise continued disdainfully. "Or maybe the notoriety. Probably both."

Penelope watched her nemesis, holding court on the other side of the room. Her regular crowd of cronies milled about, but they were joined by new people, as well, most likely curious about the Whistledown gossip. "Well, she's succeeded with the notoriety, at least."

Eloise nodded her agreement. "I cannot even imagine why she was invited. There is certainly no love lost between the two of you, and none of us like her."

"Colin insisted upon it."

Eloise turned to her with gaping jaw. "Why?"

Penelope suspected that the main reason was Cressida's recent claim to be Lady Whistledown; most of the *ton* wasn't sure whether or not she was lying, but no one was willing to deny her an invitation to an event, just in case she really was telling the truth.

And Colin and Penelope shouldn't have had any reason to know for certain otherwise.

But Penelope couldn't reveal this to Eloise, so she told her the rest of the story, which was still the truth. "Your mother didn't want to cause any gossip by cutting her, and Colin also said . . ."

She blushed. It was really too sweet.

"What?" Eloise demanded.

Penelope couldn't speak without smiling. "He said he wanted Cressida to be forced to watch me in my triumph."

"Oh. My. Word." Eloise looked as if she might need to sit down. "My brother is in love."

Penelope's blush turned a furious red.

"*He is,*" Eloise exclaimed. "He must be. Oh, you must tell me. Has he said so?"

There was something both wonderful and horrible in listening to Eloise gush. On the one hand, it was always lovely to share life's most perfect moments with one's best friend, and Eloise's joy and excitement were certainly contagious.

But on the other hand, they weren't necessarily warranted, because Colin didn't love her. Or at least he hadn't said so.

But he acted like he did! Penelope clung to that thought, trying to focus on that, rather than the fact that he'd never said the words.

Actions spoke louder than words, didn't they?

And his actions made her feel like a princess.

"Miss Featherington! Miss Featherington!"

Penelope looked to her left and beamed. That voice could belong to no one other than Lady Danbury.

"Miss Featherington," Lady D said, poking her cane through the crowd until she was standing right in front of Penelope and Eloise.

"Lady Danbury, how nice to see you."

"Heh heh heh." Lady Danbury's wrinkled face became almost young again from the force of her smile. "It's always nice to see me, regardless of what anyone else says. And *you*, you little devil. Look what you did."

"Isn't it the *best*?" Eloise asked.

Penelope looked to her closest friend. For all her mixed emotions, Eloise was truly, honestly, and forever would be thrilled for her. Suddenly it didn't matter that they were standing in the middle of a crowded ballroom, with everyone staring at her as if she were some sort of specimen on a biology plate. She turned and gave Eloise a fierce hug, whispering, "I do love you," in her ear.

"I know you do," Eloise whispered back.

Lady Danbury banged her cane—loudly—on the floor. "I'm still standing here, ladies!"

"Oh, sorry," Penelope said sheepishly.

"It's all right," Lady D said, with an uncharacteristic level of indulgence. "It's rather nice to see two girls who'd rather embrace than stab each other in the back, if you must know."

"Thank you for coming over to congratulate me," Penelope said.

"I wouldn't have missed this for the world," Lady Danbury said. "Heh heh heh. All these fools, trying to figure out what you did to get him to marry you, when all you really did was be yourself."

Penelope's lips parted, and tears pricked her eyes. "Why, Lady Danbury, that's just about the nicest—"

"No, no," Lady D interrupted loudly, "none of that. I haven't the time nor the inclination for sentiment."

But Penelope noticed that she'd pulled out her handkerchief and was discreetly dabbing her eyes.

"Ah, Lady Danbury," Colin said, returning to the group and sliding his arm possessively through Penelope's. "Good to see you."

"Mr. Bridgerton," she said in curt greeting. "Just came over to congratulate your bride."

"Ah, but I am surely the one who deserves the congratulations."

"Hmmmph. Truer words, and all that," Lady D said. "I think you might be right. She's more of a prize than anyone realizes."

"I realize," he said, his voice so low and deadly serious that Penelope thought she might faint from the thrill of it.

"And if you'll excuse us," Colin continued smoothly, "I must take my fiancée over to meet my brother—"

"I've met your brother," Penelope interrupted.

"Consider it tradition," he said. "We need to officially welcome you to the family."

"Oh." She felt rather warm inside at the thought of becoming a Bridgerton. "How lovely."

"As I was saying," Colin said, "Anthony would like to make a toast, and then I must lead Penelope in a waltz."

"Very romantic," Lady Danbury said approvingly.

"Yes, well, I am a romantic sort," Colin said airily.

Eloise let out a loud snort.

He turned to her with one arrogantly arched brow. "I am."

"For Penelope's sake," she retorted, "I certainly hope so."

"Are they always like this?" Lady Danbury asked Penelope.

"Most of the time."

Lady D nodded. "That's a good thing. My children rarely even speak to one another. Not out of any ill will, of course. They just have nothing in common. Sad, really."

Colin tightened his hand on Penelope's arm. "We really must be going."

"Of course," she murmured, but as she turned to walk toward Anthony, whom she could see across the room, standing near the small orchestra, she heard a loud and sudden commotion at the door.

"Attention! Attention!"

The blood drained from her face in under a second. "Oh, no," she heard herself whisper. This wasn't supposed to happen. Not tonight, anyway.

"Attention!"

Monday, her mind screamed. She'd told her printer Monday. At the Mottram ball.

"What is going on?" Lady Danbury demanded.

Ten young boys were racing into the room, nothing more than urchins, really, holding sheaves of paper, tossing them about like large rectangles of confetti.

"Lady Whistledown's final column!" they all yelled. "Read it now! Read the truth."

Chapter 17

C olin Bridgerton was famous for many things.

He was famous for his good looks, which was no surprise; all the Bridgerton men were famous for their good looks.

He was famous for his slightly crooked smile, which could melt a woman's heart across a crowded ballroom and had even once caused a young lady to faint dead away, or at least to swoon delicately, then hit her head on a table, which did produce the aforementioned dead faint.

He was famous for his mellow charm, his ability to set anyone at ease with a smooth grin and an amusing comment.

What he was *not* famous for, and in fact what many

people would have sworn he did not even possess, was a temper.

And, in fact, due to his remarkable (and heretofore untapped) self-control, no one was going to get a glimpse of it that night, either, although his soon-to-be wife might wake up the next day with a *serious* bruise on her arm.

"Colin," she gasped, looking down at where he was gripping her.

But he couldn't let go. He knew he was hurting her, he knew it wasn't a terribly nice thing that he was hurting her, but he was so damned *furious* at that moment, and it was either squeeze her arm for all he was worth or lose his temper in front of five hundred of their nearest and dearest acquaintances.

All in all, he thought he was making the right choice.

He was going to kill her. As soon as he figured out some way to remove her from this godforsaken ballroom, he was absolutely going to kill her. They had agreed that Lady Whistledown was a thing of the past, that they were going to let matters lie. This was not supposed to happen. She was inviting disaster. Ruin.

"This is fabulous!" Eloise exclaimed, snatching a newssheet from the air. "Absolutely, positively smashing. I'll bet she came out of retirement to celebrate your engagement."

"Wouldn't that be nice?" Colin drawled.

Penelope said nothing, but she looked very, very pale.

"Oh, my heavens!"

Colin turned to his sister, whose mouth was hanging open as she read the column.

"Grab one of those for me, Bridgerton!" Lady Danbury ordered, swatting him in the leg with her cane. "Can't believe she's publishing on a Saturday. Must be a good one."

Colin leaned down and picked up two pieces of paper from the floor, handing one to Lady Danbury and looking down at the one in his hand, even though he was fairly certain he knew exactly what it would say.

He was right.

There is nothing I despise more than a gentleman who thinks it amusing to give a lady a condescending pat on the hand as he murmurs, "It is a woman's prerogative to change her mind." And indeed, because I feel one should always support one's words with one's actions, I endeavor to keep my opinions and decisions steadfast and true.

Which is why, Gentle Reader, when I wrote my

column of 19 April, I truly intended it to be my last. However, events entirely beyond my control (or indeed my approval) force me to put my pen to paper one last time.

Ladies and Gentleman, This Author is NOT Lady Cressida Twombley. She is nothing more than a scheming imposter, and it would break my heart to see my years of hard work attributed to one such as her.

LADY WHISTLEDOWN'S SOCIETY PAPERS,
24 APRIL 1824

"This is the best thing I have ever seen," Eloise said in a gleeful whisper. "Maybe I am a bad person at heart, because I have never before felt such happiness at another person's downfall."

"Balderdash!" Lady Danbury said. "I *know* I am not a bad person, and I find this delightful."

Colin said nothing. He didn't trust his voice. He didn't trust himself.

"Where is Cressida?" Eloise asked, craning her neck. "Does anyone see her? I'll bet she's already fled. She must be mortified. I would be mortified if I were her."

"You would never be her," Lady Danbury said. "You're much too decent a person."

Penelope said nothing.

"Still," Eloise continued jovially, "one almost feels sorry for her."

"But only almost," Lady D said.

"Oh, for certain. Barely almost, truth be told."

Colin just stood there, grinding his teeth into powder.

"And I get to keep my thousand pounds!" cackled Lady Danbury.

"Penelope!" Eloise exclaimed, jostling her with her elbow. "You haven't said a word. Isn't this marvelous?"

Penelope nodded and said, "I can't believe it."

Colin's grip on her arm tightened.

"Your brother's coming," she whispered.

He looked to his right. Anthony was striding toward him, Violet and Kate hot on his heels.

"Well, this rather upstages us," Anthony said as he drew up alongside Colin. He nodded at the ladies present. "Eloise, Penelope, Lady Danbury."

"I don't think anyone is going to listen to Anthony's toast now," Violet said, glancing about the room. The buzz of activity was relentless. Errant newssheets still floated in the air, and all about them, people were slipping on the ones that had already landed on the floor. The hum of the whispers was constant and almost grating, and Colin felt like the top of his skull was going to blow off.

He had to get away. Now. Or at least as soon as possible.

His head was screaming and he felt too hot in his own skin. It was almost like passion, except this wasn't passion, it was fury, and it was outrage, and it was this awful, black feeling that he'd been betrayed by the one person who should have stood by him without question.

It was strange. He knew that Penelope was the one with the secret, the one with the most to lose. This was about her, not him; he knew that, intellectually, at least. But somehow that had ceased to matter. They were a team now, and she had acted without him.

She had no right to put herself in such a precarious position without consulting him first. He was her husband, or would be, and it was his God-given duty to protect her whether she desired it or not.

"Colin?" his mother was saying. "Are you well? You look a bit odd."

"Make the toast," he said, turning to Anthony. "Penelope isn't feeling well, and I need to take her home."

"You're not feeling well?" Eloise asked Penelope. "What's wrong? You didn't say anything."

To Penelope's credit, she managed a rather credible, "A bit of a headache, I'm afraid."

"Yes, yes, Anthony," Violet said, "do go ahead and make the toast now so that Colin and Penelope may have their dance. She really can't leave until you do."

Anthony nodded his agreement, then motioned for Colin and Penelope to follow him to the front of the ballroom. A trumpeter let out a loud squawk on his horn, signaling the partygoers to be quiet. They all obeyed, probably because they assumed the ensuing announcement would be about Lady Whistledown.

"Ladies and gentlemen," Anthony said loudly, accepting a flute of champagne from a footman. "I know that you are all intrigued by Lady Whistledown's recent intrusion into our party, but I must entreat you all to remember our purpose for gathering here tonight."

It should have been a perfect moment, Colin thought dispassionately. It was to have been Penelope's night of triumph, her night to shine, to show the world how beautiful and lovely and smart she really was.

It was his night to make his intentions well and truly public, to make sure that everyone knew that he had chosen her, and just as importantly, that she had chosen him.

And all he wanted to do was take her by the shoulders and shake her until he ran out of strength. She was jeopardizing everything. She was putting her very future at risk.

"As the head of the Bridgerton family," Anthony continued, "it gives me great joy whenever one of my siblings chooses a bride. Or groom," he added with a smile, nodding toward Daphne and Simon.

Colin looked down at Penelope. She was standing very straight and very still in her dress of ice-blue satin. She wasn't smiling, which must have looked odd to the hundreds of people staring at her. But maybe they would just think she was nervous. There were hundreds of people staring at her, after all. Anyone would be nervous.

Although if one was standing right next to her, as Colin was, one could see the panic in her eyes, the rapid rise and fall of her chest as her breathing grew faster and more erratic.

She was scared.

Good. She should be scared. Scared of what could happen to her if her secret came out. Scared of what *would* happen to her once they had a chance to talk.

"Therefore," Anthony concluded, "it gives me great pleasure to lift my glass in a toast to my brother Colin, and his soon-to-be bride, Penelope Featherington. To Colin and Penelope!"

Colin looked down at his hand and realized that

388 · JULIA QUINN

someone had placed a glass of champagne in it. He lifted his glass, started to raise it to his lips, then thought the better of it and touched it to Penelope's mouth instead. The crowd cheered wildly, and he watched as she took a sip, and then another and another, forced to keep drinking until he removed the glass, which he did not do until she was finished.

Then he realized that his childish display of power had left him without a drink, which he badly needed, so he plucked Penelope's glass from her hand and downed it in a single gulp.

The crowd cheered even harder.

He leaned down and whispered in her ear, "We're going to dance now. We're going to dance until the rest of the party joins us and we're no longer the center of attention. And then you and I will slip outside. And then we will talk."

Her chin moved in a barely perceptible nod.

He took her hand and led her onto the dance floor, placing his other hand at her waist as the orchestra began the first strains of a waltz.

"Colin," she whispered, "I didn't mean for this to happen."

He affixed a smile on his face. This was supposed to be his first official dance with his intended, after all. "Not now," he ordered.

"But—"

"In ten minutes, I will have a great deal to say to you, but for right now, we are simply going to dance."

"I just wanted to say—"

His hand tightened around hers in a gesture of unmistakable warning. She pursed her lips and looked at his face for the briefest of moments, then looked away.

"I should be smiling," she whispered, still not looking at him.

"Then smile."

"*You* should be smiling."

"You're right," he said. "I should."

But he didn't.

Penelope felt like frowning. She felt like crying, in all honesty, but somehow she managed to nudge her lips up at the corners. The entire world was watching her—her entire world, at least—and she knew they were examining her every move, cataloguing each expression that crossed her face.

Years she'd spent, feeling like she was invisible and hating it. And now she'd have given anything for a few brief moments of anonymity again.

No, not anything. She wouldn't have given up Colin. If having him meant that she would spend the rest of her life under close scrutiny from the *ton,* it would be worth it. And if having to endure his anger and disdain at a time like this was to be a part of marriage as well, then that would be worth it, too.

She'd known that he would be furious with her for publishing one last column. Her hands had been shaking as she'd rewritten the words, and she'd been terrified the entire time she'd been at St. Bride's Church (as well as the ride to and from), sure that he was going to jump out at her at any moment, calling off the wedding because he couldn't bear to be married to Lady Whistledown.

But she'd done it anyway.

She knew he thought she was making a mistake, but she simply could not allow Cressida Twombley to take the credit for her life's work. But was it so much to ask that Colin at least make the attempt to see it all from her point of view? It would have been hard enough allowing anyone to pretend to be Lady Whistledown, but Cressida was unbearable. Penelope had worked too hard and endured too much at Cressida's hands.

Plus, she knew that Colin would never jilt her once their engagement became public. That was part of the reason she'd specifically instructed her publisher to have the papers delivered on *Monday* to the Mottram ball. Well, that and the fact that it seemed terribly wrong to do it at her own engagement ball, especially when Colin was so opposed to the idea.

Damn Mr. Lacey! He'd surely done this to maximize circulation and exposure. He knew enough about society from reading Whistledown to know that a Bridgerton engagement ball would be the most coveted invitation of the season. Why this should matter, she didn't know, since increasing interest in *Whistledown* would not lead to more money in his pocket; *Whistledown* was well and truly through, and neither Penelope nor Mr. Lacey would receive another pound from its publication.

Unless . . .

Penelope frowned and sighed. Mr. Lacey must be hoping that she would change her mind.

Colin's hand tightened at her waist, and she looked back up. His eyes were on hers, startlingly green even in the candlelight. Or maybe it was just that she knew they were so green. She probably would have thought them emerald in the dark.

He nodded toward the other dancers on the floor, which was now crowded with revelers. "Time to make our escape," he said.

She returned his nod with one of her own. They had already told his family that she wasn't feeling well and wanted to go home, so no one would think overmuch of their departure. And if it wasn't quite *de rigeur* for them to be alone in his carriage, well, sometimes rules were stretched for affianced couples, especially on such romantic evenings.

A bubble of ridiculous, panicky laughter escaped her lips. The night was turning out to be the least romantic of her life.

Colin looked at her sharply, one arrogant brow raised in question.

"It's nothing," Penelope said.

He squeezed her hand, although not terribly affectionately. "I want to know," he said.

She shrugged fatalistically. She couldn't imagine what she could do or say to make the night any worse than it already was. "I was just thinking about how this evening was supposed to be romantic."

"It could have been," he said cruelly.

His hand slipped from its position at her waist, but he held on to her other hand, grasping her fingers lightly to weave her through the crowd until they stepped through the French doors out onto the terrace.

"Not here," Penelope whispered, glancing anxiously back toward the ballroom.

He didn't even dignify her comment with a reply, instead pulling her farther into the inky night, drifting around a corner until they were quite alone.

But they didn't stop there. With a quick glance to

make sure that no one was about, Colin pushed open a small, unobtrusive side door.

"What's this?" Penelope asked.

His answer was a little shove at the small of her back, until she was fully inside the dark hallway.

"Up," he said, motioning to the steps.

Penelope didn't know whether to be scared or thrilled, but she climbed the stairs anyway, ever aware of Colin's hot presence, right at her back.

After they'd climbed several flights, Colin stepped ahead of her and pushed open a door, peeking out into the hall. It was empty, so he stepped out, pulling her along with him, dashing quietly through the hall (which Penelope now recognized as the family's private chambers) until they reached a room she had never before entered.

Colin's room. She'd always known where it was. Through all her years of coming here to visit with Eloise, she'd never once done more than trail her fingers along the heavy wood of the door. It had been years since he'd lived here at Number Five on a permanent basis, but his mother had insisted upon maintaining his room for him. One never knew when he might need it, she'd said, and she'd been proven right earlier that season when Colin had returned from Cyprus without a house under lease.

He pushed open the door and pulled her inside after him. But the room was dark, and she was stumbling, and when she stopped moving it was because his body was right there in front of hers.

He touched her arms to steady her, but then he didn't let go, just held her there in the dark. It wasn't an embrace, not really, but the length of her body was touching the length of his. She couldn't see anything, but she could feel him, and she could smell him, and she could hear his breathing, swirling through the night air, gently caressing her cheek.

It was agony.

It was ecstasy.

His hands slid slowly down her bare arms, torturing her every nerve, and then, abruptly, he stepped away.

Followed by—silence.

Penelope wasn't sure what she had expected. He would yell at her, he would berate her, he would order her to explain herself.

But he was doing none of those things. He was just standing there in the dark, forcing the issue, forcing her to say something.

"Could you . . . could you light a candle?" she finally asked.

"You don't like the dark?" he drawled.

"Not now. Not like this."

"I see," he murmured. "So you're saying you might like it like this?" His fingers were suddenly on her skin, trailing along the edge of her bodice.

And then they were gone.

"Don't," she said, her voice shaking.

"Don't touch you?" His voice grew mocking, and Penelope was glad that she couldn't see his face. "But you're mine, aren't you?"

"Not yet," she warned him.

"Oh, but you are. You saw to that. It was rather clever timing, actually, waiting until our engagement ball to make your final announcement. You knew I didn't want you to publish that last column. I forbade it! We agreed—"

"We never agreed!"

He ignored her outburst. "You waited until—"

"We never agreed," Penelope cried out again, needing to make it clear that she had not broken her word. Whatever else she had done, she had not lied to him. Well, aside from keeping *Whistledown* a secret for nearly a dozen years, but he certainly hadn't been alone in that deception. "And yes," she admitted, because it didn't seem right to start lying now, "I knew you wouldn't jilt me. But I hoped—"

Her voice broke, and she was unable to finish.

"You hoped what?" Colin asked after an interminable silence.

"I hoped that you would forgive me," she whispered. "Or at least that you would understand. I always thought you were the sort of man who . . ."

"What sort of man?" he asked, this time after the barest hint of a pause.

"It's my fault, really," she said, sounding tired and sad. "I've put you on a pedestal. You've been so nice all these years. I suppose I thought you were incapable of anything else."

"What the hell have I done that hasn't been nice?" he demanded. "I've protected you, I've offered for you, I've—"

"You haven't tried to see this from my point of view," she interrupted.

"Because you're acting like an idiot!" he nearly roared.

There was silence after that, the kind of silence that grates at ears, gnaws at souls.

"I can't imagine what else there is to say," Penelope finally said.

Colin looked away. He didn't know why he did so; it wasn't as if he could see her in the dark, anyway. But there was something about the tone of her voice that made him uneasy. She sounded vulnerable, tired.

Wishful and heartbroken. She made him want to understand her, or at least to try, even though he *knew* she had made a terrible mistake. Every little catch in her voice put a damper on his fury. He was still angry, but somehow he'd lost the will to display it.

"You are going to be found out, you know," he said, his voice low and controlled. "You have humiliated Cressida; she will be beyond furious, and she's not going to rest until she unearths the real Lady Whistledown."

Penelope moved away; he could hear her skirts rustling. "Cressida isn't bright enough to figure me out, and besides, I'm not going to write any more columns, so there will be no opportunity for me to slip up and reveal something." There was a beat of silence, and then she added, "You have my promise on that."

"It's too late," he said.

"It's not too late," she protested. "No one knows! No one knows but you, and you're so ashamed of me, I can't bear it."

"Oh, for the love of God, Penelope," he snapped, "I'm not ashamed of you."

"Would you *please* light a candle?" she wailed.

Colin crossed the room and fumbled in a drawer for a candle and the means with which to light it. "I'm not ashamed of you," he reiterated, "but I do think you're acting foolishly."

"You may be correct," she said, "but I have to do what I think is right."

"You're not thinking," he said dismissively, turning and looking at her face as he sparked a flame. "Forget, if you will—although I cannot—what will happen to your reputation if people find out who you really are. Forget that people will cut you, that they will talk about you behind your back."

"Those people aren't worth worrying about," she said, her back ramrod straight.

"Perhaps not," he agreed, crossing his arms and staring at her. Hard. "But it will hurt. You will not like it, Penelope. And *I* won't like it."

She swallowed convulsively. Good. Maybe he was getting through to her.

"But forget all of that," he continued. "You have spent the last decade insulting people. Offending them."

"I have said lots of very nice things as well," she protested, her dark eyes glistening with unshed tears.

"Of course you have, but those aren't the people you are going to have to worry about. I'm talking about the angry ones, the insulted ones." He strode forward and grabbed her by her upper arms. "Penelope," he said urgently, "there will be people who want to *hurt* you."

His words had been meant for her, but they turned around and pierced his own heart.

He tried to picture a life without Penelope. It was impossible.

Just weeks ago she'd been . . . He stopped, thought. What *had* she been? A friend? An acquaintance? Someone he saw and never really noticed?

And now she was his fiancée, soon to be his bride. And maybe . . . maybe she was something more than that. Something deeper. Something even more precious.

"What I want to know," he asked, deliberately forcing the conversation back on topic so his mind wouldn't wander down such dangerous roads, "is why you're not jumping on the perfect alibi if the point is to remain anonymous."

"Because remaining anonymous isn't the point!" she fairly yelled.

"You want to be found out?" he asked, gaping at her in the candlelight.

"No, of course not," she replied. "But this is my work. This is my life's work. This is all I have to show for my life, and if I can't take the credit for it, I'll be *damned* if someone else will."

Colin opened his mouth to offer a retort, but to his surprise, he had nothing to say. *Life's work*. Penelope had a life's work.

He did not.

She might not be able to put her name on her work, but when she was alone in her room, she could look at her back issues, and point to them, and say to herself, *This is it. This is what my life has been about.*

"Colin?" she whispered, clearly startled by his silence.

She was amazing. He didn't know how he hadn't realized it before, when he'd already known that she was smart and lovely and witty and resourceful. But all those adjectives, and a whole host more he hadn't yet thought of, did not add up to the true measure of her.

She was amazing.

And he was . . . Dear God above, he was jealous of her.

"I'll go," she said softly, turning and walking toward the door.

For a moment he didn't react. His mind was still frozen, reeling with revelations. But when he saw her hand on the doorknob, he knew he could not let her go. Not this night, not ever.

"No," he said hoarsely, closing the distance between

them in three long strides. "No," he said again, "I want you to stay."

She looked up at him, her eyes two pools of confusion. "But you said—"

He cupped her face tenderly with his hands. "Forget what I said."

And that was when he realized that Daphne had been right. His love hadn't been a thunderbolt from the sky. It had started with a smile, a word, a teasing glance. Every second he had spent in her presence it had grown, until he'd reached this moment, and he suddenly *knew*.

He loved her.

He was still furious with her for publishing that last column, and he was bloody ashamed of himself that he was actually jealous of her for having found a life's work and purpose, but even with all that, he loved her.

And if he let her walk out the door right now, he would never forgive himself.

Maybe this, then, was the definition of love. When you wanted someone, needed her, adored her still, even when you were utterly furious and quite ready to tie her to the bed just to keep her from going out and making more trouble.

This was the night. This was the moment. He was

brimming with emotion, and he had to tell her. He had to *show* her.

"Stay," he whispered, and he pulled her to him, roughly, hungrily, without apology or explanation.

"Stay," he said again, leading her to his bed.

And when she didn't say anything, he said it for a third time.

"Stay."

She nodded.

He took her into his arms.

This was Penelope, and this was love.

Chapter 18

The moment Penelope nodded—the moment before she nodded, really—she knew that she had agreed to more than a kiss. She wasn't sure what had made Colin change his mind, why he had been so angry one minute and then so loving and tender the next.

She wasn't sure, but the truth was—she didn't care.

One thing she knew—he wasn't doing this, kissing her so sweetly, to punish her. Some men might use desire as a weapon, temptation as revenge, but Colin wasn't one of them.

It just wasn't in him.

He was, for all his rakish and mischievous ways, for all his jokes and teasing and sly humor, a good and noble man. And he would be a good and noble husband.

She knew this as well as she knew herself.

And if he was kissing her passionately, lowering her to his bed, covering her body with his own, then it was because he wanted her, cared enough to overcome his anger.

Cared for her.

Penelope kissed him back with every ounce of her emotion, every last corner of her soul. She had years and years of love for this man, and what she lacked in technique, she made up in fervor. She clutched at his hair, writhed beneath him, unmindful of her own appearance.

They weren't in a carriage or his mother's drawing room this time. There was no fear of discovery, no need to make sure that she looked presentable in ten minutes.

This was the night she could show him everything she felt for him. She would answer his desire with her own, and silently make her vows of love and fidelity and devotion.

When the night was through, he would know that she loved him. She might not say the words—she might not even whisper them—but he would know.

Or maybe he already knew. It was funny; it had been so easy to hide her secret life as Lady Whistledown, but so unbelievably hard to keep her heart from her eyes every time she looked at him.

"When did I start needing you so much?" he whispered, raising his head very slightly from hers until the tips of their noses touched and she could see his eyes, dark and colorless in the dim candlelight, but so very green in her mind, focusing on hers. His breath was hot, and his gaze was hot, and he was making her feel hot in areas of her body she never even allowed herself to think about.

His fingers moved to the back of her gown, moving expertly along the buttons until she felt the fabric loosening, first around her breasts, then around her ribs, then around her waist.

And then it wasn't even there at all.

"My God," he said, his voice a mere shadow louder than breath, "you're so beautiful."

And for the first time in her life, Penelope truly believed that it might be true.

There was something very wicked and titillating about being so intimately bared before another human being, but she didn't feel shame. Colin was looking at her so warmly, touching her so reverently, that she could feel nothing but an overwhelming sense of destiny.

His fingers skimmed along the sensitive skin at the outside edge of her breast, first teasing her with his fingernails, then stroking her more gently as his fingertips returned to their original position near her collarbone.

Something tightened within her. She didn't know if it was his touch or the way he was looking at her, but something was making her change.

She felt strange, odd.

Wonderful.

He was kneeling on the bed beside her, still fully clothed, gazing down at her with a sense of pride, of desire, of ownership. "I never dreamed you would look like this," he whispered, moving his hand until his palm was lightly grazing her nipple. "I never dreamed I would want you this way."

Penelope sucked in her breath as a spasm of sensation shot through her. But something in his words was unsettling, and he must have seen her reaction in her eyes, because he asked, "What is it? What is wrong?"

"Nothing," she started to say, then checked herself. Their marriage ought to be based on honesty, and she did neither of them a service by withholding her true feelings.

"What did you think I would look like?" she asked quietly.

He just stared at her, clearly confused by her question.

"You said you never dreamed I would look this

way," she explained. "What did you think I would look like?"

"I don't know," he admitted. "Until the last few weeks, honestly I don't think I thought about it."

"And since then?" she persisted, not quite sure why she needed him to answer, just knowing that she did.

In one swift moment he straddled her, then leaned down until the fabric of his waistcoat scraped her belly and breasts, until his nose touched hers and his hot breath swarmed across her skin.

"Since then," he growled, "I've thought of this moment a thousand times, pictured a hundred different pairs of breasts, all lovely and desirable and full and begging for my attention, but nothing, and let me repeat this in case you didn't quite hear me the first time, *nothing* comes close to reality."

"Oh." It was really all she could think to say.

He shrugged off his jacket and waistcoat until he was clad only in his fine linen shirt and breeches, then did nothing but stare at her, a wicked, wicked smile lifting one corner of his lips as she squirmed beneath him, growing hot and hungry under his relentless gaze.

And then, just when she was certain that she couldn't take it for one more second, he reached out and covered her with both his hands, squeezing lightly as he tested the weight and shape of her. He moaned raggedly, then sucked in his breath as he adjusted his fingers so that her nipples popped up between them.

"I want to see you sitting up," he groaned, "so I can see them full and lovely and large. And then I want to crawl behind you and cup you." His lips found her ear and his voice dropped to a whisper. "And I want to do it in front of a mirror."

"Now?" she squeaked.

He seemed to consider that for a moment, then shook his head. "Later," he said, and then repeated it in a rather resolute tone. "Later."

Penelope opened her mouth to ask him something— she had no idea what—but before she could utter a word, he murmured, "First things first," and lowered his mouth to her breast, teasing her first with a soft rush of air, then closing his lips around her, chuckling softly as she yelped in surprise and bucked off the bed.

He continued this torture until she thought she might scream, then he moved to the other breast and repeated it all over again. But this time he'd freed up one of his hands, and it seemed to be everywhere— teasing, tempting, tickling. It was on her belly, then on her hip, then on her ankle, sliding up under her skirt.

"Colin," Penelope gasped, squirming beneath him as his fingers stroked the delicate skin behind her knee.

"Are you trying to get away or come closer?" he murmured, his lips never once leaving her breast.

"I don't know."

He lifted his head and smiled down at her wolfishly. "Good."

He climbed off of her and slowly removed the remainder of his clothing, first his fine linen shirt and then his boots and breeches. And all the while, he never once allowed his eyes to stray from hers. When he was done, he nudged her dress, already pooling about her waist, around her hips, his fingers pressing lightly against her soft bottom as he lifted her up to slide the fabric under her.

She was left before him in nothing but her sheer, whisper-soft stockings. He paused then, and smiled, too much of a man not to enjoy the view, then eased them from her legs, letting them flitter to the floor after he'd slid them over her toes.

She was shivering in the night air, and so he lay beside her, pressing his body to hers, infusing her with his warmth as he savored the silky softness of her skin.

He needed her. It was humbling how much he needed her.

He was hard, hot, and so desperately wracked with desire it was a wonder he could still see straight. And yet even as his body screamed for release, he was possessed of a strange calm, an unexpected sense of control. Somewhere along the way this had ceased to be about him. It was about her—no, it was about *them,* about this wondrous joining and miraculous love that he was only now beginning to appreciate.

He wanted her—God above, he wanted her—but he wanted her to tremble beneath him, to scream with desire, to thrash her head from side to side as he teased her toward completion.

He wanted her to love this, to love him, and to *know,* when they were lying in each other's arms, sweaty and spent, that she belonged to him.

Because he already knew that he belonged to her.

"Tell me if I do anything you don't like," he said, surprised by the way his voice was shaking over his words.

"You couldn't," she whispered, touching his cheek.

She didn't understand. It almost made him smile, probably *would* have made him smile if he weren't so concerned with making this, her first experience, a good one. But her whispered words—*you couldn't*—could mean only one thing—that she had no idea what it meant to make love with a man.

"Penelope," he said softly, covering her hand with his own, "I need to explain something to you. I could hurt you. I would never mean to, but I could, and—"

She shook her head. "You couldn't," she said again. "I know you. Sometimes I think I know you better than I know myself. And you would never do anything that would hurt me."

He gritted his teeth and tried not to groan. "Not on purpose," he said, the barest hint of exasperation tinging his voice, "but I could, and—"

"Let me be the judge," she said, taking his hand and bringing it to her mouth for a single, heartfelt kiss. "And as for the other . . ."

"What other?"

She smiled, and Colin had to blink, because he could swear she almost looked as if she were amused by him. "You told me to tell you if you did anything I didn't like," she said.

He watched her face closely, suddenly mesmerized by the way her lips were forming words.

"I promise you," she vowed, "I will like it all."

A strange bubble of joy began to rise within him. He didn't know what benevolent god had chosen to bestow her upon him, but he was thinking that he needed to be a bit more attentive next time he went to church.

"I will like it all," she said again, "because I'm with you."

He took her face in his hands, gazing down at her

as if she were the most wondrous creature ever to walk the earth.

"I love you," she whispered. "I've loved you for years."

"I know," he said, surprising himself with his words. He had known, he supposed, but he'd thrust it from his mind because her love made him uncomfortable. It was hard to be loved by someone decent and good when you didn't return the emotion. He couldn't dismiss her, because he liked her and he'd not have been able to forgive himself if he'd trampled on her emotions. And he couldn't flirt with her, for much the same reasons.

And so he had told himself that what she felt wasn't really love. It had been easier to try to convince himself that she was merely infatuated with him, that she didn't understand what true love was (as if he did!), and that eventually she would find someone else and settle down into a happy and contented life.

Now that thought—that she might have married another—nearly left him paralyzed with fear.

They were side by side, and she was staring at him with her heart in her eyes, her entire face alive with happiness and contentment, as if she finally felt free now that she had spoken the words. And he realized that her expression held not one trace of expectation.

She hadn't told him she loved him simply to hear his reply. She wasn't even waiting for his answer.

She had told him she loved him simply because she wanted to. Because that was what she felt.

"I love you, too," he whispered, pressing an intense kiss against her lips before moving away so that he could see her reaction.

Penelope gazed at him for a very long while before responding. Finally, with an odd, convulsive swallow, she said, "You don't have to say that just because I did."

"I know," he replied, smiling.

She just looked at him, her widening eyes the only movement on her face.

"And you know that, too," he said softly. "You said you know me better than you know yourself. And you know I would never say the words if I didn't mean them."

And as she lay there, naked in his bed, cradled in his embrace, Penelope realized that she *did* know. Colin didn't lie, not about anything important, and she couldn't imagine anything more important than the moment they were sharing.

He loved her. It wasn't anything she'd expected, nor anything she'd even allowed herself to hope for, and yet here it was, like a bright and shining miracle in her heart.

"Are you sure?" she whispered.

He nodded, his arms drawing her closer. "I realized it this evening. When I asked you to stay."

"How . . ." But she didn't finish the question. Because she wasn't even really sure what the question was. How did he know he loved her? How had it happened? How did it make him feel?

But somehow he must have known what she could not verbalize, because he answered, "I don't know. I don't know when, I don't know how, and to be honest, I don't care. But I know this much is true: I love you, and I hate myself for not seeing the real you all these years."

"Colin, don't," she pleaded. "No recriminations. No regrets. Not tonight."

But he just smiled, placing a single finger on her lips to silence her plea. "I don't think you changed," he said. "At least not very much. But then one day I realized I was seeing something different when I looked at you." He shrugged. "Maybe I changed. Maybe I grew up."

She placed her finger on his lips, quieting him in the same manner he'd done to her. "Maybe I grew up, too."

"I love you," he said, leaning forward to kiss her. And this time she couldn't reply, because his mouth remained on hers, hungry, demanding, and very, very seductive.

He seemed to know exactly what to do. Each flick of his tongue, each nibble of his teeth sent shivers to the very core of her being, and she gave herself over to the pure joy of the moment, to the white-hot flame of desire. His hands were everywhere, and she felt him everywhere, his fingers on her skin, his leg nudging its way between hers.

He was pulling her closer, rolling her on top of him as he slid onto his back. His hands were on her bottom, pulling her so tightly against him that the proof of his desire seared itself into her skin.

Penelope gasped at the astounding intimacy of it all, but her breath was caught by his lips, still kissing her with fierce tenderness.

And then she was on her back, and he was on top of her, and the weight of him was pressing her into the mattress, squeezing the air from her lungs. His mouth moved to her ear, then to her throat, and Penelope felt herself arching beneath him, as if she could somehow curve her body closer to his.

She didn't know what she was supposed to do, but she knew she had to move. Her mother had already conducted her "little talk," as she'd put it, and she'd told Penelope that she must lie still beneath her husband and allow him his pleasures.

But there was no way she could have remained motionless, no way she could have stopped her hips from pressing up against him, nor her legs from wrapping around his. And she didn't want to *allow* him his pleasures—she wanted to encourage them, to share them.

And she wanted them for herself as well. Whatever this was, building inside of her—this tension, this desire—it needed release, and Penelope couldn't imagine that that moment, that those feelings wouldn't be the most exquisite of her life.

"Tell me what to do," she said, urgency making her voice hoarse.

Colin spread her legs wide, running his hands along her sides until they reached her thighs and squeezed. "Let me do everything," he said, breathing hard.

She grabbed at his buttocks, pulling him closer. "No," she insisted. "Tell me."

He stopped moving for the barest of moments, looking at her in surprise. "Touch me," he said.

"Where?"

"Anywhere."

Her hands on his bottom relaxed slightly, and she smiled. "I *am* touching you."

"Move," he groaned. "Move them."

She let her fingers drift to his thighs, swirling gently as she felt the soft springiness of hair. "Like this?"

He nodded jerkily.

Her hands slid forward, until they were dangerously close to his member. "Like this?"

Abruptly, he covered one of her hands with his. "Not now," he said harshly.

She looked at him in confusion.

"You'll understand later," he grunted, spreading her legs even wider before sliding his hand between their bodies and touching her most intimate place.

"Colin!" she gasped.

He smiled devilishly. "Did you think I wouldn't touch you like this?" As if to illustrate his point, one of his fingers began to dance across her sensitive flesh, causing her to arch off the bed, her hips actually lifting them both before sagging back down as she shuddered with desire.

His lips found her ear. "There's much more," he whispered.

Penelope didn't dare ask what. This was already an awful lot more than her mother had mentioned.

He slid one finger inside her, causing her to gasp again (which caused him to laugh with delight), then began to stroke her slowly.

"Oh, my *God*," Penelope moaned.

"You're almost ready for me," he said, his breath coming faster now. "So wet, but so tight."

"Colin, what are you—"

He slid another finger inside, effectively ending any chance she had for intelligent speech.

She felt stretched wide, and yet she loved it. She must be very wicked, a wanton at heart, because all she wanted was to spread her legs wider and wider until she was completely open to him. As far as she was concerned, he could do anything to her, touch her in any way he pleased.

Just as long as he didn't stop.

"I can't wait much longer," he gasped.

"Don't wait."

"I need you."

She reached up and grasped his face, forcing him to look at her. "I need you, too."

And then his fingers were gone. Penelope felt oddly hollow and empty, but only for a second, because then there was something else at her entrance, something hard and hot, and very, very demanding.

"This may hurt," Colin said, gritting his teeth as if he expected pain himself.

"I don't care."

He had to make this good for her. He had to. "I'll

be gentle," he said, although his desire was now so fierce he had no idea how he could possibly keep such a promise.

"I want you," she said. "I want you and I need something and I don't know what."

He pushed forward, just an inch or so, but it felt like she was swallowing him whole.

She went silent beneath him, her only sound her breath running raggedly across her lips.

Another inch, another step closer to heaven. "Oh, Penelope," he moaned, using his arms to hold himself above her so as not to crush her with his weight. "Please tell mc this feels good. *Please*."

Because if she said otherwise, it was going to kill him to pull out.

She nodded, but said, "I need a moment."

He swallowed, forcing his breath through his nose in short bursts. It was the only way he could concentrate on holding back. She probably needed to stretch around him, to allow her muscles to relax. She'd never taken a man before, and she was so exquisitely tight.

All the same, he couldn't wait until they'd had a chance to do this enough so that he didn't have to hold back.

When he felt her relax slightly beneath him, he pushed forward a bit more, until he reached the undeniable proof of her innocence. "Oh, God," he groaned. "This is going to hurt. I can't help it, but I promise you, it's only this one time, and it won't hurt much."

"How do you know?" she asked him.

He closed his eyes in agony. Trust Penelope to question him. "Trust me," he said, weaseling out of the question.

And then he thrust forward, embedding himself to the hilt, sinking into her warmth until he knew he was home.

"Oh!" she gasped, her face showing her shock.

"Are you all right?"

She nodded. "I think so."

He moved slightly. "Is this all right?"

She nodded again, but her face looked surprised, maybe a little dazed.

Colin's hips began to move of their own volition, unable to remain still when he was so obviously near to a climax. She was pure perfection around him, and when he realized that her gasps were of desire and not of pain, he finally let himself go and gave in to the overwhelming desire surging through his blood.

She was quickening beneath him, and he prayed that he could hold out until she climaxed. Her breath was fast and hot, and her fingers were pressing relentlessly into his shoulders, and her hips were squirming under him, whipping his need into a near-frenzy.

And then it came. A sound from her lips, sweeter than anything ever to touch his ears. She cried out his name as her entire body tensed in pleasure, and he thought—*Someday I will watch her. I will see her face when she reaches the height of pleasure.*

But not today. He was already coming, and his eyes were shut with the fierce ecstasy of it all. Her name was ripped from his lips as he thrust one last time, then slumped atop her, completely bereft of strength.

For a full minute there was silence, nothing but the rise and fall of their chests as they fought for breath, waited for the tremendous rush of their bodies to settle down into that tingly bliss one feels in the arms of one's beloved.

Or at least that was what Colin thought this must be. He had been with women before, but he had only just realized that he had never made love until he'd laid Penelope onto his bed and begun their intimate dance with a single kiss upon her lips.

This was like nothing he'd ever felt before.

This was love.

And he was going to hold on with both hands.

Chapter 19

It was not very difficult to get the wedding date pushed forward.

It occurred to Colin as he was returning to his home in Bloomsbury (after sneaking an extremely disheveled Penelope into her own house in Mayfair), that there might be a very good reason why they should be married sooner rather than later.

Of course, it was quite unlikely that she would become pregnant after only one encounter. And, he had to admit, even if she did become pregnant, the child would be an eight-month baby, which wasn't too terribly suspect in a world full of children born a mere six months or so following a wedding. Not to mention that first babies were usually late (Colin was uncle to enough nieces and nephews to know this to be true), which would make the baby an eight-and-a-half-month baby, which wasn't unusual at all.

So really, there was no urgent need to move up the wedding.

Except that he wanted to.

So he had a little "talk" with the mothers, in which he conveyed a great deal without actually saying anything explicit, and they hastily agreed to his plan to rush the wedding.

Especially since he *might* have *possibly* misled them to believe that his and Penelope's intimacies had occurred several weeks prior.

Ah, well, little white lies really weren't such a large transgression when they were told to serve the greater good.

And a hasty wedding, Colin reflected as he lay in bed each night, reliving his time with Penelope and fervently wishing she were there beside him, *definitely* served the greater good.

The mothers, who had become inseparable in recent days as they planned the wedding, initially protested the change, worrying about unsavory gossip (which in this case would have been entirely true), but Lady Whistledown came, somewhat indirectly, to their rescue.

The gossip surrounding Lady Whistledown and

Cressida Twombley and whether the two were actually the same person raged like nothing London had heretofore seen or heard. In fact, the talk was so ubiquitous, so utterly impossible to escape, that no one paused to consider the fact that the date of the Bridgerton-Featherington wedding had been altered.

Which suited the Bridgertons and the Featheringtons just fine.

Except, perhaps, for Colin and Penelope, neither of whom were especially comfortable when talk turned to Lady Whistledown. Penelope was used to it by now, of course; nary a month had gone by in the past ten years when someone had not made idle speculation in her presence about the identity of Lady Whistledown. But Colin was still so upset and angry over her secret life that she'd grown uncomfortable herself. She'd tried to broach the subject with him a few times, but he'd become tight-lipped and told her (in a very un-Colin-like tone) that he didn't want to talk about it.

She could only deduce that he was ashamed of her. Or if not of her, precisely, then of her work as Lady Whistledown. Which was like a blow to her heart, because her writing was the one segment in her life that she could point to with a great sense of pride and accomplishment. She had *done* something. She had, even if she could not put her own name on her work, become a wild success. How many of her contemporaries, male or female, could claim the same?

She might be ready to leave Lady Whistledown behind and live her new life as Mrs. Colin Bridgerton, wife and mother, but that in no way meant that she was ashamed of what she had done.

If only Colin could take pride in her accomplishments as well.

Oh, she believed, with every fiber of her being, that he loved her. Colin would never lie about such a thing. He had enough clever words and teasing smiles to make a woman feel happy and content without actually uttering words of love hc did not feel. But perhaps it was possible—indeed, after regarding Colin's behavior, she was now sure it was possible—that someone could love another person and still feel shame and displeasure with that person.

Penelope just hadn't expected it to hurt quite so much.

They were strolling through Mayfair one afternoon, just days before the wedding, when she attempted to broach the subject once again. Why, she didn't know, since she couldn't imagine that his attitude would have miraculously changed since the last time she'd mentioned it, but she couldn't seem to stop herself. Besides, she was hoping that their position out in public, where all the world could see them, would force Colin to keep a smile on his face and listen to what she had to say.

She gauged the distance to Number Five, where they were expected for tea. "I think," she said, estimating that she had five minutes of conversation before he could usher her inside and change the subject, "that we have unfinished business that must be discussed."

He raised a brow and looked at her with a curious but still very playful grin. She knew exactly what he was trying to do: use his charming and witty personality to steer the conversation where he wanted it. Any minute now, that grin would turn boyishly lopsided, and he would say something designed to change the topic without her realizing, something like—

"Rather serious for such a sunny day."

She pursed her lips. It wasn't precisely what she'd expected, but it certainly echoed the sentiment.

"Colin," she said, trying to remain patient, "I wish you wouldn't try to change the subject every time I bring up Lady Whistledown."

His voice grew even, controlled. "I don't believe I heard you mention her name, or I suppose I should say *your* name. And besides, all I did was compliment the fine weather."

Penelope wanted more than anything to plant her feet firmly on the pavement and yank him to a startling halt, but they were in public (her own fault, she supposed, for choosing such a place to initiate the conversation) and so she kept walking, her gait smooth and sedate, even as her fingers curled into tense little fists. "The other night, when my last column was published—you were furious with me," she continued.

He shrugged. "I'm over it."

"I don't think so."

He turned to her with a rather condescending expression. "And now you're telling me what I feel?"

Such a nasty shot could not go unreturned. "Isn't that what a wife is supposed to do?"

"You're not my wife yet."

Penelope counted to three—no, better make that ten—before replying. "I am sorry if what I did upset you, but I had no other choice."

"You had every choice in the world, but I am certainly not going to debate the issue right here on Bruton Street."

And they *were* on Bruton Street. Oh, *bother*, Penelope had completely misjudged how quickly they were walking. She only had another minute or so at the most before they ascended the front steps to Number Five.

"I can assure you," she said, "that you-know-who will never again emerge from retirement."

"I can hardly express my relief."

"I wish you wouldn't be so sarcastic."

He turned to face her with flashing eyes. His expression was so different from the mask of bland boredom that had been there just moments earlier that Penelope nearly backed up a step. "Be careful what you wish for, Penelope," he said. "The sarcasm is the only thing keeping my real feelings at bay, and believe me, you don't want *those* in full view."

"I think I do," she said, her voice quite small, because in truth she wasn't sure that she did.

"Not a day goes by when I'm not forced to stop and consider what on earth I am going to do to protect you should your secret get out. I love you, Penelope. God help me, but I do."

Penelope could have done without the plea for God's help, but the declaration of love was quite nice.

"In three days," he continued, "I will be your husband. I will take a solemn vow to protect you until death do us part. Do you understand what that means?"

"You'll save me from marauding minotaurs?" she tried to joke.

His expression told her he did not find that amusing.

"I wish you wouldn't be so angry," she muttered.

He turned to her with a disbelieving expression, as if he didn't think she had the right to mutter about

anything. "If I'm angry, it's because I did not appreciate finding out about your last column at the same time
as everyone else."

She nodded, catching her bottom lip between her
teeth before saying, "I apologize for that. You certainly
had the right to know ahead of time, but how could I
have told you? You would have tried to stop me."

"Exactly."

They were now just a few houses away from Number
Five. If Penelope wanted to ask him anything more,
she would have to do it quickly. "Are you sure—" she
began, then cut herself off, not certain if she wanted to
finish the question.

"Am I sure of what?"

She gave her head a little shake. "It's nothing."

"It's obviously not nothing."

"I was just wondering . . ." She looked to the side,
as if the sight of the London cityscape could somehow
give her the necessary courage to continue. "I was just
wondering . . ."

"Spit it out, Penelope."

It was unlike him to be so curt, and his tone prodded her into action. "I was wondering," she said, "if
perhaps your unease with my, er . . ."

"Secret life?" he supplied in a drawl.

"If that is what you want to call it," she acceded. "It

had occurred to me that perhaps your unease does not stem entirely from your desire to protect my reputation should I be found out."

"What, precisely," he asked in a clipped tone, "do you mean by that?"

She'd already voiced her question; there was nothing to do now but supply complete honesty. "I think you're ashamed of me."

He stared at her for three full seconds before answering, "I'm not ashamed of you. I told you once already I wasn't."

"What, then?"

Colin's steps faltered, and before he realized what his body was doing, he was standing still in front of Number Three, Bruton Street. His mother's home was only two houses away, and he was fairly certain they were expected for tea about five minutes ago, and . . .

And he couldn't quite get his feet to move.

"I'm not ashamed of you," he said again, mostly because he couldn't bring himself to tell her the truth— that he was jealous. Jealous of her achievements, jealous of her.

It was such a distasteful feeling, such an unpleasant emotion. It ate at him, creating a vague sense of shame every time someone mentioned Lady Whistledown, which, given the tenor of London's current gossip, was about ten times each day. And he wasn't quite certain what to do about it.

His sister Daphne had once commented that he always seemed to know what to say, how to set others at ease. He'd thought about that for several days after she'd said it, and he'd come to the conclusion that his ability to make others feel good about themselves must stem from his own sense of self.

He was a man who had always felt supremely comfortable in his own skin. He didn't know why he was so blessed—perhaps it was good parents, maybe simple luck. But now he felt awkward and uncomfortable and it was spilling into every corner of his life. He snapped at Penelope, he barely spoke at parties.

And it was all due to this detestable jealousy, and its attendant shame.

Or was it?

Would he be jealous of Penelope if he hadn't already sensed a lack in his own life?

It was an interesting psychological question. Or at least it would be if it were about anyone else but him.

"My mother will be expecting us," he said curtly, knowing that he was avoiding the issue, and hating himself for it, but quite unable to do anything else. "And your mother will be there as well, so we had better not be late."

"We're already late," she pointed out.

He took her arm and tugged her toward Number Five. "All the more reason not to dally."

"You're avoiding me," she said.

"How can I be avoiding you if you're right here on my arm?"

That made her scowl. "You're avoiding my question."

"We will discuss it later," he said, "when we are not standing in the middle of Bruton Street, with heaven knows whom staring at us through their windows."

And then, to demonstrate that he would brook no further protest, he placed his hand at her back and steered her none-too-gently up the steps to Number Five.

One week later, nothing had changed, except, Penelope reflected, her last name.

The wedding had been magical. It was a small affair, much to the dismay of London society. And the wedding night—well, that had been magical, too.

And, in fact, marriage was magical. Colin was a wonderful husband—teasing, gentle, attentive . . .

Except when the topic of Lady Whistledown arose.

Then he became . . . well, Penelope wasn't sure

what he became, except that he was not himself. Gone was his easy grace, his glib tongue, everything wonderful that made him the man she'd loved for so very long.

In a way, it was almost funny. For so long, all of her dreams had revolved around marrying this man. And at some point those dreams had come to include her telling him about her secret life. How could they not? In Penelope's dreams, her marriage to Colin had been a perfect union, and that meant complete honesty.

In her dreams, she sat him down, shyly revealed her secret. He reacted first with disbelief, then with delight and pride. How remarkable she was, to have fooled all of London for so many years. How witty to have written such clever turns of phrase. He admired her for her resourcefulness, praised her for her success. In some of the dreams, he even suggested that he become her secret reporter.

It had seemed the sort of thing Colin would enjoy, just the sort of amusing, devious task that he would relish.

But that wasn't the way it had turned out.

He said he wasn't ashamed of her, and maybe he even thought that was true, but she couldn't quite bring herself to believe him. She'd seen his face when he swore that all he wanted was to protect her. But protectiveness was a fierce, burning feeling, and when Colin was talking about Lady Whistledown, his eyes were shuttered and flat.

She tried not to feel so disappointed. She tried to tell herself that she had no right to expect Colin to live up to her dreams, that her vision of him had been unfairly idealized, but . . .

But she still wanted him to be the man she'd dreamed of.

And she felt so guilty for every pang of disappointment. This was Colin! Colin, for heaven's sake. Colin, who was as close to perfect as any human being could ever hope to be. She had no right to find fault with him, and yet . . .

And yet she did.

She wanted him to be proud of her. She wanted it more than anything in the world, more even than she'd wanted *him* all those years when she'd watched him from afar.

But she cherished her marriage, and awkward moments aside, she cherished her husband. And so she stopped mentioning Lady Whistledown. She was tired of Colin's hooded expression. She didn't want to see the tight lines of displeasure around his mouth.

It wasn't as if she could avoid the topic forever; any trip out into society seemed to bring mention of her alter ego. But she didn't have to introduce the subject at home.

And so, as they sat at breakfast one morning, chatting amiably as they each perused that morning's newspaper, she searched for other topics.

"Do you think we shall take a honeymoon trip?" she asked, spreading a generous portion of raspberry jam on her muffin. She probably ought not to eat so much, but the jam was really quite tasty, and besides, she always ate a lot when she was anxious.

She frowned, first at the muffin and then at nothing in particular. She hadn't realized she was so anxious. She'd thought she'd been able to push the Lady Whistledown problem to the back of her mind.

"Perhaps later in the year," Colin replied, reaching for the jam once she was through with it. "Pass me the toast, would you?"

She did so, silently.

He glanced up, either at her or over at the plate of kippers—she couldn't be sure. "You look disappointed," he said.

She supposed she should be flattered that he'd looked up from his food. Or maybe he was looking at the kippers and she just got in the way. Probably the latter. It was difficult to compete with food for Colin's attention.

"Penelope?" he queried.

She blinked.

"You looked disappointed?" he reminded her.

"Oh. Yes, well, I am, I suppose." She gave him a faltering smile. "I've never been anywhere, and you've been everywhere, and I guess I thought you could take me someplace you especially liked. Greece, perhaps. Or maybe Italy. I've always wanted to see Italy."

"You would like it," he murmured distractedly, his attention more on his eggs than on her. "Venice especially, I think."

"Then why don't you take me?"

"I will," he said, spearing a pink piece of bacon and popping it into his mouth. "Just not now."

Penelope licked a bit of jam off her muffin and tried not to look too crestfallen.

"If you must know," Colin said with a sigh, "the reason I don't want to leave is . . ." He glanced at the open door, his lips pursing with annoyance. "Well, I can't say it here."

Penelope's eyes widened. "You mean . . ." She traced a large W on the tablecloth.

"Exactly."

She stared at him in surprise, a bit startled that he had brought up the subject, and even more so that he didn't seem terribly upset by it. "But why?" she finally asked.

"Should the secret come out," he said cryptically, just in case there were any servants about, which there usually were, "I should like to be in town to control the damage."

Penelope deflated in her chair. It was never pleasant to be referred to as damage. Which was what he had done. Well, indirectly, at least. She stared at her muffin, trying to decide if she was hungry. She wasn't, not really.

But she ate it, anyway.

Chapter 20

A few days later, Penelope returned from a shopping expedition with Eloise, Hyacinth, and Felicity to find her husband seated behind his desk in his study. He was reading something, uncharacteristically hunched as he pored over some unknown book or document.

"Colin?"

His head jerked up. He must not have heard her coming, which was surprising, since she hadn't made any effort to soften her steps. "Penelope," he said, rising to his feet as she entered the room, "how was your, er, whatever it was you did when you went out?"

"Shopping," she said with an amused smile. "I went shopping."

"Right. So you did." He rocked slightly from foot to foot. "Did you buy anything?"

"A bonnet," she replied, tempted to add *and three diamond rings,* just to see if he was listening.

"Good, good," he murmured, obviously eager to get back to whatever it was on his desk.

"What are you reading?" she asked.

"Nothing," he replied, almost reflexively, then he added, "Well, actually it's one of my journals."

His face took on a strange expression, a little sheepish, a little defiant, almost as if he were embarrassed that he'd been caught, and at the same time daring her to ask more.

"May I look at it?" she asked, keeping her voice soft and, she hoped, unthreatening. It was strange to think that Colin was insecure about anything. Mention of his journals, however, seemed to bring out a vulnerability that was surprising . . . and touching.

Penelope had spent so much of her life regarding Colin as an invincible tower of happiness and good cheer. He was self-confident, handsome, well liked, and intelligent. How easy it must be to be a Bridgerton, she'd thought on more than one occasion.

There had been so many times—more than she could count—that she'd come home from tea with Eloise and her family, curled up on her bed, and wished that she'd been born a Bridgerton. Life was easy for them. They were smart and attractive and rich and everyone seemed to like them.

And you couldn't even hate them for living such splendid existences because they were so *nice.*

Well, now she was a Bridgerton, by marriage if not by birth, and it was true—life *was* better as a Bridgerton, although that had less to do with any great change in herself than it did because she was madly in love with her husband, and by some fabulous miracle, he actually returned the emotion.

But life wasn't perfect, not even for the Bridgertons.

Even Colin—the golden boy, the man with the easy smile and devilish humor—had raw spots of his own. He was haunted by unfulfilled dreams and secret insecurities. How unfair she had been when she'd pondered his life, not to allow him his weaknesses.

"I don't need to see it in its entirety," she reassured him. "Maybe just a short passage or two. Of your own choosing. Perhaps something you especially like."

He looked down at the open book, staring blankly, as if the words were written in Chinese. "I wouldn't know what to pick out," he mumbled. "It's all the same, really."

"Of course it's not. I understand that more than anyone. I—" She suddenly looked about, realized the door was open, and quickly went to shut it. "I've written countless columns," she continued, "and I assure you, they are not all the same. Some I adored." She smiled nostalgically, remembering the rush of contentment and pride that washed over her whenever she'd written what she thought was an especially good installment. "It was lovely, do you know what I mean?"

He shook his head.

"That feeling you get," she tried to explain, "when you just *know* that the words you've chosen are exactly right. And you can only really appreciate it after you've sat there, slumped and dejected, staring at your blank sheet of paper, not having a clue what to say."

"I know *that*," he said.

Penelope tried not to smile. "I know you know the first feeling. You're a splendid writer, Colin. I've read your work."

He looked up, alarmed.

"Just the bit you know about," she assured him. "I would never read your journals without your invitation." She blushed, remembering that that was exactly how she'd read the passage about his trip to Cyprus. "Well, not now, anyway," she added. "But it was *good*, Colin. Almost magical, and somewhere inside of you, you have to know that."

He just stared at her, looking like he simply didn't know what to say. It was an expression she'd seen on countless faces, but never on *his* face, and it was so very odd and strange. She wanted to cry, she wanted to throw her arms around him. Most of all, she was gripped by an intense need to restore a smile to his face.

"I know you must have had those days I described," she insisted. "The ones when you know you've written something good." She looked at him hopefully. "You know what I mean, don't you?"

He made no response.

"You do," she said. "I know you do. You can't be a writer and not know it."

"I'm not a writer," he said.

"Of course you are." She motioned to the journal. "The proof is right there." She stepped forward. "Colin, please. Please may I read a little bit more?"

For the first time, he looked undecided, which Penelope took as a small victory. "You've already read almost everything *I've* ever written," she cajoled. "It's really only fair to—"

She stopped when she saw his face. She didn't know how to describe it, but he looked shuttered, cut off, utterly unreachable.

"Colin?" she whispered.

"I'd rather keep this to myself," he said curtly. "If you don't mind."

"No, of course I don't mind," she said, but they both knew she was lying.

Colin stood so still and silent that she had no choice but to excuse herself, leaving him alone in the room, staring helplessly at the door.

He'd hurt her.

It didn't matter that he hadn't meant to. She'd reached out to him, and he'd been unable to take her hand.

And the worst part was that he knew she didn't understand. She thought he was ashamed of her. He'd told her that he wasn't, but since he'd not been able to bring himself to tell her the truth—that he was jealous—he couldn't imagine that she'd believed him.

Hell, he wouldn't have believed him, either. He'd clearly looked like he was lying, because in a way, he was lying. Or at least withholding a truth that made him uncomfortable.

But the minute she'd reminded him that he'd read everything she'd written, something had turned ugly and black inside of him.

He'd read everything she'd written because she'd *published* everything she'd written. Whereas his scribblings sat dull and lifeless in his journals, tucked away where no one would see them.

Did it matter what a man wrote if no one ever read it? Did words have meaning if they were never heard?

He had never considered publishing his journals until Penelope had suggested it several weeks earlier; now the thought consumed him day and night (when he wasn't consumed with Penelope, of course). But he was gripped by a powerful fear. What if no one wanted to publish his work? What if someone did publish it, but only because his was a rich and powerful family? Colin wanted, more than anything, to be his own man, to be known for his accomplishments, not for his name or position, or even his smile or charm.

And then there was the scariest prospect of all: What if his writing was published but no one liked it?

How could he face that? How would he exist as a failure?

Or was it worse to remain as he was now: a coward?

Later that evening, after Penelope had finally pulled herself out of her chair and drunk a restorative cup of tea and puttered aimlessly about the bedchamber and finally settled against her pillows with a book that she couldn't quite make herself read, Colin appeared.

He didn't say anything at first, just stood there and smiled at her, except it wasn't one of his usual smiles—the sort that light from within and compel their recipient to smile right back.

This was a small smile, a sheepish smile.

A smile of apology.

Penelope let her book rest, spine up, on her belly.

"May I?" Colin inquired, motioning to the empty spot beside her.

Penelope scooted over to the right. "Of course," she murmured, moving her book to the night table next to her.

"I've marked a few passages," he said, holding forward his journal as he perched on the side of the bed. "If you'd like to read them, to"—he cleared his throat—"offer an opinion, that would be—" He coughed again. "That would be acceptable."

Penelope looked at the journal in his hand, elegantly bound in crimson leather, then she looked up at him. His face was serious, and his eyes were somber, and although he was absolutely still—no twitching or fidgeting—she could tell he was nervous.

Nervous. Colin. It seemed the strangest thing imaginable.

"I'd be honored," she said softly, gently tugging the book from his fingers. She noticed that a few pages were marked with ribbons, and with careful fingers, she opened to one of the selected spots.

14 March 1819
The Highlands are oddly brown.

"That was when I visited Francesca in Scotland," he interrupted.

Penelope gave him a slightly indulgent smile, meant as a gentle scolding for his interruption.

"Sorry," he mumbled.

One would think, at least one from England would think, that the hills and dales would be a rich emerald green. Scotland resides, after all, on the same isle, and by all accounts suffers from the same rain that plagues England.

I am told that these strange beige hills are called tablelands, and they are bleak and brown and desolate.

And yet they stir the soul.

"That was when I was rather high up in elevation," he explained. "When you're lower, or near the lochs, it's quite different."

Penelope turned to him and gave him a look.

"Sorry," he mumbled.

"Maybe you'd be more comfortable if you didn't read over my shoulder?" she suggested.

He blinked in surprise.

"I would think you've already read all this before." At his blank stare, she added, "So you don't need to read it now." She waited for a reaction and got none. "So you don't need to hover over my shoulder," she finally finished.

"Oh." He inched away. "Sorry."

Penelope eyed him dubiously. "Off the bed, Colin."

Looking much chastened, Colin pushed himself off the bed and flopped into a chair in the far corner of the room, crossing his arms and tapping his foot in a mad dance of impatience.

Tap tap tap. Tappity tap tap tap.

"Colin!"

He looked up in honest surprise. "What?"

"Stop tapping your foot!"

He looked down as if his foot were a foreign object. "Was I tapping it?"

"Yes."

"Oh." He pulled his arms in more tightly against his chest. "Sorry."

Penelope refocused her attention on the journal.

Tap tap.

Penelope jerked head up. "Colin!"

He planted his feet down firmly on the carpet. "I couldn't help myself. Didn't even realize I was doing it." He uncrossed his arms, resting them on the upholstered side of the chair, but he didn't look relaxed; the fingers on both of his hands were tense and arched.

She stared at him for several moments, waiting to see if he was truly going to be able to hold still.

"I won't do it again," he assured her. "I promise."

She gave him one last assessing stare, then turned her attention back to the words in front of her.

As a people, the Scots despise the English, and many would say rightfully so. But individually, they are quite warm and friendly, eager to share a glass of whisky, a hot meal, or to offer a warm place to sleep. A group of Englishmen—or, in truth, any Englishman in any sort of uniform—will not find a warm welcome in a Scottish village. But should a lone Sassenach amble down their High Street—the local population will greet him with open arms and broad smiles.

Such was the case when I happened upon Inveraray, upon the banks of Loch Fyne. A neat, wellplanned town that was designed by Robert Adam when the Duke of Argyll decided to move the entire village to accommodate his new castle, it sits on the edge of the water, its whitewashed buildings in neat rows that meet at right angles (surely a strangely ordered existence for one such as I, brought up amid the crooked intersections of London).

I was partaking of my evening meal at the George Hotel, enjoying a fine whisky instead of the usual ale one might drink at a similar establishment in England, when I realized that I had no idea how to get to my next destination, nor any clue how long it would take to get there. I approached the proprietor (one Mr. Clark), explained my intention to visit Blair Castle, and then could do nothing but blink in wonder and confusion as the rest of the inn's occupants chimed in with advice.

"Blair Castle?" Mr. Clark boomed. (He was a booming sort of man, not given to soft speech.) "Well, now, if ye're wanting to go to Blair Castle, ye'll certainly be wanting to head west toward Pitlochry and then north from there."

This was met by a chorus of approval—and an equally loud echo of disapproval.

"Och, no!" yelled another (whose name I later learned was MacBogel). "He'll be having to cross

Loch Tay, and a greater recipe for disaster has never been tasted. Better to head north now, and then move west."

"Aye," chimed in a third, "but then he'll be having Ben Nevis in his way. Are you saying a mountain is a lesser obstacle than a puny loch?"

"Are you calling Loch Tay puny? I'll be telling you I was born on the shores of Loch Tay, and no one will be calling it puny in my presence." (I have no idea who said this, or indeed, almost everything forthwith, but it was all said with great feeling and conviction.)

"He doesn't need to go all the way to Ben Nevis. He can turn west at Glencoe."

"Oh, ho, ho, and a bottle of whisky. There isn't a decent road heading west from Glencoe. Are you trying to kill the poor lad?"

And so on and so forth. If the reader has noticed that I stopped writing who said what, it is because the din of voices was so overwhelming that it was impossible to tell anyone apart, and this continued for at least ten minutes until finally, old Angus Campbell, eighty years if he was a day, spoke, and out of respect, everyone quieted down.

"What he needs to do," Angus wheezed, "is travel south to Kintyre, turn back north and cross

*the Firth of Lorne to Mull so that he can scoot
out to Iona, sail up to Skye, cross over to the main-
land to Ullapool, back down to Inverness, pay his
respects at Culloden, and from there, he can proceed south to Blair Castle, stopping in Grampian if
he chooses so he can see how a proper bottle of
whisky is made."*

*Absolute silence met this pronouncement. Fi-
nally, one brave man pointed out, "But that'll take
months."*

*"And who's saying it won't?" old Campbell said,
with the barest trace of belligerence. "The Sassenach is here to see Scotland. Are you telling me he
can say he's done that if all he's done is taken a
straight line from here to Perthshire?"*

*I found myself smiling, and made my decision
on the spot. I would follow his exact route, and
when I returned to London, I would know in my
heart that I knew Scotland.*

Colin watched Penelope as she read. Every now and
then she would smile, and his heart would leap, and
then suddenly he realized that her smile had become
permanent, and her lips were puckering as if she were
suppressing a laugh.

Colin realized he was smiling, too.

He'd been so surprised by her reaction the first time she'd read his writing; her response had been so passionate, and yet she'd been so analytical and precise when she spoke to him about it. It all made sense now, of course. She was a writer, too, probably a better one than he, and of all the things she understood in this world, she understood words.

It was hard to believe it had taken him this long to ask for her advice. Fear, he supposed, had stopped him. Fear and worry and all those stupid emotions he'd pretended were beneath him.

Who would have guessed that one woman's opinion would become so important to him? He'd worked on his journals for years, carefully recording his travels, trying to capture more than what he saw and did, trying to capture what he *felt*. And he'd never once showed them to anyone.

Until now.

There had been no one he'd wanted to show them to. No, that wasn't true. Deep down, he'd wanted to show them to a number of people, but the time had never seemed right, or he thought they would lie and say something was good when it wasn't, just to spare his feelings.

But Penelope was different. She was a writer. She was a damned good one, too. And if she said his journal entries were good, he could almost believe that it was true.

She pursed her lips slightly as she turned a page, then frowned as her fingers couldn't find purchase. After licking her middle finger, she caught hold of the errant page and began to read again.

And smiled again.

Colin let out a breath he didn't realize he'd been holding.

Finally, she laid the book down in her lap, leaving it open to the section she'd been reading. Looking up, she said, "I assume you wanted me to stop at the end of the entry?"

It wasn't quite what he'd expected her to say, and that befuddled him. "Er, if you want to," he stammered. "If you want to read more, that would be fine, I guess."

It was as if the sun had suddenly taken up residence in her smile. "Of *course* I want to read more," she gushed. "I can't wait to see what happened when you went to Kintyre and Mull and"—frowning, she checked the open book—"and Skye and Ullapool and Culloden and Grampian"—she glanced back down at the book again—"oh, yes, and Blair Castle, of course, if you ever made it. I assume you were planning to visit friends."

He nodded. "Murray," he said, referring to a school chum whose brother was the Duke of Atholl. "But I should tell you, I didn't end up following the exact route prescribed by old Angus Campbell. For one thing, I didn't even find roads connecting half the places he mentioned."

"Maybe," she said, her eyes growing dreamy, "that is where we ought to go for our honeymoon trip."

"Scotland?" he asked, thoroughly surprised. "Don't you want to travel someplace warm and exotic?"

"To one who has never traveled more than one hundred miles from London," she said pertly, "Scotland *is* exotic."

"I can assure you," he said with a smile as he walked across the room and perched on the edge of the bed, "that Italy is *more* exotic. And more romantic."

She blushed, which delighted him. "Oh," she said, looking vaguely embarrassed. (He wondered how long he'd be able to embarrass her with talk of romance and love and all the splendid activities that went with them.)

"We'll go to Scotland another time," he assured her. "I usually find myself heading north every few years or so to visit Francesca, anyway."

"I was surprised that you asked for my opinion," Penelope said after a short silence.

"Who else would I ask?"

"I don't know," she replied, suddenly very interested in the way her fingers were plucking at the bedcovers. "Your brothers, I suppose."

He laid his hand on hers. "What do *they* know about writing?"

Her chin lifted and her eyes, clear, warm, and brown, met his. "I know you value their opinions."

"That is true," he acceded, "but I value yours more."

He watched her face closely, as emotions played across her features. "But you don't like my writing," she said, her voice hesitant and hopeful at the same time.

He moved his hand to the curve of her cheek, holding it there gently, making sure that she was looking at him as he spoke. "Nothing could be further from the truth," he said, a burning intensity firing his words. "I think you are a marvelous writer. You cut right into the essence of a person with a simplicity and wit that is matchless. For years, you have made people laugh. You've made them wince. You've made them *think*, Penelope. You have made people think. I don't know what could be a higher achievement.

"Not to mention," he continued, almost as if he couldn't quite stop now that he'd gotten started, "that you write about *society*, of all things. You write about society, and you make it fun and interesting and witty, when we all know that more often than not it's beyond dull."

For the longest time, Penelope couldn't say anything. She had been proud of her work for years, and had secretly smiled whenever she had heard someone reciting from one of her columns or laughing at one of her quips. But she'd had no one with whom to share her triumphs.

Being anonymous had been a lonely prospect.

But now she had Colin. And even though the world would never know that Lady Whistledown was actually plain, overlooked, spinster-until-the-last-possible-moment Penelope Featherington, *Colin* knew. And Penelope was coming to realize that even if that wasn't all that mattered, it was what mattered most.

But she still didn't understand his actions.

"Why, then," she asked him, her words slow and carefully measured, "do you grow so distant and cold every time I bring it up?"

When he spoke, his words were close to a mumble. "It's difficult to explain."

"I'm a good listener," she said softly.

His hand, which had been cradling her face so lovingly, dropped to his lap. And he said the one thing she never would have expected.

"I'm jealous." He shrugged helplessly. "I'm so sorry."

"I don't know what you mean," she said, not intending to whisper, but lacking the voice to do anything else.

"Look at yourself, Penelope." He took both of her hands in his and twisted so that they were facing one another. "You're a huge success."

"An anonymous success," she reminded him.

"But *you* know, and *I* know, and besides, that's not what I'm talking about." He let go of one of her hands, raking his fingers through his hair as he searched for words. "You have done something. You have a body of work."

"But you have—"

"What do I have, Penelope?" he interrupted, his voice growing agitated as he rose to his feet and began to pace. "What do I have?"

"Well, you have me," she said, but her words lacked force. She knew that wasn't what he meant.

He looked at her wearily. "I'm not talking about that, Penelope—"

"I know."

"—I need something I can point to," he said, right on top of her soft sentence. "I need a purpose. Anthony has one, and Benedict has one, but I'm at odds and ends."

"Colin, you're not. You're—"

"I'm tired of being thought of as nothing but an—" He stopped short.

"What, Colin?" she asked, a bit startled by the disgusted expression that suddenly crossed his face.

"Christ above," he swore, his voice low, the S hissing from his lips.

Her eyes widened. Colin was not one for frequent profanity.

"I can't believe it," he muttered, his head moving jerkily to the left, almost as if he was flinching.

"What?" she pleaded.

"I complained to you," he said incredulously. "I complained to you about Lady Whistledown."

She grimaced. "A lot of people have done that, Colin. I'm used to it."

"I can't believe it. I complained to you about how Lady Whistledown called me charming."

"She called me an overripe citrus fruit," Penelope said, attempting levity.

He stopped his pacing for just long enough to shoot her an annoyed look. "Were you laughing at me the whole time I was moaning about how the only way I would be remembered by future generations was in *Whistledown* columns?"

"No!" she exclaimed. "I would hope you know me better than that."

He shook his head in a disbelieving manner. "I can't believe I sat there, complaining to you that I had no accomplishments, when you had all of *Whistledown*."

She got off the bed and stood. It was impossible just to sit there while he was pacing like a caged tiger. "Colin, you couldn't have known."

"Still." He let out a disgusted exhale. "The irony would be beautiful, if it weren't directed at me."

Penelope parted her lips to speak, but she didn't know how to say everything that was in her heart. Colin had so many achievements, she couldn't even begin to count them all. They weren't something you could pick up, like an edition of *Lady Whistledown's Society Papers*, but they were just as special.

Perhaps even more so.

Penelope remembered all the moments he had made people smile, all the times he had walked past all of the popular girls at balls and asked a wallflower to dance. She thought of the strong, almost magical bond he shared with his siblings. If those weren't achievements, she didn't know what was.

But she knew that those weren't the sorts of milestones he was talking about. She knew what he needed: a purpose, a calling.

Something to show the world that he was more than they thought he was.

"Publish your travel memoirs," she said.

"I'm not—"

"Publish them," she said again. "Take a chance and see if you soar."

His eyes met hers for a moment, then they slid back down to his journal, still clutched in her hands. "They need editing," he mumbled.

Penelope laughed, because she knew she had won. And he had won, too. He didn't know it yet, but he had.

"Everyone needs editing," she said, her smile broadening with each word. "Well, except me, I guess," she teased. "Or maybe I did need it," she added with a shrug. "We'll never know, because I had no one to edit me."

He looked up quite suddenly. "How did you do it?"

"How did I do what?"

His lips pursed impatiently. "You know what I mean. How did you do the column? There was more to it than the writing. You had to print and distribute. Someone had to have known who you were."

She let out a long breath. She'd held these secrets so long it felt strange to share them, even with her husband. "It's a long story," she told him. "Perhaps we should sit."

He led her back to the bed, and they both made themselves comfortable, propped up against the pillows, their legs stretched out before them.

"I was very young when it started," Penelope began. "Only seventeen. And it happened quite by accident."

He smiled. "How does something like that happen by accident?"

"I wrote it as a joke. I was so miserable that first season." She looked up at him earnestly. "I don't know if you recall, but I weighed over a stone more back then, and it's not as if I'm fashionably slender now."

"I think you're perfect," he said loyally.

Which was, Penelope thought, part of the reason she thought he was perfect as well.

"Anyway," she continued, "I wasn't terribly happy, and so I wrote a rather scathing report of the party I'd been to the night before. And then I did another, and another. I didn't sign them Lady Whistledown; I just wrote them for fun and hid them in my desk. Except one day, I forgot to hide them."

He leaned forward, utterly rapt. "What happened?"

"My family were all out, and I knew they'd be gone

for some time, because that was when Mama still thought she could turn Prudence into a diamond of the first water, and their shopping trips took all day."

Colin rolled his hand through the air, signaling that she should get to the point.

"Anyway," Penelope continued, "I decided to work in the drawing room because my room was damp and musty because someone—well, I suppose it was me— left the window open during a rainstorm. But then I had to . . . well, you know."

"No," Colin said abruptly. "I don't know."

"Attend to my business," Penelope whispered, blushing.

"Oh. Right," he said dismissively, clearly not interested in that part of the story, either. "Go on."

"When I got back, my father's solicitor was there. And he was reading what I wrote. I was horrified!"

"What happened?"

"I couldn't even speak for the first minute. But then I realized he was laughing, and it wasn't because he thought I was foolish, it was because he thought I was good."

"Well, you *are* good."

"I know that now," she said with a wry smile, "but you have to remember, I was seventeen. And I'd said some pretty horrid things in there."

"About horrid people, I'm sure," he said.

"Well, yes, but still . . ." She closed her eyes as all the memories swam through her head. "They were popular people. Influential people. People who didn't like me very much. It didn't really matter that they were horrid if what I said got out. In fact, it would have been worse because they were horrid. I would have been ruined, and I would have ruined my entire family along with me."

"What happened then? I assume it was his idea to publish."

Penelope nodded. "Yes. He made all the arrangements with the printer, who in turn found the boys to deliver. And it was his idea to give it away for free for the first two weeks. He said we needed to addict the *ton*."

"I was out of the country when the column began," Colin said, "but I remember my mother and sisters telling me all about it."

"People grumbled when the newsboys demanded payment after two weeks for free," Penelope said. "But they all paid."

"A bright idea on the part of your solicitor," Colin murmured.

"Yes, he was quite savvy."

He picked up on her use of the past tense. "Was?"

She nodded sadly. "He passed on a few years ago. But

he knew he was ill and so before he died he asked me if I wanted to continue. I suppose I could have stopped then, but I had nothing else in my life, and certainly no marriage prospects." She looked up quickly. "I don't mean to—That is to say—"

His lips curved into a self-deprecating smile. "You may scold me all you wish for not having proposed years ago."

Penelope returned his smile with one of her own. Was it any wonder she loved this man?

"But," he said rather firmly, "only if you finish the story."

"Right," she said, forcing her mind back to the matter at hand. "After Mr—" She looked up hesitantly. "I'm not certain I should say his name."

Colin knew she was torn between her love and trust for him, and her loyalty to a man who had, in all probability, been a father to her once her own had departed this earth. "It's all right," he said softly. "He's gone. His name doesn't matter."

She let out a soft breath. "Thank you," she said, chewing on her lower lip. "It's not that I don't trust you. I—"

"I know," he said reassuringly, squeezing her fingers with his. "If you want to tell me later, that's fine. And if you don't, that will be fine as well."

She nodded, her lips tight at the corners, in that strained expression people get when they are trying hard not to cry. "After he died, I worked directly with the publisher. We set up a system for delivery of the columns, and the payments continued the way they had always been made—into a discreet account in my name."

Colin sucked in his breath as he thought about how much money she must have made over the years. But how could she have spent it without incurring suspicion? "Did you make any withdrawals?" he asked.

She nodded. "After I'd been working about four years, my great-aunt passed away and left her estate to my mother. My father's solicitor wrote the will. She didn't have very much, so we took my money and pretended it was hers." Penelope's face brightened slightly as she shook her head in bewilderment. "My mother was surprised. She'd never dreamed Aunt Georgette had been so wealthy. She smiled for months. I've never seen anything like it."

"It was very kind of you," Colin said.

Penelope shrugged. "It was the only way I could actually use my money."

"But you gave it to your mother," he pointed out.

"She's my mother," she said, as if that ought to explain everything. "She supported me. It all trickled down."

He wanted to say more, but he didn't. Portia Featherington was Penelope's mother, and if Penelope wanted to love her, he wasn't going to stop her.

"Since then," Penelope said, "I haven't touched it. Well, not for myself. I've given some money to charities." Her face took on a wry expression. "Anonymously."

He didn't say anything for a moment, just took the time to think about everything she had done in the last decade, all on her own, all in secret. "If you want the money now," he finally said, "you should use it. No one will question your suddenly having more funds. You're a Bridgerton, after all." He shrugged modestly. "It's well known that Anthony settled ample livings upon all of his brothers."

"I wouldn't even know what to do with it all."

"Buy something new," he suggested. Didn't all women like to shop?

She looked at him with an odd, almost inscrutable expression. "I'm not sure you understand how much money I have," she said hedgingly. "I don't think I could spend it all."

"Put it aside for our children, then," he said. "I've been fortunate that my father and brother saw fit to provide for me, but not all younger sons are so lucky."

"And daughters," Penelope reminded him. "Our

daughters should have money of their own. *Separate* from their dowries."

Colin had to smile. Such arrangements were rare, but trust Penelope to insist upon it. "Whatever you wish," he said fondly.

She smiled and sighed, settling back against the pillows. Her fingers idly danced across the skin on the back of his hand, but her eyes were far away, and he doubted she was even aware of her movements.

"I have a confession to make," she said, her voice quiet and even just a touch shy.

He looked at her doubtfully. "Bigger than *Whistledown*?"

"Different."

"What is it?"

She dragged her eyes off of the random spot on the wall she seemed to be focused upon and gave him her full attention. "I've been feeling a bit"—she chewed on her lip as she paused, searching for the right words—"impatient with you lately. No, that's not right," she said. "Disappointed, really."

An odd feeling began to prickle in his chest. "Disappointed how?" he asked carefully.

Her shoulders gave a little shrug. "You seemed so upset with me. About Whistledown."

"I already told you that was because—"

"No, please," she said, placing a gently restraining hand on his chest. "Please let me finish. I told you I thought it was because you were ashamed of me, and I tried to ignore it, but it hurt so much, really. I thought I knew who you were, and I couldn't believe that person would think himself so far above me that he would feel such shame at my achievements."

He stared at her silently, waiting for her to continue.

"But the funny thing is . . ." She turned to him with a wise smile. "The funny thing is that it wasn't because you were ashamed at all. It was all because you wanted something like that for your own. Something like *Whistledown.* It seems silly now, but I was so worried because you weren't the perfect man of my dreams."

"No one is perfect," he said quietly.

"I know." She leaned over and planted an impulsive kiss on his cheek. "You're the imperfect man of my heart, and that's even better. I'd always thought you infallible, that your life was charmed, that you had no worries or fears or unfulfilled dreams. But that wasn't really fair of me."

"I was never ashamed of you, Penelope," he whispered. "Never."

They sat in companionable silence for a few moments, and then Penelope said, "Do you remember when I asked you if we might take a belated honeymoon trip?"

He nodded.

"Why don't we use some of my Whistledown money for that?"

"*I* will pay for the honeymoon trip."

"Fine," she said with a lofty expression. "You may take it out of your quarterly allowance."

He stared at her in shock, then hooted with laughter. "You're going to give me pin money?" he asked, unable to control the grin that spread across his face.

"Pen money," she corrected. "So you can work on your journals."

"Pen money," he mused. "I like that."

She smiled and placed her hand on his. "I like you."

He squeezed her fingers. "I like you, too."

Penelope sighed as she settled her head on his shoulder. "Is life supposed to be this wonderful?"

"I think so," he murmured. "I really do."

Chapter 21

One week later, Penelope was sitting at the desk in her drawing room, reading Colin's journals and making notes on a separate piece of paper whenever she had a question or comment. He had asked her to help him edit his writing, a task she found thrilling.

She was, of course, overjoyed that he had entrusted this critical job to her. It meant he trusted her judgment, thought she was smart and clever, felt that she could take what he had written and make it even better.

But there was more to her happiness than that. She'd needed a project, something to do. In the first days after giving up *Whistledown*, she'd reveled in her new-found free time. It was like having a holiday for the first time in years. She'd read like mad—all those novels and books she'd purchased but never gotten around to reading. And she'd taken long walks, ridden her horse in the park, sat in the small courtyard behind her house on Mount Street, enjoying the fine spring weather and tipping her face up toward the sun for a minute or so at a time—long enough to bask in the warmth, but not so long as to turn her cheeks brown.

Then, of course, the wedding and its myriad details had consumed all of her time. So she really hadn't had much opportunity to realize what might be missing in her life.

When she had been doing the column, the actual writing of it hadn't taken too terribly long, but she always had to be on the alert, watching and listening. And when she wasn't writing the column she was thinking about writing the column or desperately trying to remember some clever turn of phrase until she could get home and jot it down.

It had been mentally engaging, and she hadn't realized how much she'd missed having her mind challenged until now, when she'd finally been given the opportunity again.

She was jotting down a question about Colin's description of a Tuscan villa on page 143 in volume two of his journals when the butler knocked discreetly on the open door to alert her to his presence.

Penelope smiled sheepishly. She tended to absorb

herself entirely in her work, and Dunwoody had learned through trial and error that if he wanted to get her attention, he had to make some noise.

"A visitor to see you, Mrs. Bridgerton," he said.

Penelope looked up with a smile. It was probably one of her sisters, or maybe one of the Bridgerton siblings. "Really? Who is it?"

He stepped forward and handed her a card. Penelope looked down and gasped, first in shock, and then in misery. Engraved in classic, stately black on a creamy white background were two simple words: Lady Twombley.

Cressida Twombley? Why on earth would she come calling?

Penelope began to feel uneasy. Cressida would never call unless it was for some unpleasant purpose. Cressida never did anything unless it was for an unpleasant purpose.

"Would you like me to turn her away?" Dunwoody asked.

"No," Penelope said with a sigh. She wasn't a coward, and Cressida Twombley wasn't going to turn her into one. "I'll see her. Just give me a moment to put my papers away. But . . ."

Dunwoody stopped in his tracks and cocked his head slightly to the side, waiting for her to go on.

"Oh, never mind," Penelope muttered.

"Are you certain, Mrs. Bridgerton?"

"Yes. No." She groaned. She was dithering and it was one more transgression to add to Cressida's already long list of them—she was turning Penelope into a stammering fool. "What I mean is—if she's still here after ten minutes, would you devise some sort of emergency that requires my presence? My *immediate* presence?"

"I believe that can be arranged."

"Excellent, Dunwoody," Penelope said with a weak smile. It was, perhaps, the easy way out, but she didn't trust herself to be able to find the perfect point in the conversation to insist that Cressida leave, and the last thing she wanted was to be trapped in the drawing room with her all afternoon.

The butler nodded and left, and Penelope shuffled her papers into a neat stack, closing Colin's journal and setting it on top so that the breeze from the open window couldn't blow the papers off the desk. She stood and walked over to the sofa, sitting down in the center, hoping that she looked relaxed and composed.

As if a visit from Cressida Twombley could ever be called relaxing.

A moment later, Cressida arrived, stepping through

the open doorway as Dunwoody intoned her name. As always, she looked beautiful, every golden hair on her head in its perfect place. Her skin was flawless, her eyes sparkled, her clothing was of the latest style, and her reticule matched her attire to perfection.

"Cressida," Penelope said, "how surprising to see you." *Surprising* being the most polite adjective she could come up with under the circumstances.

Cressida's lips curved into a mysterious, almost feline smile. "I'm sure it is," she murmured.

"Won't you sit down?" Penelope asked, mostly because she had to. She'd spent a lifetime being polite; it was difficult to stop now. She motioned to a nearby chair, the most uncomfortable one in the room.

Cressida sat on the edge of the chair, and if she found it less than pleasing, Penelope could not tell from her mien. Her posture was elegant, her smile never faltered, and she looked as cool and composed as anyone had a right to be.

"I'm sure you're wondering why I'm here," Cressida said.

There seemed little reason to deny it, so Penelope nodded.

And then, abruptly, Cressida asked, "How are you finding married life?"

Penelope blinked. "I beg your pardon?"

"It must be an amazing change of pace," Cressida said.

"Yes," Penelope said carefully, "but a welcome one."

"Mmmm, yes. You must have a dreadful amount of free time now. I'm sure you don't know what to do with yourself."

A prickling feeling began to spread along Penelope's skin. "I don't understand your meaning," she said.

"Don't you?"

When it became apparent that Cressida required an answer, Penelope replied, somewhat testily, "No, I don't."

Cressida was silent for a moment, but her cat-with-cream expression spoke volumes. She glanced about the room until her eyes fell on the writing desk where Penelope had so recently been sitting. "What are those papers?" she inquired.

Penelope's eyes flew to the papers on the desk, stacked neatly under Colin's journal. There was no way that Cressida could have known that they were anything special. Penelope had already been seated on the sofa when Cressida had entered the room. "I fail to see how my personal papers could be of your concern," she said.

"Oh, do not take offense," Cressida said with a little tinkle of laughter that Penelope found rather frightening. "I was merely making polite conversation. Inquiring about your interests."

"I see," Penelope said, trying to fill the ensuing silence.

"I'm very observant," Cressida said.

Penelope raised her brows in question.

"In fact, my keen powers of observation are quite well known among the very best circles of society."

"I must not be a link in those impressive circles, then," Penelope murmured.

Cressida, however, was far too involved in her own speech to acknowledge Penelope's. "It's why," she said in a thoughtful tone of voice, "I thought I might be able to convince the *ton* that I was really Lady Whistledown."

Penelope's heart thundered in her chest. "Then you admit that you're not?" she asked carefully.

"Oh, I think you know I'm not."

Penelope's throat began to close. Somehow—she'd never know how—she managed to keep her composure and say, "I beg your pardon?"

Cressida smiled, but she managed to take that happy expression and turn it into something sly and cruel. "When I came up with this ruse, I thought: *I can't lose.* Either I convince everyone I'm Lady Whistledown or they won't believe me and I look very cunning when I say that I was just pretending to be Lady Whistledown in order to ferret out the true culprit."

Penelope held very silent, very still.

"But it didn't quite play out the way I had planned. Lady Whistledown turned out to be far more devious and mean-spirited than I would have guessed." Cressida's eyes narrowed, then narrowed some more until her face, normally so lovely, took on a sinister air. "Her last little column turned me into a laughingstock."

Penelope said nothing, barely daring to breathe.

"And then . . ." Cressida continued, her voice dropping into lower registers. "And then you—*you!*—had the effrontery to insult me in front of the entire *ton*."

Penelope breathed a tiny sigh of relief. Maybe Cressida didn't know her secret. Maybe this was all about Penelope's public insult, when she'd accused Cressida of lying, and she'd said—dear God, what had she said? Something terribly cruel, she was sure, but certainly well deserved.

"I might have been able to tolerate the insult if it had come from someone else," Cressida continued. "But from someone such as you—well, that could not go unanswered."

"You should think twice before insulting me in my own home," Penelope said in a low voice. And then she added, even though she hated to hide behind her husband's name, "I am a Bridgerton now. I carry the weight of their protection."

Penelope's warning made no dent in the satisfied mask that molded Cressida's beautiful face. "I think you had better listen to what I have to say before you make threats."

Penelope knew she had to listen. It was better to know what Cressida knew than to close her eyes and pretend all was well. "Go on," she said, her voice deliberately curt.

"You made a critical mistake," Cressida said, pointing her index finger at Penelope and wagging it back and forth in short tick-tocky motions. "It didn't occur to you that I *never* forget an insult, did it?"

"What are you trying to say, Cressida?" Penelope had wanted her words to seem strong and forceful, but they came out as a whisper.

Cressida stood and walked slowly away from Penelope, her hips swaying slightly as she moved, the motion almost like a swagger. "Let me see if I can remember your exact words," she said, tapping one finger against her cheek. "Oh, no, no, don't remind me. I'm sure it will come to me. Oh, yes, I recall now." She turned around to face Penelope. "I believe you said you'd always liked Lady Whistledown. And then—and to give you credit, it was an evocative, memorable turn of phrase—you said that it would break your heart if she turned out to be someone like Lady Twombley." Cressida smiled. "Which would be me."

Penelope's mouth went dry. Her fingers shook. And her skin turned to ice.

Because while she hadn't remembered exactly what she'd said in her insult to Cressida, she did remember what she'd written in that last, final, column, the one which had been mistakenly distributed at her engagement ball. The one which—

The one which Cressida was now slapping down onto the table in front of her.

Ladies and Gentleman, This Author is NOT Lady Cressida Twombley. She is nothing more than a scheming imposter, and it would break my heart to see my years of hard work attributed to one such as her.

Penelope stared down at the words even though she knew each one by heart. "What do you mean?" she asked, even though she knew her attempt to pretend that she didn't know exactly what Cressida meant was futile.

"You're smarter than that, Penelope Featherington," Cressida said. "You know I know."

Penelope kept staring at the single, incriminating sheet of paper, unable to tear her eyes from those fateful words—

It would break my heart.

Break my heart.

Break my heart.

Break my—

"Nothing to say?" Cressida asked, and even though Penelope could not see her face, she felt her hard, supercilious smile.

"No one will believe you," Penelope whispered.

"I can barely believe it myself," Cressida said with a harsh laugh. "You, of all people. But apparently you had hidden depths and were a bit more clever than you let on. Clever enough," she added with noticeable emphasis, "to know that once I light the spark of this particular piece of gossip, the news will spread like wildfire."

Penelope's mind whirled in dizzying, unpleasant circles. Oh, God, what was she going to tell Colin? How would she tell him? She knew she had to, but where would she find the words?

"No one will believe it at first," Cressida continued. "You were right about that. But then they'll start to think, and slowly but surely, the pieces of the puzzle will fall into place. Someone will remember that they said something to you that ended up in a column. Or that you were at a particular house party. Or that they'd seen Eloise Bridgerton snooping about, and doesn't everyone know that the two of you tell each other everything?"

"What do you want?" Penelope asked, her voice low and haunted as she finally lifted her head to face her enemy.

"Ah, now, there's the question I've been waiting for." Cressida clasped her hands together behind her back and began to pace. "I've been giving the matter a great deal of thought. In fact, I put off coming here to see you for almost a full week until I could decide upon the matter."

Penelope swallowed, uncomfortable with the notion that Cressida had known her deepest secret for nearly a week, and she'd been blithely living her life, unaware that the sky was about to come crashing down.

"I knew from the outset, of course," Cressida said, "that I wanted money. But the question was—how much? Your husband is a Bridgerton, of course, and so he has ample funds, but then again, he's a younger son, and not as plump in the pocket as the viscount."

"How much, Cressida?" Penelope ground out. She

knew that Cressida was drawing this out just to torture her, and she held little hope that she would actually name a figure before she was good and ready.

"Then I realized," Cressida continued, ignoring Penelope's question (and proving her point), "that you must be quite wealthy, too. Unless you're an utter fool—and considering your success at hiding your little secret for so long, I've revised my initial opinion of you, so I don't think you are—you'd have to have made a fortune after writing the column for all those years. And from all outward appearances"—she gave a scornful glance to Penelope's afternoon dress—"you haven't been spending it. So I can only deduce that it is all sitting in a discreet little bank account somewhere, just waiting for a withdrawal."

"How much, Cressida?"

"Ten thousand pounds."

Penelope gasped. "You're mad!"

"No." Cressida smiled. "Just very, very clever."

"I don't have ten thousand pounds."

"I think you're lying."

"I can assure you I'm not!" And she wasn't. The last time Penelope had checked her account balance, she'd had £8246, although she supposed that with interest, it had grown by a few pounds since then. It was an enormous sum of money, to be sure, enough to keep any reasonable person happy for several lifetimes, but it wasn't ten thousand, and it wasn't anything she wished to hand over to Cressida Twombley.

Cressida smiled serenely. "I'm sure you'll figure out what to do. Between your savings and your husband's money, ten thousand pounds is a paltry sum."

"Ten thousand pounds is *never* a paltry sum."

"How long will you need to gather your funds?" Cressida asked, completely ignoring Penelope's outburst. "A day? Two days?"

"Two days?" Penelope echoed, gaping. "I couldn't do it in two weeks!"

"Aha, so then you *do* have the money."

"I don't!"

"One week," Cressida said, her voice turning sharp. "I want the money in one week."

"I won't give it to you," Penelope whispered, more for her own benefit than Cressida's.

"You will," Cressida replied confidently. "If you don't, I'll ruin you."

"Mrs. Bridgerton?"

Penelope looked up to see Dunwoody standing in the doorway.

"There is an urgent matter which requires your attention," he said. "Immediately."

"Just as well," Cressida said, walking toward the

door. "I'm done here." She walked through the doorway, then turned around once she reached the hall, so that Penelope was forced to look at her, perfectly framed in the portal. "I'll hear from you soon?" she inquired, her voice mild and innocent, as if she were talking about nothing more weighty than an invitation to a party, or perhaps the agenda for a charity meeting.

Penelope gave her a little nod, just to be rid of her.

But it didn't matter. The front door may have thunked shut, and Cressida might be gone, but Penelope's troubles weren't going anywhere.

Chapter 22

Three hours later, Penelope was still in the drawing room, still sitting on the sofa, still staring into space, still trying to figure out how she was going to solve her problems.

Correction: problem, singular.

She had only one problem, but for the size of it, she might as well have had a thousand.

She wasn't an aggressive person, and she couldn't remember the last time she had a violent thought, but at that moment, she could have gladly wrung Cressida Twombley's neck.

She watched the door with a morose sense of fatalism, waiting for her husband to come home, knowing that each ticking second brought her closer to her moment of truth, when she would have to confess everything to him.

He wouldn't say, *I told you so.* He would never say such a thing.

But he would be thinking it.

It never occurred to her, not even for a minute, that she might keep this from him. Cressida's threats weren't the sort of thing one hid from one's husband, and besides, she was going to need his help.

She wasn't certain what she needed to do, but whatever it was, she didn't know how to do it alone.

But there was one thing she knew for sure—she didn't want to pay Cressida. There was no way Cressida would be satisfied with ten thousand pounds, not when she thought she could get more. If Penelope capitulated now, she'd be handing money over to Cressida for the rest of her life.

Which meant that in one week's time, Cressida Twombley would tell all the world that Penelope Featherington Bridgerton was the infamous Lady Whistledown.

Penelope reckoned she had two choices. She could lie, and call Cressida a fool, and hope that everyone believed her; or she could try to find some way to twist Cressida's revelation to her advantage.

But for the life of her, she didn't know how.

"Penelope?"

Colin's voice. She wanted to fling herself into his arms, and at the same time, she could barely bring herself to turn around.

"Penelope?" He sounded concerned now, his footsteps increasing in speed as he crossed the room. "Dunwoody said that Cressida was here."

He sat next to her and touched her cheek. She turned and saw his face, the corners of his eyes crinkled with worry, his lips, slightly parted as they murmured her name.

And that was when she finally allowed herself to cry.

Funny how she could hold herself together, keep it all inside until she saw him. But now that he was here, all she could do was bury her face in the warmth of his chest, snuggle closer as his arms wrapped around her.

As if somehow he could make all her problems go away by his presence alone.

"Penelope?" he asked, his voice soft and worried. "What happened? What's wrong?"

Penelope just shook her head, the motion having to suffice until she could think of the words, summon the courage, stop the tears.

"What did she do to you?"

"Oh, Colin," she said, somehow summoning the energy to pull herself far enough back so that she could see his face. "She knows."

His skin went white. "How?"

Penelope sniffled, wiping her nose with the back of her hand. "It's my fault," she whispered.

He handed her a handkerchief without ever taking his eyes off of her face. "It's not your fault," he said sharply.

Her lips slid into a sad smile. She knew that his harsh tone was meant for Cressida, but she deserved it as well. "No," she said, her voice laced with resignation, "it is. It happened exactly as you said it would. I wasn't paying attention to what I wrote. I slipped up."

"What did you do?" he asked.

She told him everything, starting with Cressida's entrance and ending with her demands for money. She confessed that her poor choice of words was going to be her ruin, but wasn't it ironic, because it really did feel like her heart was breaking.

But the whole time she spoke, she felt him slipping away. He was listening to her, but he wasn't there with her. His eyes took on a strange, faraway look, and yet they were narrowed, intense.

He was plotting something. She was sure of it.

It terrified her.

And thrilled her.

Whatever he was planning, whatever he was thinking, it was all for her. She hated that it had been her stupidity that had forced him into this dilemma, but she couldn't stem the tingle of excitement that swept across her skin as she watched him.

"Colin?" she asked hesitantly. She'd been done speaking for a full minute, and still he hadn't said anything.

"I'll take care of everything," he said. "I don't want you to worry about a thing."

"I assure you that that is impossible," she said with shaking voice.

"I take my wedding vows quite seriously," he replied, his tone almost frighteningly even. "I believe I promised to honor and keep you."

"Let me help you," she said impulsively. "Together we can solve this."

One corner of his mouth lifted into a hint of a smile. "Have you a solution?"

She shook her head. "No. I've been thinking all day, and I don't know . . . although . . ."

"Although what?" he asked, his brows rising.

Her lips parted, then pursed, then parted again as she said, "What if I enlisted the aid of Lady Danbury?"

"You're planning to ask her to pay off Cressida?"

"No," she said, even though the tone of his voice

told her that his had not been a serious question. "I'm going to ask her to be me."

"I beg your pardon?"

"Everyone thinks she's Lady Whistledown, anyway," Penelope explained. "At least, quite a lot of people do. If she were to make an announcement—"

"Cressida would refute it instantly," Colin interrupted.

"Who would believe Cressida over Lady Danbury?" Penelope turned to him with wide, earnest eyes. "I wouldn't dare cross Lady Danbury in any matter. If she were to say she was Lady Whistledown, I'd probably believe her myself."

"What makes you think you can convince Lady Danbury to lie for you?"

"Well," Penelope replied, chewing on her lower lip, "she likes me."

"She likes you?" Colin echoed.

"She does, rather. I think she might like to help me, especially since she detests Cressida almost as much as I do."

"You think her fondness for you will lead her to lie to the entire *ton*?" he asked doubtfully.

She sagged in her seat. "It's worth asking."

He stood, his movements abrupt, and walked to the window. "Promise me you won't go to her."

"But—"

"Promise me."

"I promise," she said, "but—"

"No buts," he said. "If we need to, we'll contact Lady Danbury, but not until I have a chance to think of something else." He raked his hand through his hair. "There must be something else."

"We have a week," she said softly, but she didn't find her words reassuring, and it was difficult to imagine that Colin did, either.

He turned around, his about-face so precise he might have been in the military. "I'll be back," he said, heading for the door.

"But where are you going?" Penelope cried out, jumping to her feet.

"I have to think," he said, pausing with his hand on the doorknob.

"You can't think here with me?" she whispered.

His face softened, and he crossed back to her side. He murmured her name, tenderly taking her face in his hands. "I love you," he said, his voice low and fervent. "I love you with everything I am, everything I've been, and everything I hope to be."

"Colin . . ."

"I love you with my past, and I love you for my future." He bent forward and kissed her, once, softly, on the lips. "I love you for the children we'll have and for the years we'll have together. I love you for every one of my smiles, and even more, for every one of your smiles."

Penelope sagged against the back of a nearby chair.

"I love you," he repeated. "You know that, don't you?"

She nodded, closing her eyes as her cheeks rubbed against his hands.

"I have things to do," he said, "and I won't be able to concentrate if I'm thinking about you, worrying if you're crying, wondering if you're hurt."

"I'm fine," she whispered. "I'm fine now that I've told you."

"I will make this right," he vowed. "I just need you to trust me."

She opened her eyes. "With my life."

He smiled, and suddenly she knew that his words were true. Everything would be all right. Maybe not today and maybe not tomorrow, but soon. Tragedy couldn't coexist in a world with one of Colin's smiles.

"I don't think it will come to that," he said fondly, giving her cheek one affectionate stroke before returning his arms to his sides. He walked back to the door, turning the moment his hand touched the knob. "Don't forget about my sister's party tonight."

Penelope let out a short groan. "Do we have to? The last thing I want to do is go out in public."

"We have to," Colin said. "Daphne doesn't host balls very often, and she'd be crushed if we did not attend."

"I know," Penelope said with a sigh. "I know. I knew it even as I complained. I'm sorry."

He smiled wryly. "It's all right. You're entitled to a bit of a bad mood today."

"Yes," she said, trying to return the smile. "I am, aren't I?"

"I'll be back later," he promised.

"Where are you—" she started to ask, then caught herself. He obviously didn't want questions just then, even from her.

But to her surprise, he answered, "To see my brother."

"Anthony?"

"Yes."

She nodded encouragingly, murmuring, "Go. I will be fine." The Bridgertons had always found strength in other Bridgertons. If Colin felt he needed his brother's counsel, then he should go without delay.

"Don't forget to prepare for Daphne's ball," he reminded her.

She gave him a halfhearted salute and watched as he left the room.

Then she moved to the window to watch him walk by, but he never appeared. He must have headed straight out the back to the mews. She sighed, allowing her bottom to rest against the windowsill for support. She hadn't realized just how much she'd wanted to catch one last glimpse of him.

She wished she knew what he was planning.

She wished she could be sure he even had a plan.

But at the same time, she felt oddly at ease. Colin would make this right. He'd said he would, and he never lied.

She knew that her idea to enlist the aid of Lady Danbury wasn't a perfect solution, but unless Colin came up with a better idea, what else could they do?

For now, she would try to push it all from her mind. She was so weary, and so very tired, and right now what she needed was to close her eyes and think of nothing but the green of her husband's eyes, the shining light of his smile.

Tomorrow.

Tomorrow she would help Colin solve their problems.

Today she would rest. She would take a nap and pray for sleep and try to figure out how she would face all of society this evening, knowing that Cressida would be there, watching and waiting for her to make a false move.

One would think that after nearly a dozen years of pretending she was nothing more than the wallflowerish Penelope Featherington, she'd be used to playing roles and hiding her true self.

But that was when her secret had been safe. Everything was different now.

Penelope curled up on the sofa and closed her eyes.

Everything was different now, but that didn't mean that it had to be worse, did it?

Everything would be fine. It would. It had to.

Didn't it?

Colin was starting to regret his decision to take a carriage over to his brother's house.

He'd wanted to walk—the vigorous use of his legs and feet and muscles seemed the only socially acceptable outlet for his fury. But he'd recognized that time was of the essence, and even with traffic, a carriage could convey him to Mayfair faster than could his own two feet.

But now the walls seemed too close and the air too thick, *and goddamn it,* was that an overturned milkwagon blocking the street?

Colin poked his head out the door, hanging out of the carriage even as they were still rolling to a halt. "God above," he muttered, taking in the scene. Broken glass littered the street, milk was flowing everywhere, and he couldn't tell who was screeching louder—the horses, which were still tangled in the reins, or the ladies on the pavement, whose dresses had been completely splattered with milk.

Colin jumped down from his carriage, intending to help clear the scene, but it quickly became apparent that Oxford Street would be a snarl for at least an hour, with or without his help. He checked to make sure that the milkwagon horses were being properly cared for, informed his driver that he would be continuing on foot, and took off walking.

He stared defiantly in the faces of each person he passed, perversely enjoying the way they averted their gaze when faced with his obvious hostility. He almost wished one of them would make a comment, just so he could have someone to lash out at. It didn't matter that the only person he really wanted to throttle was Cressida Twombley; by this point anyone would have made a fine target.

His anger was making him unbalanced, unreasonable. Unlike himself.

He still wasn't certain what had happened to him

when Penelope had told him of Cressida's threats. This was more than anger, greater than fury. This was physical; it coursed through his veins, pulsed beneath his skin.

He wanted to hit someone.

He wanted to kick things, put his fist through a wall.

He'd been furious when Penelope had published her last column. In fact, he'd thought he couldn't possibly experience a greater anger.

He was wrong.

Or perhaps it was just that this was a different sort of anger. Someone was trying to hurt the one person he loved above all others.

How could he tolerate that? How could he allow it to happen?

The answer was simple. He couldn't.

He had to stop this. He had to *do* something.

After so many years of ambling through life, laughing at the antics of others, it was time to take action himself.

He looked up, somewhat surprised that he was already at Bridgerton House. Funny how it no longer seemed like home. He'd grown up here, but now it was so obviously his brother's house.

Home was in Bloomsbury. Home was with Penelope.

Home was anywhere with Penelope.

"Colin?"

He turned around. Anthony was on the pavement, obviously returning from an errand or appointment.

Anthony nodded toward the door. "Were you planning to knock?"

Colin looked blankly at his brother, just then realizing that he'd been standing perfectly still on the steps for God only knew how long.

"Colin?" Anthony asked again, his brow furrowing with concern.

"I need your help," Colin said. It was all he needed to say.

Penelope was already dressed for the ball when her maid brought in a note from Colin.

"Dunwoody got it from the messenger," the maid explained before bobbing a quick curtsy and leaving Penelope to read the note in privacy.

Penelope slid her gloved finger under the envelope flap and nudged it open, pulling out the single sheet of paper on which she saw the fine, neat handwriting that had become so familiar to her since she'd started editing Colin's journals.

I will make my own way over to the ball this evening. Please proceed to Number Five. Mother, Elo-

ise, and Hyacinth are waiting to accompany you to
Hastings House.

All my love,
Colin

For someone who wrote so well in his journals, he wasn't much of a correspondent, Penelope thought with a wry smile.

She stood, smoothing out the fine silk of her skirts. She'd chosen a dress of her favorite color—sage green—in hopes that it might lend her courage. Her mother had always said that when a woman looked good, she felt good, and she rather thought her mother was right. Heaven knows, she'd spent a good eight years of her life feeling rather *bad* in the dresses her mother had insisted looked good.

Her hair had been dressed in a loosely upswept fashion that flattered her face, and her maid had even combed something through the strands (Penelope was afraid to ask what) that seemed to bring out the red highlights.

Red hair wasn't very fashionable, of course, but Colin had once said he liked the way the candlelight made her hair more colorful, so Penelope had decided that this was one case upon which she and fashion would have to disagree.

By the time she made her way downstairs, her carriage was waiting for her, and the driver had already been instructed to take her to Number Five.

Colin had clearly taken care of everything. Penelope wasn't sure why this surprised her; he wasn't the sort of man who forgot details. But he was preoccupied today. It seemed odd that he would have taken the time to send instructions to the staff about her delivery to his mother's house when she could have conveyed the order just as well herself.

He had to be planning something. But what? Was he going to intercept Cressida Twombley and have her shipped off to a penal colony?

No, too melodramatic.

Maybe he'd found a secret about her, and was planning to cross-blackmail her. Silence for silence.

Penelope nodded approvingly as her carriage rolled along Oxford Street. That had to be the answer. It was just like Colin to come up with something so diabolically fitting and clever. But what could he possibly have unearthed about Cressida in so short a time? In all her years as Lady Whistledown, she'd never heard even a whisper of anything truly scandalous attached to Cressida's name.

Cressida was mean, and Cressida was petty, but she'd never stepped outside the rules of society. The only truly daring thing she'd ever done was claim to be Lady Whistledown.

The carriage turned south into Mayfair, and a few minutes later, they came to a stop in front of Number Five. Eloise must have been watching at the window, because she virtually flew down the steps and would have crashed into the carriage had the driver not stepped down at that precise moment and blocked her path.

Eloise jumped from foot to foot as she waited for the driver to open the carriage door; in fact, she looked so impatient that Penelope was surprised she didn't brush past him and wrench the door open herself. Finally, ignoring the driver's offer of help, she climbed into the carriage, nearly tripping on her skirts and tumbling to the floor in the process. As soon as she'd righted herself, she looked both ways, her face pursed into an extremely furtive expression, and yanked the door shut, nearly taking off the driver's nose in the process.

"What," Eloise demanded, "is going on?"

Penelope just stared at her. "I could ask the same of you."

"You could? Why?"

"Because you nearly knocked over the carriage in your haste to climb inside!"

"Oh," Eloise sniffed dismissively. "You have only yourself to blame for that."

"Me?"

"Yes, you! I want to know what's going on. And I need to know tonight."

Penelope was quite certain that Colin would not have told his sister about Cressida's blackmail demands, not unless his plan was to have Eloise harangue Cressida to death. "I don't know what you mean," she said.

"You *have* to know what I mean!" Eloise insisted, glancing back up toward the house. The front door was opening. "Oh, bother. Mother and Hyacinth are coming already. *Tell* me!"

"Tell you *what*?"

"Why Colin sent us that abominably cryptic note instructing us to stick to you like *glue* all evening."

"He did?"

"Yes, and may I point out that he underlined the word *glue*?"

"And here I thought the emphasis was yours," Penelope said dryly.

Eloise scowled. "Penelope, this is not the time to poke fun at me."

"When *is* the time?"

"Penelope!"

"Sorry, I couldn't resist."

"Do you know what the note was about?"

Penelope shook her head. Which wasn't a complete

lie, she told herself. She really didn't know what Colin had planned for this evening.

Just then the door opened, and Hyacinth bounded in. "Penelope!" she said with great enthusiasm. "*What* is going on?"

"She doesn't know," Eloise said.

Hyacinth shot her sister an annoyed look. "It figures you'd sneak out here early."

Violet poked her head in. "Are they quarreling?" she asked Penelope.

"Just a little," Penelope replied.

Violet sat next to Hyacinth across from Penelope and Eloise. "Very well, it's not as if I could stop them, anyway. But do tell, what did Colin mean when he instructed us to stick to you like glue?"

"I'm sure I don't know."

Violet's eyes narrowed, as if assessing Penelope's honesty. "He was quite emphatic. He underlined the word *glue,* you know."

"I know," Penelope replied, just as Eloise said, "I told her."

"He underlined it twice," Hyacinth added. "If his ink had been any darker, I'm sure I would have had to go out and slaughter a horse myself."

"Hyacinth!" Violet exclaimed.

Hyacinth just shrugged. "It's all very intriguing."

"Actually," Penelope said, eager to change the subject, or at least to twist it slightly, "what I'm wondering is, what will Colin wear?"

That got everyone's attention.

"He left home in his afternoon clothes," Penelope explained, "and didn't come back. I can't imagine your sister would accept anything less than full evening kit for her ball."

"He'll have borrowed something from Anthony," Eloise said dismissively. "They're precisely the same size. Same as Gregory, actually. Only Benedict is different."

"Two inches taller," Hyacinth said.

Penelope nodded, feigning interest as she glanced out the window. They'd just slowed down, the driver presumably trying to navigate through the crush of carriages that were choking Grosvenor Square.

"How many people are expected tonight?" Penelope asked.

"I believe five hundred were invited," Violet replied. "Daphne doesn't host parties very often, but what she lacks in frequency she makes up for in size."

"I'll say," Hyacinth muttered. "I hate crowds. I'm not going to be able to get a decent breath tonight."

"I'm lucky you were my last," Violet told her with

weary affection. "I'd not have had the energy for any more after you, I'm sure."

"Pity I wasn't first, then," Hyacinth said with a cheeky smile. "Think of all the attention I could have had. Not to mention the fortune."

"You're already quite the heiress as it is," Violet said.

"And you always manage to find your way to the center of attention," Eloise teased.

Hyacinth just grinned.

"Did you know," Violet said, turning to Penelope, "that all of my children are going to be in attendance tonight? I can't remember the last time we were all together."

"What about your birthday party?" Eloise asked.

Violet shook her head. "Gregory wasn't able to get away from university."

"We're not expected to line up according to height and sing a festive tune, are we?" Hyacinth asked, only half joking. "I can see us now: The Singing Bridgertons. We'd make a fortune on the stage."

"You're in a punchy mood tonight," Penelope said to her.

Hyacinth shrugged. "Just getting myself ready for my upcoming transformation into glue. It seems to require a certain mental preparedness."

"A gluey frame of mind?" Penelope inquired mildly.

"Precisely."

"We must get her married off soon," Eloise said to her mother.

"You first," Hyacinth shot back.

"I'm working on it," Eloise said cryptically.

"What?" The word's volume was rather amplified by the fact that it exploded from three mouths at once.

"That's all I'm going to say," Eloise said, and in such a tone of voice that they all knew she meant it.

"I will get to the bottom of *this*," Hyacinth assured her mother and Penelope.

"I'm sure you will," Violet replied.

Penelope turned to Eloise and said, "You don't stand a chance."

Eloise just lifted her chin in the air and looked out the window. "We're here," she announced.

The four ladies waited until the driver had opened the door, and then one by one they alighted.

"My goodness," Violet said approvingly, "Daphne has truly outdone herself."

It was difficult not to stop and look. All of Hastings House was ablaze with light. Every window had been adorned with candles, and outdoor sconces held torches, as did a fleet of footmen who were greeting the carriages.

"It's too bad Lady Whistledown isn't here," Hyacinth said, her voice for once losing its cheeky edge. "She would have loved this."

"Maybe she *is* here," Eloise said. "In fact, she probably is."

"Did Daphne invite Cressida Twombley?" Violet asked.

"I'm sure she did," Eloise said. "*Not* that I think she's Lady Whistledown."

"I don't think anyone thinks that any longer," Violet replied as she lifted her foot onto the first step. "Come along, girls, our night awaits."

Hyacinth stepped forward to accompany her mother, while Eloise fell into line beside Penelope.

"There's magic in the air," Eloise said, looking around as if she'd never seen a London ball before. "Do you feel it?"

Penelope just looked at her, afraid that if she opened her mouth, she'd blurt out all of her secrets. Eloise was right. There was something strange and electric about the night, a crackling sort of energy—the kind one felt just before a thunderstorm.

"It almost feels like a turning point," Eloise mused,

"as if one's life could change completely, all in one night."

"What are you saying, Eloise?" Penelope asked, alarmed by the look in her friend's eyes.

"Nothing," Eloise said with a shrug. But a mysterious smile remained upon her lips as she hooked her arm through Penelope's and murmured, "Let's be off. The night awaits."

Chapter 23

Penelope had been to Hastings House a number of times, both for formal parties and more casual visits, but never had she seen the stately old building look more lovely—or more magical—than it did that evening.

She and the Bridgerton ladies were among the first to arrive; Lady Bridgerton had always said that it was rude for family members even to consider fashionably late entrances. It was nice to be so early, though; Penelope was actually able to see the decorations without having to push through crushing crowds.

Daphne had decided not to use a theme for her ball, unlike the Egyptian ball last week and the Grecian one the week before. Rather, she had decorated the house with the same simple elegance with which she lived her everyday life. Hundreds of candles adorned the walls and tables, flickering in the night, reflecting off the enormous chandeliers that hung from the ceilings. The windows were swathed in a shimmery, silvery fabric, the sort of thing one might imagine a fairy to wear. Even the servants had changed their livery. Penelope knew that the Hastings servants usually wore blue and gold, but tonight their blue was adorned with silver.

It could almost make a woman feel like a princess in a fairy tale.

"I wonder how much this cost," Hyacinth said, eyes wide.

"Hyacinth!" Violet scolded, batting her daughter on the arm. "You know that it's impolite to ask about such things."

"I didn't ask," Hyacinth pointed out, "I wondered. And besides, it's only Daphne."

"Your sister is the Duchess of Hastings," Violet said, "and as such she has certain responsibilities to her station. You would do well to remember that fact."

"But wouldn't you agree," Hyacinth said, linking her arm around her mother's and giving her hand a little squeeze, "that it's more important simply to remember that she's my sister?"

"She has you there," Eloise said with a smile.

Violet sighed. "Hyacinth, I declare that you will be the death of me."

"No, I won't," Hyacinth replied. "Gregory will."

Penelope found herself stifling a laugh.

"I don't see Colin here yet," Eloise said, craning her neck.

"No?" Penelope scanned the room. "That's surprising."

"Did he tell you that he would be here before you arrived?"

"No," Penelope replied, "but for some reason I rather thought he would."

Violet patted her arm. "I'm sure he'll be here soon, Penelope. And then we'll all know what this big secret is that has him insisting we remain by your side. Not," she added hastily, her eyes widening with alarm, "that we view it as any sort of *chore*. You know we adore your company."

Penelope gave her a reassuring smile. "I know. The feeling is mutual."

There were only a few people ahead of them in the receiving line, so it wasn't very long before they were able to greet Daphne and her husband Simon.

"*What*," Daphne asked without preamble, just as soon as she was sure her other guests were out of earshot, "is going on with Colin?"

Since the question appeared to be directed mostly at her, Penelope felt compelled to say, "I don't know."

"Did he send you a note as well?" Eloise asked.

Daphne nodded. "Yes, we're to keep an eye on her, he said."

"It could be worse," Hyacinth said. "We're to stick to her like glue." She leaned forward. "He underlined *glue*."

"And here I thought I wasn't a chore," Penelope quipped.

"Oh, you're not," Hyacinth said breezily, "but there's something rather enjoyable about the word *glue*. Slides off the tongue rather pleasingly, don't you think? Glue. Glooooooo."

"Is it me," Eloise asked, "or has she gone mad in the head?"

Hyacinth ignored her with a shrug. "Not to mention the drama of it. I feel as if I'm a part of some grand espionage plot."

"Espionage," Violet groaned. "Heaven help us all."

Daphne leaned forward with great drama. "Well, he told *us*—"

"It's not a competition, wife," Simon put in.

She shot him an annoyed look before turning back to her mother and sisters and saying, "He told us to make sure she stays away from Lady Danbury."

"Lady Danbury!" they all exclaimed.

Except for Penelope, who had a very good idea why Colin might want her to stay away from the elderly countess. He must have come up with something better than her plan to convince Lady Danbury to lie and tell everyone that *she* was Lady Whistledown.

It had to be the double-blackmail theory. What else could it be? He must have uncovered some horrible secret about Cressida.

Penelope was almost giddy with delight.

"I thought you were rather good friends with Lady Danbury," Violet said to her.

"I am," Penelope replied, trying to act perplexed.

"This is very curious," Hyacinth said, tapping her index finger against her cheek. "Very curious indeed."

"Eloise," Daphne suddenly put in, "you're very quiet tonight."

"Except for when she called me mad," Hyacinth pointed out.

"Hmmm?" Eloise had been staring off into space—or perhaps at something behind Daphne and Simon—and hadn't been paying attention. "Oh, well, nothing to say, I suppose."

"*You?*" Daphne asked doubtfully.

"Precisely what I was thinking," Hyacinth said.

Penelope agreed with Hyacinth, but she decided to keep that to herself. It wasn't like Eloise not to weigh in with an opinion, especially not on a night like this, which was growing more and more shrouded with mystery as each second passed.

"You all were saying everything so well," Eloise said. "What could I have possibly added to the conversation?"

Which struck Penelope as very odd. The sly sarcasm was in character, but Eloise *always* thought she had something to add to a conversation.

Eloise just shrugged.

"We should be moving along," Violet said. "We're beginning to hold up your other guests."

"I shall see you later," Daphne promised. "And—Oh!"

Everyone leaned in.

"You will probably want to know," she whispered, "that Lady Danbury is not here yet."

"Simplifies my job," Simon said, looking a bit weary of all the intrigue.

"Not mine," Hyacinth said. "I still have to stick to her—"

"—like glue," they all—including Penelope— finished for her.

"Well, I do," Hyacinth said.

"Speaking of glue," Eloise said as they stepped away from Daphne and Simon, "Penelope, do you think you can make do with only two batches for a bit? I should like to step out for a moment."

"I will go with you," Hyacinth announced.

"You can't both go," Violet said. "I'm certain Colin didn't want Penelope left with only *me*."

"May I go when she's back, then?" Hyacinth grimaced. "It's not something I can avoid."

Violet turned to Eloise expectantly.

"What?" Eloise demanded.

"I was waiting for you to say the same thing."

"I'm far too dignified," Eloise sniffed.

"Oh, please," Hyacinth muttered.

Violet groaned. "Are you certain you wish us to remain by your side?" she asked Penelope.

"I didn't think I had a choice," Penelope replied, amused by the interchange.

"Go," Violet said to Eloise. "Just hurry back."

Eloise gave her mother a nod, and then, much to everyone's surprise, she reached forward and gave Penelope a quick hug.

"What was that for?" Penelope asked with an affectionate smile.

"No reason," Eloise replied, her returning grin rather like one of Colin's. "I just think this is going to be a special night for you."

"You do?" Penelope asked carefully, unsure of what Eloise might have figured out.

"Well, it's obvious *something* is afoot," Eloise said. "It's not like Colin to act with such secrecy. And I wanted to offer my support."

"You'll be back in just a few minutes," Penelope said. "Whatever is going to happen—if indeed anything is going to happen—you're not likely to miss it."

Eloise shrugged. "It was an impulse. An impulse born from a dozen years of friendship."

"Eloise Bridgerton, are you growing sentimental on me?"

"At this late date?" Eloise said with a look of mock outrage. "I think not."

"Eloise," Hyacinth interrupted, "will you *leave*? I can't wait all night."

And with a quick wave, Eloise was off.

For the next hour, they just milled about, mingling with the other guests, and moving—Penelope, Violet, and Hyacinth—as one giant being.

"Three heads and six legs have we," Penelope remarked as she walked toward the window, the two Bridgerton women bustling right alongside her.

"I beg your pardon?" Violet asked.

"Did you really want to look out the window," Hyacinth muttered, "or were you just testing us? And *where* is Eloise?"

"Mostly just testing you," Penelope admitted. "And I'm sure Eloise was detained by some other guest. You know as well as I that there are many people here from whom it is rather difficult to extract oneself from conversation."

"Hmmph," was Hyacinth's reply. "Someone needs to recheck her definition of *glue.*"

"Hyacinth," Penelope said, "if you need to excuse yourself for a few minutes, please do go ahead. I shall be just fine." She turned to Violet. "You as well. If you need to leave, I promise I shall remain right here in the corner until you return."

Violet looked at her in horror. "And break our word to Colin?"

"Er, did you actually give him your word?" Penelope asked.

"No, but it was implied in his request, I'm sure. Oh, look!" she suddenly exclaimed. "There he is!"

Penelope tried to signal discreetly at her husband, but all her attempts at circumspection were drowned out by Hyacinth's vigorous wave and holler of, "Colin!"

Violet groaned.

"I know, I know," Hyacinth said unrepentantly, "I must be more ladylike."

"If you know it," Violet said, sounding every inch the mother she was, "then why don't you *do* it?"

"What would be the fun in that?"

"Good evening, ladies," Colin said, kissing his mother's hand before smoothly taking his place beside Penelope and sliding his arm around her waist.

"Well?" Hyacinth demanded.

Colin merely quirked a brow.

"Are you going to *tell* us?" she persisted.

"All in good time, dear sister."

"You're a wretched, wretched man," Hyacinth grumbled.

"I say," Colin murmured, looking about, "what happened to Eloise?"

"That's a very good question," Hyacinth muttered, just as Penelope said, "I'm sure she'll be back soon."

He nodded, not looking terribly interested. "Mother," he said, turning toward Violet, "how have you been?"

"You've been sending cryptic notes all over town," Violet demanded, "and you want to know how I've *been*?"

He smiled. "Yes."

Violet actually started wagging her finger at him,

something she'd forbidden her own children from ever doing in public. "Oh, no, you don't, Colin Bridgerton. You are not going to get out of explaining yourself. I am your mother. Your mother!"

"I am aware of the relation," he murmured.

"You are not going to waltz in here and distract me with a clever phrase and a beguiling smile."

"You think my smile is beguiling?"

"Colin!"

"But," he acceded, "you did make an excellent point."

Violet blinked. "I did?"

"Yes. About the waltz." He cocked his head slightly to the side. "I believe I hear one beginning."

"I don't hear anything," Hyacinth said.

"Don't you? Pity." He grabbed Penelope's hand. "Come along, wife. I do believe this is our dance."

"But no one is dancing," Hyacinth ground out.

He flashed her a satisfied smile. "They will be."

And then, before anyone had a chance to comment, he'd yanked on Penelope's hand, and they were weaving through the crowds.

"Didn't you want to waltz?" Penelope asked breathlessly, right after they'd passed the small orchestra, the members of whom appeared to be taking an extended break.

"No, just to escape," he explained, slipping through a side door and pulling her along with him.

A few moments later they had ascended a narrow staircase and were secreted in some small parlor, their only light the flickering torches that blazed outside the window.

"Where are we?" Penelope asked, looking around.

Colin shrugged. "I don't know. It seemed as good a place as any."

"Are you going to tell me what is going on?"

"No, first I'm going to kiss you."

And before she had a chance to respond to that (not that she would have protested!) his lips found hers in a kiss that was hungry and urgent and tender all in one.

"Colin!" she gasped, in that split second when he took a breath.

"Not now," he murmured, kissing her again.

"But—" this was muffled, lost against his lips.

It was the sort of kiss that enveloped her, from her head to her toes, from the way his teeth nibbled her lips, to his hands, squeezing her bottom and sliding across her back. It was the sort of kiss that could easily have turned her knees to water and led her to swoon on the sofa and allow him to do anything to her, the more wicked the better, even though they were mere yards away from over five hundred members of the *ton,* except—

"Colin!" she exclaimed, somehow breaking her mouth free of his.

"Shush."

"Colin, you have to stop!"

He looked like a lost puppy. "Must I?"

"Yes, you must."

"I suppose you're going to say it's because of all the people just next door."

"No, although that's a very good reason to consider restraint."

"To consider and then reject, perhaps?" he asked hopefully.

"No! Colin—" She pulled herself from his arms and moved several feet away, lest his nearness tempt her into forgetting herself. "Colin, you need to tell me what is going on."

"Well," he said slowly, "I *was* kissing you. . . ."

"That's not what I meant, and you know it."

"Very well." He walked away, his footsteps echoing loudly in her ears. When he turned back around, his expression had turned deadly serious. "I have decided what to do about Cressida."

"You have? What? Tell me."

His face took on a slightly pained expression. "Actually, I think it might be best if I didn't tell you until the plan is under way."

She stared at him in disbelief. "You're not serious."

"Well . . ." He was looking longingly at the door, clearly hoping for an escape.

"Tell me," she insisted.

"Very well." He sighed, then sighed again.

"Colin!"

"I'm going to make an announcement," he said, as if that would explain everything.

At first she said nothing, thinking that maybe it would all become clear if she just waited a moment and thought about it. But that didn't work, and so she asked, her words slow and careful, "What sort of announcement?"

His face turned resolute. "I'm going to tell the truth."

She gasped. "About me?"

He nodded.

"But you can't!"

"Penelope, I think it's best."

Panic began to rise within her, and her lungs felt impossibly tight. "No, Colin, you can't! You can't do that! It's not your secret to reveal!"

"Do you want to pay Cressida for the rest of your life?"

"No, of course not, but I can ask Lady Danbury—"

"You're not going to ask Lady Danbury to lie on your behalf," he snapped. "That's beneath you and you know it."

Penelope gasped at his sharp tone. But deep down, she knew he was right.

"If you were so willing to allow someone else to usurp your identity," he said, "then you should have just allowed Cressida to do it."

"I couldn't," she whispered. "Not her."

"Fine. Then it's time we both stood up and faced the music."

"Colin," she whispered, "I'll be ruined."

He shrugged. "We'll move to the country."

She shook her head, desperately trying to find the right words.

He took her hands in his. "Does it really matter so much?" he said softly. "Penelope, I love you. As long as we're together, we'll be happy."

"It's not that," she said, trying to tug her hand from his so that she could wipe the tears from her eyes.

But he wouldn't let go. "What, then?" he asked.

"Colin, you'll be ruined, too," she whispered.

"I don't mind."

She stared at him in disbelief. He sounded so flip, so casual about something that would change his entire life, alter it in ways he couldn't possibly imagine.

"Penelope," he said, his voice so reasonable she could barely stand it, "it's the only solution. Either we tell the world, or Cressida does."

"We could pay her," she whispered.

"Is that what you really want to do?" he asked. "Give her all the money you've worked so hard to earn? You might as well have just let her tell the world she was Lady Whistledown."

"I can't let you do this," she said. "I don't think you understand what it means to be outside of society."

"And you do?" he countered.

"Better than you!"

"Penelope—"

"You're trying to act as if it doesn't matter, but I know you don't feel that way. You were so angry with me when I published that last column, all because you thought I shouldn't have risked the secret getting out."

"As it turns out," he remarked, "I was right."

"See?" she said urgently. "Do you see? You're still upset with me over that!"

Colin let out a long breath. The conversation was not moving in the direction he'd hoped. He certainly hadn't intended for her to throw his earlier insistence that she not tell anyone about her secret life back in his face. "If you hadn't published that last column," he said, "we wouldn't be in this position, that is true, but the point is now moot, don't you think?"

"Colin," she whispered. "If you tell the world I'm Lady Whistledown, and they react the way we think they will, you'll never see your journals published."

His heart stood still.

Because that was when he finally understood her.

She had told him before that she loved him, and she had shown her love as well, in all the ways he'd taught her. But never before had it been so clear, so frank, so raw.

All this time she'd been begging him not to make the announcement—it had all been for him.

He swallowed against the lump that was forming in his throat, fought for words, fought even for breath.

She reached out and touched his hand, her eyes pleading, her cheeks still wet with tears. "I could never forgive myself," she said. "I don't want to destroy your dreams."

"They were never my dreams until I met you," he whispered.

"You don't want to publish your journals?" she asked, blinking in confusion. "You were just doing it for me?"

"No," he said, because she deserved nothing less than complete honesty. "I do want it. It *is* my dream. But it's a dream you gave me."

"That doesn't mean I can take it away."

"You're not."

"Yes, I—"

"No," he said forcefully, "you're not. And getting my work published . . . well, it doesn't hold a candle to my real dream, which is spending the rest of my life with you."

"You'll always have that," she said softly.

"I know." He smiled, and then it turned rather cocky. "So what do we have to lose?"

"Possibly more than we could ever guess."

"And possibly less," he reminded her. "Don't forget that I'm a Bridgerton. And you are now, too. We wield a bit of power in this town."

Her eyes widened. "What do you mean?"

He shrugged modestly. "Anthony is prepared to give you his full support."

"You told Anthony?" she gasped.

"I had to tell Anthony. He's the head of the family. And there are very few people on this earth who would dare to cross him."

"Oh." Penelope chewed on her lower lip, considering all this. And then, because she had to know: "What did he say?"

"He was surprised."

"I expected as much."

"And rather pleased."

Her face lit up. "Really?"

"And amused. He said he had to admire someone who could keep a secret like that for so many years. He said he couldn't wait to tell Kate."

She nodded. "I suppose you'll have to make an announcement now. The secret is out."

"Anthony will hold his counsel if I ask him to," Colin said. "That has nothing to do with why I want to tell the world the truth."

She looked at him expectantly, warily.

"The truth is," Colin said, tugging on her hand and pulling her close, "I'm rather proud of you."

She felt herself smiling, and it was so strange, because just a few moments earlier, she couldn't imagine ever smiling again.

He leaned down until his nose touched hers. "I want everyone to know how proud I am of you. By the time I'm through, there won't be a single person in London who doesn't recognize how clever you are."

"They may still hate me," she said.

"They may," he agreed, "but that will be their problem, not ours."

"Oh, Colin," she sighed. "I do love you. It's an excellent thing, really."

He grinned. "I know."

"No, I really do. I thought I loved you before, and I'm sure I did, but it's nothing like what I feel now."

"Good," he said, a rather possessive gleam appearing in his eyes, "that's the way I like it. Now come with me."

"Where?"

"Here," he said, pushing open a door.

To Penelope's amazement, she found herself on a small balcony, overlooking the entire ballroom. "Oh. Dear. God," she gulped, trying to yank him back into the darkened room behind them. No one had seen them yet; they could still make their escape.

"Tsk tsk," he scolded. "Bravery, my sweet."

"Couldn't you post something in the paper?" she whispered urgently. "Or just tell someone and allow the rumor to spread?"

"There's nothing like a grand gesture to get the point across."

She swallowed convulsively. As gestures went, this was going to be grand. "I'm not very good at being the center of attention," she said, trying to remember how to breathe in a normal rhythm.

He squeezed her hand. "Don't worry. I am." He looked out over the crowd until his eyes found those of their host, his brother-in-law, the Duke of Hastings. At Colin's nod, the duke began to move toward the orchestra.

"Simon knows?" Penelope gasped.

"I told him when I arrived," Colin murmured absently. "How do you think I knew how to find the room with the balcony?"

And then the most remarkable thing happened. A veritable fleet of footmen appeared as if from nowhere and began handing tall flutes of champagne to every guest.

"Here's ours," Colin said approvingly, picking up two glasses that were waiting in the corner. "Just as I asked."

Penelope took hers silently, still unable to comprehend all that was unfolding around her.

"It's probably a little flat by now," Colin said in a conspiratorial sort of whisper that she knew was meant to set her at ease. "But it's the best I could do under the circumstances."

As Penelope clutched Colin's hand in terror, she

watched helplessly as Simon quieted the orchestra and directed the throng of partygoers to turn their attention to his brother and sister on the balcony.

His brother and sister, she thought in wonder. The Bridgertons really did inspire a bond. She never thought she'd see the day when a duke referred to her as his sister.

"Ladies and gentlemen," Colin announced, his strong, confident voice booming throughout the hall, "I would like to propose a toast to the most remarkable woman in the world."

A low murmur spread across the room, and Penelope stood frozen, watching everyone watching her.

"I am a newlywed," Colin continued, beguiling the partygoers with his lopsided smile, "and therefore you are all required to indulge me in my lovesick ways."

Friendly laughter rippled through the crowd.

"I know that many of you were surprised when I asked Penelope Featherington to be my wife. I was surprised myself."

A few unkind titters wafted through the air, but Penelope held herself perfectly still, completely proud. Colin would say the right thing. She knew he would. Colin always said the right thing.

"I wasn't surprised that I had fallen in love with her," he said pointedly, giving the crowd a look that dared them to comment, "but rather that it had taken so long.

"I've known her for so many years, you see," he continued, his voice softening, "and somehow I'd never taken the time to look inside, to see the beautiful, brilliant, witty woman she'd become."

Penelope could feel the tears trickling down her face, but she couldn't move. She could barely breathe. She had expected him to reveal her secret, and instead he was giving her this incredible gift, this spectacular declaration of love.

"Therefore," Colin said, "with all of you here as my witnesses, I would like to say—Penelope—" He turned to her, taking her free hand in his, and said:

"I love you. I adore you. I worship the ground you walk upon."

He turned back out to the crowd, lifted his glass, and said, "To my wife!"

"To your wife!" they all boomed, caught up in the magic of the moment.

Colin drank, and Penelope drank, even though she couldn't help but wonder when he was going to tell them all the real reason for this announcement.

"Put down your glass, dear," he murmured, plucking it from her fingers and setting it aside.

"But—"

"You interrupt far too much," he scolded, and then he swept her into a passionate kiss, right there on the balcony in front of the entire *ton*.

"Colin!" she gasped, once he gave her a chance to breathe.

He grinned wolfishly as their audience roared its approval.

"Oh, and one last thing!" he called to the crowd.

They were now stamping their feet, hanging on his every word.

"I'm leaving the party early. Right now, as a matter of fact." He shot a wicked, sideways grin at Penelope. "I'm sure you'll understand."

The men in the crowd hooted and hollered as Penelope turned beet red.

"But before I do, I have one last thing to say. One last little thing, in case you still don't believe me when I tell you that my wife is the wittiest, cleverest, most enchanting woman in all of London."

"Nooooo!" came a voice from the back, and Penelope knew it was Cressida.

But even Cressida was no match for the crowd, none of whom would let her pass, or even listen to her cries of distress.

"You might say that my wife has two maiden names,"

he said thoughtfully. "Of course you all knew her as Penelope Featherington, as did I. But what you didn't know, and what even I was not clever enough to figure out until she told me herself . . ."

He paused, waiting for silence to fall over the room.

". . . is that she is also the brilliant, the witty, the breathtakingly magnificent—Oh, you all know who I am talking about," he said, his arm sweeping out toward the crowd.

"I give you my wife!" he said, his love and pride flowing across the room. "Lady Whistledown!"

For a moment there was nothing but silence. It was almost as if no one even dared to breathe.

And then it came. Clap. Clap. Clap. Slow and methodical, but with such force and determination that everyone had to turn and look to see who had dared to break the shocked silence.

It was Lady Danbury.

She had shoved her cane into someone else's arms and was holding her arms high, clapping loud and proud, beaming with pride and delight.

And then someone else began to clap. Penelope jerked her head to the side to see who . . .

Anthony Bridgerton.

And then Simon Basset, the Duke of Hastings.

And then the Bridgerton women, and then the Featherington women, and then another and another and more and more until the entire room was cheering.

Penelope couldn't believe it.

Tomorrow they might remember to be angry with her, to feel irritated at having been fooled for so many years, but tonight . . .

Tonight all they could do was admire and cheer.

For a woman who had had to carry out all of her accomplishments in secret, it was everything she'd ever dreamed of.

Well, almost everything.

Everything she'd truly ever dreamed of was standing next to her, his arm around her waist. And when she looked up at him, at his beloved face, he was smiling down at her with such love and pride that her breath caught in her throat.

"Congratulations, Lady Whistledown," he murmured.

"I prefer Mrs. Bridgerton," she replied.

He grinned. "Excellent choice."

"Can we leave?" she whispered.

"Right now?"

She nodded.

"Oh, *yes*," he said enthusiastically.

And no one saw them for several days.

Epilogue

Bedford Square, Bloomsbury
London, 1825

"It's here! It's here!"

Penelope looked up from the papers spread over her desk. Colin was standing in the doorway of her small office, jumping from foot to foot like a schoolboy.

"Your book!" she exclaimed, jumping to her feet as quickly as her rather ungainly body would allow. "Oh, Colin, let me see. Let me see. I can't wait!"

He couldn't contain his grin as he handed her his book.

"Ohhhh," she said reverently, holding the slim,

leather-bound volume in her hands. "Oh, my." She held the book up to her face and inhaled deeply. "Don't you just love the smell of new books?"

"Look at this, look at this," he said impatiently, pointing to his name on the front cover.

Penelope beamed. "Look at that. And so elegant, too." She ran her finger over the words as she read, "*An Englishman in Italy,* by Colin Bridgerton."

He looked ready to burst with pride. "It looks good, doesn't it?"

"It looks better than good, it looks perfect! When will *An Englishman in Cyprus* be available?"

"The publisher says every six months. They want to release *An Englishman in Scotland* after that."

"Oh, Colin, I'm so proud of you."

He drew her into his arms, letting his chin rest on top of her head. "I couldn't have done it without you."

"Yes, you could," she replied loyally.

"Just be quiet and accept the praise."

"Very well," she said, grinning even though he couldn't see her face, "you couldn't. Clearly, you could never have been published without such a talented editor."

"You won't hear any disagreement from me," he said softly, kissing the top of her head before he let her go. "Sit down," he added. "You shouldn't be on your feet for so long."

"I'm fine," she assured him, but she sat down, anyway. Colin had been overly protective since the first moment she'd told him she was pregnant; now that she was only a month from her due date, he was insufferable.

"What are these papers?" he asked, glancing down at her scribblings.

"This? Oh, it's nothing." She started to gather them into piles. "Just a little project I was working on."

"Really?" He sat down across from her. "What is it?"

"It's . . . well . . . actually . . ."

"What is it, Penelope?" he asked, looking exceedingly amused by her stammers.

"I've been at loose ends since I finished editing your journals," she explained, "and I found I rather missed writing."

He was smiling as he leaned forward. "What are you working on?"

She blushed; she wasn't sure why. "A novel."

"A novel? Why, that's brilliant, Penelope!"

"You think so?"

"Of course I think so. What is it called?"

"Well, I've only written a few dozen pages," she said, "and there's much work to be done, but I think, if I don't decide to change it overmuch, that I will call it *The Wallflower*."

His eyes grew warm, almost misty. "Really?"

"It's a little bit autobiographical," she admitted.

"Just a little bit?" he returned.

"Just a little."

"But it has a happy ending?"

"Oh, yes," she said fervently. "It *has* to."

"It has to?"

She reached her hand across the table and rested it atop his. "Happy endings are all I can do," she whispered. "I wouldn't know how to write anything else."

Dear Reader,

Have you ever wondered what happened to your favorite characters after you closed the final page? Wanted just a little bit more of a favorite novel? I have, and if the questions from my readers are any indication, I'm not the only one. So after countless requests from Bridgerton fans, I decided to try something a little different, and I wrote a "2nd Epilogue" for each of the novels. These are the stories that come after the stories.

At first, the Bridgerton 2nd Epilogues were available exclusively online; later they were published (along with a novella about Violet Bridgerton) in a collection called The Bridgertons: Happily Ever After. *Now, for the first time, each 2nd Epilogue is being included with the novel it follows. I hope you enjoy Penelope and Colin as they continue their journey.*

Warmly,
Julia Quinn

Romancing
Mister Bridgerton:
The 2nd Epilogue

"*You didn't tell her?*"
Penelope Bridgerton would have said more, and in fact would have liked to say more, but words were difficult, what with her mouth hanging slack. Her husband had just returned from a mad dash across the south of England with his three brothers, in pursuit of his sister Eloise, who had, by all accounts, run off to elope with—

Oh, dear God.

"Is she married?" Penelope asked frantically.

Colin tossed his hat on a chair with a clever little twist of his wrist, one corner of his mouth lifting in a satisfied smile as it spun through the air on a perfect horizontal axis. "Not yet," he replied.

So she hadn't eloped. But she *had* run away. And

she'd done it in secret. Eloise, who was Penelope's closest friend. Eloise, who told Penelope everything. Eloise, who apparently *didn't* tell Penelope everything, had run off to the home of a man none of them knew, leaving a note assuring her family that all would be well and not to worry.

Not to worry????

Good heavens, one would think Eloise Bridgerton knew her family better than that. They had been frantic, every last one of them. Penelope had stayed with her new mother-in-law while the men were searching for Eloise. Violet Bridgerton had put up a good front, but her skin was positively ashen, and Penelope could not help but notice the way her hands shook with every movement.

And now Colin was back, acting as if nothing was amiss, answering none of her questions to her satisfaction, and beyond all that—

"How could you not have told her?" she said again, dogging his heels.

He sprawled into a chair and shrugged. "There really wasn't an appropriate time."

"You were gone five days!"

"Yes, well, not all of them were with Eloise. A day's travel on either end, after all."

"But—but—"

Colin summoned just enough energy to glance about the room. "Don't suppose you ordered tea?"

"Yes, of course," Penelope said reflexively, since it had not taken more than a week of marriage to learn that when it came to her new husband, it was best to always have food at the ready. "But Colin—"

"I did hurry back, you know."

"I can see that," she said, taking in his dampened, windblown hair. "Did you ride?"

He nodded.

"From Gloucestershire?"

"Wiltshire, actually. We retired to Benedict's."

"But—"

He smiled disarmingly. "I missed you."

And Penelope was not so accustomed to his affection that she did not blush. "I missed you, too, but—"

"Come sit with me."

Where? Penelope almost demanded. Because the only flat surface was his lap.

His smile, which had been charm personified, grew more heated. "I'm missing you right now," he murmured.

Much to her extreme embarrassment, her gaze moved instantly to the front of his breeches. Colin let out a bark of laughter, and Penelope crossed her arms. "*Don't*, Colin," she warned.

"Don't what?" he asked, all innocence.

"Even if we weren't in the sitting room, and even if the draperies weren't open—"

"An easily remedied nuisance," he commented with a glance to the windows.

"And *even*," she ground out, her voice growing in depth, if not quite in volume, "were we not expecting a maid to enter at any moment, the poor thing staggering under the weight of your tea tray, the fact of the matter is—"

Colin let out a sigh.

"—you *have not answered my question!*"

He blinked. "I've quite forgotten what it was."

A full ten seconds elapsed before she spoke. And then: "I'm going to kill you."

"Of that, I'm certain," he said offhandedly. "Truly, the only question is when."

"Colin!"

"Might be sooner rather than later," he murmured. "But in truth, I thought I'd go in an apoplexy, brought on by bad behavior."

She stared at him.

"*Your* bad behavior," he clarified.

"I didn't have bad behavior before I met you," she retorted.

"Oh, ho, ho," he chortled. "Now *that* is rich."

And Penelope was forced to shut her mouth. Because, blast it all, he was right. And that was what all of this was about, as it happened. Her husband, after entering the hall, shrugging off his coat, and kissing her rather soundly on the lips (in front of the butler!), had blithely informed her, "Oh, and by the by, I never did tell her you were Whistledown."

And if there was anything that might count as bad behavior, it had to be over ten years as the author of the now infamous *Lady Whistledown's Society Papers*. Penelope had, in her pseudonymous guise, managed to insult just about everyone in society, even herself. (Surely, the *ton* would have grown suspicious if she had never poked fun at herself, and besides, she really did look like an overripe citrus fruit in the dreadful yellows and oranges her mother had always forced her to wear.)

Penelope had "retired" just before her marriage, but a blackmail attempt had convinced Colin that the best course of action was to reveal her secret in a grand gesture, and so he had announced her identity at his sister Daphne's ball. It had all been very romantic and very, well, *grand*, but by the end of the night it had become apparent that Eloise had disappeared.

Eloise had been Penelope's closest friend for years, but even she had not known Penelope's big secret. And now she still didn't. She'd left the party before Colin had announced it, and he apparently had not seen fit to say anything once he'd found her.

"Frankly," Colin said, his voice holding an uncharacteristic strain of irritability, "it's less than she deserved, after what she put us through."

"Well, yes," Penelope murmured, feeling rather disloyal even as she said it. But the entire Bridgerton clan had been mad with worry. Eloise had left a note, it was true, but it had somehow got mixed into her mother's correspondence, and an entire day had passed before the family was reassured that Eloise had not been abducted. And even then, no one's mind was set at ease; Eloise may have left of her own accord, but it had taken another day of tearing her bedchamber to bits before they found a letter from Sir Phillip Crane that indicated where she might have run off to.

Considering all that, Colin did have something of a point.

"We have to go back in a few days for the wedding," he said. "We'll tell her then."

"Oh, but we can't!"

He paused. Then he smiled. "And why is that?" he asked, his eyes resting on her with great appreciation.

"It will be her wedding day," Penelope explained, aware that he'd been hoping for a far more diabolical

THE 2ND EPILOGUE · 547

reason. "She must be the center of all attention. I cannot tell her something such as *this*."

"A bit more altruistic than I'd like," he mused, "but the end result is the same, so you have my approval—"

"I don't need your approval," Penelope cut in.

"But nonetheless, you have it," he said smoothly. "We shall keep Eloise in the dark." He tapped his fingertips together and sighed with audible pleasure. "It will be a most excellent wedding."

The maid arrived just then, carrying a heavily laden tea tray. Penelope tried not to notice that she let out a little grunt when she was finally able to set it down.

"You may close the door behind you," Colin said, once the maid had straightened.

Penelope's eyes darted to the door, then to her husband, who had risen and was shutting the draperies.

"Colin!" she yelped, because his arms had stolen around her, and his lips were on her neck, and she could feel herself going quite liquid in his embrace. "I thought you wanted food," she gasped.

"I do," he murmured, tugging on the bodice of her dress. "But I want you more."

And as Penelope sank to the cushions that had somehow found their way to the plush carpet below, she felt very loved indeed.

———

Several days later, Penelope was seated in a carriage, gazing out the window and scolding herself.

Colin was asleep.

She was a widgeon for feeling so nervous about seeing Eloise again. Eloise, for heaven's sake. They had been as close as sisters for over a decade. Closer. Except, maybe . . . not quite as close as either had thought. They had kept secrets, both of them. Penelope wanted to wring Eloise's neck for not telling her about her suitor, but really, she hadn't a leg to stand on. When Eloise found out that Penelope was Lady Whistledown . . .

Penelope shuddered. Colin might be looking forward to the moment—he was positively devilish in his glee—but she felt rather ill, quite frankly. She hadn't eaten all day, and she was *not* the sort to skip breakfast.

She wrung her hands, craned her neck to get a better view out the window—she thought they might have turned onto the drive for Romney Hall, but she wasn't precisely certain—then looked back to Colin.

He was still asleep.

She kicked him. Gently, of course, because she did not think herself overly violent, but really, it wasn't fair that he had slept like a baby from the moment the carriage had started rolling. He had settled into his seat, inquired after her comfort, and then, before she'd even managed the *you* in "Very well, thank you," his eyes were closed.

Thirty seconds later he was snoring.

It really wasn't fair. He always fell asleep before she did at night as well.

She kicked him again, harder this time.

He mumbled something in his sleep, shifted positions ever so slightly, and slumped into the corner.

Penelope scooted over. Closer, closer . . .

Then she organized her elbow in a sharp point and jabbed him in the ribs.

"Wha . . . ? " Colin shot straight awake, blinking and coughing. "What? What? What?"

"I think we're here," Penelope said.

He looked out the window, then back at her. "And you needed to inform me of this by taking a weapon to my body?"

"It was my elbow."

He glanced down at her arm. "You, my dear, are in possession of exceedingly bony elbows."

Penelope was quite sure her elbows—or any part of her, for that matter—were not the least bit bony, but there seemed little to gain by contradicting him, so she said, again, "I think we're here."

Colin leaned toward the glass with a couple of sleepy blinks. "I think you're right."

"It's lovely," Penelope said, taking in the exquisitely maintained grounds. "Why did you tell me it was rundown?"

"It is," Colin replied, handing her her shawl. "Here," he said with a gruff smile, as if he weren't yet used to caring for another person's welfare in quite the way he did hers. "It will be chilly yet."

It was still fairly early in the morning; the inn at which they had slept was only an hour's ride away. Most of the family had stayed with Benedict and Sophie, but their home was not large enough to accommodate all of the Bridgertons. Besides, Colin had explained, they were newlyweds. They needed their privacy.

Penelope hugged the soft wool to her body and leaned against him to get a better look out the window. And, to be honest, just because she liked to lean against him. "I think it looks lovely," she said. "I have never seen such roses."

"It's nicer on the outside than in," Colin explained as the carriage drew to a halt. "But I expect Eloise will change that."

He opened the door himself and hopped out, then offered his arm to assist her down. "Come along, Lady Whistledown—"

"Mrs. Bridgerton," she corrected.

"Whatever you wish to call yourself," he said with a grand smile, "you're still mine. And this is your swan song."

As Colin stepped across the threshold of what was to be his sister's new home, he was struck by an unexpected sense of relief. For all his irritation with her, he loved his sister. They had not been particularly intimate while growing up; he had been much closer in age to Daphne, and Eloise had often seemed nothing so much as a pesky afterthought. But the previous year had brought them closer, and if it hadn't been for Eloise, he might never have discovered Penelope.

And without Penelope, he'd be . . .

It was funny. He couldn't imagine what he'd be without her.

He looked down at his new wife. She was glancing around the entry hall, trying not to be too obvious about it. Her face was impassive, but he knew she was taking everything in. And tomorrow, when they were musing about the events of the day, she would have remembered every last detail.

Mind like an elephant, she had. He loved it.

"Mr. Bridgerton," the butler said, greeting them with a little nod of his head. "Welcome back to Romney Hall."

"A pleasure, Gunning," Colin murmured. "So sorry about the last time."

Penelope looked to him in askance.

"We entered rather . . . suddenly," Colin explained.

The butler must have seen Penelope's expression of alarm, because he quickly added, "I stepped out of the way."

"Oh," she started to say, "I'm so—"

"Sir Phillip did not," Gunning cut in.

"Oh." Penelope coughed awkwardly. "Is he going to be all right?"

"Bit of swelling around the throat," Colin said, unconcerned. "I expect he's improved by now." He caught her glancing down at his hands and let out a chuckle. "Oh, it wasn't me," he said, taking her arm to lead her down the hall. "I just watched."

She grimaced. "I think that might be worse."

"Quite possibly," he said with great cheer. "But it all turned out well in the end. I quite like the fellow now, and I rather—Ah, Mother, there you are."

And sure enough, Violet Bridgerton was bustling down the hall. "You're late," she said, even though

Colin was fairly certain they were not. He bent down to kiss her proffered cheek, then stepped to the side as his mother came forward to take both of Penelope's hands in hers. "My dear, we need you in back. You are the matron of honor, after all."

Colin had a sudden vision of the scene—a gaggle of chatty females, all talking over one another about minutiae he couldn't begin to care about, much less understand. They told each other everything, and—

He turned sharply. "Don't," he warned, "say a word."

"I beg your pardon." Penelope let out a little huff of righ-teous indignation. "I'm the one who said we couldn't tell her on her wedding day."

"I was talking to my mother," he said.

Violet shook her head. "Eloise is going to kill us."

"She nearly killed us already, running off like an idiot," Colin said, with uncharacteristic shortness of temper. "I've already instructed the others to keep their mouths shut."

"Even Hyacinth?" Penelope asked doubtfully.

"Especially Hyacinth."

"Did you bribe her?" Violet asked. "Because it won't work unless you bribe her."

"Good Lord," Colin muttered. "One would think I'd joined this family yesterday. Of course I bribed her." He turned to Penelope. "No offense to recent additions."

"Oh, none taken," she said. "What did you give her?"

He thought about his bargaining session with his youngest sister and nearly shuddered. "Twenty pounds."

"Twenty pounds!" Violet exclaimed. "Are you mad?"

"I suppose you could have done better," he retorted. "And I've only given her half. I wouldn't trust that girl as far as I could throw her. But if she keeps her mouth shut, I'll be another ten pounds poorer."

"I wonder how far you *could* throw her," Penelope mused.

Colin turned to his mother. "I tried for ten, but she wouldn't budge." And then to Penelope: "Not nearly far enough."

Violet sighed. "I ought to scold you for that."

"But you won't." Colin flashed her a grin.

"Heaven help me," was her only reply.

"Heaven help whatever chap is mad enough to marry her," he remarked.

"I think there is more to Hyacinth than the two of you allow," Penelope put in. "You ought not to underestimate her."

"Good Lord," Colin replied, "we don't do *that*."

"You're so sweet," Violet said, leaning forward to give Penelope an impromptu hug.

"It's only through sheer force of luck she hasn't taken over the world," Colin muttered.

"Ignore him," Violet said to Penelope. "And you," she added, turning to Colin, "must head immediately to the church. The rest of the men have already gone down. It's only a five-minute walk."

"You're planning to walk?" he asked doubtfully.

"Of course not," his mother replied dismissively. "And we certainly cannot spare a carriage for you."

"I wouldn't dream of asking for one," Colin replied, deciding that a solitary stroll through the fresh morning air was decidedly preferable to a closed carriage with his female relations.

He leaned down to kiss his wife's cheek. Right near her ear. "Remember," he whispered, "no telling."

"I can keep a secret," she replied.

"It's far easier to keep a secret from a thousand people than it is from just one," he said. "Far less guilt involved."

Her cheeks flushed, and he kissed her again near her ear. "I know you so well," he murmured.

He could practically hear her teeth gnashing as he left.

———————

"Penelope!"

Eloise started to jump from her seat to greet her, but Hyacinth, who was supervising the dressing of her hair, jammed her hand on her shoulder with a low, almost menacing, "*Down.*"

And Eloise, who normally would have slain Hyacinth with a glare, meekly resumed her seat.

Penelope looked to Daphne, who appeared to be supervising Hyacinth.

"It has been a long morning," Daphne said.

Penelope walked forward, pushed gently past Hyacinth, and carefully embraced Eloise so as not to muss her coiffure. "You look beautiful," she said.

"Thank you," Eloise replied, but her lips were trembling, and her eyes were wet and threatening to spill over at any moment.

More than anything, Penelope wanted to take her aside and tell her that everything was going to be all right, and she didn't *have* to marry Sir Phillip if she didn't want to, but when all was said and done, Penelope *didn't* know that everything was going to be all right, and she rather suspected that Eloise did have to marry her Sir Phillip.

She'd heard bits and pieces. Eloise had been in residence at Romney Hall for over a week without a chaperone. Her reputation would be in tatters if it got out, which it surely would. Penelope knew better than anyone the power and tenacity of gossip. Plus, Penelope had heard that Eloise and Anthony had had A Talk.

The matter of the wedding, it seemed, was final.

"I'm so glad you're here," Eloise said.

"Goodness, you know I would never miss your wedding."

"I know." Eloise's lips trembled, and then her face took on that expression one makes when one is trying to appear brave and actually thinks one might be succeeding. "I know," she said again, a little more evenly. "Of course you wouldn't. But that does not lessen my pleasure in seeing you."

It was an oddly stiff sentence for Eloise, and for a moment Penelope forgot her own secrets, her own fears and worries. Eloise was her dearest friend. Colin was her love, her passion, and her soul, but it was Eloise, more than anyone, who had shaped Penelope's adult life. Penelope could not imagine what the last decade would have been like without Eloise's smile, her laughter, and her indefatigable good cheer.

Even more than her own family, Eloise had loved her.

"Eloise," Penelope said, crouching down beside her so that she might put her arm around her shoulders. She cleared her throat, mostly because she was about to ask a question for which the answer probably did not matter. "Eloise," she said again, her voice dropping to a near whisper. "Do you want this?"

"Of course," Eloise replied.

But Penelope wasn't sure she believed her. "Do you lo—" She caught herself. And she did that little thing with her mouth that tried to be a smile. And she asked, "Do you like him? Your Sir Phillip?"

Eloise nodded. "He's . . . complicated."

Which made Penelope sit down. "You're joking."

"At a time like this?"

"Aren't you the one who always said that men were simple creatures?"

Eloise looked at her with an oddly helpless expression. "I thought they were."

Penelope leaned in, aware that Hyacinth's auditory skills were positively canine. "Does he like you?"

"He thinks I talk too much."

"You do talk too much," Penelope replied.

Eloise shot her a look. "You could at least smile."

"It's the truth. But I find it endearing."

"I think he does as well." Eloise grimaced. "Some of the time."

"Eloise!" called Violet from the doorway. "We really must be on our way."

"We wouldn't want the groom to think you've run off," Hyacinth quipped.

Eloise stood and straightened her shoulders. "I've done quite enough running off recently, wouldn't you say?" She turned to Penelope with a wise, wistful smile. "It's time I began running to and stopped running from."

Penelope looked at her curiously. "What did you say?"

But Eloise only shook her head. "It's just something I heard recently."

It was a curious statement, but this wasn't the time to delve further, so Penelope moved to follow the rest of the family. After she'd taken a few steps, however, she was halted by the sound of Eloise's voice.

"Penelope!"

Penelope turned. Eloise was still in the doorway, a good ten feet behind her. She had an odd look on her face, one that Penelope could not quite interpret. Penelope waited, but Eloise did not speak.

"Eloise?" Penelope said quietly, because it looked as if Eloise *wished* to say something, just wasn't sure how. Or possibly what.

And then—

"*I'm sorry.*" Eloise blurted it out, the words rushing

across her lips with a speed that was remarkable, even for her.

"You're sorry," Penelope echoed, mostly out of surprise. She hadn't really considered what Eloise might say in that moment, but an apology would not have topped the list. "For what?"

"For keeping secrets. That wasn't well-done of me."

Penelope swallowed. *Good Lord.*

"Forgive me?" Eloise's voice was soft, but her eyes were urgent, and Penelope felt like the worst sort of fraud.

"Of course," she stammered. "It is nothing." And it *was* nothing, at least when compared to her own secrets.

"I should have told you about my correspondence with Sir Phillip. I don't know why I didn't at the outset," Eloise continued. "But then, later, when you and Colin were falling in love . . . I think it was . . . I think it was just because it was *mine.*"

Penelope nodded. She knew a great deal about wanting something of one's own.

Eloise let out a nervous laugh. "And now look at me."

Penelope did. "You look beautiful." It was the truth. Eloise was not a serene bride, but she was a glowing one, and Penelope felt her worries lift and lighten and finally disappear. All would be well. Penelope did not know if Eloise would experience the same bliss in her marriage as she'd found, but she would at least be happy and content.

And who was she to say that the new married couple wouldn't fall madly in love? Stranger things had happened.

She linked her arm through Eloise's and steered her out into the hall, where Violet had raised her voice to heretofore unimagined volumes.

"I think your mother wants us to make haste," Penelope whispered.

"Eloeeeeeeeeeeeese!" Violet positively bellowed. "NOW!"

Eloise's brows rose as she gave Penelope a sideways glance. "Whatever makes you think so?"

But they didn't hurry. Arm in arm they glided down the hall, as if it were the church aisle.

"Who would have thought we'd both marry within months of each other?" Penelope mused. "Weren't we meant to be old crones together?"

"We can still be old crones," Eloise replied gaily. "We shall simply be married old crones."

"It will be grand."

"Magnificent!"

"Stupendous!"

"We shall be leaders of crone fashion!"

"Arbiters of cronish taste."

"What," Hyacinth demanded, hands on hips, "are the two of you talking about?"

Eloise lifted her chin and looked down her nose at her. "You're far too young to understand."

And she and Penelope practically collapsed in a fit of giggles.

"They've gone mad, Mother," Hyacinth announced.

Violet gazed lovingly at her daughter and daughter-in-law, both of whom had reached the unfashionable age of twenty-eight before becoming brides. "Leave them alone, Hyacinth," she said, steering her toward the waiting carriage. "They'll be along shortly." And then she added, almost as an afterthought: "You're too young to understand."

After the ceremony, after the reception, and after Colin was able to assure himself once and for all that Sir Phillip Crane would indeed make an acceptable husband to his sister, he managed to find a quiet corner into which he could yank his wife and speak with her privately.

"Does she suspect?" he asked, grinning.

"You're terrible," Penelope replied. "It's her *wedding*."

Which was not one of the two customary answers to a yes-or-no question. Colin resisted the urge to let out an impatient breath, and instead offered a rather smooth and urbane "By this you mean . . . ?"

Penelope stared at him for a full ten seconds, and then she muttered, "I don't know what Eloise was talking about. Men are *abysmally* simple creatures."

"Well . . . *yes*," Colin agreed, since it had long been obvious to him that the female mind was an utter and complete mystery. "But what has that got to do with anything?"

Penelope glanced over both shoulders before dropping her voice to a harsh whisper. "Why would she even be thinking about Whistledown at a time like this?"

She had a point there, loath as Colin was to admit it. In his mind, this had all played out with Eloise somehow being aware that she was the only person who didn't know the secret of Lady Whistledown's identity.

Which was ridiculous to be sure, but still, a satisfying daydream.

"Hmmmm," he said.

Penelope looked at him suspiciously. "What are you thinking?"

"Are you certain we cannot tell her on her wedding day?"

"Colin . . ."

"Because if we *don't*, she's sure to find out from

*some*one, and it doesn't seem fair that we not be present to see her face."

"Colin, *no*."

"After all you've been through, wouldn't you say you deserve to see her reaction?"

"No," Penelope said slowly. "No. No, I wouldn't."

"Oh, you sell yourself too cheaply, my darling," he said, smiling benevolently at her. "And besides that, think of Eloise."

"I fail to see what else it is I have been doing all morning."

He shook his head. "She would be devastated. Hearing the awful truth from a complete stranger."

"It's not awful," Penelope shot back, "and how do you know it would be a stranger?"

"We've sworn my entire family to secrecy. Who else does she know out in this godforsaken county?"

"I rather like Gloucestershire," Penelope said, her teeth now charmingly clenched. "I find it delightful."

"Yes," he said equably, taking in her furrowed brow, pinched mouth, and narrowed eyes. "You look delighted."

"Weren't you the one who insisted we keep her in the dark for as long as humanly possible?"

"*Humanly possible* being the phrase of note," Colin replied. "*This* human"—he gestured rather unnecessarily to himself—"finding it quite impossible to maintain his silence."

"I can't believe you've changed your mind."

He shrugged. "Isn't it a man's prerogative?"

At that her lips parted, and Colin found himself wishing he'd found a corner as private as it was quiet, because she was practically begging to be kissed, whether she knew it or not.

But he was a patient man, and they did still have that comfortable room reserved at the inn, and there was still much mischief to be made right here at the wedding. "Oh, Penelope," he said huskily, leaning in more than was proper, even with one's wife, "don't you want to have some fun?"

She flushed scarlet. "Not *here*."

He laughed aloud at that.

"I wasn't talking about that," she muttered.

"Neither was I, as a matter of fact," he returned, completely unable to keep the humor off his face, "but I *am* pleased that it comes to mind so readily." He pretended to glance about the room. "When do you think it would be polite to leave?"

"Definitely not yet."

He pretended to ponder. "Mmmm, yes, you're probably correct at that. Pity. But"—at that he pretended to brighten—"it does leave us time to make mischief."

Again, she was speechless. He liked that. "Shall we?" he murmured.

"I don't know what I'm going to do with you."

"We need to work on this," he said, giving his head a shake. "I'm not sure you fully understand the mechanics of a yes-or-no question."

"I think you should sit down," she said, her eyes now taking on that glint of cautious exhaustion usually reserved for small children.

Or adult fools.

"And then," she continued, "I think you should remain in your seat."

"Indefinitely?"

"*Yes.*"

Just to torture her, he sat. And then—

"*Nooooo*, I think I'd rather make mischief."

Back to his feet he was, and striding off to find Eloise before Penelope could even attempt to lunge for him.

"Colin, *don't!*" she called out, her voice echoing off the walls of the reception room. She managed to yell—of course—at the precise moment when every other wedding guest paused to take a breath.

A roomful of Bridgertons. What were the odds?

Penelope jammed a smile on her face as she watched two dozen heads swivel in her direction. "Nothing about it," she said, her voice coming out strangled and chirpy. "So sorry to disturb."

And apparently Colin's family was well used to his embarking on something requiring the rejoinder "Colin, don't!" because they all resumed their conversations with barely another glance in her direction.

Except Hyacinth.

"Oh, blast," Penelope muttered under her breath, and she raced forward.

But Hyacinth was quick. "What's going on?" she asked, falling into stride beside Penelope with remarkable agility.

"Nothing," Penelope replied, because the last thing she wanted was Hyacinth adding to the disaster.

"He's going to tell her, isn't he?" Hyacinth persisted, let out an "*Euf??*" and an "Excuse me," when she pushed past one of her brothers.

"No," Penelope said firmly, darting around Daphne's children, "he's not."

"He *is*."

Penelope actually stopped for a moment and turned. "Do any of you ever listen to anyone?"

"Not me," Hyacinth said cheerfully.

Penelope shook her head and moved forward, Hyacinth hot on her heels. When she reached Colin, he was standing next to the newlyweds and had his arms linked through Eloise's and was smiling down at her as if he had never once considered:

   a. Teaching her to swim by tossing her in a lake.
   b. Cutting off three inches of her hair while she slept.

or

   c. Tying her to a tree so that she did not follow him to a local public inn.

Which of course he had, all three of them, and two he'd actually done. (Even Colin wouldn't have dared something so permanent as a shearing.)

"Eloise," Penelope said, somewhat breathless from trying to shake off Hyacinth.

"Penelope." But Eloise's voice sounded curious. Which did not surprise Penelope; Eloise was no fool, and she was well aware that her brother's normal modes of behavior did not include beatific smiles in her direction.

"Eloise," Hyacinth said, for no reason Penelope could deduce.

"Hyacinth."

Penelope turned to her husband. "Colin."

He looked amused. "Penelope. Hyacinth."

Hyacinth grinned. "Colin." And then: "Sir Phillip."

"Ladies." Sir Phillip, it seemed, favored brevity.

"Stop!" Eloise burst out. "What is going on?"

"A recitation of our Christian names, apparently," Hyacinth said.

"Penelope has something to say to you," Colin said.

"I don't."

"She does."

"I *do*," Penelope said, thinking quickly. She rushed forward, taking Eloise's hands in her own. "Congratulations. I'm so happy for you."

"That's what you needed to say?" Eloise asked.

"Yes."

"*No*."

And from Hyacinth: "I am enjoying myself immensely."

"Er, it's very kind of you to say so," Sir Phillip said, looking a bit perplexed at her sudden need to compliment the host. Penelope closed her eyes for a brief moment and let out a weary sigh; she was going to need to take the poor man aside and instruct him on the finer points of marrying into the Bridgerton family.

And because she did know her new relations so well, and she knew that there was no way she was going to avoid revealing her secret, she turned to Eloise and said, "Might I have a moment alone?"

"With me?"

It was enough to make Penelope wish to strangle someone. Anyone. "Yes," she said patiently, "with you."

"And me," Colin put in.

"And me," Hyacinth added.

"*Not* you," Penelope said, not bothering to look at her.

"But still me," Colin added, looping his free arm through Penelope's.

"Can this wait?" Sir Phillip asked politely. "This is her wedding day, and I expect that she does not wish to miss it."

"I know," Penelope said wearily. "I'm so sorry."

"It's all right," Eloise said, breaking free of Colin's grasp and turning to her new husband. She murmured a few words to him that Penelope could not hear, then said, "There is a small salon just through that door. Shall we?"

She led the way, which suited Penelope because it gave her time to say to Colin, "You will say nothing."

He surprised her by nodding, and then, maintaining his silence, he held open the door for her as she entered the room behind Eloise.

"This won't take long," Penelope said apologetically. "At least, I hope it won't."

Eloise said nothing, just looked at her with an expression that was, Penelope had just enough presence of mind to notice, uncharacteristically serene.

Marriage must agree with her, Penelope thought, because the Eloise *she* knew would have been chomping at the bit at such a moment. A big secret, a mystery to be revealed—Eloise loved that sort of thing.

But she was just standing there, calmly waiting, a light smile touching her features. Penelope looked to Colin in confusion, but he was apparently taking her instructions to heart, and his mouth was clamped firmly shut.

"Eloise," Penelope began.

Eloise smiled. A bit. Just at the corners, as if she wanted to smile more. "Yes?"

Penelope cleared her throat. "Eloise," she said again, "there is something I must tell you."

"Really?"

Penelope's eyes narrowed. Surely the moment did not call for sarcasm. She took a breath, tamping down the urge to fire off an equally dry rejoinder, and said, "I did not wish to tell you on your wedding day"—at this she *speared* her husband with a glare—"but it seems I have no choice."

Eloise blinked a few times, but other than that, her placid demeanor did not change.

"I can think of no other way to say it," Penelope plodded on, feeling positively sick, "but while you were gone . . . That is to say, the night you left, as a matter of fact . . ."

Eloise leaned forward. The movement was slight, but Penelope caught it, and for a moment she thought— Well, she didn't think anything clearly, certainly nothing that she could have expressed in a proper sentence. But she did get a feeling of unease—a different sort of unease than the one she was already feeling. It was a suspicious sort of unease, and—

"I am Whistledown," she blurted out, because if she waited any longer she thought her brain might explode.

And Eloise said, "I know."

Penelope sat down on the nearest solid object, which happened to be a table. "You know."

Eloise shrugged. "I know."

"How?"

"Hyacinth told me."

"*What?*" This from Colin, looking fit to be tied. Or perhaps more accurately, fit to tie Hyacinth.

"I'm sure she's at the door," Eloise murmured, with a nod. "In case you want to—"

But Colin was one step ahead of her, wrenching open the door to the small salon. Sure enough, Hyacinth tumbled in.

"Hyacinth!" Penelope said disapprovingly.

"Oh, please," Hyacinth retorted, smoothing her skirts. "You didn't think I wouldn't eavesdrop, did you? You know me better than that."

"I'm going to wring your neck," Colin ground out. "We had an agreement."

Hyacinth shrugged. "I don't really need twenty pounds, as it happens."

"I already *gave* you ten."

"I know," Hyacinth said with a cheerful smile.

"Hyacinth!" Eloise exclaimed.

"Which isn't to say," Hyacinth continued modestly, "that I don't *want* the other ten."

"She told me last night," Eloise explained, her eyes narrowing dangerously, "but only after informing me that she knew who Lady Whistledown was, and in fact the whole of society knew, but that the knowledge would cost me twenty-*five* pounds."

"Did it not occur to you," Penelope asked, "that if the whole of society knew, that you could simply have asked someone else?"

"The whole of society wasn't in my bedchamber at two in the morning," Eloise snapped.

"I am thinking of buying a hat," Hyacinth mused. "Or maybe a pony."

Eloise shot her a nasty look, then turned to Penelope. "Are you really Whistledown?"

"I am," Penelope admitted. "Or rather—" She looked over at Colin, not exactly certain why she was doing so except that she loved him so much, and he knew her so well, and when he saw her helpless little wobbly smile, he would smile in return, no matter how irate he was with Hyacinth.

And he did. Somehow, amidst everything, he knew what she needed. He always did.

Penelope turned back to Eloise. "I *was*," she amended. "No longer. I've retired."

But of course Eloise already knew that. Lady W's letter of retirement had circulated long before Eloise had left town.

"For good," Penelope added. "People have asked, but I shan't be induced to pick up my quill again." She paused, thinking of the scribblings she'd embarked upon at home. "At least not as Whistledown." She looked at Eloise, who had sat down next to her on the table. Her face was somewhat blank, and she hadn't said anything in *ages*—well, ages for Eloise, at least.

Penelope tried to smile. "I am thinking of writing a novel, actually."

Still nothing from Eloise, although she was blinking quite rapidly, and her brow was scrunched up as if she were thinking quite hard.

And so Penelope took one of her hands and said the one thing she was really feeling. "I'm sorry, Eloise."

Eloise had been staring rather blankly at an end table, but at that, she turned, her eyes finding Penelope's. "You're sorry?" she echoed, and she sounded dubious, as if sorry couldn't possibly be the correct emotion, or at least, not *enough* of it.

Penelope's heart sank. "I'm so sorry," she said again. "I should have told you. I should have—"

"Are you *mad*?" Eloise asked, finally seeming to snap to attention. "Of *course* you should not have told me. I could never have kept this a secret."

Penelope thought it rather remarkable of her to admit it.

"I am so *proud* of you," Eloise continued. "Forget the writing for a moment—I cannot even fathom the logistics of it all, and someday—when it is not my wedding day—I shall insist upon hearing every last detail."

"You were surprised, then?" Penelope murmured.

Eloise gave her a rather dry look. "To put it mildly."

"I had to get her a chair," Hyacinth supplied.

"I was already sitting down," Eloise ground out.

Hyacinth waved her hand in the air. "Nevertheless."

"Ignore her," Eloise said, focusing firmly on Penelope. "Truly, I cannot begin to tell you how impressed I am—now that I've got over the shock, that is."

"Really?" It hadn't occurred to Penelope until that very moment just how much she'd wished for Eloise's approval.

"Keeping us all in the dark for so long," Eloise said, shaking her head with slow admiration. "From me. From *her*." She jabbed a finger in Hyacinth's direction. "It's really very well-done of you." At that she leaned forward and enveloped Penelope in a warm hug.

"You're not angry with me?"

Eloise moved back and opened her mouth, and Penelope could see that she'd been about to say, "No," probably to be followed by "Of course not."

But the words remained in Eloise's mouth, and she just sat there, looking slightly thoughtful and surprised until she finally said . . . "No."

Penelope felt her brows lift. "Are you certain?" Because Eloise didn't sound certain. She didn't much sound like Eloise, to be honest.

"It would be different if I were still in London," Eloise said quietly, "with nothing else to do. But this—" She glanced around the room, gesturing rather vaguely toward the window. "*Here*. It's just not the same. It's a different life," she said quietly. "I'm a different person. A little bit, at least."

"Lady Crane," Penelope reminded her.

Eloise smiled. "Good of you to remind me of that, Mrs. Bridgerton."

Penelope almost laughed. "Can you believe it?"

"Of you, or me?" Eloise asked.

"Both."

Colin, who had been keeping a respectful distance— one hand firmly clamped around Hyacinth's arm to keep *her* at a respectful distance—stepped forward. "We should probably return," he said quietly. He held out his hand, and helped first Penelope, then Eloise, to her feet. "You," he said, leaning forward to kiss his sister on the cheek, "should *certainly* return."

Eloise smiled wistfully, the blushing bride once again, and nodded. With one last squeeze of Penelope's hands, she brushed past Hyacinth (rolling her eyes as she did so) and made her way back to her wedding party.

Penelope watched her go, linking her arm in Colin's and leaned gently into him. They both stood there in contented silence, idly watching the now empty doorway, listening to the sounds of the party wafting through the air.

"Do you think it would be polite if we left?" he murmured.

"Probably not."

"Do you think Eloise would mind?"

Penelope shook her head.

Colin's arms tightened around her, and she felt his lips gently brush her ear. "Let's go," he said.

She did not argue.

On the twenty-fifth of May, in the year 1824, precisely one day after the wedding of Eloise Bridgerton to Sir Phillip Crane, three missives were delivered to the room of Mr. and Mrs. Colin Bridgerton, guests at the Rose and Bramble Inn, near Tetbury, Gloucestershire. They arrived together; all were from Romney Hall.

"Which shall we open first?" Penelope asked, spreading them before her on the bed.

Colin yanked off the shirt he'd donned to answer the knock. "I defer to your good judgment as always."

"As always?"

He crawled back into bed beside her. She was remarkably adorable when she was being sarcastic. He couldn't think of another soul who could carry that off. "As whenever it suits me," he amended.

"Your mother, then," Penelope said, plucking one of the letters off the sheet. She broke open the seal and carefully unfolded the paper.

Colin watched as she read. Her eyes widened, then her brows rose, then her lips pinched slightly at the corners, as if she were smiling despite herself. "What does she have to say?" he asked.

"She forgives us."

"I don't suppose it would make any sense for me to ask for what."

Penelope gave him a stern look. "For leaving the wedding early."

"You told me Eloise wouldn't mind."

"And I'm sure she did not. But this is your *mother*."

"Write back and assure her that should she ever remarry, I will stay to the bitter end."

"I will do no such thing," Penelope replied, rolling her eyes. "I don't think she expects a reply, in any case."

"Really?" Now he was curious, because his mother always expected replies. "What did we do to earn her forgiveness, then?"

"Er, she mentioned something about the timely delivery of grandchildren."

Colin grinned. "Are you blushing?"

"No."

"You *are*."

She elbowed him in the ribs. "I'm not. Here, read it yourself if you are so inclined. I shall read Hyacinth's."

"I don't suppose she returned my ten pounds," Colin grumbled.

Penelope unfolded the paper and shook it out. Nothing fluttered down.

"That minx is lucky she's my sister," he muttered.

"What a bad sport you are," Penelope chided. "She bested you, and rather brilliantly, too."

"Oh, please," he scoffed. "I did not see *you* praising her cunning yesterday afternoon."

She waved off his protests. "Yes, well, some things are more easily seen in hindsight."

"What does she have to say?" Colin asked, leaning over her shoulder. Knowing Hyacinth, it was probably some scheme to extort more money from his pockets.

"It's rather sweet, actually," Penelope said. "Nothing nefarious at all."

"Did you read both sides?" Colin asked dubiously.

"She only wrote on one side."

"Uncharacteristically uneconomical of her," he added, with suspicion.

"Oh, heavens, Colin, it is just an account of the wedding after we left. And I must say, she has a superior eye for humor and detail. She would have made a fine Whistledown."

"God help us all."

The last letter was from Eloise, and unlike the other

two, it was addressed to Penelope alone. Colin was curious, of course—who wouldn't be? But he moved away to allow Penelope her privacy. Her friendship with his sister was something he held in both awe and respect. He was close to his brothers—extremely so. But he had never seen a bond of friendship quite so deep as that between Penelope and Eloise.

"Oh!" Penelope let out, as she turned a page. Eloise's missive was a good deal longer than the previous two, and she'd managed to fill two sheets, front and back. "That minx."

"What did she do?" Colin asked.

"Oh, it was nothing," Penelope replied, even though her expression was rather peeved. "You weren't there, but the morning of the wedding she kept apologizing for keeping secrets, and it never even occurred to me that she was trying to get me to admit to keeping secrets of my own. Made me feel wretched, she did."

Her voice trailed off as she read through another page. Colin leaned back against the fluffy pillows, his eyes resting on his wife's face. He liked watching her eyes move from left to right, following the words. He liked watching her lips move as she smiled or frowned. It was rather amazing, actually, how contented he felt, simply watching his wife read.

Until she gasped, that was, and turned utterly white.

He shoved himself up on his elbows. "What is it?"

Penelope shook her head and groaned. "Oh, she is devious."

Privacy be damned. He grabbed the letter. "What did she say?"

"Down there," Penelope said, pointing miserably at the bottom. "At the end."

Colin brushed her finger away and began to read. "Good Lord, she's wordy," he muttered. "I can't make heads or tails of it."

"Revenge," Penelope said. "She says my secret was bigger than hers."

"It was."

"She says she's owed a boon."

Colin pondered that. "She probably is."

"To even the score."

He patted her hand. "I'm afraid that's how we Bridgertons think. You've never played a sporting game with us, have you?"

Penelope moaned. "She said she is going to consult *Hyacinth*."

Colin felt the blood leave his face.

"I know," Penelope said, shaking her head. "We'll never be safe again."

Colin slid his arm around her and pulled her close. "Didn't we say we wanted to visit Italy?"

"Or India."

He smiled and kissed her on the nose. "Or we could just stay here."

"At the Rose and Bramble?"

"We're supposed to depart tomorrow morning. It's the last place Hyacinth would look."

Penelope glanced up at him, her eyes growing warm and perhaps just a little bit mischievous. "I have no pressing engagements in London for at least a fortnight."

He rolled atop her, tugging her down until she was flat on her back. "My mother did say she would not forgive us unless we produced a grandchild."

"She did not put it in quite so uncompromising terms."

He kissed her, right on the sensitive spot behind her earlobe that always made her squirm. "Pretend she did."

"Well, in that case—oh!"

His lips slid down her belly. "Oh?" he murmured.

"We had best get to—oh!"

He looked up. "You were saying?"

"To work," she just barely managed to get out.

He smiled against her skin. "Your servant, Mrs. Bridgerton. Always."

About the Author

#1 *New York Times* bestselling author **JULIA QUINN** began writing one month after graduating from college and, aside from a brief stint in medical school, she has been tapping away at her keyboard ever since. Her novels have been translated into thirty-seven languages and are beloved the world over. A graduate of Harvard and Radcliffe Colleges, she lives with her family in the Pacific Northwest.

Meet the Bridgerton Family

The Bridgertons are by far the most prolific family in the upper echelons of society. Such industriousness on the part of the viscountess and the late viscount is commendable, although one can find only banality in their choice of names for their children. Anthony, Benedict, Colin, Daphne, Eloise, Francesca, Gregory, and Hyacinth (orderliness is, of course, beneficial in all things, but one would think that intelligent parents would be able to keep their children straight without needing to alphabetize their names).

It has been said that Lady Bridgerton's dearest goal is to see all of her offspring happily married, but truly, one can only wonder if this is an impossible feat. Eight children? Eight happy marriages? It boggles the mind.

~*Lady Whistledown's Society Papers,*
Summer 1813

The Duke and I

Who?

Daphne Bridgerton
and the Duke of Hastings.

What?

A sham courtship.

Where?

London, of course. Where else could
one pull off such a thing?

Why?

They each have their reasons,
neither of which includes
falling in love . . .

The Viscount Who Loved Me

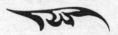

The season has opened for the year of 1814, and there is little reason to hope that we will see any noticeable change from 1813. The ranks of society are once again filled with Ambitious Mamas, whose only aim is to see their Darling Daughters married off to Determined Bachelors. Discussion amongst the Mamas fingers Lord Bridgerton as this year's most eligible catch, and indeed, if the poor man's hair looks ruffled and windblown, it is because he cannot go anywhere without some young miss batting her eyelashes with such vigor and speed as to create a breeze of hurricane force. Perhaps the only young lady not interested in Lord Bridgerton is Miss Katharine Sheffield, and in fact, her demeanor toward the viscount occasionally borders on the hostile.

And that is why, Dear Reader, This Author feels a match between Anthony Bridgerton and Miss Sheffield would be just the thing to enliven an otherwise ordinary season.

~Lady Whistledown's Society Papers,
13 April 1814

An Offer From a Gentleman

The 1815 season is well under way, and while one would think that all talk would be of Wellington and Waterloo, in truth, there is little change from the conversations of 1814, which centered around that most eternal of society topics—marriage.

As usual, the matrimonial hopes among the debutante set center upon the Bridgerton family, most specifically the eldest of the available brothers, Benedict. He might not possess a title, but his handsome face, pleasing form, and heavy purse appear to have made up for that lack handily. Indeed, This Author has heard, on more than one occasion, an Ambitious Mama saying of her daughter: "She'll marry a duke . . . or a Bridgerton."

For his part, Mr. Bridgerton seems most uninterested in the young ladies who frequent society events. He attends almost every party, yet he does nothing but watch the doors, presumably waiting for some special person.

Perhaps . . .

A potential bride?

~Lady Whistledown's Society Papers,
12 July 1815

Romancing Mister Bridgerton

April is nearly upon us, and with it a new social season here in London. Ambitious Mamas can be found at dress shops all across town with their Darling Debutantes, eager to purchase that one magical evening gown that they simply know will mean the difference between marriage and spinsterhood.

As for their prey—the Determined Bachelors—Mr. Colin Bridgerton once again tops the list of desirable husbands, even though he is not yet back from his recent trip abroad. He has no title, that is true, but he is in abundant possession of looks, fortune, and, as anyone who has ever spent even a minute in London knows, charm.

But Mr. Bridgerton has reached the somewhat advanced age of three-and-thirty without ever showing an interest in any particular young lady, and there is little reason to anticipate that 1824 will be any different from 1823 in this respect.

Perhaps the Darling Debutantes—and perhaps more importantly their Ambitious Mamas—would do well to look elsewhere. If Mr. Bridgerton is looking for a wife, he hides that desire well.

On the other hand, is that not just the sort of challenge a debutante likes best?

~Lady Whistledown's Society Papers,
26 March 1824

To Sir Phillip, With Love

. . . I know you say I shall someday like boys, but I say never! NEVER!!! With three exclamation points!!!

~from Eloise Bridgerton to her mother,
shoved under Violet Bridgerton's door
during Eloise's eighth year

. . . I never dreamed that a season could be so exciting! The men are so handsome and charming. I know I shall fall in love straightaway. How could I not?

~from Eloise Bridgerton to her brother Colin,
upon the occasion of her London debut

. . . I am quite certain I shall never marry. If there was someone out there for me, don't you think I should have found him by now?

~from Eloise Bridgerton to her dear friend
Penelope Featherington, during her sixth
season as a debutante

. . . this is my last chance. I am grabbing destiny with both my hands and throwing caution to the wind. Sir Phillip, please, *please*, be all that I have imagined you to be. Because if you are the man your letters portray you to be, I think I could love you. And if you felt the same . . .

~from Eloise Bridgerton, jotted on a scrap of paper
on her way to meet Sir Phillip Crane
for the very first time

When He Was Wicked

TRUE OR FALSE?

True Michael Stirling is in love with
the one woman he cannot have.

True Michael Stirling is in love with
the one woman he cannot have.

True Michael Stirling is in love with
the one woman he cannot have.

True Michael Stirling is in love with
the one woman he cannot have.

True Michael Stirling is in love with
the one woman he cannot have.

Truth Michael Stirling is in love with
Francesca Bridgerton.

Sometimes there is only one truth that matters.

It's In His Kiss

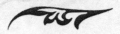

Our Cast of Characters

Hyacinth Bridgerton: The youngest of the famed Bridgerton siblings, she's a little too smart, a little too outspoken, and certainly not your average romance heroine. She's also, much to her dismay, falling in love with . . .

Gareth St. Clair: There are some men in London with wicked reputations, and there are others who are handsome as sin. But Gareth is the only one who manages to combine the two with such devilish success. He'd be a complete rogue, if not for . . .

Lady Danbury: Grandmother to Gareth, mentor to Hyacinth, she has an opinion on everything, especially love and marriage. And she'd like nothing better than to see Gareth and Hyacinth joined in holy matrimony. Luckily, she's to have help from . . .

One meddling mother, one overprotective brother, one very bad string quartet, one (thankfully fictional) mad baron, and of course, let us not forget the shepherdess, the unicorn, and Henry the Eighth.

On the Way to the Wedding

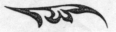

IN WHICH

FIRSTLY, Gregory Bridgerton falls in love with the wrong woman, and

SECONDLY, she falls in love with someone else, but

THIRDLY, Lucy Abernathy decides to meddle; however,

FOURTHLY, she falls in love with Gregory, which is highly inconvenient because

FIFTHLY, she is practically engaged to Lord Haselby, but

SIXTHLY, Gregory falls in love with Lucy. Which leaves everyone in a bit of a pickle.

Watch them all find their happy endings in the stunning conclusion to the

Bridgerton Series

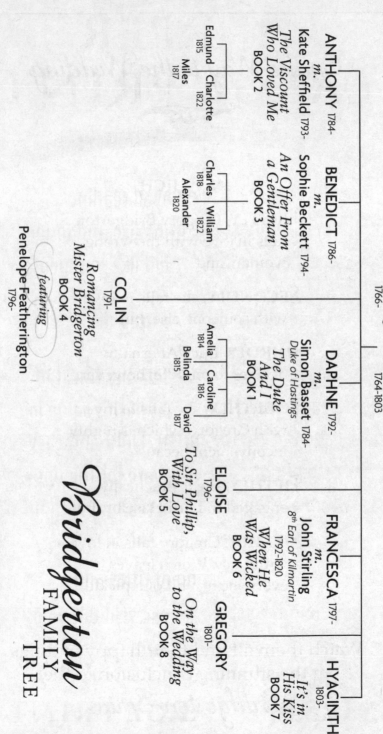

Violet Ledger *m.* EDMUND
1766- 1764-1803

ANTHONY 1784-
m.
Kate Sheffield 1793-
The Viscount Who Loved Me
BOOK 2

Edmund 1815
Miles 1817
Charlotte 1822

BENEDICT 1786-
m.
Sophie Beckett 1794-
An Offer From a Gentleman
BOOK 3

Charles 1818
William 1822
Alexander 1820

COLIN 1791-
Romancing Mister Bridgerton
BOOK 4
featuring
Penelope Featherington 1796-

DAPHNE 1792-
m.
Simon Basset 1784-
Duke of Hastings
The Duke And I
BOOK 1

Amelia 1814
Belinda 1815
Caroline 1816
David 1817

ELOISE 1796-
To Sir Phillip, With Love
BOOK 5

FRANCESCA 1797-
m.
John Stirling
8th Earl of Kilmartin
1792-1820
When He Was Wicked
BOOK 6

GREGORY 1801-
On the Way to the Wedding
BOOK 8

HYACINTH 1803-
It's in His Kiss
BOOK 7

Bridgerton FAMILY TREE

FOR MORE INFORMATION
PLEASE VISIT JULIAQUINN.COM